CHRISTMAS IN THE CABIN

A DAD'S BEST FRIEND, SECRET BABY, HOLIDAY ROMANCE

SOFIA T SUMMERS

Copyright © 2022 by Sofia T Summers
All rights reserved.

The following story contains mature themes, strong language and sexual situations. It is intended for mature readers.

No part of this book may be reproduced in any form or by any electronic or mechanical means, including information storage and retrieval systems, without written permission from the author, except for the use of brief quotations in a book review.

OTHER BOOKS BY SOFIA T SUMMERS

Forbidden Temptations Series (Age Gap Romances - this series)

Daddy's Best Friend

My Best Friend's Daddy

Daddy's Business Partner

Doctor Daddy

Secret Baby with Daddy's Best Friend

Knocked Up by Daddy's Best Friend

Pretend Wife to Daddy's Best Friend

SEAL Daddy

Fake Married to My Best Friend's Daddy

Accidental Daddy

The Grump's Girl Friday

The Vegas Accident

My Beastly Boss

My Millionaire Marine

The Wedding Dare

The Summer Getaway

The Love Edit

The Husband Lottery

Forbidden Fantasies (Reverse Harem Series)

My Irish Billionaires

Toy for the Teachers

Three Grumpy Bosses

Feasting on Her Curves

DESCRIPTION

**Driving home for Christmas, I couldn't outrun the snow or Nick Wallace.
I had travelled the world, but nothing prepared me for that fateful night in his cabin...
Not even for the baby girl who arrived eight months later.**

There were secrets pride urged me to keep.
Nick never learned about his daughter, *our* daughter,
And I kept my word that my father would never know what we did.
Their friendship didn't need to be shattered like all my hopes.

**Now, fate is calling me back home for an extended holiday season.
There will be no quick getaway this time.**

People say that time heals all wounds, but what can an all-consuming kiss do?
Everything always looks better under the glow of holiday lights,
But will the harsh light of reality be the end of everything I once craved from Nick?

SOFIA T SUMMERS

This Christmas, will I finally stop running?

PROLOGUE

DARCY

Over and over, I turned the key in the ignition. Every time I thought the engine might rumble to life, it failed me again, and all my hopefulness dwindled into helplessness. Stuck on the side of the mountain, I had another thirty minutes to get to my dad's place, but my Mustang wasn't going to make it. My dear Shelby was beautiful, but she couldn't fight the snow and ice piling up in this wild storm. She could only sit there and maybe keep me warm.

Looking at the gas gauge, I realized that wouldn't be much longer, either. The little red hand sat around the one-quarter mark. I didn't know if that was enough to keep the heat running all night long. If the gas could somehow make it to morning, I imagined the car's battery might not.

No bars on my cell phone. No chance of driving out of this ditch. Plus, I was a little too far out of the small mountain town to walk back for salvation.

"Merry freakin' Christmas to me," I muttered.

The cheerful music on the radio sounded like it was mocking me. With a huff, I pulled the key from the little slot. The speakers went dead. The heat stopped blowing from the vents, but there was enough heat in the car to keep me warm. I had my mittens and my hat . . .

I was definitely going to die. *Froze to death in her car*, the obituary would say. I could already see the local news's headlines.

"Black Sheep?"

The voice made me jump. Turning my head, a familiar pair of blue eyes met mine. I couldn't believe it.

"Nick?" I called through the icy window. "Is that you?"

I didn't need to ask. I had memorized every strand of his sandy blond hair and the crooked bridge of his nose. It was the only imperfection on his otherwise perfect face. The smile he offered always looked wry, even when he was being earnest.

With that same grin, he exclaimed, "Funny running into you out here!"

"No, it isn't!" I protested. "I'm stuck."

"Then, get out of the car!"

I scoffed. "You just want me to abandon my car?"

"It's not going anywhere!"

As I glanced through the windshield, snowflakes fatter than goose feathers were starting to cover my car. He was right. This was my one chance at a Christmas miracle.

I had to take it.

Bracing myself for the cold, I grabbed my purse from the front seat before rushing to the trunk. I shuddered against the wind, trying to unlock it with my mitten-clad hands. God, I didn't want to take them off. My fingers would be purple in seconds.

"Give me the keys," Nick insisted.

I looked over to his shoulder and then up at his face. His red knit cap had his blond hair pushed down across his intent gaze. He was used to the cold, making it easier to retrieve my suitcase and throw it in the backseat of his old blue Chevrolet. Shivering again, I didn't protest.

"I guess I should thank you," I said as Nick slid into the cab beside me. "I would probably have died out here."

"Oh, you're tougher than that, but why were you driving that thing in a snowstorm? What happened to your hatchback, and shouldn't you have some boyfriend with you? Bill mentioned you were seeing someone."

"I sold it when I left for Costa Rica. I didn't need two cars, especially when I was going to be out of the country."

"Is that where you've been?" he wondered while shifting into drive.

"Costa Rica was in the spring and South America this summer. I did a Schengen visa in Europe this fall. I got back from Copenhagen last week. That's where I left the boyfriend."

"Oh, I'm sorry."

I shook my head. "Don't be. I'm certainly not."

We had only ever been a traveling fling. He wanted to head east to New Zealand. I wanted to head home for the holidays. As fun as the guy was, there was no point in pretending we were a great love affair.

Nick laughed, flashing that teasing grin. "Did you visit that Red-Light District?"

"You're thinking of Amsterdam, and do you think I'm the kind of person to visit brothels and sex shops?"

"No, Black Sheep, you've never been that kind of girl."

"Darcy." I sighed. "Why can't you ever call me Darcy?"

He chuckled again, turning around the switchback edge of the mountain. It didn't matter that we could barely see. Nick knew these roads like the back of his hand. He probably had every inch of Banner Elk and the surrounding mountains memorized. I just had to settle into my seat and try to keep calm.

It was never easy being around him, especially in close quarters.

"What?" he teased. "You don't like your old nickname?"

"It was fine back in the day, but I'm twenty-five now."

"How about Darlin' Darcy Rose?" Nick persisted with his game. "I can't call you that anymore either?"

I shifted in my seat, averting my eyes. "I would prefer you didn't."

"Fine, Darcy it is then."

"Thank you." I paused, glancing out the window. "So . . . why were you in town, anyway?"

"I was picking up my mail before the post office closed. I needed some odds and ends from the store. You know, the usual."

Nick turned right when he should have turned left.

"This isn't the way to my dad's."

He shook his head. "Oh, I'm not taking you out to your dad's."

"What?" I turned to watch the road's fork vanish from view. "Nick, he doesn't know where I am! My phone wasn't working back there! Just let me out. I've got bars now. I can call him."

"You want me to leave you out on the side of a road . . . on Christmas Eve . . . in the dark . . . in a snowstorm?"

As he laughed, I remembered hoping to be home in time for Christmas Eve dinner, but I figured that was a pipe dream.

"I'm sure Dad could come get me."

"Visibility is getting worse by the minute. You really want your father out in this?"

"No," I mumbled begrudgingly.

Nick flashed a triumphant grin. "That's what I thought. Now, my cabin is only ten minutes from here. You can spend the night with me, and I'll take you over to your dad's house in the morning. You'll be there just in time to dump out your stocking and eat your special Christmas breakfast. I promise."

"Fine. It's not like I have much of a choice, anyway."

"No, you don't."

Surrendering, I crossed my arms over my chest and wondered, "When did you even get this cabin?"

"I got rid of my grandparents' old trailer. I used the land to build this place last year."

"I guess I have been away for a while, then."

The truck rumbled. The road shifted from smooth asphalt to uneven gravel. Nick slowed to a crawling pace as we passed through trees and caught glimpses of Christmas lights glowing in the night. At the far end, we rounded a patch of woods and came into a clearing where a log cabin sat with a green metal roof, a big stone chimney, and a carport on the side.

The little cabin looked like a haven in the dark, gray night. The winds whipped around us. I hated to open the truck door, but I told myself it was safer inside. Everything would be better if I just got inside the house, so in a rush, Nick grabbed my suitcase from the back and led me through the side door. The mudroom had hooks on the walls and a place for our boots. Passing by the washer and dryer, we stepped into the kitchen that felt undeniably warm.

It wasn't just the temperature. The place was just so *cozy*. I recognized half of the furniture from his grandparents' place, like the old kitchen table and the China hutch complete with blue Wedgwood plates. Even the olive-green cabinets had their charm, but I couldn't rest easily in the space.

Nick's hair still fell across his eyes. His cheeks were pink from the winter's icy cold. I had run all over the world, but I couldn't escape him, not here, not in this storm.

"I got a lasagna at the store," he declared while setting down his paper grocery bag. "I was planning to bake it for dinner. That okay?"

"I'm good with lasagna," I assured him.

"Good. You can take the bed upstairs. I'll sleep on the couch."

My shoulders slumped. I had to protest.

"No, Nick, I can't put you out."

"It's no big deal," he insisted while unpacking his groceries. "I fall asleep on the couch all the time watching television. Just go upstairs. You can put your stuff down and get comfortable."

"Okay, okay."

I didn't need many directions. There was only a loft over the back of the house. Walking past the bathroom and behind the couch, I caught sight of the little Christmas tree covered in colorful lights and old ornaments sitting just beside the fireplace. The bedroom overlooked the living room with its large bed and simple furnishings. Nick had never been the kind of man to need much, but he did have a few things around from his past. I was pretty sure the patchwork quilt was something his Grandma Peggy had made.

Not dwelling on the man's bed, I got myself out of my cold jeans and sweater, trading them for leggings and my oversized Duke sweatshirt. It was big enough that it didn't matter if I wore a bra. My chest just looked like a heap of heathered gray cotton. With my wild thicket of dark hair pulled up into a bun, I decided there was nothing attractive about this outfit.

Nick Wallace would never want me anyway, cute pajamas or otherwise.

After calling Dad to explain, I followed my nose back downstairs to the kitchen. Nick might not have been trying, but I hated how good he looked with his flannel's sleeves rolled up to his elbows. I could see the tattoos scattered across his right arm, including the bright petals of a blooming red rose.

His backside in those jeans didn't help, either.

"Need any help?" I asked while forcing my voice not to crack.

He slid the lasagna into the oven, and the heavy metal door creaked shut. Nick set a timer.

"You could cut up some lettuce."

I tried to joke. "I didn't know you ate salad. I always took you for a meat and potatoes man."

Fortunately, he chuckled. "I don't mind eating a few green leaves every so often. Besides, I'm not a teenager anymore. I can't just eat crap and expect to fit in my pants."

"Yeah, I know that feeling."

Nick definitely wasn't a teenager. He was in his late thirties and about fourteen years too old for me, but that didn't change how my heart fluttered when he got close. It didn't change how I leaned into the smell of the clean scents of aftershave and pine tar soap. I swallowed hard.

"You got anything to drink?" I asked while working hard to chop up the romaine.

"I, um, have some sweet tea and some beer."

"You got anything stronger?"

"Whiskey?"

"Sounds great," I replied with a forced smile. "Let's put a little tea in that and call it a cocktail."

"All right," Nick agreed. "What's botherin' you, then?"

"Bothering me?"

"You always get jittery when something's bothering you, and I've never known you to drink anything stronger than a shandy."

"Well, I'm not that girl anymore. I enjoy plenty of cocktails now, especially margaritas and palomas."

"That doesn't mean something's not botherin' you."

I grumbled to myself. Of course, Nick had to be the guy who gave me my first drink. Shaking my head, I forced away the unhelpful thought. I couldn't just melt into a puddle on his kitchen floor.

"I just feel bad about not getting home tonight," I lied.

"Don't worry too much," Nick tried to assure me. "I'm sure your Uncle Mickey and Aunt Erin are keepin' your dad company tonight."

"Yeah, they're probably playing card games and listening to Dad's old Christmas cassettes."

I could see it all in my mind's eye, letting my muscles and my worries ease themselves. Everything felt easier by the time we sat down to dinner. I was already working on my second spiked sweet tea, and Nick was nursing a beer. Our little salad and take-and-bake lasagna tasted pretty good.

"Merry Christmas Eve, Darcy," he offered, clinking his bottle to my glass.

"Merry Christmas Eve," I repeated before gulping back more of my tea.

"So, it's only seven thirty. What do you want to do?"

I wanted to bury myself under his quilt and forget where I was.

"We could watch a movie," I suggested instead. "Or . . . we could play a card game, or um, you got checkers?"

"I've got a deck of cards, no checkers."

"Well then, I guess this night is ruined."

Nick rolled his eyes and offered that wry grin. "Sure, it is, Black Sheep."

I rolled my eyes at the old nickname but said nothing. He was letting me sleep in his bed for the night. He was feeding me dinner. I couldn't complain. I just needed a third sweet tea to get over it.

With *It's A Wonderful Life* playing in the background, Nick and I found ourselves playing our fourth game of Go Fish on the plush brown couch. We played by the light of the Christmas tree and the fire burning in the heavy stone fireplace while a red plaid blanket covered my lap. On the little screen in the corner, George and Mary were finally getting hitched.

"You got any threes?" I asked Nick.

"Go Fish."

I reached over to the coffee table, a slab of heavy wood straight from the trunk. The bark still ran along the rough edges, but I didn't focus on the piece of furniture. My tipsy head was too excited.

"I fished my wish!" I exclaimed too giddily, laying down a book of threes. "Now, do you have any queens?"

"Here," Nick surrendered.

Handing over his two queens, it was only a matter of seconds before I was declared the winner, but we only could play the same game for so long before the fun faded.

"I think that's enough Go Fish," Nick declared, gathering the cards.

"What now, then?"

His head turned toward the television. "We could just watch the movie."

As I settled myself down, George Bailey's honeymoon began. Rain poured down outside his house like the snow falling down outside. I watched as his new wife smiled at him. My body curled tighter against the end of the couch.

"You know, I ran into Kevin Booth when I was at the grocery store," Nick remarked. "He asked about you, wanted to know if I knew where you were."

Kevin Booth took me to my senior prom. We were together for less than a month, and he was my only foray into dating in high school.

"Why would he ask about me?"

Nick shrugged. "Maybe he's still into you. Why? You don't like him anymore? I thought he was your first crush. I've certainly never heard of you dating anyone else."

George and Mary were heading to bed. They looked so happy together.

"He wasn't my first crush," I blurted out.

"Then, who was?"

"Nobody you know."

"I've served beer to just about everyone within fifty miles of here," he remarked in disbelief. "I'm sure I know him."

"No, you really don't."

He prodded my shoulder. "Come on, don't lie to me."

"*Nick.*"

"Is it really that big of a deal? It's ancient history."

No, it damn well wasn't.

"I thought we were gonna watch this movie."

"We will," he said with a chuckle, "right after you tell me who you liked instead of Kevin."

I knew exactly what I was doing, but I'd had too much whiskey to care.

"You, okay?" I huffed before taking a gulp of my drink.

There was no sense of shame as I turned to meet Nick's surprised eyes. It was the most serious I'd ever seen on him. His Southern lilt grew thicker with the rasp of his voice.

"What are you talkin' about?"

"I liked you, Nick. You were always the good-looking bartender at my dad's bar, and well, you were always nice to me. That didn't help. I was eighteen and foolish. Honestly, what did you expect?"

Apparently, whiskey was a truth serum for me. I used my last scrap of good sense to decide to never drink it again.

"You think I'm . . . *good-lookin'*?"

God, Nick's baritone voice sounded like whiskey tasted—strong, dark, and damn intoxicating.

"Does that make you uncomfortable?"

"No," he said. "You're just Black Sheep."

"You also called me 'Darling Darcy Rose.'"

"It's just a nickname," he insisted, quickly at a loss for words. "You were always hanging around the bar. You were Bill's daughter. It didn't mean . . . I never . . . I–I think you've had too much to drink."

"No, I haven't. I could touch my toes right now. I could do it and sing a whole song in French."

"Darcy, you don't—"

I cut him off by trying to stand, but I hadn't prepared for getting caught up in the blanket. I wasn't ready for anything. All too quickly, I stumbled and found myself falling into Nick's capable arms. His face was inches from mine, and my hand managed to press into his strong thigh. My fingers were inches from the bulge in his dark jeans.

Was it always that big or is he just happy to see me?

"I really shouldn't be taking advantage of you," I mumbled. "You've had two beers tonight."

"Three," Nick amended.

"I'm not drunk, but you probably are. I should, uh, just go to bed."

"Yes, you should."

And yet, my whole body was frozen in place. The heat rising up my spine should have me thawed out, but I couldn't move away. I was trapped in the steely-blue cage that was Nick's gaze. I could see the chiseled lines of his face and smell the scent of aftershave looming on his neck.

Back in the kitchen, a cuckoo clock chimed midnight.

"Merry Christmas, Nick," I offered softly.

His chest rose and fell with labored breath. "Why did you say those things?"

"Because you asked."

"What, would you do anything I asked of you?"

"Maybe."

He exhaled heavily. *"Darcy..."*

Nick muttered my name like a curse, but he didn't push me away. Nothing could stop our lips from meeting. It felt as inevitable as the snowstorm outside. One kiss became two, and two turned into more. Growing dizzy and light, my head fell against the throw pillows. I could feel Nick's calloused hands sliding under my sweatshirt and cupping my breasts. I didn't stop myself from moaning into his mouth.

It was everything I'd always wanted. All those years of pining finally culminated in this.

"We shouldn't be doing this," he muttered, his kisses wandering down to my throat.

I could feel his bulge growing hard against my thigh. No matter what he said, I could feel how Nick wanted me, even if I didn't totally believe it. It was right there in his hungry kiss and roving hands, but it still didn't feel real.

"Don't stop," I whispered.

"Hell, Darcy."

The scene became a mixture of golden, dim light and cold shadows. The fire began to die out as our clothes became a pile on the floor. Every time Nick exposed a new piece of me, his mouth devoured the skin. His broad frame consumed mine, and I was nothing but happily helpless under him.

I had found my haven in the snow. He was six-foot-four and smelled like winter and smoke. My fingers could run freely through his hair and down his tanned chest, and I didn't think to hide. It was never like me to shy away. I could only let my legs spread wider as Nick's hand began to feel me out. He found me dripping wet, ready, and willing. His two fingers traced my folds with slow intention.

"You shouldn't be this beautiful," Nick growled. "I shouldn't want you like this."

I pleaded in a whisper, "Let me have you this once. It'll only be one time."

His lips crashed against mine again, and our bodies connected. I felt every inch of him push into me. As I shut my eyes, my head fell back. My hips knew how to move. My hands knew to anchor themselves against his shoulders. Every piece of me began to move on instinct while pleasure built up inside me. It grew like a fire, sparking and flourishing into a raging swell of flames in my heart.

That's what we were—shadows and skin, bone and smoke. Nick rocked me into the deepest climax I'd ever known, and he left nothing but the bones on my skin. Breathless and gasping, I inhaled the scent of the wood fire as my eyes opened. Shadows grew over us together.

I never made it to bed that night. In the morning, the sunrise woke me. Squinting my eyes, I took in a deep breath scented with pine soap, salt on skin, and the ashes of a cold hearth. The world outside looked white, and I was pinned between the back of the couch and Nick's naked frame. His tattooed arm fastened me against him over our blanket.

"Darcy?" I heard Nick grumble as he opened his eyes. "Dammit. Damn it all."

His swears sounded nothing like the night before. There was no wry smile on his face or touch of affection. In a rush, I felt him pull away from me before finding his boxers and jeans. The world quickly grew cold. I wrapped the blanket around me to keep warm, but it wasn't enough.

"I shouldn't've let this happen," he muttered in a rush. "We'd both been drinking. I should've known better. God, what would Bill think? After all he's done for me, I wouldn't blame him for shootin' me dead."

The fire had gone out. My heart froze over.

"You're right," I declared quickly, unable to listen to any more of Nick's muttering. "We had both been drinking. It was stupid, and nobody will ever know, especially Dad."

Buttoning his jeans, Nick looked at me with apologetic eyes. "Darcy..."

No warmth lingered in the sound.

"It's fine," I insisted, standing with the blanket. "I'm gonna get dressed so you can take me home."

Not waiting for more, I hurried upstairs and promised that nobody would know how my heart broke that Christmas morning, especially Nick Wallace.

CHAPTER ONE

NICK - TWO YEARS LATER

I felt it the moment the heat kicked off. With the bar quiet and still, there was no reason to leave it on for my sake. I could throw on my leather flight jacket and keep working alone in the back office. My fingers thumbed through the paper bills with the ease of doing it a million times before.

This was the order of my life. It's what I knew, and it's where I always expected to be.

"Nick?" a familiar voice called out. "I saw your truck parked out back!"

"I'm in the office!" I shouted.

Footsteps sounded on the concrete floor. Then, Bill Steward's dark eyes met mine with a small smile forming under his graying mustache. He scratched his nose while appraising the scene. Our two bodies took up most of the free space in the small office.

"What are you doin' here so late on a Friday night?" Bill wondered, watching me take down the cheap painting to put his cash in the safe. "It's nearly midnight."

"I could say the same about you. I see you're wearing your good flannel."

He chuckled low and deep like some kind of Southern Santa. "It was poker night over at my brother's. I figured the guys deserved a shirt without too many holes in it."

"So you dressed up for them," I joked. "How nice of you."

We laughed lightly together as the last of the money got tucked away. The safe door shut with a loud click, and like always, I hung the painting back up and straightened it twice. I could still remember the first night Bill let me do this as his new manager. Over a decade had passed, but in some ways, it only felt like last week.

"Was business good tonight?" Bill asked me then.

"Yeah, per usual," I replied. "People seem to be liking this new fish fry special on Fridays. More faces are becoming weekly regulars, and our old regulars seem to like it too."

"That's thanks to your good thinkin', you know. If you got any more bright ideas, feel free to give 'em to me, and speaking of dinners..."

"Yes?"

"Will you be coming to the house for Thanksgiving?"

Turning toward the desk, I tried to move like nothing was amiss. I logged out of the desktop computer and began to file the paid expense reports away in the tall filing cabinet.

"You aren't going to Durham for the holiday?"

"Naw, Darcy's coming here for the week this time. She talked about going to see her mother in Oregon, but it's not gonna work out. She's gonna drive over Sunday afternoon and stay until the next Sunday. Honestly, I can't remember the last time she stayed so long, but I ain't complaining."

My heart clenched at the name. I spent a long time trying to get that name out of my head, but I could never escape it. Her eyes still reflected the firelight. The memory of her touch made me weak. It was such a stark contrast from the cold shoulder and icy looks she left me with the next day. Across from me at her father's dinner table,

CHRISTMAS IN THE CABIN

Darcy spent that Christmas as if I didn't exist, and honestly, it was for the best.

I wasn't sure I could trust myself around her anymore. Once I had her my grasp, it felt impossible to let go, but I did. I did it for Darcy's sake and for the man standing in the doorway, not that he even knew it. I never gave her a second glance when she was younger. Darcy Rose Steward was just the plucky young girl who would sip sodas and do her calculus homework in one of the back booths of the bar. Things changed after she left for college. Bit by bit, she became someone else, someone Darcy was always meant to be, and certainly too good for the likes of this little mountain town.

She was especially too good for the likes of me.

"Are you sure you'll have room?" I remarked, trying to keep my voice light.

"You know I always do for you, Nick."

I smiled. Bill had always been generous to me. Scratching the back of my head, I knew there was no reason I could give to refuse. I didn't have anyone waiting at home for me. Ten years had passed since I'd had anyone else at home, and if I didn't agree, the only Thanksgiving dinner awaiting me would be some takeout or a frozen meal. Bill knew it too.

He would never be harsh and point out my lack of family. With his hands in his coat pockets, Bill patiently waited for an answer. He wasn't going to pressure or belittle me. Still, the truth lingered in the brief silence. Darcy would just have to suffer through another dinner with me, and once dessert was eaten, I'd quickly get out of her thick curls for as many years as I possibly could.

"Sure, I'll be there. Thanks, Bill."

He flashed a friendly grin. "Of course. Now, come on. Let's get this place locked up and get ourselves home. My armchair's callin' my name."

As Bill offered a hand turning out the lights and double-checking his bar, a dozen different thoughts raced through my mind. What was I going to tell Darcy when I finally faced her again? Would she be happy to see me? If she gave me *that look* again, staring into my soul and stripping me bare, would I be able to survive it?

I was so wrapped up in myself that I almost ran into Bill. The emergency light glowed over us as he opened the back door just as I absently reached for the handle.

"I've got it," he told me. "Brace yourself, though. The wind's pickin' up."

He wasn't kidding. The cold November air smelled of ice and damp leaves settling in the woods around us. I pulled my knit cap from my back pocket and handed Bill my set of keys. Out in the gravel lot, there wasn't much to see but our two vehicles parked side by side and the dumpster under the streetlight, yet the wincing expression on Bill's face was new. He rubbed his chest as he handed me back the keys.

"You okay, Bill?"

Quickly, he nodded, dropping his hand back to his side.

"I'm fine," he said. "Mickey made some enchiladas for dinner tonight, and I think he got a little heavy-handed with his canned jalapeños. Washing it down with a can of beer probably didn't help me either. It's just indigestion."

"I figured you'd have a stomach of steel after all these years."

"No part of me is as good as it used to be. Each mornin', I've got a new surprise of what's gonna be sore next."

"Sounds like something to look forward to."

Bill shook his head. "Don't go wishin' your life away, boy. I'd kill to be forty-one again."

"You make it sound like I'm still twenty-one."

"To me, Nick, you are."

Was I really still so young in his eyes? When Bill looked at me, did he see the teenager he met doing court-appointed community service or the young bar back, frantic on his first Saturday night? These days, I only saw the silver hairs hiding among the fading blond and the fine lines settling around my face. I never considered myself a vain man, but each morning, I saw every reminder in the mirror that I wasn't young anymore.

That's what made it so easy for Darcy to sweep me under her rug. When she was sober with her eyes wide open, she could see how much more life had in store for her. She was traveling the world and building a life all on her own. I wasn't going to stake her to these rocky grounds, and just like Bill's wincing expression, Thanksgiving dinner would probably be nothing.

Saying goodbye to Bill, I hopped into the cab of my old Scottsdale and steeled myself for what was coming for me. Darcy would be in town for seven days. She would be gone before I knew it, and nothing would pass between us beyond a few minutes of conversation and some dinner rolls. Even if it put me in an early grave, I refused to make the same mistake twice.

CHAPTER TWO

DARCY

I had already checked my packing list twice, but a third time would keep me from getting paranoid on the highway. Running down the yellow pad, I checked off my clothes, my toiletries, my work bag, two bottles of my favorite wine, and a massive suitcase and tote bag filled with things for my petite partner in crime. Sipping her iced coffee, my neighbor and tenant, Margie, smiled at me from across my kitchen island.

"I think you have everything you could possibly need for the week," she remarked teasingly. "I think you could survive the apocalypse with all the stuff in your car."

I shrugged. "With a baby, you know any Tuesday can turn into the apocalypse. It just depends on her mood."

"That was definitely true with my twins! God, it's so funny seeing them with babies of their own now."

"Does it feel like just desserts?"

"Sometimes, yes," she confessed.

With her ginger pixie-cut and wide grin, Margie was a recent divorcee with two cats and a penchant for jokes about wine. She had them scattered on kitsch things all over her half of our duplex. Last Christmas, she'd even given me a pair of tea towels which read something like, *Part of me says I should stop drinking like this, but the other part of me says, "Don't listen to her, she's drunk.*

That was Margie. She was a liberated middle-aged woman, happy to be a fun grandma and pick up my mail when I was gone. As for me, I was at the beginning of my journey with motherhood. My baby girl sat across the room, flipping through one of her soft books. She wiggled and moved like a metronome to the music playing, and when one of her pages squeaked, she showed off her baby teeth with an excited smile.

"Willa!" I chimed. "I think it's time we put on our shoes! You wanna get ready to go see Grandpa?"

Dropping her book, she stood as she exclaimed, "Go!"

Her small hands reached up and over her playpen walls. She was more than ready to leave to see her Grandpa. Stumbling over her own feet, Willa eagerly climbed the pen and toddled over toward the garage door. She crawled up on the shoe bench and lifted her legs for me.

"I'm coming. I'm coming," I told her cheerfully.

Willa had always been restless and often willful. She always wanted to do things her small body wasn't ready for as a baby, like lifting her head when her neck didn't have the strength. At night, she'd fight her tired hazel eyes, and even when I was pregnant with her, Willa grew impatient enough to come about three weeks early. She had always been a fighter, even beating out my birth control pills to exist.

"Mama!" She fretted when I didn't move fast enough.

"I've got you all worked up, haven't I?" I teased.

As I kneeled down in front of my daughter, Margie laughed behind us. "You mentioned Grandpa. What did you expect? I wouldn't mind seeing Bill myself."

"I'll tell Dad you say hi," I assured her. "Thanks again for covering for me. Like I mentioned, the lawn guys will be over tomorrow. The hanging plants in the sunroom will probably only have to be watered once, and you can leave any mail and packages on the dining table."

"I worked in a preschool for thirty years and raised two girls," Margie reminded me. "I think I can handle your empty house."

"Oh, I know you can. I don't know what I'd do without you next door."

She shrugged. "I'm sure you'd figure it out. It takes a while, but every mom does."

From the day I realized I was pregnant, life felt more and more like an improv show. I managed to get this duplex built and find Margie to rent next door. Unable to travel anymore while working remotely, my days of waking up in hostels and coworking spaces were traded for mornings in my sunroom office and weekends at Mommy and Me classes. It wouldn't have worked without the kindness of others, like my very understanding supervisor and Margie's occasional babysitting for deductions on her rent, but I was making it work.

I never had to put Willa in some overpriced daycare. With the rent money, I could cut back my hours to work thirty hours and week, and no matter what hurdle came next, I always found a way forward. This was going to be my longest trip home in years, but I knew I could make it work too. Willa and I would enjoy our Thanksgiving like nothing was amiss. As long as I kept a low profile, nobody would wonder where her father was . . . or *who* he was.

That was how I liked it.

"Go!" Willa chimed again.

With her small sneakers velcroed into place, Willa squirmed off the bench and pointed to the garage door. She was ready to go on her first big trip to the mountains, not even looking back to wave goodbye to Margie.

"Say bye-bye to Miss Margie," I reminded Willa while reaching for her pink denim jacket and hat. "Can you wave to her?"

Willa turned and waved, but her gaze went back to the doorknob in a flash. She was more than ready for me to buckle her into her car seat and head out. With the car loaded and the house shut tight, I couldn't put off our trip any longer. Margie waved goodbye to us

CHRISTMAS IN THE CABIN

again from the shared porch of our twin houses. As my fingers tapped against the steering wheel, brown fall leaves piled up under the hollow trees we drove past, heading toward the highway. The hills would grow into ancient rolling mountains before I knew it. My heart already felt the pull of switchback country roads and pines growing over the steep rock.

A piece of me always missed my childhood home, but these days, anxiety mingled with happy memories of my youth. I should've been excited to see my dad. I hadn't hugged him since Willa's first birthday in August. He'd already bought our turkey and was talking about what we would have for our special breakfast. But when a new text came in from him, the robotic voice of my car recited my worst fear.

Got your bedroom ready, it read aloud. *Also, I talked with Nick Friday night. He'll be coming to Thanksgiving this year.*

I groaned so loudly that Willa sat taller in her car seat, looking alive from the back.

"Mommy's okay," I assured her with a forced smile.

Adjusting the music, I skipped the upbeat folk tune for something more mellow, more suited to my brooding. I'd planned to avoid him at all costs, yet that was impossible now. I had quietly hoped he would say no. I didn't want to hear people's questions about Willa, his more so than anyone else's. Nick never knew I got pregnant. He had no clue that he was a father, and it was his own stupid fault.

Part of me hadn't gotten over how he'd cast me aside that Christmas morning. I was off on the other side of the world when I realized I was pregnant. Coming back from Thailand, I went home to celebrate Easter and my father's birthday, but Nick never showed his face once. Dad said he had work. Then, Nick was feeling bad. The excuses were easy to believe, yet I couldn't.

Nick didn't want to face me again, and if he couldn't bear to look me in the eyes, how was he going to take becoming a father? I had been willing to set aside my injured pride. For the sake of honesty, I would have given him a chance, but the more I considered it, the more I realized I was better off staying in Durham.

I already had the plans to build a home base for myself and create some passive income. There was a better school system and more entertainment and things to do. It was a good place to raise a little girl, and I couldn't imagine Nick packing up his cabin to become a part of modern suburbia. Boone was a big enough city in his eyes, and it was mostly a comfortable college town. I wasn't sure you could even call it a city.

He couldn't keep leaving my ego black and blue. Perhaps I could've called him, forcing him to listen, but I didn't want to fight for a man who'd refused to hold onto me. I couldn't waste my energy with a baby on the way.

Looking back on it all, my knuckles grew white against the steering wheel. Two years hadn't changed my lingering resentment. If anything, my bitterness sharpened like steel blades, ready to fight against a man who might dare to offer a cheap apology. It wasn't like I had to tell Nick anything anymore. I had kept my promise to him and lied to my father, after all.

Dad believed the guy I'd been seeing that fall was Willa's father. I said that he was back home in Australia, and I wasn't keen on spending the rest of my life shipping my daughter around the world. For Dad, it wasn't hard to believe. He and my mom had met while he was taking a summer road trip across Route Sixty-Six. Their romance ran out when the road did, but that didn't keep me from showing up.

With Mom being a chronic wanderer and an airline stewardess by trade, Dad had always been my primary caregiver. He taught me how to read and helped me with my science fair projects. Mom sent me birthday gifts and holiday cards in the mail, and these days, I tried to see her at least once a year. One week out of the fifty-two was the most she ever seemed to carve out for me. I didn't begrudge her for it. I just . . . I knew where we stood.

She was never going to be the parent that cut crusts off her kid's sandwiches, and Nick wasn't the kind to give up his peace of mind for the chaos of bustling city roads, preschool parent drama, and home-owner associations. Life pulled us all in different directions. Still, that didn't mean Willa's life wasn't a happy one. She sipped her milk and mumbled her garbled speech as we reached the mountains. Her feet kicked to the tempo of our music. I just hoped she never inherited my chronic struggle of always forgetting something before a trip.

I hadn't missed anything on my packing list. This time, I forgot to fill up my gas tank, and there wasn't a station at every corner around these parts. The needle teetering around E began to taunt me.

"Crap on a cracker," I muttered under my breath.

My quickest stop was a little place I'd been a million times before. The unassuming local gas station was known for their cheese biscuits and the high schoolers who would buy them before heading to class. The grease from the baked chunks of cheddar bled through the paper bags, and as I pulled up, I saw three kids eagerly rushing out with their snacks and biscuits in tow. Hustling toward the black SUV parked beside me, I knew they had to be tourists. Their four kids came hustling out of the glass door.

"We got them!" one yelled in a nasally Northern accent.

As I quickly went about my business, it wasn't long before the hulking black beast of a car pulled away, and my heart stopped. There was only one other vehicle at the station. It was an eighties truck, light blue, with rust in a few faint places. The sight of it had me frozen in place.

He can't really be here. It can't happen like this.

My eyes shot to Willa in the backseat, blissfully ignorant, before they flew toward the small white brick building. There was a tall figure in a dark leather flight jacket. I could make out a red knit cap too. With my hand squeezing the gas nozzle, the fuel couldn't come out fast enough.

CHAPTER THREE

NICK

"Here you are, Nick," the plump gray-haired woman said with a smile. "Enjoy."

"Thanks, Hilda. Hope you and yours have a good Thanksgiving."

"You too, sweetie!"

The gas station felt louder than usual with the pack of children running around. They had been just ahead of me, ordering two biscuits apiece, before pulling drinks from the glass cases and gum from the shelves. The narrow aisles were filled with the flurry of their activity, and I was happy to let them push ahead toward the register. Outside, their dad looked like he was going to fall asleep pumping his gas.

"Thank you!" they all chimed at different times. "Bye!"

Change and snacks in hand, the kids hustled past me and out of the store. Their feet thumped against the cheap linoleum floor, leaving the security bell to ring in their wake. I had already gotten my country ham biscuit and black coffee. Now, I just had to deal with the teenage cashier looking sullen behind the register. The point of sale system looked to be about the only thing that had changed in the last forty years there. The brown wooden walls and posters stuck up behind him all seemed the same.

"Can you put forty bucks on pump four?" I asked.

The cashier ran a hand over his oily black hair and nodded. "Yeah, sure."

I debated not asking. I needed to get to the bar and look over the receipts and prep some food orders for the next day, but the bartender in me couldn't help it. Pulling out my debit card, I looked the teenager up and down.

"What's got you down?"

"Nothin' much," he mumbled, swiping my card for me. "It just sucks to be here sometimes."

I thought nothing could fix the frown on his face, but it only took one casual look through the storefront window. Turning his head to the left, the teenager blinked twice and grinned, showing off his neon braces. I wondered what could make him look so eager. A few guesses went through my mind, but none of them were *her*.

I'd seen her so many times that after a while, I stopped believing my eyes. I didn't recognize the silver Subaru or the gray wool coat she wore, but I'd know that thicket of coiled curls anywhere. With her hip-hugging jeans and pink cheeks, Darcy looked better than any one of my mirages and further from my reach than ever before. Every bone in my body twisted under the pressure.

Should I go say something? Did she even know I was going to be coming over for Thanksgiving? Of course, she had to know, but I didn't have a clue how she felt about it.

"She's got a real nice rack, doesn't she?" the cashier remarked, forcing me to break my gaze.

It was my turn to frown now. A fiery flash of resentment coursed through me. Glaring at him, I watched the boy's stupid grin fall.

"That doesn't give you the right to comment on it," I growled. "How do you think she'd feel if she heard you say that?"

"Sorry, geez."

I rolled my eyes. "I don't need to hear your apology. Just shut up and hand me my receipt."

Of course, he didn't notice how I couldn't disagree. Her open coat showed off the V-neck sweater she wore underneath. Only a blind man would miss the full feature it highlighted.

Were they somehow bigger than before?

"Here's your receipt," the kid said, shoving an old pen across the counter.

I couldn't decide whether I wanted to rush through signing my name. With every stroke of my signature, my heart beat faster. Did I honestly want to see her like this? Was I ready for the rejection? It turned out it didn't matter.

Darcy pulled away just as I pushed open the glass door. Standing there, I watched her turn and head off down the road toward her father's house. She must have seen my truck. It was the only one there, yet her eyes had been so focused on her task. Perhaps she hadn't noticed.

Maybe she really had put me out of her mind once and for all.

Trying to shake it off, I headed over to the bar to do inventory and double-check everything before the holiday week began, eating my quick afternoon meal on the way. I couldn't let things fall by the wayside just because people were going to be stuffing their faces with turkey and pie. Our usual schedule would be thrown off. Still, I knew how to make it work. I could do my old bar back duties and save someone else the trouble.

The bar always looked strange on Sundays. Unzipping my coat, I didn't bother to lock the back door. There was nobody around to worry about, and the bar's desolate quiet was a far cry from the rowdy Saturday night before. The pool tables were untouched, and the small kitchen didn't feel cramped. Heading toward the walk-in, I pulled back the latch and grabbed the clipboard.

Maybe she had seen me and didn't know what to say.

Running a hand over my face, I felt two years of this strange torture weighing down on my back. It made my shoulders slump and my muscles ache. Back then, I told myself what I needed to keep my worst impulses at bay. I said Darcy's dismissive looks were because she had scratched an itch with me and found herself dissatisfied. She wrote me off as a stupid mistake that she didn't want to deal with again, as she should have. Still, a small voice whispered in the back of my head.

I heard it every morning and night. Its one line echoed in the place where dreams and reality met, but with the days counting down to Thanksgiving, I began to hear it more. It nagged me, standing there in the chill of the bar's old metal fridge and through every one of my mundane tasks.

What if I was wrong?

Darcy had good reasons to forget me. Her world was elsewhere, and my feet were rooted right there against the mountainside. With my past and my history, this life was the best I could ask for.

Almost twenty-five years had passed since I broke the law out of desperation. Foolish naivety told me it would be fine. I wasn't hurting anyone. Driving a car up the coast felt so innocent in the moment, but even as the seasons changed and years went by, I never fully escaped the whispers or the memories of fear that I was going to waste my youth behind bars.

Sheer dumb luck and a lenient judge stopped that from ever coming true, but Bill Steward was the man who made sure I didn't go back to that life. He didn't listen to the whispers of small town skeptics. He put his faith in a dumb kid who'd made an even dumber mistake, and how did I repay him? I let a few drinks and one lone look into her dark eyes get the better of me.

If Bill knew what I'd done, he would kill me on sight. I wouldn't blame him, either. I'd probably give him the rope to string me up and the shovel to dig my grave. No amount of hard work and time would wash me clean of that guilt. Every time I heard her name or remembered the soft, tickling feeling of her breath against my neck, I knew I'd never escape.

It was four days until I had to face Darcy again. Going through the motions of my work, I told myself to spend every minute steeling myself against her. I had to learn to keep my cool or I'd come undone all over again. Even thinking about it, I found myself coming out of my jacket thanks to the stifling heat.

I told myself I had four long days, but that was a lie. Time wasn't on my side. It never had been.

Cleaning out the ice maker, I heard the heavy door fall shut. The click of boot heels tapped against the concrete floor, and something inside me just knew. I didn't have time to brace myself against the Molotov cocktail of pining and regret.

I didn't even have four minutes.

CHAPTER FOUR

DARCY

There was a time when my grandmother slept where I stood. As a little girl, I could sneak into her big bed and bury myself under her quilts early in the morning before the sun ever rose. I recalled when my dad and Uncle Mickey built the bookcases into the wall for me and moved my things into the bedroom. Once upon a time, my grandfather ordered this house kit not long after he married Grandma.

Family history lived in every pine floorboard and piece of furniture, and as I tucked my underthings away in the dresser drawer, I knew I could never feel old in this place. The mountains were too ancient, and there were just too many memories. Even the smell of my father's spaghetti sauce took me back.

"Now, the secret is just a little bit of sugar," Dad explained to Willa. "Canned tomatoes are too acidic. It's all those preservatives that do it, so you gotta cut it just a tad."

I doubted she knew what he said, but Willa stared all the same. Propped up in the crook of his arm, she had one hand curled around his shirt collar. She leaned toward the old Dutch oven set on the gas stove. Of course, Dad didn't usually measure out his herbs in little glass bowls. He usually fished his different jars out of the burgundy cabinets and eyeballed it, but to let Willa help, he set down his spoon, picked up the oregano, and let her sprinkle it into the pot.

The sleeves of her floral shirt were pushed up to her elbows like Dad's plaid shirt. She focused her bright eyes in concentration. All the while, I leaned against the kitchen door frame, watching them work together.

"I've just finished unpacking our stuff," I declared. "I wouldn't have minded keeping Willa in my room."

"Oh, it was way easier to clean up the den. Besides, I can just imagine Willa pullin' all those books off your shelves," Dad answered with a small laugh. "Those trophies ain't exactly safe for babies, either."

"I keep meaning to put them in the attic."

My days participating in the trivia bowl and science fairs were long over, but I had a feeling Dad liked to see the silver and gold plastic trophies. The was one bronze medal and a ribbon from my few years of horseback riding. I just never took to horses like I did to fun facts.

"Ah, naw, leave 'em there," he insisted. "They aren't hurtin' anyone where they are."

"I noticed you got my old crib out of the attic, though."

Dad beamed, handing Willa some more parsley to dump into the pot. "That was your crib first. I had to get a new mattress, but I think that thing looks better than anything you'd find in those new fancy baby boutiques. They just don't make 'em like that anymore."

"No, they don't. Thanks for doing it, though. I wish I could've helped you."

"You were busy getting yourself and my favorite little butter bean here, but if you wanna help me . . ."

"Yeah?"

"You wanna run over to the bar and pick somethin' up? I've got to send some stuff over to my accountant tomorrow morning. Otherwise, I might not get my quarterly taxes paid, and Uncle Sam might come for me in January."

I folded my arms over my chest. "Wouldn't you want to go grab it yourself? I could watch the pasta sauce while you're gone."

"But Willa and I are having fun here! It's not every day I get to spend time with her."

"What about me?" I wondered jokingly. "Am I old news now?"

"No, you're my favorite daughter, my favorite *very helpful* daughter. It won't take you but an hour, and if you go, you can take your Shelby."

"Wait, really?"

My eyes lit up like Willa's. Once my pregnant stomach struggled to fit behind the wheel of that car, I knew I needed something more family friendly, but I never had the heart to sell my Mustang. Dad, Uncle Mickey, and I had all fixed it up together. It was part of me and our history, so I decided to leave it in the safety of my father's barn out back. My toes were already tapping in my ankle boots, eager to feel the pedals under the sole of my foot.

I didn't love going to the bar these days. Like my bedroom and a hundred other places in this small town, the ghosts of my past still lingered there. Spending too much around them allowed those shadows to sneak back under my skin, and I became someone I didn't necessarily want to be.

"You're sure nobody's there?" I asked Dad. "It'll just be a quick pickup?"

He nodded. "It's just one folder of expense invoices and employee salaries. I got it all together and left it by mistake on Friday. When I saw Nick, I just forgot what I was doin'. My brain isn't what it used to be."

I wasn't going to get into it with him about the beauty and convenience of digital files and cloud-based sharing systems. We'd been there and done that one time too many.

"You're fifty-seven, not eighty-seven," I said instead.

"But I'm not gettin' any younger here."

"Fine, fine, you have fun with Willa. I'll go and be back in an hour at the latest. You say it's in a folder, right?"

"Bright green and labeled. You won't miss it on the desk."

"Okay," I agreed, kissing his cheek and my daughter's.

As I shrugged into my coat, the two waved from the stove. The sun was already beginning to set. The vibrant shades of pink and violet made the mountains that much darker, but they were nothing compared to the cherry-red car with white racing stripes. Its interior smelled like old leather and freedom. Shifting her into gear, Shelby rumbled to life, swelling with the excitement inside me.

There was nothing as liberating as a fast car with a full tank of gas.

Coasting around rocky curves, I hummed along to the radio already playing holiday music. Nobody could touch me here. I could talk to myself, laugh at my thoughts, and enjoy the sweeping landscape before it got too dark. However, the delight was lost the moment I parked the car around the side of the old backwater bar.

"Looks like nothing has changed," I mumbled while pulling my keys from the ignition.

The old steel building's sign wasn't lit up in the gravel lot it shared with the auto shop and garage next door. Steward's Repair was as much an institution to the locals as Bill's, and half the beauty was that the leaf peepers and tourists rarely ever stopped there. It didn't look like much from the outside. However, the sight of that same blue truck meant everything to me.

Nick had to be here. I could turn back around and tell Dad I didn't see it, but I had lied enough to my father in the last few years. Besides, perhaps it was better I face him now and rip off the pesky bandage.

The clock in my head began turning backward. My heels dug into the gravel mixed with the red mountain clay. Every cheap gray stone crunched underfoot as I felt myself going back in time. I was lucky the bar was closed for Sunday. With everyone gone, I didn't get so nauseous when I opened the back door. Everything remained frozen in time... but not me.

I wasn't the nerdy, lovesick teenager anymore, and I didn't have to be afraid of facing Nick Wallace. Still, my feet slowly stepped down the hall, wondering if he might pop up at every other corner. He wasn't in the back office or the kitchen. Hesitantly, I peeked into the large, empty bar to see if I could find Nick or even notice a change in my father's decor.

Being my grandpa's old garage, the bar had an industrial look city snobs loved to mimic in their overpriced lofts. Steel beams painted black ran along the ceiling. The concrete floors showed decades of wear and tear. Countless cars had been fixed up in this place before my family built the new repair shop next door, so oil spill stains were permanently splotched against the polished gray. The collection of neon lights and rusting vintage placards hung in all their usual places, and even the same old deep-fried menu was written out across the chalkboard above the bar nearby.

It was all just as I remembered it. Weaving through the mismatched tables and chairs, I remembered eating dinner at every single table at one point or another, scarfing down French fries while trying to do homework. If the kitchen had been open, I might have ordered a plate of those fries. I had no appetite, though.

My stomach was knotted up too badly. My throat grew dry. Nick's tall figure rose up from behind the counter, ice scoop and bucket in hand. Clearly, he had been cleaning. He hadn't expected company, either.

"Um . . . hey, Nick," I greeted him, already regretting looking for him in the first place.

His blue eyes looked like a frozen lake I could skate across. They were both sparkling and impenetrable, and they chilled me to the bone. Even as he wiped his hands and looked away, small shivers continued to shoot up my spine.

"Well, well." He chuckled as if to ease the tension. "Black Sheep, have you any wool?"

"No wool. I came for some papers for Dad and noticed your truck outside."

My feet dared to take one step and then another. In his fitted black T-shirt, Nick reminded me why so many women fawned over him, even me. I glimpsed the red rose tattoo amid the sleeve of art covering his right arm. The muscles underneath were as defined as a heavyweight prizefighter ready for the championship match. A scar on his scruffy jawline made it seem like he had been fighting on more than one occasion, or maybe he'd cut himself working here.

There were so many pieces of his life that I didn't know. Way back when, I wanted to ask about the tattoos, the faded scars, and the pensive looks, but now, I knew to bite my tongue. Nothing good would come from it. There were already enough scars here, both seen and unseen.

"He could've picked it up tomorrow," Nick pointed out.

"That's what I said, but you know my dad. He won't get any sleep tonight. He'll be up worrying about it."

He nodded once. "Yeah, I know Bill."

Straightening his broad shoulders, Nick stood to his full six-foot frame. A cleaning rag remained in his white-knuckled fists, but he couldn't wring out his anxiety. Nick just had to dump the old ice in the bar sink and keep moving.

My mouth opened to speak, but I didn't know what to say anymore. There was a time when Nick and I talked like old friends. I'd come home from college. He'd ask me all about it, listening as he served beer from the tap and wrangled the bar staff. We used to be able to talk about anything, but standing there, clicking my heels together, I realized how hollow most of it was.

Nick and I used to talk about everything and nothing at the same time.

"I hope the drive here wasn't too bad," he finally remarked.

"Oh, no, there were just a few idiots on the highway today."

A small smile toyed at the corners of his lips. "There's always gotta be at least one."

"I don't think the highway would function without them."

Nick chuckled softly. It was everything and nothing again.

The words that mattered caught in the back of my throat. I made a quick escape to go grab the file, but it only saved me for a few minutes. Nick was already done with whatever to-do list he'd made for himself. Meeting me in the hallway, he shrugged into his old flight jacket, and I had to fight the urge to fix the shearling collar for him.

I couldn't touch him. I could hardly look at him for more than a minute without sweating.

"Lemme just . . ." he mumbled over the din of my pounding heart.

He was too close. I felt on edge and uncertain, and the folder in my hands was seconds from being ripped apart. I thought he was about to touch me for a moment, yet reaching across the wall, Nick flipped the light switch. My panic was for nothing. The hall became washed in a dull yellow emergency light.

"Did you get everything you needed?" he asked then.

I nodded quickly. "Yeah, I think I did."

It took a moment for my vision to adjust to the new darkness. I could make out the path, yet my footsteps didn't move quickly enough. I needed air that was fresh and far from the one-of-a-kind smell of the old bar and a faint hint of pine.

The back door opened. Putting space between Nick and me, I felt the icy evening did me a favor. It let me shake off the burning heat lingering on my back and release the growing tension in my body. Light shined from the nearby streetlamp like a beacon, and my soft exhalation of breath looked like a plume of smoke.

"I guess this is where I leave you," Nick remarked, locking the door behind us.

His rugged face softened for a minute. Everything about him was so intense that quiet moments somehow seemed more nerve-wracking. His colorful eyes glinted, and my heart clenched in response.

"I'll see you on Thursday, then."

"Or sooner," he replied. "That's the funny thing about small towns. They only seem to get smaller until you can't help but bump into people."

"That's true."

No matter where I went, I couldn't hide myself or Willa. Nick was going to see her. Questions wouldn't be avoided, yet the man had so few questions for me now. I mean, I hadn't seen him in almost two years. My conversation wasn't sparkling, but he'd never once asked how I was.

He was the one who turned away. *He* never looked back.

Jitters began to boil over into frustration. A hundred different emotions simmered under my skin, and none of them felt good.

Just tell him, a small voice cried inside me.

"Don't forget we're having dinner at five," I blurted out instead.

Then, I turned on my heels and stalked off to my car. Nick said nothing. I figured it wasn't good running into me. I couldn't have looked well. There was no sign or show of reaching out. He only left me to throw open my car door and hide myself inside. With my self-inflicted anger, I shifted into reverse to head home. The holiday radio station wasn't so fun anymore.

I checked my mirrors out of habit, knowing nothing was there to hit in the empty lot. I glanced down to shift into drive, but I noticed Nick one last time in the rearview mirror. He was wringing that red knit beanie in his hands. His feet remained rooted there in the gravel, never moving an inch.

Anger was a cheap excuse and pathetic armor. My shoulders slumping, I shook my head and turned away. If Nick had wanted to tell me something, he should have done it two years ago. The hollow pang of longing wasn't enough to make me surrender, not then or now. I didn't care how it gnawed at me. Driving off into the night, I was done looking back.

CHAPTER FIVE

NICK

She was there in the cab of my truck as I drove home and curled up again on my couch. It didn't matter how many hours ticked by that night. Every trace of Darcy haunted me. Her polished fingers had me in a chokehold, trying to force the four little words I was too cowardly to admit.

I've missed you, Darcy.

Over the years, I'd imagined what it would be like to see her. I practiced what I might say and do, but in those few minutes, I wasted hours of planning. The promises I made to myself kept me from saying anything more. My comments became idiotic and dull, and while her eyes appraised me, her expression gave away nothing.

I couldn't tell what Darcy thought of me anymore. I only knew how her ghost followed a half-step behind me around the cabin and every step up the stairs. The darkness didn't send her away. She wouldn't even let me sleep.

As she sat at the edge of my bed, the mirage of Darcy watched me toss and turn. She crossed her legs and studied me with those unflinching eyes. I had never seen anything else like them. About the color of black coffee, Darcy's eyes showed how the wheels of her mind turned endlessly. She'd never once seemed vacant or bored. No, those eyes could stare into my soul and pick me apart in a second. Burying my head under the blankets couldn't hide me. Those eyes and that soft voice followed me into my dreams with ease.

Nick...

It'll only be one time.

Nobody will ever know.

The sight of her in the empty bar mingled with her words from the past. Her profile glowed in the low light. She was back in her old college sweatshirt, not the expensive wool coat from before. I didn't know which version of her had me more beguiled. Every angle and mood held me captive, and I surrendered to every one of them.

With my hands burying themselves in her hair, I pulled us both against the wall of the bar's back hallway. Clothes or pretense couldn't hold me back. It didn't stop Darcy either. Taking hold of me, those pink nails curled around my neck and dug into my skin. I could feel the red marks she left behind, but my mind was too preoccupied with pulling her back into my arms to sense any pain. Fixated on the taste of her lips, I felt myself being consumed by her.

Darcy was all I could touch, all I could see. I longed to ravage every inch of her with such wild desperation. Broken and remade, I felt myself wrapping around Darcy's finger as she smiled at me for the first time in ages. Her fingers trailed down my chest and curled around my length. She had me in her palm and refused to let go. I didn't want to let go of the vision either.

It was all I had of her. Only a ghost of Christmas past could fill the hollow ache in my heart, satiating every silent desire I still carried like a torch. As unrelenting as Darcy herself, the flame refused to go out.

Merry Christmas, Nick.

My body jolted forward. Between gasping breaths, my eyes grew wider. Darcy wasn't there, not in my bed nor in the cabin, yet her effect on me hadn't changed. She had my skin covered in a fine mist of cold sweat and my body aroused. In my sleep, I'd fallen to pieces. Every piece of me felt heavy against the mattress, but I pulled back the covers anyway. My feet hit the frozen floorboards. Even the soles of my feet burned.

I hoped a cool shower might wash away the illicit thoughts. With water running down my back, I longed to forget it all, but that never happened. Months of agony proved it to be a pipe dream. I had been here so many times, yet after seeing her there, the wanting became so much worse. No amount of soap could scrub it away. Deep down, I knew I couldn't leave the shower without some kind of relief.

The dreams had been flashes, quick and unclear, but shutting my eyes, I sensed Darcy so clearly. The weight of my body was over her naked frame. My hands studied every curve as my fingertips pressed into her soft skin. With a ragged sigh, I reached down to find my rock hard shaft. My thumb rolled over my tip, mimicking Darcy in my dreams. I let myself get lost in her. My back pressed against the white shower wall, and forgetting everything else, I shut my eyes and shut out the worries.

She was beside me, against me, and as I found my rhythm, I allowed myself to believe that I didn't have to let her go. My hand moved up and down, gently twisting before I quickened my pace. Darcy never left me. She was there in my bed and under the running water. Her chest brushed against me. Her lips moved over my ear.

Don't stop.

It's what she wanted. I couldn't give up. Against her, *inside* her, I was ready to fall to my knees and give her everything I had. I remembered my hum of delight against her lips. I felt Darcy's pleasure reverberate through her body and back into mine. My muscles stiffened at the overwhelming euphoria building within me, but I refused to relent. I clenched my jaw and moved at a rapid-fire pace even quicker than my racing pulse.

This was the only place I could surrender, the only time I could admit the truth.

Then, before I knew it, my release took hold of me and the ghost of Darcy let go. The evidence of what I'd done washed down the drain, and as my shoulders slumped, I took in one deep breath and then another. No eyes studied me as I turned off the shower and wrapped a towel around my waist. Over the bathroom vanity, the steamed-up mirror didn't show the truth in my eyes, but it didn't matter. I felt it in my heart and deep within my bones.

I had never gotten over Darcy or that night. Seeing her brought it all back to the surface, pouring out of my aching heart and taking over every corner of my mind. I couldn't hide from my desires. Darcy herself didn't need to know how I pined for her, but there was no kidding myself. I should've found someone else. I needed to put her in my past, yet something had never let me.

Darcy had her fingers wrapped around more than my throat. She'd taken hold of something inside me that I didn't quite understand. It shouldn't have been so hard to shake her, but I couldn't. In many ways, I didn't want to be set free of this agony.

It was all I really had.

Opening the bathroom door, I glanced around the dim living room coming to life in the first rays of gray morning light. The cabin felt still and silent, and even if she existed merely as a figment of my imagination, having Darcy was better than no one at all. I usually enjoyed the peace and quiet. There was no getting distracted in the business of the day or even a need to speak, yet the silence sometimes spoke volumes.

First, my mother went.

Then, it was Grandpa Jim when I was sixteen, and Grandma Peggy ten years later.

I had grown so used to the nights alone, but there was a time I remembered having people with me at the kitchen table. Darcy could've been any woman. Perhaps my isolation was masquerading as desire, pinning itself onto the one woman I happened to find lost in a rare Christmas snowstorm. That's what I had to tell myself. As I began to fix my morning coffee, I repeated the words over and over in my head.

This isn't about Darcy. My feelings are mine alone to solve. She didn't need to get tangled up in my problems, and besides that, she deserved far better than me.

CHAPTER SIX

DARCY

For a moment, I thought I smelled salt and pine. My eyes remained closed, yet I could have sworn I felt a toned arm draped over my blankets and waist. A faint memory of Nick's couch came back to me. I remembered how Nick held onto me and never let me fall even as he slept. I wondered what changed when we woke up that Christmas morning.

That question had been quietly plaguing me ever since, but now wasn't the time to dwell on it. My alarm was going off. Willa had to be awake. Pulling back the bed covers, I found no man's arm to pull away. I tiptoed out of my old bedroom in peace.

"Good morning, Willa girl," I whispered to her. "Are you ready to start the day?"

Clicking on a nearby lamp, my daughter's face lit up with sleepy-eyed excitement. She clung to her favorite plush pig with one hand and reached for me with the other. I had to fix the scrunched up arms of her star-printed pajamas, though. They were already getting too small for her. Soon enough, she would have to get another set of bigger clothes, but the snugness didn't bother Willa. She let me check her diaper before heading to the kitchen. Willa knew exactly how our Monday morning would go, even if we were at Dad's house.

Together, we'd have our breakfast before getting ready, and as I went through my morning meeting, Willa would have something to occupy her curious mind. I was thinking that play dough and cartoons could do the trick today.

"But first, breakfast," I declared, settling her into her high chair.

Buckling her up, I clicked on the light over the old gas stove. The back door hinges squeaked, and I heard heavy boots coming off and getting kicked aside. Dad smiled as he saw us.

"Looks like I'm just in time," he greeted us before kissing the top of Willa's head. "You need twelve eggs?"

"How about five?" I replied. "Two for me, two for you, and one for Willa."

"And you know what would go good with that? Some bacon!"

I shook my head. This was coming from the man with cholesterol problems and a doctor who urged him to eat a more heart-healthy diet. Years of fried food, beers, and smoking cigarettes in his youth had done nothing for him. He'd quit smoking by the time I came along, but the damage had already been done.

"What about fruit?" I suggested instead. "We could make some cinnamon apples and toast with the bread I brought."

"Bacon could be real good with that too, you know. I wouldn't mind a sausage, either."

"Just fish me some of your apples out of the fridge, Dad."

There was no stopping a grown man from eating what he wanted. Moving around the little country kitchen together, Dad sliced three pieces of toast and cut up the Granny Smiths into a saucepan. He sprinkled in some cinnamon and brown sugar and set it to simmer.

"Do you remember when we planted that apple tree?" Dad remarked fondly. "You weren't much older than Willa, I think."

"I was three. Then, when I was five, you and Grandma decided to put that chicken coop under it."

"And now, my hens are enjoyin' the shade and fallen apples every fall."

Smiling with pride, Dad lived such a different life from mine. There wasn't a grocery store around the corner here. For Dad, it was a good twenty-minute drive to get back to any of the surrounding small towns, and he was one of the luckier ones. It made far more sense for him to keep a small garden in the summertime and fruit trees in the fall. Fish fillets were wrapped and stocked in the chest freezer out back, and all had been caught by Dad and Uncle Mickey on one of their afternoon fishing trips.

Many people would look at this way of living and consider in more trouble than it's worth, and maybe even frustrating, but there was a quiet ease as we fixed our plates and sat down together. There was no cacophony of city noise or cars rushing past the house. Out here, everything felt so . . . *still*.

"What's on your docket for today?" Dad asked, biting into the bacon he fixed for himself anyway.

"I've got my usual departmental weekly meeting," I explained. "That's first thing at nine, and then, I'm getting started on some new website pages and updating a client's landing page. It's the usual, nothing special."

"Are you writing code with HTML or JavaScript today?"

Bringing my coffee mug to my lips, I couldn't hide my laughter or growing grin.

"Do you even know what that means?" I asked.

"No, not really. I've just heard you use those words. Did I get it right?"

"Sort of. I'll be coding with JavaScript, actually. It's very popular, but it's a different kind of language than HTML."

"How so?"

As Willa played with her cooked apples, I reached over to cut them into smaller bites, not that it did much good. She just shoved even more into her mouth until she had stuffed chipmunk cheeks.

"One bite at a time, Willa," I reminded her before turning back to Dad. "JavaScript's like . . . it's like the studs of a house. It's the structure and the framework, and HTML would be more like the drywall and paint. It's the content you actually see on the page."

"Oh, I get what you're sayin'."

"Do you? Honestly, I wasn't sure it made much sense."

"No, it did," he assured me. "If you've got this meeting, you want me to take Willa for the morning?"

I swallowed a mouthful of scrambled eggs. "I was just going to set up her playpen and give her some activities until snack time."

"Naw, let her run wild with me! Nick's got opening up the bar under control. I won't have to go in until later this afternoon."

I tried not to dwell on his name. Truth be told, workdays often held like a high wire act for me. I had to keep one hand on my laptop and the other ready for Willa. I champed at the bit for any chance to get Willa out and about instead of cooped up with me.

People often suggested daycare, friends and nosy co-workers alike, but even with my generous salary, the options I had seen looked more like infant prisons than places dedicated to nurturing care. There would be one worker for every twelve babies. If I knew Willa was stuck in a place like that, how would I get any more work done than I already did? Between play dates, Margie, and me, Willa had far more to do than sit in a crib most of the day.

"Well, Dad, if you're sure . . ."

"Of course, I'm sure! You go on and get dressed. Willa and I will take it from here."

My father was the last person who needed coaching about taking care of a little girl. By the time I had on my leggings and best sweater, Dad was already buttoning up Willa's coat and getting her pumped up to play in the back yard. I couldn't remember the last time I didn't have to juggle work and my daughter's morning routine.

I guessed . . . never? As long as she had been alive, it had been her and me. I didn't really know what a difference a second pair of hands could make.

You know who might like to help you? He's always been capable. He's always been a hard worker. You only have to tell him.

Grabbing my laptop from my bedroom, I shook the thought away. I didn't have time to agonize. My morning meeting was due to start in ten minutes.

"Go give your momma a kiss, Willa," Dad told her. "She needs the luck for work."

She toddled over in her navy duffle coat with its sweet wooden toggles. Between it and her red pom hat, she almost looked like Paddington Bear.

Cute... just like her father.

I swallowed back the words and accepted the kiss on the cheek. The guilt had been my companion for long enough that I'd learned to ignore it. Bringing my laptop to life at the dining table, I slipped in my earbuds and sighed. I'd given Willa all that I could, yet I couldn't get past the secret wish that she'd have more in her life.

The answer stared back at me, his reflection caught in my rearview mirror. I didn't know how I would make it through this week without all these feelings spilling out.

"Good morning, everyone!" my supervisor, Chris, chimed on the screen. "I hope you're all ready for a short work week. I'm gonna make this as painless as possible, so just bear with me here for ten minutes."

I had work to do and money to earn. With my speaker on mute, I listened to the progress reports of last week while prepping my screen for my daily tasks. A few minutes in the meeting turned into a few hours of typing and testing code. I didn't expect my text notifications to pop up in the far corner, one that came with a picture.

It showed a terrace overlooking a garden shaded by palm trees with white patio umbrellas popped up to provide guests shade as they worked. The green flora was absurdly bright, lush and gorgeous. Looking at the face in the far corner, I couldn't see much of her face behind her large Jackie-O shades, but I would know that bobbed strawberry-blonde hair and wide grin anywhere.

Back in Phuket made me think of you, so I snapped this pic this afternoon! I read underneath the photo. *Staying in the cabanas isn't the same without you next door, but I'll be coming back stateside next month for the holidays. Maybe we can meet up? I could fly into your airport like before. I'd love to see you and Willa. I'll bet she's gotten so big!*

I wasn't the kind of mother to plaster my child's face all over the internet, but I happily sent back a picture of Willa in a pumpkin patch from the month before. Propped up on a hay bale, Willa squinted and grinned up at the camera, showing off the gaps between her baby teeth. I instantly got back a row of heart emojis.

Sam Rutledge was the best friend I'd made while traveling. We met in Bali at a retreat in Canngu. We both got the giggles during a morning yoga class and agreed to get lunch together after. The rest was history.

Both single women and coders from the States, it was easy for us to bond, but it was even better when she and I decided to bunk together for a while. She made my rooms half the cost and our weekends twice as fun. She was even with me in Mexico when I realized that my nausea wasn't from the water but from morning sickness. One year of travels and a night together on our bathroom floor made it feel like I had known Sam for a lifetime.

She's so precious!!! Sam messaged back.

Smiling to myself, I typed, *We're in the mountains visiting my dad right now, but definitely text me when you get your flight details. I'd love to see you and hear about your island hopping this fall.*

The thought of seeing Sam was the exact distraction I needed. I began to forget about where I was, only that Willa was safe and I could work in peace. By the time Dad caught my attention, another two hours had passed without my realizing. I pulled out my left earbud.

"Yeah, Dad?"

"I'm fixin' sandwiches for Willa and me," he told me. "Can I make you one too?"

Looking at the clock, it was nearly one, and my stomach quietly growled at the thought. I saved my spot and nodded.

"That would be great. I'll be there in just a sec."

"Don't worry. Willa and I've got it under control."

Dad chuckled under his breath, remembering this sight from a million times before. He would catch me picking at my nail polish as I studied at that same dining table. At midnight, he'd tell me to close up shop and head to bed, but there was always one more page to read or one new thing to learn. The more I learned, the dumber I felt. With so much to see and do, there were never enough hours in the day, but I had to press pause every once in a while.

At the very least, I had to eat, didn't I?

I couldn't bounce back from running myself into the ground anymore. I was too old for all-nighters and overdoses of caffeine. I had to take things slower, enjoying what time I had with the people I loved most.

In the kitchen, Dad had his radio playing the local public station, playing the sounds of a classical symphony through the occasional fuzz of white noise. It brought back memories of my childhood where Dad would heat tomato soup on the stove and fix us a grilled cheese sandwich to share, but today, it looked like we were all getting our own.

"Some things never change, do they?" I offered with a teasing smile.

Dad reached into his pantry cabinet and pulled out two cans of soup. "Well, look how you turned out. If a bit of classical radio and soup made you so smart, it can work on Willa. Lord knows, you didn't get it from me."

"Says the man who graduated from high school in three years."

Opening the cans, he shook his head. "I was just ready to get out and earn my keep."

"And that doesn't make you smart?"

"It makes me resourceful and efficient."

"Two words you'd use for a smart person," I countered, but looking at him, my smile faltered. "Are you, um, feeling okay?"

"Yeah, why?"

"It looks like Willa maybe tired you out."

It was worse than that. Dad breathed too hard for a man buttering sandwich bread. She was over in her high chair, and I walked over to finger comb Willa's hat hair, but it didn't make me forget the worn look in my father's eyes. He even flexed his shoulders in some kind of discomfort. He could smile all he liked, but something wasn't right.

My Thanksgiving with him wasn't going to be as cut and dry as I hoped.

"I guess some things do change," Dad tried to joke. "I'm not exactly thirty anymore, darlin'. Between pickin' the last of the apples and entertainin' Willa, I got a bit of a workout in the yard. That's all. It looks like I should've spent that time at the store. I've still got stuff on the list to buy for Thursday."

"Did she have you running in circles?"

"No, the chickens did, though."

I tried to laugh along, but I still asked, "Would you talk to your doctor about this?"

"Oh, I don't need to bother him."

"You wouldn't be. Please, just do it for me."

"All right, all right," he surrendered. "Now, you want to fix us somethin' to drink?"

I crossed the kitchen to kiss my father's cheek.

"Thank you, Dad."

Under his mustache, Dad smiled more tenderly. We had been a bonded pair for so long. Guys had come and gone, but Dad was always there with a listening ear and a kind word. He was my biggest advocate and supporter. Even if Dad thought nothing of it, I didn't want to risk everything he meant to me, not when I'd already lost the chance to keep the one man I wanted more than any other.

Dad would see his doctor, get an answer, and move forward like always. Willa and I weren't going to lose him, not this holiday season or anytime soon. As long as I could do something about it, everything would be absolutely fine.

CHAPTER SEVEN

NICK

It probably could have waited.

With the holiday, Bill was spending more time away from the bar than usual, keeping him from the office and the questions. People started asking about the annual New Year's Eve party hosted by the bar. Before I became a manager, Bill had learned the hard way that the event needed tickets thanks to a jam-packed bar and a visit from an unhappy fire marshal, but now, our regulars had already started asking when they could get their names on the list.

I could have told everyone to be patient, but their urgency became mine. Driving out to Bill's, I came prepared with a proposal for the year's party and armed against the thought of seeing Darcy again. Bill said she was working from his house, so I had to figure that she would be shut up in the office. Pulling up to the little house on the hill, it seemed luck was on my side for a change. That shiny silver Subaru Darcy drove now was nowhere in sight.

Seeing Darcy in the driver's seat of her old car had been a sight for sore eyes and a knife in my chest all at once. It was if we'd gone back in time for one brief moment where I hadn't ruined things between us. Darcy was still just Bill's daughter, the one who would stop by the bar and tell me all about college and living in the city. She looked so alive back then.

"Hey, I wasn't expecting you!" Bill called from across the yard.

He shut the steel garage door behind himself before walking over to me. With his usual friendly smile on his face, Bill wiped his hands with an old rag. The sleeves of his old Army sweatshirt were pushed up high to his elbows. Bill hadn't inherited his father's deep love of cars like his brother had, but that didn't mean the man couldn't be handy with a wrench. There seemed to be nothing Bill Steward couldn't fix.

Shutting my truck door, I answered, "I've got some work stuff to go over with you. You working on Darcy's Mustang for her? If it's a bad time..."

"Oh, no, it's all good. I just finished changing the oil in my old Ford," he explained. "I've gotta keep it runnin' smooth if I want to teach Willa to drive in that thing like I did Darcy."

Wait... *who?*

I followed Bill up the front porch steps, my head close to hurting from confusion. Who was Willa? Was I supposed to know that name?

"Willa?" I repeated as Bill opened the door.

"You know, Darcy's little girl." He said like it was so obvious. "They're off getting some stuff for Thanksgiving dinner, so I guess you'll finally get to meet her on Thursday. I would've picked the groceries up myself. Darcy insisted I call my doctor's office, though. I think she'd got it in her head that I've got somethin' wrong with me, like all men my age don't start gettin' weird aches and pains..."

Stepping into the living room, I unzipped my coat and stared at the scene laid out before me. Bill hadn't been expecting company. I didn't even come over to his place that much, but last night, he'd mentioned that he wouldn't be coming in again until Friday evening. He said things were busy at his place.

I didn't realize those things included a small child.

There was a tiny pink jacket hung up on one of the wall hooks. I hung my coat beside it. Plush toys and books were on the old plaid couch, and a sippy cup sat abandoned on the antique coffee table. Had I really been so blind?

As my muscles grew heavy, I walked closer to the corner fireplace mantel where Bill had his family pictures. Two small photographs sat in the newest frames. One had Darcy with a tired smile, holding a tiny baby dressed like a pumpkin. The other showed them beside a cake lit up with one lone candle, and staring at it, I recognized the smile she used to offer me. It made gravity feel ten times as heavy.

I had always assumed that Darcy was still traveling, but that had only made an ass of me. Looking back, I had avoided the subject of Darcy for so long. I knew nothing about her life anymore. Guilt kept her name out of my mouth. An old flickering flame forced me to turn away. I blinded myself to what was right under my nose, but I had to ask.

Forcing out the words, I asked, "When was this taken?"

Bill never murdered me, so he couldn't have known. Perhaps Darcy was seeing someone now. God, I hoped she was.

"Last August," Bill answered through my hurricane of emotions. "Willa had just turned one. I wish I had more pictures of her, but with phones these days, nobody thinks to print one out."

"Did Willa's dad take these?"

Bill's warm smile faded. The lips under his mustache drew themselves into a hard line.

"Hell no. That Kiwi or Aussie bastard is back on the other side of the world," he grumbled. "He could travel all over Europe for the hell of it, but he can't damn well bother to get on a plane for his own kid."

The answers began adding up my head. Darcy had been seeing someone that fall. If she was born in August, it meant Darcy had gotten pregnant in November.

That's what it had to be, right? Counting back the months in my head, that was the only logic I could come up with. It let my body relax ever so slightly.

"I didn't realize he wasn't in the picture," I remarked as if I'd always known, like I hadn't been averting my gaze from Darcy when she was merely a photograph. "That's a shame."

Shame didn't cut it. That idiot didn't know what he was missing. He was a cold-hearted fool if he really left Darcy and this doe-eyed girl behind. Who would ever take a family like that for granted?

Settling into his recliner, Bill scoffed. "Darcy and I have agreed to not talk about it anymore, but I don't think the moron's involved at all. He doesn't send her money, a card, nothin'. I mean, I get that not everyone needs to get married and have that picket-fence life. I didn't with Darcy's mom. It's not like she's little miss homemaker either, but dammit, she tried her best. She sees her daughter. She sent us money back when Darcy was little and visited. Seriously, what kind of man doesn't show up for his kid?"

I plopped myself down on the couch and dropped my papers on the coffee table.

"A bastard," I had to agree. "A really stupid bastard."

Looking over to Bill, it was the first time in my life I'd ever seen him so obviously angry. His brown eyes grew flinty. His jaw clenched. Cursing under his breath, Bill unconsciously rubbed at his chest in the same spot as before, but that didn't keep him from simmering with frustration and resentment.

"If I ever meet him, I'm gonna wring his neck like the chicken he is," he said.

"He'd definitely deserve it."

Silently, I knew I'd be right there beside Bill. I hated anyone who hurt her. I always had. Back when people gave Darcy a hard time at the bar, I always found myself stepping in. She never needed my help. She probably didn't want it. That didn't change the flash of fury I'd feel, but this? The picture Bill painted had me boiling.

I couldn't fathom any fool not wanting a life with her and a child *they made*. If I weren't too old, if I weren't the wrong kind of man in a dozen different ways, I would've been over the moon to have someone like her. Bill probably wouldn't be keen on having a son-in-law like me, whether I was forty-one or thirty-one. No man was good enough for his girl. He'd sworn that time and again when she was young.

Darcy had too much going for her to be stuck here.

She was too smart and too talented to only be someone's wife.

No foolish boy would hold her back from all that she could be, not the good ol' boys who gave her sideways glances and certainly not me.

"You didn't come here to hear me gripe," Bill realized, pulling me out of my red haze. "You said you had some proposals for our big New Year's Eve party?"

I blinked twice, trying to remember what he meant.

"Oh, uh, yeah," I finally realized. "I've got some possible menu items for the night and drink specials, and I've got a few ideas about advertising it online. I've been lookin' into possibly starting up a website for the bar. I know we get by with word of mouth, but it might be good to be online just a little bit. It could help us advertise and maybe get in some new faces."

Bill almost smiled. "I'm sure Darcy would love that. She's always gettin' on me about the newfangled technology and online stuff. She near 'bout twisted my arm to get that fancy point of sale system."

"Well, she wasn't wrong. It's certainly helped with overhead and cutting back on waste."

She was always clever like that. Darcy didn't need anyone's help to carry her own. She certainly didn't need some deadweight bastard, either. If anyone could raise a child by themselves, it was Darling Darcy Rose Steward with her rose-petal lips and thorny temper. That old flame began flickering inside me again at the thought.

I had to turn away from the light. Focusing on the work in front of me, I forced myself back into the dark. Darcy didn't need me fighting for her or even glancing her way. If I let that flame get out of hand, it would only lead to trouble, and that couldn't happen.

I refused to be the bastard who held her back.

CHAPTER EIGHT

DARCY

Pacing around the kitchen, I struggled to hold back my growing nerves. I was running on about four hours of sleep. My head buzzed, overcaffeinated and on edge. With Dad and Willa in the living room watching the dog show, I could pretend that I was starting prep on my sides and getting out the turkey Dad had dry brined for us, but really, I kept forgetting what I was supposed to be doing. Everything was taking twice as long.

"Where's that stupid knife?" I muttered to myself.

Of course, it was on the breakfast table in the corner . . . right where I had been cutting up the pile of carrots and Brussels sprouts just five minutes earlier. That was too easy of an answer, though. Why would I ever look there?

I felt my mind unraveling in real time. Nick wasn't due to arrive for another four hours or so, yet my eyes kept flitting over toward the sink's window. I counted down every minute in my head while trying to keep track of the to-do list I'd thankfully jotted down. Wiping my fingers on a dishcloth, I grabbed the knife and checked off *Vegetable*

Prep. It was time for me to start cutting up lemons for inside the turkey.

I just had to find the lemons first.

"Hey, darlin', why don't you let me help you?"

Dad stood in the kitchen doorway with Willa already toddling ahead. Her arms wrapped around my leg before she tugged.

"I guess it's about your snack time," I realized. "Come on, baby girl."

"And you still haven't changed out of your pajamas," Dad added.

Looking down, I realized he was right. I was still in my waffle-knit joggers and matching blue top. Had I ever even washed my face or brushed my teeth after breakfast? If I was still in my pajamas, I definitely hadn't showered.

Willa eagerly crawled into her high chair before plopping herself down. She didn't care one bit that her mother was going into panic mode. She looked up at me with pleading eyes that got wider every second I didn't hand her some food.

"*Mama*," she pleaded.

"I hear you, Willa," I promised her. "I'll get your snack."

The sliced banana wasn't much, but my daughter stopped complaining. She didn't mind it when I leaned down to kiss the top of her head or how I lingered there. With a deep inhale, I shut my eyes and went back to those first days of her life.

I had been so nervous when I was pregnant. On my own, I didn't know what kind of parent I would be, but when Willa fell asleep on my chest for the first time, I rested my hand on her tiny back and breathed in that new baby smell. All the worries began to look so small. I knew it wouldn't be easy. For Willa, though, I would figure it out.

We figured it out then. I could figure it out now.

Cementing my resolve, I went to get ready for the day and the hours slipped by. Dad and I took turns entertaining Willa as our dinner cooked, and before I knew it, headlights were sweeping through the front windows. Dad was lighting a fire in our fireplace, and the high, boisterous sound of my aunt came bursting through the back door.

"Where's my sweet niece at?" she exclaimed in her faded Louisiana drawl. "I've brought the pie!"

There were a lot of ways to describe Erin Steward. Rowdy, boisterous, and spitfire all suited, but my uncle always settled on "live wire". With her short bottle-blonde hair that stuck out at the ends and megawatt smile, live wire certainly suited her.

"Well, I guess if you've got sweets, I can at least give you a hug," I declared as our eyes met.

"There you are!" she shouted. "Give me some sugar, you precious girl!"

Kissing her cheek, I leaned down to hug her short, stocky frame. Uncle Mickey stepped through the door as we pulled apart, showing off his gap-toothed grin. His hands were full of Tupperware containers and casserole dishes.

"We've got a whole second feast here," he teased. "Your aunt don't know nothin' about bringin' just a few sides."

"Well, somebody had to make your mom's stuffing recipe, and I figured we should have the cranberry relish to go with the turkey."

I laughed. "You know there's only going to be five of us, right?"

"And little Willa!" Aunt Erin reminded me. "Where is that sweet girl?"

"Right here," Dad called, stepping into the warm, crowded kitchen.

"Oh, let me have her!"

Willa happily toyed with the sequins on my aunt's seasonal pumpkin sweater. In a minute, the house had become noisy and crowded. There wasn't enough space on the kitchen counters for all the food, so the breakfast table had to be cleared, and the pine floors squeaked and groaned under all the shuffling feet. Uncle Mickey had to step back out for a pitcher of sweet tea, but he came in with something more.

"Look who just pulled up!" he announced from the mudroom.

The screen door slapped shut. The back door squeaked, and with four steady footsteps, he appeared. Nick stood there in a navy fisherman's sweater that brought out the blue of his eyes. My palms grew hot under such a cloudless sky. There was no shade or place to hide, and no matter how many times I wiped my hands on my corduroy skirt, I couldn't rub the heat away.

Willa was in my aunt's arms by the stove. Nick *saw* her. He glanced over to watch how Aunt Erin brushed the tendrils of brown hair from her forehead, and I couldn't do anything but smile politely.

"Hey, Nick," I offered weakly.

His expression didn't change. For Christ's sake, why wasn't he panicking? I swallowed back my anxiety for the second time, but he only turned to set down his casserole dish before shrugging out of that same old leather jacket. I worked to keep my jaw from going slack.

Shouldn't this have been a bigger moment? Didn't he have at least one question?

"Have you met Willa, Nick?" Aunt Erin asked him like I wasn't dying where I stood.

He shook his head. "No, but um, I made a sweet potato casserole."

"She's the cutest thing, isn't she?" my aunt persisted. "I'd let you hold her, but I haven't had my fill of her yet. Come on, Willa. Let's go see what kind of toys your mama brought with her! Won't that be fun?"

Willa grinned at the thought, setting off with Aunt Erin and leaving us alone. Uncle Mickey must have gone back out to the car. I never saw where he went. I could only slide my hands into the pockets of my skirt and try to remain calm.

"Thanks for the casserole," I remarked. "I–I thought you might be surprised to see a kid here."

Nick's calm expression didn't change. "Well, your picture's on the mantel."

"Oh . . . *right*."

All the anxiety in me deflated. I wasn't surprised my father had fed him my old excuses, but deep down, I imagined that Nick might suspect *something*. He never thought to question or ask. In all my panic, I didn't know what to expect, but this wasn't it. It just made everything worse for Nick to look so good while acting so unaffected. Pushing up his sweater sleeves to his elbows, Nick glanced around the kitchen.

"So, is there anything I can help with?"

I let Nick take the silverware and napkins into the dining room, putting space and one measly wall between us. Dad, in his fresh tartan plaid shirt, showed up with his younger brother and was chattering about taking my car to some show. Uncle Mickey was the local car club's president, after all. He needed to make a good showing.

Talk of vintage cars and work filled the small house and surrounded the dining table. In a whirlwind, we all managed to get our plates and find our seats. Willa was easy to manage. Her high chair was buckled down at one of the ends, and with both of our plates in hand, I was the last to walk into the dining room. Dad was at the far end. My aunt and uncle took up one side of the dining table, meaning the only chair left was . . .

"Go on and sit down next to Nick," Dad told me.

Sandwiched right between Nick and the daughter he didn't realize was his. I sank down into the antique oak chair, and my heart sank in tandem. In another life, this would've been the perfect scene. The house was warm. Our table was covered with cider bottles, bread, and all kinds of toppings. Dad even had a fire going in the living room nearby, and with Nick so close, I could've reached for his free hand over the tablecloth. I would have pulled it into my lap, knowing it was all mine. It all looked so perfect in my head.

That wasn't my reality, though. Sitting there, I focused on minding Willa as my uncle announced that he and my aunt would be off visiting my cousin for Christmas. It wasn't much of a surprise. With their son, Jordan, off in the military, they took whatever chances they could to see him. I quietly listened until Aunt Erin set her eyes on me.

"Can you pass me the cranberry relish, Darcy?" she asked.

"Yeah, sure."

I reached over the table toward her extended hand, offering her the glass dish that smelled or cranberry and orange. Her eyes sparked with a new thought.

"You know, we're not leaving until the day after your birthday," she explained. "Maybe we could get together before then and celebrate you too. Our flight's out of the Raleigh airport, so we'll be in your neck of the woods!"

Running a hand through my hair, I had to admit, "That might be nice."

"We just don't see much of you these days, not that we saw you when you were off jet-setting around! I don't even remember the last time your curls were so long. With your hair like this, you look just like Andie MacDowell!" Aunt Erin gushed, clearly hopped up on good food and hard cider. "Her hair is all graying now, but your hair's got the same texture and color like when she was young. Doesn't she look like Andie, Mickey?"

My uncle swallowed his bite of green bean casserole. "Have I met her? Is she in your board game club?"

"No, the actress from *St. Elmo's Fire* and *Groundhog Day* and, well, a bunch of other stuff!" she insisted. "Come on! You know who I'm talking about."

"Oh, right," he agreed before looking at me down the table. "Your aunt's wrong, though, Darcy. You're much prettier."

I narrowed my eyes teasingly. "Are you trying to butter me up into passing you another roll?"

"Maybe..."

I grabbed the bread basket and reached over the table. Uncle Mickey's smile grew.

"Here. Take two."

Aunt Erin wasn't wrong. Our curls were the same, sure, but that was about where the similarities ended. I didn't have her glamorous model height or lithe figure. My five-foot-six frame was always curvy or full-figured or whatever the trendy word was for it. A girl couldn't grow up on sweet tea and biscuits and expect to be as skinny as a bean pole, not that I ever wanted to be.

I liked who I was. The freckles on my shoulders and nose were old friends now, and while I had my vanity, I would never let it take control of me. If some snob or jerk had a problem with my hips, that was their problem, not mine. The buzzed part of me just wished the man to my left would give them a second glance.

That's how I knew to stop drinking the cider and switch to water.

"Now, I want to hear more about your Christmas plans," I declared, looking back to Aunt Erin. "You mentioned you're going out to Hawaii? He's still stationed there, right?"

With her glass already by her lips, Aunt Erin nearly spat out her wine in excitement. "Oh! It's going to be twelve days of Christmas in paradise! Now that Jordan's renting a place off base and I'm retired from teaching, we're going to be able to see so much more of him. I don't even remember the last time we all spent a Christmas together. He was stationed over in the Middle East and then, he was somewhere off in Europe. Gosh, it's gotta be three years now!"

"Have you got any big plans while you're there, then?"

"Well, Jordan's mentioned he's been seeing a local girl for the last six months, and they've invited us over to their Christmas cookout." Aunt Erin's beaming face stretched from ear to ear. "Our boy hasn't said anything, but I think it's a sign!"

Uncle Mickey chuckled. "Why would he need to say anything? You've been hollerin' the obvious from the rooftops all week. Lord, Erin, I'll bet the girl can hear you all the way in Oahu."

"Well, if she can, Jordan's girlfriend wouldn't know it's my voice, would she?"

Their talk of whale watching tours and Hawaiian barbecue consumed the rest of the dinner conversation, but it couldn't drown out the growing need making my fingertips tingle and my hands heavy. How easy would it have been to slip my hand into Nick's lap? I could trace the length of his thigh or weave his fingers with mine. The thought alone of one small, innocent touch made my heart skip a beat. One sideways glance of his perfect blue eyes had me forgetting how to breathe. Sitting there, pretending I wasn't affected by having him so close, it became a sweet and torturous agony.

I couldn't bear his getting closer. I didn't want to let him go, either. Throwing back the last of my wine, it all became too much.

CHRISTMAS IN THE CABIN

"I think it's about time for pie!" I chimed, nearly jumping from my chair.

I managed to get the pumpkin pie and enough breathing room to make it through the last twenty minutes of dessert. By then, it was time for Willa's bath and bed. I made sure to linger and read an extra book for her, waiting until she was soundly asleep. Still, that didn't keep me from finding my aunt, uncle, and dad playing cards together around the dining table or Nick alone in the kitchen.

He loaded dirty dishes into our dishwasher. With his sleeves pushed up again and a towel thrown over his shoulder, he looked so ordinary and so devastating all at once. The flash of a red rose tattoo caught my attention, its red petals unfolding over his lavender-blue veins. He brushed back those stray pieces of fallen blond hair, and though we were only a few feet apart, I knew we had miles to go before I ever found peace with him.

"You don't have to do that," I tried to say, but my voice didn't have the resolve I needed.

"You and Bill worked hard on dinner all day," he insisted quietly. "This is the least I can do. Besides, those three are too cutthroat at that canasta game for the likes of me."

I tried to smile, but my lips couldn't manage it. I rocked back on my feet. Nick looked me over before loading up one last casserole dish.

"Can I get you something to drink?" he offered.

I knitted my eyebrows together. "What?"

"You look like you could use something stronger than cider, and I am a bartender. Although, I can't help but think I'm the problem here. If you want me to go . . ."

"No, it's not that," I half-lied. "I–I'm . . . It's been a long day."

Alone with him, I realized I was waiting again for the questions that weren't coming. Nick simply finished his chore. I tried to put some food in plastic containers, but getting closer to him felt like a mistake. Though I stuck by the oven, tension lingered around us like the mountain fog, undeniable and unfailing. Each day brought much of the same, but Nick and I used to be pretty good friends before . . .

"I can't keep doing this," he suddenly declared with a frustrated sigh.

"Cleaning up the kitchen?" I asked, playing dumb as I swallowed hard. "I said you didn't have to. If you want to go sit in the dining room, I can finish up in here."

His voice dropped lower. "I'm talking about us. I mean what's happening right now."

This was my opening, my one chance to admit every secret I'd been keeping. I didn't even have to tell him now. My mind racing, I imagined asking him to meet me later or to just follow me outside. I'd have to get him alone. I would need to be sure there was enough privacy to explain.

The idea left as quickly as it came.

"You can't expect things to stay the same," I muttered under my breath. "We can't just go back."

"But this feels like some kind of cold war, and though things . . . *happened*, I don't want to be at odds with you. I mean, I liked it better when we could actually talk."

"We're talking now."

Setting down the dish towel, Nick shook his head. "You know what I mean, Darcy. You must remember how things used to be."

"Yeah, I know."

Nick had changed the course of my life. He'd changed *me*, and he couldn't even see it. I wanted to be angry. The bitterness inside me insisted that I lash out, but how could I blame him? I'd become a good liar . . . too good, apparently. My only chance to make amends had to begin with burying a hatchet. I couldn't expect him to read my mind or know what I needed even before I did.

"I do miss talking with you," I admitted, daring to take one step closer. "Sometimes, I think about how I'd sit at the bar on slow weeknights and keep you company. I'd convince you to have a drink with me during closing."

"That's how I got this tattoo."

"I remember . . ."

Not thinking, I let Nick take another step toward me. He put his body within arms' reach, and my fingertips took on a mind of their own. They reached out. Tracing the thornless stem trailing up the middle of his forearm, I let my eyes slowly meet his. They looked too blue and too crystal clear. All the answers I needed lived right there. They had frozen over under the ice I'd put there.

Nick might have pulled back that morning, but now I was the one pushing him away. Nothing happened the same way twice. Still, I took in a deep breath, smelling pine soap and a nearby wood fire. Some things hadn't changed.

"I don't expect things to be perfect," he told me softly, "but can we work on making it better?"

Rich with a low rasp, the question invited me to inch closer. It was like well-worn velvet or a favorite pair of jeans. It was a sound to slip into, warming me from within. The blue ice began to thaw out. My eyes couldn't help but flicker toward his mouth, and though fear begged me to pull away, my fingers stayed against his arm.

I whispered, "I'd like to try."

A thin veil of air kept us apart. With a slight turn of my head, our lips would meet again. We only had to close the distance. I only had to shut my eyes and find my way back to who Nick and I were supposed to be.

CHAPTER NINE

NICK

Her lips had been so close to mine that I felt their heat. My chest ached for a relief only Darcy could possibly provide. I saw her veil of lashes as her eyes slowly shut, and for a moment, I wondered what the sugar and spice of the holiday tasted like on her lips. I was seconds from falling when Erin popped up, looking to refresh her glass.

I still couldn't decide whether it was a blessing or a curse.

That Saturday night, I wiped down the bar for about the hundredth time, watching as the bar backs served up the new holiday-themed drinks. Reindeer ales and spiced lagers were all the rage this small-business Saturday.

"Can I get two Red-Nose Ales, please?" a perky girl asked, leaning against the bar.

Flashing a ten-dollar bill, the girl looked like a fairy with pink hair. Glancing over to where her three friends sat, I took her money and made a mental note of where her friends gestured from the back booth. It was right where Darcy used to sit. She'd bring in her homework while her Dad worked, and remembering her poring over those books, the memory stirred something inside me.

"Enjoy," I told the girl, pushing two bottles and the change her way.

She flashed a grin and hurried back to her friends. Nobody was complaining. Everyone behind the bar kept working hard. Bill and I almost didn't need to be there, and silently, I wished Bill would go home.

It wasn't just the struggle of facing him, either. Back in his old office chair, Bill wouldn't stop rubbing his chest as he looked over the timesheets for the last week. His eyes didn't seem to be focusing, and the pill bottle on the desk wasn't a good sign.

"How are the books lookin'?" I asked, grabbing more cash for the register.

"Fine."

"I was thinking maybe we could hire a few new seasonal bartenders and bussers. If it's going to be this busy every weekend, it looks like we might be short-staffed."

"Fine," he muttered again.

I shut the safe and set down the bound stack of fives. Waiting for Bill to look up, I watched him. He didn't notice.

"What's wrong, Bill?" I finally had to ask. "And please, don't tell me it's Mexican food. You and I've both been eating the same leftovers for the last two days."

He grumbled quietly. It could've been about me, the pain, or both. Trying to drop his hand, Bill had no way of hiding his discomfort.

"It usually goes away by now," he confessed. "I mean, I feel some twinges when I've been workin' outside, or on a walk, but when I settle down, it does too."

"How long have you been back here trying to get it to stop?"

Bill looked toward the clock on the wall. "I guess . . . about an hour."

He had that doctor's appointment coming up, but the longer I appraised Bill, the more I realized a few more days of letting this slide might just be the death of him. If I let something bad happen to Bill, no doubt, Darcy would kill me.

"You need to get this looked at," I decided aloud. "Go to the emergency room in Boone. The urgent care in town is probably closed, but that place is always open."

"I don't know..."

The hospital in the old college town wasn't exactly the best in the business, but it was better than him sitting here hurting. Pulling his old tan coat off its hook, I shook my head in refusal.

"Bill, this isn't exactly up for debate. I—"

"No." He sighed raggedly. "I don't know if I can drive that far."

It would be a good forty minutes from here. The dark night had already settled over the mountains. If he wasn't feeling well, I understood how the drive might be somewhat daunting, but this was more than anxiety. Bill stood, flexing his shoulders as the pain grew and fighting back a frown.

Forget driving to Boone. In his state, I wouldn't trust Bill to drive out of the parking lot.

"Give me five minutes to tell Zoe we're heading out," I insisted.

The assistant manager had been working there for almost a year now. She handled customers and closing better than anyone else, and with the bar in her hands, I took Bill out to my truck. He slumped back into his seat, listening to the engine rumble to life. Warm air blasted through the speakers, but it didn't fight off the chill running down my spine.

Someone was going to have to call Darcy.

"Hey, darlin'," Bill greeted her over his phone.

I counted my lucky stars that he felt well enough to call her, but his explanation remained vague.

"It's nothin' serious. You don't need to come out," he insisted.

"Dad," I heard Darcy say before something else undecipherable.

A beat of silence followed. Frowning, Bill looked over at me.

"She wants to talk to you."

I took the cell phone from his hands and stared ahead at the dark road curving around the mountain. We were close to the highway now. It would be a straight shot into town from there.

"On a scale of one to ten, how bad does he look?" Darcy asked, not mincing her words.

"Um . . . which is worse?"

"Ten."

"I'd say seven," I answered honestly. "I'm not taking him just to be polite."

"You mean he couldn't take himself?"

"Yes."

Darcy groaned on her end. I could hear the rustle of something. She had to be on the move.

"Look, I've got to get Willa together," she explained hurriedly. "It's too late to call my aunt or uncle to come over, so will you be there until I can get to the hospital?"

"Of course."

Though it changed nothing, Bill piped up, saying, "Darcy doesn't need to come out all this way."

"I'm gonna be about half an hour behind y'all," she estimated, not caring about her father's insistence. "Just . . . just keep him in one piece until I can get there, will you?"

"I'll do my best."

Her voice grew quiet. "Thank you, Nick."

It killed me when she talked like that. When Darcy lowered her guard, she felt more tempting and dangerous. It was as if I would agree to anything she asked. Although, it wasn't the time to come undone. I needed to focus on getting Bill to the hospital, for his sake and hers.

When the light of the hospital's sign came into view, it felt like salvation for only a second. Bill immediately got sent off to an examination room, and since I wasn't family, I waited anxiously in the lobby. The teal upholstered chair squeaked as I fidgeted. Every breath I took smelled sterile, and the white tile floors looked freshly waxed. Off in a corner, a housekeeper decorated a tabletop Christmas tree to bring cheer to this desolate place.

The world kept turning around me, yet I found myself waiting for her. Like the second hand of a clock, my knee bounced until I saw her dark eyes come around the corner. Willa slumped into her mother's arms half-asleep. In her pumpkin pajamas, the little girl hardly registered where she was, but her mother was wide-eyed and verging on wild.

"How is he?" she asked.

I stood from my chair out of habit. "I haven't heard anything since they took him back. Whatever it is, I think it can't have helped that he ignored it."

"Just like Dad," Darcy muttered under breath. "His stubbornness is going to kill him."

"Mr. Wallace?" the stocky nurse who checked Bill called.

"I'm here," I told her, already moving to where she stood with her clipboard. "This is William Steward's daughter, Darcy."

The nurse smiled politely. "Nice to meet you. Mr. Steward's just gotten out of his scans and has been admitted to a room. If you'd like to follow me, you can see him now."

We stepped quickly down the shadowed halls of the emergency department until we reached a low-lit room. Its window overlooked the parking lot. Bill was already settled into the bed with a pale blue gown on. His usual clothes were in a bag on a nearby table, and different machines beeped all around him. I stood with my back against the wall, letting Darcy take the lone armchair.

"I said you didn't have to come," Bill insisted. "It's nearly midnight."

Darcy rolled her eyes. "Hey to you too, Dad."

Moving on, Bill quietly told us about the tests they took, sticking some tiny tube in his arms and injecting dye into his chest. Darcy didn't flinch. She waited with a quiet, determined look until the doctor arrived, never once letting go of Willa. When the balding man in the white coat appeared, her dark eyes flashed with awareness, and his explanations were far more detailed than Bill's cryptic answers.

"It looks like your father has stable angina," the old doctor explained. "There seems to be plaque build-up around his stint he received several years ago. It's not uncommon. We're seeing it more and more these days, but like I said, it's stable."

"Stable?" Darcy echoed.

"That means his chest pains occur when he's triggered by exercise or any number of strains on his system," he explained. "Now, as long as it remains stable, there's no reason some medication and a few lifestyle changes won't mitigate the symptoms. He can live a perfectly normal life as long as it stays stabilized."

"And if it doesn't?" I had to ask.

The doctor took in a deep breath and turned to Bill in the bed. "If it becomes unstable, Mr. Steward, you'll have to undergo a heart bypass. Hopefully, it won't come to that for a long time or at all, but for tonight, I'd like to keep you under observation and run another scan in the morning. It will give us a more thorough understanding of the best way to proceed."

"Guess I can't argue, can I?" Bill tried to joke.

Darcy quickly answered, "Not if I have anything to say about it."

Though she yawned as the doctor left, I knew Darcy wouldn't have slept for a second without laying eyes on her father. She appraised him and the situation, letting the wheels of her mind turn. I kept quiet in the corner.

"I'm not going to leave tomorrow," she said to Bill. "I'll call Margie and tell her I'm staying an extra few days."

"Oh, Darcy, you don't need to take care of me."

"It's not all about you, Dad. I'm not going to be able to sit still in Durham until I know we're over this hurdle and that your chest pains are under control."

He held up his hand like a white flag of surrender. "All right, all right. Just go home for tonight. There's no way Willa's gonna get a good night's sleep here. Lord knows, I won't."

"Fine," she agreed quietly before moving to kiss her father's forehead. "Try and get some rest. We'll see you tomorrow."

Her smile fell as we walked down the quiet hall. The lights made Willa grumble in her mother's arms. Slowly, Darcy rubbed her back without missing a beat, her feet still falling in line with mine. It seemed a shame that Darcy had to do it all on her own. Between her kid, her dad, and everything else, she was the only person I knew who could keep it all going, but that didn't mean she didn't deserve some help.

"Let me drive you home," I offered before considering it.

We were close to the doors now. The dark parking lot was just a few feet away.

"You don't have a car seat in your truck."

I shrugged. "We'll take yours and come back for mine in the morning."

"How will you get home, then?"

"I'll sleep on your dad's couch."

"You won't fit on it. You're too tall."

"I'll be okay."

Darcy pursed her lips, tightening them as she refused to yawn. I'd been prepared to stay up until one o'clock for work, but I imagined she'd been up early that morning with Willa. Stubbornness had always run in the Steward family, though.

"Come on, Black Sheep," I tried to tease. "You know you're tired."

"Well, I guess it wouldn't hurt."

Not complaining about the nickname, Darcy pulled her keys from her coat pocket and put them in my palm. It took a second for her to show me where the signals were, but on the highway, everything settled down. Willa slept in the back while Darcy's tired eyes stared at the road ahead. Things weren't normal between us, but this situation was beyond our being uncomfortable around each other. The anxiety had to be set aside.

"I'll need to go back to Durham on Monday," she murmured to herself. "I didn't bring enough stuff to stay this long. Maybe if I call Aunt Erin, she can watch Willa, but I've got a video call with the graphic design team that afternoon. If I go on Tuesday, I . . ."

She was spiraling. Reaching over, I squeezed Darcy's shoulder, stopping her before her tired mind went over the edge. Her dark eyes flashed toward me, shooting straight for my heart. I had to look away. It overwhelmed me to glimpse everything hidden behind her eyes.

"Don't worry about that right now," I insisted gently. "Your dad's got a washing machine, and you've got time. Things will be much easier to figure out in the morning."

That's what I had to keep telling myself. In the dark of the car, the lines I'd drawn became harder to see. My attention would flick from

Darcy leaning her head against the car window over to the sight of Willa in the rearview mirror. Something about it held the comfort of familiarity like . . . like another life I could've had.

It followed me all the way to Bill's house and into the living room. Hanging up our coats, I heard Darcy talking softly to Willa in the next room. The house felt quiet and maybe a little too warm . . . or perhaps that was just me. A flush of heat rose up my neck at the sight of her. Darcy pulled back her hair with the tie from around her wrist, and for the first time, I got to see what she had been hiding underneath that coat.

Darcy was back in those black leggings that hugged every inch of her legs and hips. She ran her hands over her waist absentmindedly, glancing around the room as she pushed up against the fabric of her lavender T-shirt. My fingers had been there once. They itched to go there again. Clearing my throat, I glanced down toward the sofa.

"You don't need to stay up on my account. There's a blanket and pillows here already. I'm good."

Darcy must've been reading here on the couch. There was a mug with nothing but a cold tea bag inside it next to a D.H. Lawrence novel I didn't know.

"No, it's . . ." she said before seeming to change her words. "I wanted to say thanks for tonight. If you hadn't taken him there, I . . . I honestly don't want to think about it."

A low rasp laced itself in my words as I replied, "You know I've always cared about you. That's nothing new."

I meant to say "you all", but I knew I was right deep down. Before she spread her wings and left town, Darcy had been important to me. She was so much more than the girl I knew, more than a man's daughter. Still, that yearning to protect had always been there, even if *how* I wanted to care for her looked different.

Memories of Thanksgiving night came creeping back. They danced around all those secret dreams and that one stolen night. If Darcy wanted someone to care about her, I was right there. Every inch of me felt willing, even if it shouldn't have.

She took one step closer and then another, still toying with the hem of her shirt. The house felt too quiet. It began to melt away until Darcy was all I saw.

"You shouldn't have to sleep on this little couch, not after a night like this," she whispered. "You offered me your bed once, you know."

"But will you be in it too?"

The truth was slipping out of me like water flowing through my fingers. I couldn't hold onto it. My grip on my resolve weakened. Knowing there was no one but us there made everything that much harder to ignore. Darcy tilted her head up to me. Her words softened as she spoke.

"If you want."

Those three little words had me falling to pieces. Too tired to fight, I let my hands fly where they wanted, sliding to her waist as our lips inched closer together. Our lips moved slowly together and then all at once. As Darcy laced her arms over my shoulders, I knew there would be no turning back.

CHAPTER TEN

DARCY

It killed me when Nick was kind. More than his good looks or his rugged charm, I couldn't take it when he acted so gallant and chivalrous. It brought out something selfish in me. Not wanting to sleep alone, I refused to let him rest there on the old tweed couch, not when his hands could slide under my shirt. He kissed me with all the power of chances not taken. My heart pounding, I reveled in how Nick cupped the sides of my breasts and let my tongue brush against his lower lip.

They said time healed all wounds, but what about a kiss or a touch? Could a night with Nick be the balm I needed? I refused to believe such a man could be so willfully cruel.

This was all a misunderstanding, a voice whispered inside me. *Give him the chance to make it right.*

Every word caught in my throat. I needed to tell him, but more than that, I needed *him*. Even if it wounded my pride to admit it, I was done pretending I didn't crave the weight of his body pressed against mine, even if it only lasted for one more night.

"Come to bed," I whispered between kisses, already stepping away from the living room toward my room. "I don't want to be alone."

Nick didn't argue. Tangled together and never letting go, we were slow dancing in a strange sort of way, moving to the tempo of my quickening heartbeat. I couldn't begin to count how many times I'd craved this. In the last two years alone, I would lie awake in the dark wondering what it would be like to peel back his black Henley and undo the button of his jeans. No memory did it justice.

Nick had never pressed me against the short hallway. With his lips moving away from mine, I felt his kiss graze over my jaw and dip down to my neck. I longed to get lost in the sensation, melting away from the rest of the world. Nick pushed his fingers under the thin fabric of my bralette. He was already undoing the hooks before he ever got off my shirt.

"I told myself I wouldn't do this again," he confessed breathlessly. "I was supposed to get over you."

"Do you want to stop?"

I could force myself to forget. I'd done it plenty of times before, but his words had me wondering about all the conversations we'd never had. Every bone in my body protested, echoing Nick's reply.

Nearly growling, he cursed, "Fuck, no."

Our revelations would have to wait. Rattled and tired, we both needed an anchor in that dark, cold night. Nick's hunger was just as potent as mine. With his hands roving over me, I felt his fingerprints making their mark on my skin as I lured us both toward the open door. My pajamas were scattered across the floor where I'd dressed in a rush, not that he noticed.

His eyes fixed themselves on me alone. Dangerous and determined, Nick's expression held me as his hands pulled away to peel back the pieces of fabric keeping us apart. Our clothes became a trail of breadcrumbs on the floor. Our kisses grew more desperate as the burning fever simmered underneath our skin.

My shirt and bra came off in one fell swoop, hitting the bedroom wall. My thumbs hooked under the waistband of Nick's jeans, dropping them to the floor. The push and pull took hold of us until my knees hit the edge of the bed.

"You're gonna be the goddamn death of me," Nick said under his breath. "You'll have to bury me out back."

"I'm pretty sure we've got a shovel somewhere."

He laughed at that, the sound decadent and tempting. He must have known how he had me like putty in his palm. Nick's wolfish grin spread over his handsome face as he spread me out over the rumpled bed. Ready to consume me, body and soul, Nick guided my hands over my head as he kissed me again, and I melted deeper into the mattress. His lips trailed back down the hollow of my throat and toward my breasts. I felt his fingertips outlining my curves, barely touching my skin. They set every piece of me on fire.

"Don't you dare stop now," I muttered without thinking.

Nick tugged at my leggings, the last scrap of clothing keeping us apart. My feet lifted willingly, and at long last, I was bare before him. Too many nights had passed since I'd had Nick like this. With every labored breath, our chests brushed against each other and I lay there helpless in the moment. I invited Nick to let his mouth graze over one breast and then the other.

"Don't worry," he insisted, moving from left to right. "I couldn't stop even if I tried."

Past the point of no return, we let every excuse and pretense fall away. Nick and I were just two people now. One of us hungered to kiss and taste. The other prayed to be devoured. Nick made his meal of me in that darkened room, and with my fingernails digging into my palms, I stifled back a whimper.

The whole mountain didn't have to know what we were doing.

Nick made it difficult not to let out a high and breathless gasp. He knew just how to let his lips wander over my stomach while spreading my legs ever so slightly. I felt the heat of his breath before he kissed my inner thigh, and I began to forget everything but the pleasure he provided. I knew nothing but the sensation of his tongue pressing into my slick folds before circling my clit. My hips gently bucked against the feeling.

"God, *Nick*."

He relished my reaction. I didn't dare move or let my hands wander to his hair, but my legs moved on instinct. They curled around his shoulders, slowly writhing in euphoria. I was too close to coming out of my burning skin. I refused to let the night end here.

"Let me have you," I pleaded quietly.

As Nick groaned, the hum of it vibrated against my skin, forcing me to bite my lip and not cry out. I felt him move out from between my legs. I hadn't even realized how my eyes were tightly shut, but when they opened, I saw a side of Nick I almost didn't recognize.

It sparked behind the blue of his eyes. I felt it as his rock-hard length brushed against me. Nick Wallace craved this as badly I craved him. With one look, I glimpsed the deepest depths of Nick's desire, and I found myself ready to drown in them all.

"Always so perfect," Nick whispered so quietly I nearly missed it.

He didn't give me the chance to protest. After all, I was only a woman. I'd made plenty of mistakes in my life, and I had more than a few silvering stretchmarks. Nick had eyes. He had to know, yet there wasn't time to argue. My hand was all too eager to reach down. Finally, my fingers could move over his tip. Nick dripped with desire as I guided him into me. Our bodies connected, and I felt the sweetest agony savoring every inch of him. My body stretched and shifted, welcoming him closer. I let out another moan, and Nick stole it in a kiss.

"God, you feel good," I said the second he pulled away.

He flashed that devastating smile. "I was about to say the same thing, darlin'."

Without much effort, Nick found his rhythm. He moved slowly at first, feeling every rock and thrust. My arms fell back over my head again. Nick let his fingers lace with mine, and as he stole another soft moan from my lips, his pace quickened.

My spine began to arch. My entire body longed to twist and writhe, but it had nowhere to go. I was happily trapped under him and getting lost in the ecstasy of it all. The burning heat pooled at my center. It rose higher and higher, but I held on for dear life. I refused to let go until it became impossible. When I couldn't kiss Nick back any longer, he kissed me anyway, stealing every ragged gasp and moan.

Then, it crashed over me. My toes curled, and my grip tightened around Nick's hands. The sweet relief quaked through me, and a second later, Nick's release flowed into me like an aftershock. Every muscle in my body grew limp, and a foolish smile spread over my face. Nick collapsed beside me, yet he pulled me with him. There in the darkness, he held onto me as the air dried the fine mist of sweat on our skin.

"I . . . I think there's a spare toothbrush you can borrow," I recalled hazily.

Nick offered a lazy grin, asking, "Are you tryin' to tell me somethin'?"

"Yeah, that if you're gonna stay over, you deserve the chance to wash your face and brush your teeth."

It didn't take us long to find our way under the covers. The house was getting too cold to move slowly, especially with the floorboards freezing the soles of my feet. Nick wasn't bothered by my cold feet, though. He just draped his arm over my body like he'd done it a million times before while his tall frame consumed the better part of my double bed.

With my eyes closed, I felt how his body curled around mine. His grip rooted me there. I didn't move throughout the night, and when I woke at dawn, every one of my muscles had turned into stone. It took a long minute for me to remember where I actually was. Caught between dreams and reality, I quietly questioned whether the moment was real.

Nick took in a deep breath behind me, and I realized last night *had* happened.

Dad was in the hospital.

Nick was in my bed.

Slowly, I twisted around onto my stomach under his arm. Something inside me still didn't believe it, not until I met the blue of his eyes. They were bright even in the faint light peeking through the curtains. A smile toyed at the corners of his lips, and his expression softened. With his hair falling across his eyes, Nick looked about ten years younger.

"Hey," he muttered.

"Hi," I whispered back. "Did you sleep okay?"

His palm pressed flat against my back, sliding slowly over my bare skin. Nick felt unbelievably warm. I was so tempted to forget the question and kiss him, but something told me not to press my luck. One night of indulgence didn't guarantee anything more.

"Pretty good. How about you?"

I nodded. "Yeah, I slept fine."

"When does Willa wake up?"

My heart skipped a beat. The more he said her name, the more I knew I had to tell him, but I hated to burst this quiet bubble we'd made. Nick didn't deserve a rude awakening so early in the morning.

"She's probably up already," I admitted. "I rarely have to wake her up myself."

"I guess you need to go get her, then."

Still, Nick kept his arm over me. The memory of his confession the night before came creeping back.

"I was supposed to get over you."

I'd never thought to ask if there was someone else. I didn't consider how Nick had spent the last two years. All that time, he didn't reach out, but maybe I hadn't left his mind. Perhaps the ghosts of holidays past had haunted Nick like they had haunted me.

When he did let me go, I felt the reluctance in his body and heard it in his grumbling sigh. I found my sleepshirt on the floor, and walking down the hallway and back into the living room, I hastily buttoned it up. The drafty house was too cold to be walking around without clothes. Nick's body heat wasn't radiating into me any longer.

"Good morning, Willa girl," I greeted her softly, seeing her sleepy eyes open. "Are you ready for breakfast?"

She readily pushed back her blanket and pulled herself up against the wooden spindles of her crib. She pressed her cheek against my shoulder, yawning so that her breath tickled my neck. Last night's excitement had definitely ruined her rest.

"After we eat, we're gonna go to the hospital to get Grandpa," I told her. "Then, we're all gonna have a very lazy Sunday. I think we've earned it."

Leaving her makeshift room, I led us to the kitchen and toward the sounds of someone else. Nick was there in his black flannel and jeans, both haphazardly thrown on. He added coffee grounds to the machine while I settled Willa into her special seat. We moved about the kitchen quietly, each of us set in our tasks. Nick fixed two cups of coffee and three pieces of toast. I scrambled some eggs. It was such a small thing, but it was the kind of morning we'd never had.

The truth tingled against my lips. Itching to come out, the words had to be forced back. Nick and I didn't have enough time to hash out all the missed mornings and days gone by, but when would there ever be a good time? When would this ever feel easier? Across the breakfast table, I studied how Nick propped his elbows on the table and sipped his mug of black coffee. My hands and feet longed to reach for his, and silently, I wished we could skip the heartache and fall into quiet, comfortable patterns like these.

"I think we're beyond pretending this was a one-time thing," he admitted while buttering his toast. "I . . . I don't know what we are, but—"

I interjected, "We don't have to label it. If we're not explaining it to anyone, there's not much of a reason, and it's not like Willa will tell on us. She's good at keeping secrets."

"How many words does she actually know?"

"She knows plenty, but she can only say, like, three."

"I guess our secrets are very safe with her, then," he remarked with a lone laugh. "It would just be nice to explain it to myself."

Wiping breadcrumbs from Willa's cheeks, I felt another pang of regret, but I forced it away. Breakfast needed to be cleared away. I had to put on some real clothes. On the drive back to the hospital, I let music fill the spaces between small talk as Nick drove again.

"There it is," he declared when his old blue truck came into view.

He parked beside it, letting himself out into the cold. Even in his day-old clothes, he still looked handsome. The faint scruff on his jaw shadowed his face, but it made me wish I'd held onto him for one minute longer. Saying goodbye by the hood of my car didn't feel like enough.

"Thanks again," I offered. "I'm not sure how the next few days are going to look, but I'm glad you were there for this one."

Nick smiled softly. "You know I'm happy to help. Whatever you need, just call me. You're gonna have your hands full, and besides work, what else do I have going on?"

"Friends?" I suggested. "A social life?"

He chuckled. "I get enough of people working at the bar. I'm a hermit in the making."

"Don't be so sure."

Nick took it as a joke, but one day soon, he'd know what I meant. We were both done pretending. Nick wasn't going to deny his attraction, and I wouldn't lie to myself. Clearly, my crush on Nick had aged like liquor, only getting stronger as the years went by. It made me feel like a cheater and a fool. I just wasn't sure who I'd been fooling more.

When Nick kissed me, my chest quietly ached. His lips tasted like bitter coffee, and his fingers brushed back my curls. He tucked them behind my ears when he pulled away.

"Take care of yourself, Black Sheep."

"You too, Nick."

Tears begged to well in my eyes and spill out, but instead, I smiled softly. I refused to let the pain consume me as it had before. Still, he'd have to know.

This was more than Nick learning how we shared a daughter. When the time came, I'd be forced to swallow my pride, and Nick Wallace would have to face how he broke my heart.

CHAPTER ELEVEN

NICK

Bill ended up being prescribed a handful of pills and serious bed rest. Taking it easy at home, he left me in charge of the bar for the week, trusting that I knew the business better than he did.

"You spend more time there than me," he commented over the phone. "With all this newfangled technology, I'm probably better off lettin' you run the place and be what people call a 'silent investor' . . . like I could learn to shut my mouth!"

He laughed at his own self-deprecation, but I knew Bill had been training me for that very reason. Darcy would never want the bar, not in a million years. Although, Bill could sell it to someone he trusted. He could sign his life's work away to someone who would appreciate the history and the traditions of the place. I didn't know how Bill had picked me out as that person. I'd been trying for years to live up to his expectations, but when Darcy looked my way, all those feeble attempts were blown apart.

She called. I came running.

Pulling up to Bill's place that next Sunday morning, I knew not to make sense of it. It would only lead to an awful headache. I didn't need to describe how I felt when Darcy stepped out the front door with Willa in tow. They looked like two peas in a pod in their matching knit caps. Grabbing Willa's hands, Darcy bounced her from step to step, making the girl laugh all the way down. I wasn't sure which one of them was smiling more.

Darcy looked so alive and radiant with a grin that stretched from each pearl-adorned ear, so unabashed, it took me back for a split second. The sight of her underneath me with that wide, satisfied smile. Even in the darkened room, it caught me, holding me for heartbeat until I couldn't take it anymore.

I longed to be the man who made her smile like that every damn day.

"Hey, thanks again for coming with us," she called out to me. "I know I could've done this on my own, but it seemed a shame not to take Willa out to the farm. It's been a tradition of ours for a long time."

The afternoon before, Darcy had texted me, wondering if I would go with her to one of the Christmas tree farms. Bill had been getting his Frasier firs there for years. I'd seen the pictures of Darcy when she looked more like Willa, small and excited for an adventure. It had been surreal messaging back and forth with her that week over her father and random little things. It was the most we'd talked in years, and in a way, it felt like old times. I could already feel myself getting selfish, dreading the day she'd pack up and go back to her city. As long as Darcy was around, I planned to steal every second that I could.

"It's no trouble, I'm happy to come," I assured her. "I can buy a wreath for myself or something."

Settling her daughter and backpack into the back seat, Darcy remarked, "Oh, that's something else we should get. Dad's door could use it. He told me to take his checkbook before lying down, but like hell, I'm gonna use his money."

"Guess we should get out of here before he notices. Do you want me to give you the keys?"

"Really, Nick?" She teasingly rolled her eyes. "I get you want to be the alpha-male driver or whatever, but seriously, I know how to drive. You don't need to chauffeur me anytime we're together."

"All right, I get it."

I held up my hands in surrender, and before long, we were on the road and heading north. Darcy often flitted her attention to her rearview mirror to the little girl wiggling along to the holiday music. It was some modern pop-style tune I didn't really know, yet Willa bopped along anyway. Turning my head, I watched her feet bounce to the tempo. She didn't keep perfect time. The world outside distracted her, but Willa wiggled anyway.

"Is she always like this or does she just really love Christmas?" I asked.

I settled back into my seat and set my eyes on Darcy. Her hands twisted around the steering wheel as she stared ahead at the road.

"Um, well, she's always liked music," Darcy slowly began to explain. "She likes anything with an upbeat tempo, but she'll listen quietly to light piano music or those instrumental pop covers some string groups do. These days, I play the music more for her than me. She's not old enough yet, but I think she'll do well taking music lessons or doing dance."

"My mother played the piano," I remarked causally. "She used to teach lessons and play for weddings and stuff like that. She always wanted me to learn, but I don't think I inherited the talent for it."

It was an old memory, all faded around the edges. There was a time when remembering my mother came with melancholy and a hollow ache in my chest, but enough years had passed. I could remember the good and not let it be tainted by the bitter end. My eyes glancing toward the massive sign for the Highlands Lodge, I heard a faint pitch in Darcy's reply.

"Did she? I forgot about that."

I shrugged, watching a ski shop come into view. "I do too, sometimes."

Looking back, I recalled how she used to quietly regret not going to some school for music. Her clouded blue eyes would grow distant, and she'd talk about all the things she wished to be. She could've been a professional pianist or gone on to be a certified music teacher, not just one who taught the odd lesson between waitressing shifts.

But you've gotta have money for that.

That's what she said about so many things.

The line had been burned into my brain. If you had to choose between school and food for supper, supper always won. Mom tried a lot of ways to escape that life, but watching her, I learned some places and lives couldn't be escaped. She only turned her blue eyes into water and wore down her spirit into dust.

"This is our exit, right?" Darcy wondered, snapping me back to reality.

I looked to where she pointed. "Yeah, that's the one."

Setting aside the shadows of what was, I focused on enjoying my time with Darcy and her daughter. I'd never spent much time with toddlers, or any kids, for that matter. They weren't exactly patrons of the bar, and I didn't have any nieces or nephews. Still, Willa seemed clever and eager. She had to hold onto her mother's hand, but she whined if we didn't let her walk on her own two feet. She wanted to wander across the grassy parking lot and toward the endless hills of fir trees. Her eyes widened at the sight of the red-roofed shop and all its holiday decorations. The month had only just begun, but here, it was Christmas Eve every day.

"Should we look at wreaths or shop for a tree first?" Darcy wondered, still holding fast to Willa's hand. "I'm up for either one."

"Let's go ahead and find y'all a tree. We can pick out some wreaths while they're getting it strapped to the car."

"All right, Willa, does that sound like a plan?"

The girl didn't answer with anything but an excited snaggle-toothed grin. Red-jacketed men roamed the grounds, answering questions with bright yellow tags in hand. As we passed by one twelve-foot fir, Willa reached toward the yellow tag.

"You can't have that, Willa," Darcy told her gently. "It means someone's bought that tree."

"Do you want a big tree like this one?" I asked anyway. "Do you think we could fit it in your Grandpa's house?"

Darcy pitched her voice into a teasing, silvery tone. "Oh, no! It's too big for us! We've got to find one that's *just right*. Right?"

"Ya!" Willa declared.

Her small voice sounded so pure and sweet. Clapping her hands, she charged ahead of us, only to plop down after ten steps. She didn't cry like I expected. With a concentrated look, she pulled herself back onto her feet.

"Need a hand?" I asked her.

I figured it was the instinct all adults felt when they saw something so small. I took two steps forward and met Willa where she stood, offering her my hand. Willa looked at it curiously, but she accepted it. She made a fist around two of my fingers with a soft grip and carried on.

"I think these might be better," I said, pointing with my free hand toward a row of six- and seven-footers.

Willa bounced on her feet. "G-go!"

"Let's go, then," Darcy agreed beside us.

I could blame Darcy's rosy cheeks on the cold air. It made sense for her hands to brush along the evergreen branches as she inspected each tree we passed, but something in her expression didn't make sense. The wheels of her mind were turning again. She looked down at Willa before drifting back to the trees. Darcy mulled over some secret, and though I knew she wouldn't tell me, I couldn't help but ask.

"Is everything okay?"

She blinked three times and put a smile on her face again. Quickly, Darcy nodded.

"Yeah, I'm good," she said.

"'Cause it looks like something's on your mind . . ."

"It's nothing, really," she insisted with a shake of her head. "I'm just thinking about everything going on right now. I, um, I guess I'll have to be doing this all again next weekend if I'm back in Durham. We'll have to get a tree for our house too."

"Oh, right."

My heart sank slowly. The sensation of Willa's hand became all the more potent. For a moment, that strange feeling of familiar comfort came creeping back, like a good dream I'd forgotten long ago. Darcy's remark woke me up.

"It won't be as fun as this place, though," she mused, trying to sound brighter. "I wonder if they've still got the hay rides and hot chocolate."

"Well, we can certainly find out."

Once we found a tree as tall as me and full around the bottom, Willa, Darcy, and I found that they had more than a hayride now. There was a petting zoo and an artisan's market filled with local crafts. A midday trip to buy a Christmas tree became a whole afternoon of entertainments. By the time we actually picked out our wreaths and headed to the outdoor register, Willa was wiped out in her mother's arms.

"I guess this is going to be her afternoon nap," Darcy said softly. "Hey, Nick, could you, uh, grab my wallet for me? It's in the front pocket of my bag."

I understood why she was so keen on coming with a spare hand. With her arms full of Willa, Darcy didn't have a way to hand over her credit card to the old woman behind the glass. I knew Darcy would have figured it out if I hadn't been there, but I liked being the one who earned her grateful smile. That selfish, foolish part of me wanted to be the one she looked to in those small moments.

Walking back to the car with two wreaths in tow, I remarked, "You know, by the time we get back to Bill's, you're not gonna have much time to make dinner. Why don't you let me take you out? My treat."

"I don't want to put you out," Darcy insisted.

"You wouldn't be. We could go over to that little Italian place in town, Antonella's? It's always good . . . unless you're gonna tell me Willa won't eat pizza or pasta."

She tried not to laugh. "I don't think I've ever met a kid who won't eat pizza."

"Then, come on. Be that old Darlin' Darcy Rose and humor me. Let me take you two out."

"What have I told you about nicknames?"

"That you love 'em."

Darcy shook her head. "You're a terrible liar."

I popped her trunk and double-checked the red binding holding down Darcy's tree on the rooftop. Darcy settled Willa into her car seat, and as the car came to life, I finally got my white flag of surrender.

"Uncle Mickey was gonna come over tonight," she admitted. "It's not like Dad'll be alone . . ."

"Just text Mickey that you're not gonna be home."

Darcy sighed. "Fine. You win. Pizza does sound good right now."

Nothing could stop the smug grin from spreading over my face. I didn't care what we ate. I could've gone anywhere. All I wanted was to steal a few more moments of their time. If Darcy was leaving, then I needed to make this one day last as long as I could.

I wasn't quite ready to wake up from the dream.

CHAPTER TWELVE

DARCY

Nick didn't need to know how much I liked the suggestion of dinner the second he voiced it. Somewhere among the rows of fir trees, I realized I'd tried to test him without realizing it. I found myself taking a step back, letting him take Willa's hand to see if he could be the man I quietly hoped he was. Perhaps this was sadistic or cruel of me, but when I saw how the two were quietly drawn to one another, I knew.

No matter what happened between us, he wouldn't deny her.

Over the red checkered tablecloth and plastic-covered menus, I tried thinking of where to begin. An Italian restaurant wasn't the place to hash things out, but we could agree to talk. I could make time to tell him the truth and maybe to let him have more time with Willa. I didn't know how easy it would be to drive back and forth, but we could make it work... couldn't we?

"I don't consider myself a picky eater," Nick commented, rolling up the sleeves of his navy flannel. "We don't even have to split a pizza, but promise me you don't want that West Coast one."

My eyes scanned the menu. "What, do you not like artichoke hearts and feta over a cauliflower crust?"

CHRISTMAS IN THE CABIN

"I don't like cauliflower in any form."

"You're in luck because neither do I," I assured him. "Half the pizza is the crust. I'm not going to ruin the experience eating something like that. How about the Al Fresco pizza, though? Can you handle tomatoes and basil?"

Nick flashed a winsome grin. "Yeah, that makes sense on a pizza."

I found myself smiling again, forgetting the pain I'd carried and the heartache I was about to cause. Under the twinkling string lights and fake plants, Nick and I fell back into our old habits. Nobody was close enough to hear our small talk over the kitsch Italian classical piped through the speakers. Willa especially didn't think anything of us from where she sat in her highchair, activity page in hand. It was just the three of us in our own bubble again, and somewhere between our starter salads and our pizza arriving, I found the nerve to tell him. It was going to be the first step forward to something better.

"You're right. She really does like pizza," Nick remarked, watching Willa gobble her bite-sized pieces of her slice. "You're just shovin' it in your cheeks, aren't you, kiddo?"

With marinara on her mouth, Willa smiled over at him before taking another piece.

"Swallow first," I instructed her. "I swear you're going to choke yourself someday."

"She's a cute kid, though."

"Yeah, it makes her think she can get away with anything. Don't you, Willa girl?"

Poking her underarm, I forced back a peal of laughter as Willa shied away from the tickling. Such happiness was so fragile and fleeting. I hated for the heavy weight of reality to crush our good day, yet it needed to be done. I set down my pizza slice and looked at Nick across the table.

"Nick, we both know that I won't be here forever," I began. "I'll have to get back to Durham eventually, but do you think that, well, if you had the time, that maybe we could—"

The words were right here on the tip of my tongue, yet suddenly, I found myself being cut off. I could've thrown my pizza crust, I was so annoyed to hear the loud voice calling my name.

"Well, look who it is!" he called loud enough for other dinner guests to turn their heads. "Darcy Rose Steward, it's been a long time."

I tried not to wince. "Hey, Kevin. Um, how's it going?"

I had maybe seen Kevin Booth once since our high school graduation and the following weekend where we broke off our unremarkable relationship. He had been someone to go with to prom. Someone to prove that I, a young woman of eighteen years, of sound body and mind, could actually get a boyfriend.

His glasses were gone, and the small pimples on his chin were now replaced with a scruffy light-brown beard. Otherwise, Kevin had hardly changed. He wore the same department-store polos and cocksure smile. As he stood over Willa in her highchair, he looked past her like she was just another ornament in the restaurant.

"You're still hanging out with same old Nick, I see," Kevin joked, but it sounded more like a jab. "I don't know the last time I've seen you anywhere other than behind Bill's bar, Nick."

It riled up something inside me I didn't like.

"Of course, I am. He's a family friend," I answered firmly. "We've been out getting stuff for Dad's place for Christmas."

Sliding his hands into his khaki slacks, Kevin replied, "Oh, yeah, I heard he wasn't doin' too well. Such a shame, really. I guess that's why you're in town, then."

"For now, yes," I told him. "I'd hate to keep you, though."

It was the polite Southern version of *get lost*, but Kevin hardly noticed. He always looked past people until they got in the way of what he wanted. I'd been that person once. Back when it was our last semester of high school, everyone presumed he'd been the top of our class. They forgot all about me in the library, taking classes online that the school couldn't offer in person. Off on my own, I beat the competition for best GPA by a wide margin. It won me the scholarships I needed to get to Duke without ruining my father, and it was a devastating blow to Kevin Booth's fragile ego. He held his scruffy chin high now, but the mountains wouldn't forget.

I wouldn't either.

"Well, if you're in town, you should come out to the Christmas party tomorrow night over at Highlands Lodge. I'm the director of Events Management there now, and my parents have put me in charge of the annual event," he declared too proudly. "You won't want to miss it."

"Thanks for asking, but I'm not sure I could come," I insisted. "I've got my daughter with me."

For the first time, Kevin was forced to look down and see Willa. His smile didn't meet his eyes, and across from me, Nick shifted in his seat. People salivated for an invitation to the annual Booth Christmas party. They always had it at their family's ski resort. It was one of the most expensive places to stay in town. It had one of the few fancy restaurants in the area and a spa where you could get things like mud facials and sea salt pedicures. The place was high-class, but that didn't mean the man who would one day inherit the place had any class of his own.

"Well, that's what sitters are for, right?" Kevin said before dismissing her again. "Even parents have to live a little, and we've got all-new ciders and beers coming over from the local brewery. Nick can come along too. You'll need a designated driver if you're gonna have a good time."

Nick took a swig from his water glass. "I'm working."

"Aren't you always?" Kevin snorted. "God, I thought they didn't send you to prison back in the day, but maybe you're doing your time at that bar. Can't you get off for one night?"

Nick's eyes froze over with a chilling kind of resentment. His jaw clenched, but he said nothing. It wasn't the first time in my life that I'd heard a joke like that. Nick's record had been expunged years ago. He never had to go to prison for his foolish mistake, but the whispers and comments followed him everywhere. It didn't matter *why* he'd done it. People just liked looking down their noses at him. He became easy to talk about.

How could he have been so stupid? They would say. *Maybe he wasn't.*

Maybe he's still doing it on the side, even if his family's gone now. I mean, he could use the money.

Like mother, like son.

Such a shame.

Peggy and Jim Wallace honestly deserved better.

I'd heard it all over the years. I never once gave it a second thought, but it pained me to see how Nick swallowed it all like a bitter pill. Studying him there, I saw why he'd retreated up into the hills. It was the only place he could breathe.

"I'll put both of your names on the list," Kevin decided without an ounce of remorse. "I hope you'll come. Like I said, it's going to be one of the best."

"I'll see what I can do," I offered half-heartedly.

"Well, I guess my fiancée should be back from the bathroom now," he remarked. "I'll go see if I can find her."

As he walked off, I muttered, "I wonder who'd have the balls to marry him. God, what a piece of work."

Nick chuckled across from me. The ice in his expression thawed.

"Didn't you used to date him?"

"For like, three months," I reminded him. "We weren't exactly Romeo and Juliet, and there weren't many options for single guys. Most of the kids seemed to be paired up and got married the year after high school."

"And more than half of them are divorced now," Nick added with a kind of bitter disappointment. "I've heard a lot of their sob stories at the bar."

"I'll bet you have, but . . . let's not talk about that."

"Are you gonna go to the party, though?"

Picking up a second slice, I dropped it on my plate. I didn't know how to answer. My first reaction was an adamant refusal, but it would be nice to eat and drink on the Booths' dime. Since Willa was born, I couldn't remember the last time I'd gone out on my own anywhere.

"Only if you're going with me," I insisted like a dare. "I'm not facing those people on my own."

Nick's gaze flashed with a quiet conspiratorial delight. My heart skipped at the sight of it.

"I'll see if Zoe can manage the bar that night," he told me, and that was that.

It wasn't until we were heading back to my dad's that I realized where our conversation had gone wrong. Kevin had interrupted one of the most important moments of my life. Well, that might have been an exaggeration, but it certainly felt that way.

Pulling up to the house, I saw Uncle Mickey's old SUV parked beside Nick's truck. The bushes along the front porch were glowing with their colorful holiday lights, and the house glowed from within. I could bet Dad and my uncle were sitting in the living room, talking about anything and everything. As I went to get Willa from the back seat, I knew this was my last chance.

"Nick, I don't know if you remember, but before Kevin showed up, I was asking you if we could maybe talk sometime."

Popping open the trunk, he asked, "Sure, but what do you wanna talk about?"

"It's just that...well..."

My floundering got in the way. This time, Uncle Mickey was stepping out the front door with an excited expression. He adjusted his old ball cap and waved.

"Your dad says you went out to get a tree!" he yelled from the porch. "I figured you might need a hand getting it down off the car!"

I couldn't be angry with his generosity or the hug he gave me, but my uncle didn't realize what he was interrupting.

"It's no big deal," I told Nick quickly. "I just thought it might be nice to talk."

There would be no trace of the truth or a kiss goodnight, not with my family around. Caught between a rock and a hard place, I knew I'd put myself there. I'd created this madness all on my own, and I was going to have to wriggle my way out.

I'd let my pride go for him. There could be no more fake smiles or hasty excuses. Nick would have to hear the whole truth, and after a day like ours, I felt desperate to have him again. I'd seen his quiet courtesy in the mornings and his hunger in the dark. I tried to forget so many times, but my eyes were wide open now. This time, Nick wasn't going to push me away.

I wouldn't let him.

CHAPTER THIRTEEN

NICK

"Thanks for going out there with her," Bill told me in the kitchen. "I know you'll keep an eye on her for me because someone definitely has to!"

He laughed, turning the steak over in his cast iron pan. Willa had already been given her fish sticks and peas all mashed together with her potatoes. In some ways, I would've happily plopped down beside her and watched her chomp and chew. Willa was bound to be more interesting than this party, but I wasn't about to disappoint her mother. After seeing the way Kevin Booth ogled her, I refused to let Darcy go alone, either.

Folding my arms, I admitted aloud, "Darcy can handle herself."

"Oh, I know that. I'm just not lookin' to bail her out tonight. You know how she can get. That girl can be sweeter than sugar or burn you faster than a jalapeño. She's not afraid to call a man out."

"Don't I know it," I muttered under my breath.

She'd looked ready to rip the hair off Kevin's head for a split second. That night in the booth, Darcy's eyes went flinty and her words grew sharp. Willa might have been Kevin's only saving grace, but walking into that small country kitchen, I felt that she was nothing short of an angel.

Darcy was back in that same wine-red miniskirt from Thanksgiving with a black sweater and sheer tights that seemed to catch the light with some kind of shimmer. She had painted her smile with some berry-colored gloss, and though I'd known for her so long, I'd never seen her hair so smooth. She had it pushed back with a thick headband and running almost to the small of her back.

"Where'd your curls go?" Bill teased, nearly making me jump.

I'd gotten lost for a moment, forgetting where I was. All I could think about was whether I wanted to show Darcy off or keep her all to myself. Either way, I'd be kidding myself, and if Bill knew what I was thinking, he'd shove me right into his oven.

"Oh, they'll be back once I shower again," she assured him with a smile.

I asked, "How'd you do it?"

"Hot air brush and a lot of patience," she teased before turning to Willa. "Now, you're gonna be a good girl for Grandpa Bill, won't you? You won't be a fuss-budget when it's bedtime, right?"

Fish stick in hand, Willa nodded, stopping to let Darcy kiss the top of her head.

"I don't expect us to stay long," she told her father, "but don't wait up for me."

Bill accepted a kiss on his cheek, saying, "Even if I wanted to, I'm not sure if I could. Between all these new pills and a movie on TV, Willa might be the one puttin' me in the crib."

Darcy rolled her eyes and smiled. "As long as you're both alive when I get back, do whatever you want."

"See ya 'round, Bill."

"Have fun, you two!" Bill called after us.

Making our goodbyes, we slipped out the back laundry room and headed out to where my truck was parked. Darcy offered up the Mustang, but beyond Darcy, their cars were the Stewards' pride and joy.

"There's talk of ice on the road tonight," I told her. "Let's stick to the truck."

It was a straight shot down the highway to reach the resort. I knew the way well, but my eyes flicked over the closer and closer we got. Darcy fidgeted on the passenger's side. She twiddled her thumbs and fussed with her long, smooth hair.

"Are you nervous?" I asked curiously, almost surprised.

"A little, honestly," she confessed. "You know what they say?"

"No."

Her head turned toward me. Her dark eyes grew intense.

"High school *never* ends."

Pulling into the Highlands Lodge, I already knew what she meant, even if I had left high school early. It didn't always matter how time had passed or if you tried to move on. To some people, you would never change.

They just wouldn't let you.

We moved through the coat check and into through the hotel designed like some Swiss chalet crossed with a rustic log cabin. People cluttered up the lobby couches and Christmas trees decorated every spare corner. The whole place smelled like gingerbread and spice.

"I guess they're hosting the local holiday baking competition again," Darcy mused beside me. "It's usually around this time of year."

"Maybe we could sneak off and go find those gingerbread houses then," I suggested jokingly, hoping to shake off the cloud growing over Darcy. "It might be more exciting than this party."

Darcy let out a long sigh. "No, we made it this far. We might as well go all the way."

"I thought we'd already done that twice."

"Oh, don't you start," she said. "We're in public, remember?"

Case in point, the second we reached the coat check, a shrill voice squealed. My head and Darcy's both snapped to attention, and a woman I almost didn't recognize came running over in her pointy heels and tight green sweater dress. Even if she was stick-thin, I wondered if she'd been melted and poured into it.

"Ohmigod, Darcy!" she shrieked. "Kevin said he ran into you at Antonella's, but I almost didn't believe him."

"Jensen." Darcy greeted her with far less enthusiasm. "It's, uh, so good to see you."

Shrugging out of her coat, she handed it to the attendant and took her ticket. I watched the scene from a foot away. Anyone would have thought the two were old friends based on how Jensen squeezed Darcy. Throwing her arms around her necklace, Jensen jingled with all her silver jewelry. The bleached-out hair was new, but I knew I'd recognized that face somewhere. She'd stopped by the bar with her dates plenty of times.

"I almost didn't recognize you without your curls!" Jensen gushed. "I heard you were off traveling for some big computer company in the Triangle. Did you leave that job or something?"

"No, no, I just work remotely," Darcy explained. "The traveling was a personal choice, but I've taken a step back from that."

Jensen's eyes widened. "Are you moving back to town, then?"

"No, I'm just in town for a little while. Dad ended up in the hospital, so I've been around just to make sure things are okay."

"Aww!" Jensen pouted her lower lip. "You've always been such a daddy's girl. I mean, I get it, though. My dad's been so great about this whole wedding business. We're having it here, of course, but there are caterers to hire and my dress to buy."

Darcy's eyebrows shot up. "Wait, are you Kevin's fiancée?"

"Yeah, didn't he tell you? Oh, all the old girls from the volleyball team are here in the ballroom. You have to come see them! They'll just die!"

Before I knew it, Jensen grabbed Darcy by the wrist, pulling her away from me. Her dark eyes turned back to find mine. Half pleading and half apologetic, Darcy's expression said everything she couldn't.

"I'll find you," she said before being dragged into the busy ballroom.

There had to be about two hundred people overflowing in the main ballroom and spilling out onto the heated patio, and I'd probably served at least half of them. The rustic chandeliers were turned down low. People crowded around the dance floor and the overstocked bar. Pushing past the warm bodies, I made my way to the mahogany bar and to a young man in a black bowtie who already looked haggard.

"Can I get a hard cider?" I asked him, shoving a few bucks into his tip jar.

"Sure," he agreed flatly.

He poured the cider into a short glass before pushing it my way. I took a long sip of it, knowing it would be the only drink I'd have tonight. I needed to make it count.

"Hey," a woman said beside me. "You're that bartender guy over at that Bill's place. I've always meant to ask your name."

"I'm Nick," I replied.

"Tara," she offered back with her hand. "You've got a great place over there. No offense to the Booths, but it's a lot more fun at Bill's."

I didn't know this woman from Eve. With chin-length ginger hair and freckled cheeks, she looked pretty, but she'd never compare to Darcy. I showed off my smile and began to play bartender.

"We don't have a DJ there, just an old jukebox, but it's good to know you like the place."

Tara leaned closer, propping her head on her fist. Her smile became even more intent. She reached for my hand, and I pulled back, pretending I didn't notice her not-so-subtle move. I took hold of my glass instead.

"I like keeping it old school," she mused. "It's so much more comfortable, and you guys behind the bar fix a hell of a drink. It's easy for a girl to kick back and *enjoy* herself."

"Did you come here tonight with anyone, Tara?"

She batted her eyelashes. "Only some friends."

"Well, I'm sorry. I came here with someone, and I'm going to have to take her home. I hope you come back by Bill's, though. I'm sure there's another guy on our team who'd love to make you a drink or two."

Her expression hinted at her disappointment, but standing taller, Tara smiled softly. She took a long drink of her wine.

"Will he be as handsome as you, Nick?"

I had to laugh. "I'll leave that for you to decide."

"I hope your date knows how lucky she is."

My laughter faded away. Motioning to the bartender again, I threw back the last of my cider and asked for a bottle of water.

"She might," I confessed in a low tone, "but I'm pretty sure I'm the lucky one."

Darcy wasn't my date. She wasn't really my anything, but in that massive room, I was the only who knew how she glowed in the dark. I'd listened to the sound of her breathing and felt her chest against mine. Even if it lasted for one night, I had Darcy before, and it made me feel luckier than any rich bastard like Kevin freaking Booth.

Wandering through the crowd again, I searched for her dark eyes. I got stopped a few times by familiar faces, but they were never hers. It wasn't until I stepped out onto the patio that I heard her voice again. Surrounded by cushioned lounge chairs, fire pits glowed in the nearby darkness. Her voice carried over the cold air and faint smoke.

"Congrats on your engagement to Jensen," she told the dark figure. "That's some rock you bought her, and I mean, we weren't really close back in the day. She looks happy, though."

God, it had to be Kevin.

"My parents are planning to retire in five years," he explained in his arrogant way. "Since it's a family business, they figured it would be best if I settled down before I took over. Marriage wasn't really in my plan right now, but it won't hurt anything."

I walked down the patio steps. Darcy sounded skeptical.

"Hurt anything?" she echoed. "What is that supposed to mean?"

Coming closer, I saw the firelight illuminating Kevin's face. I'd seen that look one too many times. Men always wore it when they had one too many drinks and were way too sure a woman would go home with them. It didn't matter what she thought or how she shied away.

Kevin laughed once. "I'll still have fun, and from what I've heard, you learned how to show a man a good time. That's how you got that baby of yours, right?"

My grip tightened around my bottle. Five seconds from water

bursting everywhere, the plastic crumpled in my hand, but Darcy was already erupting.

"You've got to be kidding me," she snapped. "You know you invited me here with Nick, right? We drove here together!"

"So? It's not like you're with that guy," Kevin scoffed even as Darcy shot up from her chair. "I figured the only way to get you to come would be to get Nick here too. He always acted like a hound around you—a little too protective."

"That's only because he cares, unlike you! All you care about is getting to stick your limp dick into anything that breathes. For Christ's sake, Jensen could be a brat in school, but she deserves better than this, and definitely better than you."

Spinning on her heels, Darcy wasn't prepared to see me standing a few paces back. I didn't know where the empty glass in her hand came from, but as our eyes met, it dropped into the grass. Her dark golden eyes widened.

"Nick, I—"

"I brought you some water," I told her.

"Oh, great, *he's* here," Kevin groaned.

I could have given that asshole a black eye, but Darcy's expression was pleading with me again. With one look, Kevin became irrelevant.

"I want to go," she said simply.

I nodded, and when I offered her my free hand, she took it without any hesitation. I felt the ice on her fingertips and saw the plume of her breath, but Darcy set her sights toward the patio. She was damn determined to get away from here without making any more of a scene.

Kevin wouldn't have it.

"Are you serious right now?" he called after us. "I don't know why you take things so seriously. You haven't changed at all! I mean, even if I was hitting on you, you should feel lucky!"

As her grip tightened against my hand, I reminded her, "He's drunk. Just ignore him for one more minute."

That's all it would have taken, but Kevin clambered after us onto the patio. The few party guests sitting around the tables with their blankets and wine started watching. Darcy's cheeks had never looked so red.

"I mean, where do you get off being such a snob?" he shouted, slurring his words. "Why would I want some piece of used goods?"

Time slowed in an instant. Before I could react, Darcy's hand let go of mine. She moved faster than I ever could, spinning on her heels. Her arm flew out, and I could've sworn I heard a gust of wind as she whipped her hand at full tilt. Her flat palm smacked against his shocked face, and when time returned to its normal speed, Kevin screamed.

"How dare you!" Darcy shouted. "You piece of sh—!"

She lunged for his throat as the others gasped around us. Darcy needed to be saved from a possible murder charge. Forgetting the idiot and his cruelty, I grabbed Darcy at the waist, and her angry retort stopped short.

"Let me go, Nick," she huffed, scrambling to sink her purple manicure into Kevin's wounded face. "Let me at him."

I shook my head, hating how I had to hoist her over my shoulder. "No, we're going. Nothing to see here, folks! Just a tipsy woman and an idiot."

Darcy groaned, slapping my back. "Don't lie! I only had one glass of wine!"

I didn't put her down until we reached the coat check, and as soon as she shoved her arms into her gray sleeves, I took her by wrist out to my truck. We could look at gingerbread houses some other Christmas. Our time here was over.

"I can't believe you just carried me out of there like that," she grumbled in my cab. "Did you not think that would be embarrassing for me?"

"It was better than your getting arrested tonight," I pointed out, handing her the water bottle I'd somehow never dropped. "Drink this."

Darcy cut her eyes at me, but she did as she was told. Taking one sip and then another, her anger fizzled out. I watched her slump into the bench seat. Her voice grew soft again.

"I knew something was up when Kevin told Jensen and her friends that he'd requested the DJ to play some song for them. He said we'd save their seats before giving me that glass of wine," she told me before taking in a deep breath. "Maybe he thought I'd be easy—easy for him to have and for Jensen to hate. If he got caught, it would've been nothing to throw me under the bus."

"Was he always that awful?"

"No." Darcy laughed bitterly, smiling anyway. "His garbage personality has aged like a fine wine. He's only gotten more self-centered with time."

Reaching over, I squeezed her shoulder. "Hey, what did you say last night? Let's not talk about that, right?"

"Right."

Her smiled brightened, and my heart broke just a little. It killed me not to hold her when she was like that. Part of me wished I'd been the one to make Kevin scream, but Darcy wouldn't want me fighting her battles. I just had to focus on making her smile again.

"The night's still pretty young," I noted. "You've got the night off, so there's no need to rush home, right? Besides, I know a place where there's plenty of alcohol and even more fried food on a Saturday night."

Laughing, her face grew warm again. Darcy played along.

"I think I've heard of this place. What's it called again?"

"It's a surprise. You sit right there, Darlin' Darcy Rose, and enjoy the ride."

She took another sip of her water. "I'll do my best, but it's your fault if I'm disappointed."

I found myself laughing as she turned on the radio. Before anyone could stop us, Darcy and I made off like two thieves in the night, forgetting the people who made her feel less than or like she didn't belong. They were the ones who didn't matter. They couldn't compare. Thorns and all, Darcy was the most captivating rose in this garden, and as long as she was with me, I wouldn't let her forget it.

CHAPTER FOURTEEN

DARCY

I had a dozen bad excuses for going to that party. I wanted to show the people there that I wasn't the quiet nerd they once knew. I wanted a chance to dress up and go out, but mostly, I longed for a chance to be with Nick again. It was so stupid.

We'd spent so many nights together without ever getting bored. After I turned twenty-one, Nick would let me keep one of the barstools warm on weeknights. I spent half of that winter break swinging my legs and sipping cans of summer shandy, hoping the taste of a warmer season would warm me up too. It was always Nick, though.

With his black shirts and pushed-back hair, he put the flush of heat on my cheeks and the warm sensation at my center. He warmed me up on the coldest December nights until my heart melted. Watching Nick unlock the back door, I felt why I could never make myself hate him, even after everything.

"The kitchen should be closing for the night," he remarked with a mischievous look. "We should be able to hide back there for a while."

The kitchen had already been closed and cleaned up for the night.

CHRISTMAS IN THE CABIN

We had free rein to hang up our coats and scrounge through the walk-in. Nick discovered spare fish fillets and potatoes, deciding what our late dinner would be.

"How do you feel about fried fish?"

"Great," I replied, already pushing up my sleeves.

In a cast iron skillet, the oil began to bubble over the gas flames while Nick chopped up some potatoes. I battered and breaded the fish. Even before I tasted it, the smell of it alone had me salivating, or maybe it was the sight of Nick.

"We make a pretty good team, darlin'," he decided.

"Do you remember the last time we spent a Saturday night at the bar together? It was the weekend after my college graduation, and I convinced you to have a drink with me."

"Of course, I do. That's when I got this damn tattoo. The whiskey told me I needed something to remember you by . . . as if you're forgettable."

That same afternoon, I'd gotten the job offer at my company in Durham. They didn't give me the option to work remotely right away, but I was excited to be working in a city. I imagined living in some kind of renovated loft with plants in every windowsill.

I had so many ideas of what my life would look like, but my daydreams about corporate life were nothing like the reality I faced. Whether I was in high school, in college, or in the office, I often found myself on the outside looking in. It didn't matter how many times I shoved my foot in the door, so I decided to take off and see what other doors might open for me.

I'd flown around the world and back again, looking for the missing piece that would make me feel like I belonged. Restless and running, I'd still found myself back here in the place that raised me, with the one man I never imagined wanting me back.

Swallowing back the memories, I reminded Nick, "That tattoo was all your idea."

"One of the few good ideas I've ever had."

I nearly told him to stop. His body was already brushing against mine. The tight kitchen had plenty of steel surfaces to lean against, but we couldn't get caught here, of all places. I had to keep being good as we sat down with our meal.

With our paper plates, we leaned against one of the prep tables with drinks in hand. It tasted better than anything served at that stupid Highlands Lodge.

"I get why people like this so much," I readily admitted. "I'd eat this every day."

Nick cracked a teasing smile. "Haven't you eaten fish tacos in Baja and fresh pasta in Italy? What's so good about this stuff?"

"It tastes like home."

Wiping his mouth, Nick balled up his paper napkin and stared down at his half-eaten plate. He seemed to be choosing his words.

"Do you miss seeing all those places?"

"Sometimes," I admitted. "It was different after coming home and settling down, but well, I remember being in the mountains of Thailand that last spring. I'd splurged on a treehouse-type place with this amazing overlook, and I remember watching the sunrise. These misty clouds had settled into the valleys. The sunlight cut through them as they began to billow up and float away, but . . ."

"But what?"

It had been the same night I'd learned I was pregnant. I stayed up all night tossing and turning, wondering what I was going to do. Then, with my blanket wrapped around my shoulders, I stepped out onto the balcony.

"It reminded me of here," I finished. "No matter where I went, there really was no place like home. It's not perfect, but a piece of me will always be here in the mountains."

It was right there living in Nick, even if he didn't know it. As the hours passed by, we sat there in the back until the bar shut down at midnight. Nick wanted to hear all about how I'd found traces of home in places like Thailand, Bolivia, and Spain, but the more I talked, the more I wanted to wrap my arms around Nick.

I longed to take him to a place that planes couldn't reach, but he had to check everyone's work out of habit. Following him into the empty bar, I watched him in the glow of the neon signs still lit up, looking for a sign myself.

We had to be more than friends. His feelings had to be more than lust. His actions and his silence fought against one another, but one had to win out. Sliding onto one of the stools, it seemed we each had a secret to share.

"Um, Nick, why don't you sit down with me for a second?" I asked him, patting the stool to my left. "Those two specks of dust aren't going anywhere."

Laughing under his breath, Nick relented, coming around the bar to settle down beside me. My heartbeat raced, but I forced my breathing to remain even. I didn't need to give myself away so quickly.

"You know that Thailand trip I talked about earlier?" I began. "The day before that, I . . . I learned that I was pregnant with Willa. I'd been up all night worrying, and when I felt conflicted, I started looking for a sign. It feels stupid to admit, but it was how I knew it was time to come back and be closer to home. It was time to start a new chapter, even if it meant leaving the life I knew behind."

"I'm sure it wasn't easy," Nick mused, his eyes drifting to some other place. "You're so good with her, you know. You're a great mother, and she's such a sweet kid. I get that it might be a sore subject, but wherever her father is, he's an idiot for letting you two go."

"Do you really think that?"

His blue eyes looked so clear and bright as they stared into mine. They didn't pour over me like water or remind me of the sky. There, studying me, Nick's eyes *burned*. They were the hottest flames melting me while his answer lured me closer.

"Of course, I do," he told me in that warm, rich baritone. "You're an amazing person, Darcy, and I . . . I care about you."

It wasn't the word I wanted, but I took it as readily as I welcomed Nick's lips against mine. His hands curled around the back of my neck, anchoring me against him. There was so much more to say, but it all could wait for a few minutes more. Everything between us grew heated. Once upon a time, I'd imagined moments just like this, one where Nick pulled me from my seat and hoisted me by the hips onto the bar.

We met eye to eye for only a heartbeat before diving back into the kiss again. My arms draped themselves over Nick's broad shoulders. Slowly, he pushed at the hem of my skirt, letting his fingers press into my inner thighs.

"If we're gonna keep doing this," Nick muttered between kisses, "we should really talk about protection."

"Says the guy already getting into my skirt."

I felt the smile on his lips and tasted the salt lingering on the tip of his tongue. As he laughed lightly, the vibration hummed against my skin, delighting me to no end.

"I've got an implant for that," I assured him. "Trust me, we're fine."

Nothing was meant to happen the same way twice. With Willa, I'd learned that pills weren't always enough, but I could rewrite history this time around. I didn't have to wake up to a broken heart. I only had to take control.

My right hand slid down over his heart, moving down Nick's chest. I slipped two fingers under the waistband of his jeans. Tracing along that fine line, I listened to his soft groan as Nick moved from my lips to the crook of my neck. He invited me to undo his zipper and find the bulge hidden under black cotton. I felt how it grew and hardened for me, giving away everything that Nick desired. I pushed past it all, using my second hand to tug away the useless fabric. The second I found his tip, Nick gripped my thigh for all he was worth.

"You like this, don't you?" I murmured breathlessly. "You like having me here . . . with me touching you just like this."

My palm wrapped around his length, slowly stroking up and down. Nick's groan became more audible. I compelled him to shove up my skirt and go for my tights. He felt close to ripping them apart.

"I've pictured it more than I want to admit," Nick muttered in a darkened tone.

I almost wanted to laugh, saying, "You and me both, baby."

From base to tip, I coaxed him to life until he became rock hard and nearly dripping with desire. My fingertips purposefully brushed

CHRISTMAS IN THE CABIN

over his balls, and Nick shuddered. He came undone for me bit by bit until there was nothing left but the madness of desperation. Nick forced me away, only to yank the clothes from my body and let his own drop to the floor. I heard my shoes hit the concrete and saw a glimpse of my tights floating through the air. Wherever they went, I was glad to see them go. I didn't want anything keeping us apart.

Nick had me in nothing but my bra when he pulled me off the bartop, forcing my legs to fasten around his waist. With my mouth against his jaw and ear, I felt him turn us around to the nearest table where he could reach me more easily, or rather, where I could find myself straddling his waist and his rigid dick.

Whispering in his ear, I wondered, "What if we break this thing?"

It was far more of an excitement than a concern. Burning and alive, I didn't care about anything but having him inside me, and catching the light in his brilliant blue eyes, I knew Nick felt the same.

"We've got more in the back, darlin'," he nearly growled. "Nobody'll ever know."

Only Nick and I would know how amazing it felt to have our bodies connect. Guiding himself into me, Nick let my hips rock against his. He anchored me once more with his hands at my waist, and I drifted into the euphoria. My clit brushed against him. My pleading moans got lost in his mouth. Gasping for air, I stole it all from his lungs, only pulling away when there was no longer enough.

"Don't stop," he urged me. "Don't give up."

My spine began to arch, and with my head falling back, I breathed, "I can't."

Even if the building around us began to burn, I had to have my pleasure. There was no escape from the chokehold of our fervent wanting. With my eyes falling shut, I felt Nick's lips move over the hollow of my throat and the tops of my breasts. It pushed me further than I'd ever known. For a moment, I thought I might give out, crumbling to pieces before we found satisfaction, but I kept going. I refused to relent until I cried out his name.

"Dammit, Nick," I pleaded with a voice I didn't know. "I . . . I . . ."

I lost all sense of words as the climax claimed me. Falling against him, it hit me like a rushing wave, but I would never be washed away. Nick had too tight a hold on me. Through his release, he wrapped his arms around my back, pulling us both back against the long table. I lay over him, listening to my pounding heart and our gasping breaths.

"Looks like the table held up," Nick muttered after a quiet minute.

"I know," I whispered. "It's so disappointing."

Nick's low laugh reverberated through my bare chest. His fingers combed through the ends of my hair. The heat had gone off in the bar. The room grew cold, but beside him, I felt undeniably warm.

"Maybe next time, we can ruin a piece of furniture," he joked.

Smiling to myself, I was elated to hear there would be a next time.

"Yeah . . . maybe."

I couldn't remember the last time I had stayed out so late, but Nick and I were in no rush to take me home. It slipped into the early hours of the morning when we finally left the bar behind. My eyelids grew heavy, and I slipped into a place that could only be a dream. With the quiet music playing and ice tapping against the windshield, everything felt so surreal.

My head nestled itself on Nick's shoulder. His spare hand rested in my lap. Nick only needed one hand to keep the truck rolling along, and every once in a while, his eyes would glance toward me. They were as blue as a clear sky after a snowstorm where the haze cleared and everything looked bright. It was my favorite color and my favorite feeling, and it all lived in him.

Yawning, I whispered softly, "Sometimes, I wish she had your eyes."

The scene faded into black until I heard the click of keys and a felt a hand leaving my lap. Taking in a deep breath, I realized we were back at my father's house. The holiday lights glowed on the front porch poles. The place looked warm from within, yet it couldn't compare to the warmth of Nick's body or the comfort of that truck cab. If Willa hadn't been inside, I might have been tempted to spend the whole night right there where I sat.

"Your dad might be up," Nick reminded me.

He was politely telling me not to linger, and with that rich rasp in his voice, I had no chance of arguing. Everything he said sounded so lovely and agreeable. I wanted Nick to count sheep for me, yet I looked into his eyes and saw something I didn't understand. It wasn't angry or cruel. Nick never was, but the depths of his blue eyes sobered me. They made my shoulders straighten and my hand reach for the door.

"Thanks for coming out with me tonight," I told him, "and, um, for saving me from myself."

"Anytime."

For a second, I didn't know what to expect with Nick still staring at me like that, but when he leaned closer, my muscles relaxed. His lips pressed against my cheek and brushed against the corner of my mouth. It made me want so much more.

"Good night, Nick."

"'Night, Black Sheep."

I pushed open the passenger door and let in a rush of freezing wind. It made me shudder as I hustled up to the porch, following the light from Nick's headlamps. I couldn't see him past the warm white glow. The freezing rain was getting heavier and the light was too bright, but I felt his eyes on me as I reached for the doorknob.

Though I couldn't see him, I turned back and waved one last time, holding onto the hope of another night. We never finished that conversation. It grew too late and my head too tired, but Nick offered me hope without knowing it. With his one small declaration, I finally started to believe that it could all work out.

CHAPTER FIFTEEN

NICK

My eyes didn't want to peel away from the table where Darcy had ridden me into oblivion. Though the bar was packed for a Thursday night and filled with noise, my ears only heard her voice. Echoes of her quiet whisper drowned everything out.

"Sometimes, I wish she had your eyes."

"Nick, can I get a whiskey sour?" a long-time regular asked. "I'd like to open a tab too."

I nodded, my mind still elsewhere. "Sure, sure."

Taking the man's card, the remark played over in my head again. I needed to pay attention. One of our usual bartenders had come down with food poisoning, so we were short-staffed. I was filling drink orders and managing the bar at the same time. Any other night, it wouldn't have been an issue, but for the last five nights, I lay awake wondering.

What did Darcy mean?

I swiped the card and poured the whiskey. My muscles could go through the motions whether or not I could think straight. Down the bar, a pair of women waved at me.

"Here, enjoy," I told the man before heading over. "Ladies, what can I get for ya?"

Even though I wasn't functioning, I recognized the woman as Ellie, the woman who ran the hair salon in Banner Elk. Her pinkish-blonde hair kind of gave her away. She grinned as she always did, acting a little too rowdy even before the alcohol.

"Nickie!" she exclaimed. "This is my cousin, June! She's getting her *graduate degree* over in Boone right now! She's going to work at colleges."

"Sounds like a good gig," I replied. "Now, Ellie, you want your usual vodka tonic?"

Ellie snickered, showing off her whitened teeth. "Oh, you know me too well!"

"And what can I get for you, June? We've got a half-price deal on all our beer taps tonight."

June's voice was mousy like her hair as she asked over the noise, "Uh, do you have something mild? I'm not much of a drinker."

"We've got a local Witbeir that's pretty smooth, and I've never had a complaint about our honeycrisp hard cider."

"I'll try the wit-beer one," she decided. "And can we get a basket of fries?"

I nodded, and heading off, I got the drinks together. My mind wandered back to Darcy, wondering what she was doing. It had to be about Willa's bedtime. Maybe Darcy was putting her down in that old crib or reading her a book. Willa's hazel eyes fought against the need to sleep, trying so hard to stay round, wide, and awake. I pictured it all in my head to the point that I nearly overfilled the pint glass.

Heading back over, I told the two, "I've got your drinks and your order in with the kitchen. Someone should bring that right out to you in a sec, okay?"

Ellie shook her head. "Oh, you're always so good, Nickie! This bar wouldn't be the same without you."

"Thanks, and you know, Ellie, it's just Nick."

"But you need a name as cute as your face!"

Other patrons nearby laughed as I teasingly rolled my eyes. The cousin tugged Ellie away, taking them over to an empty round table. In the far corner, someone got excited over at the pool table. A crowd cheered.

Zoe came hustling over. "Nick, we need another roll of quarters!"

"I'll go get it," I agreed, letting my voice dip under the noise. "Make sure Ellie gets her fries, okay? I think she might've had some wine before coming here."

Zoe sighed, running a hand over her black braided hair. "She's never been the same since her split, has she?"

"Well, you know how it goes," I mumbled. "They can't afford therapy, so they wind up here. Booze is cheaper than a psychologist."

I'd seen it time and again, but I couldn't be the man to give Ellie an ego boost. My own sanity was too close to coming apart. In the back office, the smell of my cooling coffee filled the room. I took a sip from the mug I'd nearly forgotten, ignoring the stale but sweet taste.

I would have to go see her when the bar closed. It would be late, but I couldn't keep living like this. After a while, a man could die without enough sleep, and nobody could drop me six feet under until I had my answer. Darcy had been leading up to something when I started losing myself. Distracted by her soft voice and dark eyes, I hadn't seen the obvious signs.

Bill told me she'd gotten pregnant by some guy from down under. Willa's birthday was in August, and I took it at face value. I didn't question the explanation or that first indescribable pang in my chest. The moment I saw those pictures, I wondered, and I let the story be my quick escape from horror and guilt.

What if it had all been a lie, though?

What if Darcy told her father that to cover up the secrets I'd begged her to keep?

All that time, had I gotten it so wrong?

I reached into the safe while those questions circled around me in a vicious cycle. Darcy had to be hiding something, but nothing inside me felt certain about what, exactly. I only knew the research I'd done the night before. They had all these websites for due dates and what a "full-term pregnancy" actually meant, and by looking online, I knew that Willa's birthday was at the very end of August. One of Darcy's friends had posted about the first birthday party back in the summer, and it wasn't even three weeks before her possible due date if . . .

Running a hand over my face, I groaned. My bones twisted in agony. All these hypotheticals were close to killing me, and closing time couldn't come fast enough.

Every hour felt slower than the last. I worked myself to the bone trying to block out the voices until we finally declared last call. With Zoe's help and the others', I got the bar cleaned up in record time. I threw my truck into gear like a man on the run, but I wasn't interested in escaping. That night, I flew down the curving mountain roads toward the woman with the honest-to-God answers. Only Darcy could tell me why I might have all these indescribable feelings every damn time I interacted with Willa.

I'd always known. Deep down, I felt it, but I never wanted to believe it.

I whipped into the gravel driveway and headed up toward the warm, glowing house. The lights were sparkling in the bushes again. The tree Darcy and I bought together was up in the living room window, but I couldn't have prepared myself for Darcy already throwing open the front door. Even through the darkness, I saw how her resolve was threadbare and close to falling apart. Her eyes looked too wild for her to be okay. When I shut my truck door behind me, I saw him.

Bill had his arm slung over his daughter's shoulders. His face looked pallid and gray even in all the warm lights. One step at a time, she was trying to get him to her Subaru, and all my questions were cast aside.

"Nick!" she called the second she looked up. "Dad was just going to bed when he nearly collapsed. I tried calling an ambulance, but they're gonna take forever to get out here!"

Hustling over, I took Bill's weight off her back, throwing it onto mine. I already knew where this was going. I didn't need explanations.

"Go get Willa. I'll get him in the car," I told her quickly. "Do you have your keys?"

She pulled them from the pocket of her Duke hoodie before hustling inside. I only noticed then that she was barefoot. Everything was unraveling so quickly. We didn't have time to make sense of things or talk about what happened way back when. With moccasins on her feet and Willa bundled up in her arms, Darcy came rushing out as I settled Bill into the front passenger's seat. He could hardly speak. His brown eyes were elsewhere.

"N-nick...?" he mumbled.

"Just focus on breathing, Bill," I urged him. "You've gotta keep breathing for them."

Nodding, he seemed to understand, even if his gasps got more erratic and somewhat frightening. I had to steel myself. Not even asking, I hopped into the driver's seat as Willa got buckled up. One door slammed and then another.

"I'm in," Darcy said from behind me.

The engine growled as I whipped the crossover into gear, forcing it to move faster than it liked. Leaving the little house behind, I left all my dizzying questions with it. I agonized over them plenty, but they weren't life or death... not like this.

My answers had to wait.

CHAPTER SIXTEEN

DARCY

I didn't think to ask why Nick had shown up when he did. Over dinner, Dad had been talking about going back to the bar for the weekend. It had been too long since he did a management shift, and after a day in the yard and working on his cars, Dad said he didn't feel half bad. It gave me a small shred of hope that his meds were doing their job. I thought I wouldn't have to worry so much.

We were just watching the Thursday night football game together. Dad sat in his armchair while I read one of my old books. The night felt like any other until I noticed Dad rubbing his chest. When the game ended, Dad went to tidy up the kitchen. The sight of his hand gripping the door frame would always be scorched into my brain now. Time slowed as his legs gave way, and inside, I fought between the urge to scream and the fear of scaring Willa awake.

Sitting there in another hospital room, I wasn't able to sit with my father this time. They had him on all kinds of drips, trying to get him stabilized. I heard conversation of possibly doing another procedure in the morning, but it was so hard to focus. The doctors told me he had a heart attack. Listening to the woman with wire-framed glasses,

I forced myself to hear her while I clung to Willa. I let her soft, slow breaths against my neck offer some meager comfort.

"His angina has destabilized," she explained in her quick, small voice. "To keep him from having another heart attack, he'll have to undergo a triple heart bypass in the next week. I'll have to look in our systems and see when the next available appointment is."

"Of course," I agreed with a nod.

The aging woman stepped out of the small consultation room. Now, it was just me, Willa, a few cushioned chairs, and Nick sitting beside me.

"What are you thinkin'?" he asked quietly, his Southern drawl slipping through.

He usually worked so hard to talk over it, much like me.

"That maybe we should see if it could be done in Durham," I admitted. "The hospitals there have more technology and research. The doctors there have more experience with these procedures. I mean, they're going to crack open his chest. He'll be recovering for *weeks*."

"But his people are here," Nick pointed out.

"I know. Uncle Mickey's here, and all his friends. It's just me who lives in Durham."

"And you shouldn't have to feel like you're doing this alone. I know it's not easy stayin' out here, but you know how to work from your dad's place. There will be plenty of people happy to help out."

"And I don't want him to run out of time," I added under my breath.

That was all I could think when I started pulling him up onto his feet. Every heartbeat felt like another second lost. We were at the hospital now. Dad had the doctors and treatments he needed, but in my head, I could already see where this was going. Dad was going to have to keep me around for at least another month, letting me help him in and out of bed and take part in his recovery.

Christmas was starting to feel a hell of a lot more complicated. A strong, gentle hand curled around my shoulder and neck. Its warmth washed over me, easing every tense muscle that it touched.

"He won't," Nick said. "Bill's got plenty of time left. He'll get through this. You all will."

Nodding, I met his blue eyes again. They were crystal clear and so certain. It was already so late, but there was paperwork to fill out that couldn't wait. Dad was going to have to stay overnight and possibly until his surgery. I had all the information I needed in my phone, but for God's sake, I wasn't even wearing a bra. There was no way of preparing myself for this night and these moments.

"Miss Steward?" a woman in scrubs said as she opened the small room's door.

"Here," I replied.

"I've got the admission paperwork ready for you to sign, if you'll just follow me."

"Can he come with us?" I asked without thinking.

The woman's almond-shaped eyes flicked over to Nick and back to me. If she had any ideas, she didn't share them. Her round face remained blank and her voice even.

"Yes, that's fine."

Once again, I was being shuttled to another cramped space. We were in the emergency room lobby and then this strange broom closet of a room. Now, Nick and I headed over to a cubicle where my father's health insurance could be submitted into the system with all the other random information these people demanded from my tired brain.

"I'll start by having you look over these forms and confirming that everything you see is correct," the woman instructed me.

I moved to sit in one of her blue chairs, but I didn't have a free arm or hand to spare. There were only Nick's. Looking at him, I hated how much I needed him. I told myself I could always manage on my own, but after a few days, I felt myself leaning on Nick for, well, everything.

"Can you hold Willa?" I had to ask him. "She's out cold."

Nick blinked in surprise, but cautiously, he outstretched his arms to let Willa slump against him. She squirmed for a minute in her pajamas and knit cap. Her shut eyes scrunched up, but then, her cheek got comfortable on the shearling collar of his coat. It wasn't lost on me that this was the first time Nick had ever held Willa. His arm curled around her legs to easily support her weight, and if I hadn't known better, I would've thought he'd done it a thousand times.

"Thanks," I told him before grabbing a spare pen.

The pre-op paperwork felt endless. Before I could finish with one set, the doctor popped up to confirm that Dad's operation would be next Tuesday morning. They were already talking rehab and home visits. They tried to be sympathetic. Piles of brochures and papers were put into my hands to read at home, but it was the early hours of the morning before they let us go with my father still up in one of their beds.

"They won't let Dad go home until Saturday at the earliest," I realized as we walked toward the main exit. "I'm going to need more stuff from Durham. I'll have to go back for the day tomorrow, but I can't drive like this. Maybe I could text Aunt Erin and then get in a quick nap."

"I'll watch her."

My feet squeaked to a halt on the linoleum floors. "Wait, what?"

Nick's face held the same unchanging resolve. "I can watch her tomorrow. We can go back to your place, let you get some rest, and I'll stick around and watch Willa."

"Are you sure you want to do that?"

She was still in his arms. Willa did seem to like it there, and even if some paranoid voice told me to be suspicious, there would be no better person to watch her. Nick was her father, after all. Standing there in the hospital hallway, I felt about two seconds from telling him and being done with it. That was the lack of sleep talking, though.

I needed the voices in my head to quiet down. They weren't letting me think straight.

"This isn't just about you and me," Nick insisted. "Bill's family. You're family, and if that means watching Willa for a day, I can do it."

"But you haven't slept either. You just got off a shift."

"Like you didn't work today?"

"I did," I admitted, remembering I was supposed to work again tomorrow. "Okay, okay, we'll go with your plan."

Without another word, Nick smiled softly. He leaned over to kiss my temple, lingering there for a minute. My tired body ached to lean back. I wanted to be just like Willa and tuck my head into the crook of his neck, but we had miles to go before that could happen. I had to save my solace for the moment we got home.

It was awful to need someone so badly. It went against everything I'd expected of life and myself, but I wasn't merely a working mother anymore. This need went beyond being a single parent. I had to look out for my daughter, my dad, and myself now, and at some point, I did have to work. There was no denying that I desperately needed Nick, now more than ever.

CHAPTER SEVENTEEN

NICK

After three hours of hard sleep, Darcy rolled off me to slide her moccasins back on. Shades of lavender shadowed her eyes as she called her uncle and explained the situation. He agreed to go sit at the hospital and keep an eye on Bill. With her bases covered, she wrangled her hair into a messy bun, got dressed, and told me how to take care of Willa. Her words rushed out as she fixed coffee and toast for herself.

"She's still sleeping, so don't bother getting her up until she's awake," she explained while hustling around the kitchen. "We've got plenty of leftovers in the fridge, and Willa loves television, so if you two just watch one of those holiday movie marathons or cartoons all day, that's totally fine. I'm taking the Shelby, so if there's an emergency and you need to take Willa somewhere, you'll have her car seat. I'd say that she usually has a nap after her morning and afternoon snacks, but to be real, her sleep schedule is gonna be shot to hell today. Maybe just try to get her to sleep after lunch for an hour or two, and we can get her back on track."

"And a snack's some beef jerky and a cold one, right?" I teased.

Darcy instantly frowned. "We both know the answer to that."

"A resounding yes?"

"You're lucky you're cute, but I've got to . . . *oh, dammit.*"

Glancing at her phone, Darcy groaned. She shut her eyes and took in a deep breath. What else could be going wrong in her life?

"What is it?"

"My friend Sam is flying in today to Raleigh. I said we'd catch up, but I totally forgot she texted me at all."

I fought back a yawn. "What time's she gettin' in?"

"One-thirtyish?"

"So, pick her up from the airport and have a late lunch with her. You're gonna have to eat, right?"

"But that'll make my return time even later here. If you have work, I can't—"

Putting both hands on her shoulders, I stopped Darcy and all her fretting. It was amazing to know how smart she could be. She was one of the quickest and cleverest people I knew, but she could really overthink things too.

"Darcy," I began slowly. "I messaged the assistant manager on duty tonight. He knows I'll be coming in late. Everyone at the bar understands, so it's not an issue. If you need to take an extra hour to sit and eat, that's more than fine. Do it for your sanity."

"Fine, I'll let Sam know, and Nick?"

"Yeah?"

"Thank you."

Setting down her coffee mug, Darcy wrapped her arms around my chest, pressing her cheek against me. It was nothing to let my hands slide under her black sweater. Feeling the small of her back, I quietly wished she didn't have to go. My tired bones wanted to curl around her again and forget, but there were things Darcy still needed to do.

My questions hadn't stopped plaguing me either. A kiss on my cheek was all I'd get, though.

I helped Darcy into her gray coat before sending her on her way, and before I knew it, the small shotgun-style house became oddly quiet. I sat down in the living room with my own cup of coffee, but it felt so strange to be in Bill's alone. The sound of the morning news didn't change that. When I heard Willa call, I realized I was with a child who, the more I thought about it, had to secretly be mine.

Willa was growing into the spitting image of her mother. She had the same dark curls and warm, peachy flush to her cheeks. When I opened the den door, I didn't see myself in her, but there was something I felt while studying her curious expression. I longed to give it a name, to understand what those strange hunger pangs were.

"Ma?" she asked me.

"Mama had to go on a trip," I told her. "It's you and me today. Can I take you to get some food? Come on, Willa, let's go to the kitchen."

"F–foo," she agreed, reaching up for me with her plush toy in tow.

I mimicked Darcy's habits, settling Willa into her high chair and offering a distraction. On Bill's old radio, I found a station playing more contemporary Christmas music. The horns of *Christmas Wrapping* played while I began fixing cinnamon oatmeal with some cooked apples from the fridge. Sausage patties sizzled in a pan, and getting lost in the sounds, I nearly missed how Willa was patting along to the music. She was no metronome, but the smile on her face grew wide. She showed her few baby teeth to me as I put a little plastic bowl in front of her.

"Breakfast is served!" I declared. "Please don't be too much of a critic."

Willa only whined when I kept her from digging her fingers into her oatmeal as if it were a sandbox. As we sat there at the breakfast table, I propped my elbows on the table and chewed one of the turkey sausage patties. I tried to make myself really believe it.

Willa is my daughter.

This funny, messy toddler is my child.

Darcy and I share a kid.

Until I heard the truth from Willa's mother, I couldn't make myself fully believe it, no matter how I phrased it. All the paranoia and panic from the night before had been worn out of me. I wasn't sure how I'd broach the subject with Darcy anymore. By the time breakfast ended, Willa quickly claimed my energy. I thought wrangling an entire bar of patrons could be tricky, but somehow, this felt harder. Nobody at the bar ever needed me to change their diaper.

I got her bottom clean and powdered after a few fumbling attempts. In her red leggings and striped shirt, Willa shuffled around the living room looking like a candy cane. She flipped through all her soft books as the kids' public broadcasting station played on the television. Willa flopped down to stare at a little cartoon girl and her blue cat, but after a while, Willa got restless. She grew fussy and whined.

"How about we go outside?" I suggested.

Before I could get up from the couch, Willa had already scrambled from her seat and began hustling through the house. She really was her mother's child. Willa eagerly watched the hens clucking and strutting around Bill's homemade pen. She picked up and studied dried oak leaves, and in the cold grass, Willa sat herself down to watch everything around her. Double-checking her winter coat, I sat down too.

I had memories almost like this one. When I was small, my mother sat with me in the fall leaves and taught me all the colors. We tromped through the forests until our noses turned pink and sat at the piano when it rained. Looking back, I realized how my mom was trying to make the most of what little we had when she wasn't working. My grandparents couldn't offer us much more than a home. Nobody had money to spare, but we found our ways to be content.

It was all before the car accident, Mom's neck pain, and the prescriptions. Her last scraps of happiness were torn into shreds. Our days of playing in the leaves were over as a long winter settled over my life.

Seeing me, Willa crawled over to prop herself against my outstretched legs. She made my thigh her pillow. Her light golden-brown eyes watched the clouds blowing by, and right then, I didn't know if it would be better or worse to learn that Willa was mine.

I had missed so much of her young life already. I'd missed her first moments in the world, her first word, and her first steps. Willa wouldn't remember those things, but I always would. It might be a relief to know I hadn't neglected my own child. I wouldn't have to grapple with the idea that Darcy had kept her from me, and yet, as Willa grew tired there, I realized this was the first time in over a decade that I had someone to call my own flesh and blood.

On all those quiet nights, isn't that exactly what I'd wished for? I told myself a long time ago that I was better off alone, but that didn't keep me from wanting. Everything I said didn't stop me from holding onto Darcy for all I was worth. Even if it ruined me, I clung to her more with each passing day. I grew more attached to things that could have been if we were different people, or rather, if *I* were different.

I wouldn't change a single hair on Darcy's head. I wouldn't change Willa's, either.

It was already dark by dinnertime. I bothered to turn on their Christmas tree and holiday lights before finding some dinner for Willa to eat. Scarfing down her macaroni and cheese, the noodles nearly dropped from her mouth when the sound of a car came rolling up. Willa squirmed with excitement when she saw her mother walking through the door.

"Hey, you two," she greeted us. "Did you have a good day?"

"Yeah, we made it through unscathed," I replied.

Darcy kissed Willa's temple before dropping into the empty chair. "I talked with Dad on the phone this afternoon. He's groggy. They've got him on a lot of meds, but we'll be able to go see him in the morning."

"How is he feeling, though?"

"Not too bad, all things considered. Uncle Mickey was staying until dinnertime. He says they spent the day watching old Westerns."

Already slipping into her maternal role, Darcy reached for a napkin and wiped cheese from Willa's cheeks. I didn't know how she was still smiling. She looked close to collapsing right there on the table, but Darcy persisted anyway. As I cleaned up the kitchen, she took Willa off to bed, taking extra care to linger for a few minutes more.

She didn't deserve to be bombarded, but I felt myself being torn apart. I couldn't take another night of not knowing. As Darcy stepped into the kitchen, the words came spilling out while she was simply trying to get a glass of water.

"Darcy," I said, setting down the dirty plates. "The other night, coming home from the bar . . ."

"What about it?"

Blood rushed to my head. My throat began to dry out.

"What did you mean when you wished Willa had my eyes?"

CHAPTER EIGHTEEN

DARCY

Pushing my fork through my grits, I sat in that café feeling every level of guilt. No amount of cutesy Southern decor could cheer me up.

There was guilt for not being with my father in the hospital.

Guilt for letting this insanity about Willa go on for so long.

Guilt for dumping my day's projects onto another junior developer.

I even felt bad about not being more present with Sam. Her stories about surf lessons in Spain were lost on me. Taking a bite from her quinoa bowl, she cocked her head to the side. Her eyebrows knitted together.

"What planet are you on right now?" she asked with a joking smile. "Is it nice there?"

"I wish," I muttered back, taking a sip of my latte.

"Well, you said your dad sounded good on the phone, right?" Sam offered encouragingly. "The hospital says he's doing well, even if he still needs the bypass."

Uncle Mickey had called when I was waiting in the airport terminal for Sam, telling me the semi-good news. Dad looked good for a man who'd played a coin toss with fate. The nurses liked his color and his vital signs. All in all, I should've been grateful, but I should have been there to hear it myself. Just because I needed to grab more clothes and extra stuff for work, I found myself split between two places. I was only one woman . . . one woman who was fighting the urge to call Nick Wallace.

"It's not just that. Willa's with her dad today," I confessed.

Setting down her spoon, Sam's green eyes widened as the realization sank in. She'd been there when I realized my stomach problems weren't seafood or water related. Sam knew how, when I first came back home to tell Nick, he was nowhere to be found. Only a handful of my friends knew bits and pieces of the story, but of them all, Sam was the only one who'd witnessed it. She knew my embarrassment and heartbreak better than anyone else.

"So, he knows then?"

I shook my head. "Dad fed him that line about the Australian guy I dated in Europe, but he's a family friend. He's important to me and Dad. I can't keep lying to him. It's cruel and unusual punishment, especially since . . ."

I didn't want to air all my laundry in a public restaurant, but Sam grinned anyway. She adjusted those oversized sunglasses on her head and leaned over the small bistro table. My eyes cut to the old women sipping coffee just two tables over.

"You've had sex again, haven't you?" she hissed in an excited whisper.

I sighed. "Yeah, okay, we . . . might have spent the night together once or twice."

"Twice? I thought you said he dumped you!"

"You can't be dumped by a guy you aren't dating."

The two old ladies looked our way. They didn't seem annoyed, but my cheeks flushed with embarrassment anyway. I was supposed to be the strong, independent woman who didn't rely on some stupidly handsome man. I'd been fine for so long, but maybe "fine" couldn't cut it anymore.

Going back to Thanksgiving, I told Sam about how my plans to keep Nick at arm's length turned into his keeping my bed warm. She devoured the story like her grilled veggies and ancient grains. Her bowl was clean by the time I reached up to that morning. I'd been so tempted to kiss Nick goodbye, but if our lips had met, I wasn't sure I'd make it out the door.

"It sounds like you've forgiven him for what happened," Sam mused between sips of her iced chai.

"No, I haven't," I said before wincing. "Yes? Honestly, I don't know. I've wanted to be angry with him for so long, but it's so hard. When I'm with him, I get this feeling like we could always be like this. We have a second chance to be happy, but we can't exist in a vacuum. Dad will have to know that I lied and that Nick and I, you know, *made Willa*. With his health in such a state, I–I don't know what the news will do to him."

"And living is a lie is so much better?"

"No," I had to admit. "It's the worst. As much as I tried to hate Nick, I'm hating myself that much more."

Reaching across the table, Sam took my hand and smiled sympathetically. "It's been almost two years. That's plenty of time for a change of heart, and come on, Darcy, you know men can say some really stupid things. Maybe . . . maybe he didn't really mean what came across. If he's the kind of guy you say he is, Nick would want to make up for that BS line."

"Can't we all say dumb stuff, though?"

"Hell, I definitely have! Anyone who knows me can attest to that."

Laughing lightly, it felt good to have a change of pace, but I had to go back and face the people I'd left behind. Sam was kind enough to help me pack and sort through the mound of mail left on my dining table. She had always been such a loyal friend. I thought nothing of letting her spend the night before heading down to South Carolina in a rental car.

"Order a pizza, take an insanely long shower," I encouraged her as we hugged goodbye.

"And send me more pictures of Willa!" she insisted excitedly. "I can't get enough of those chubby little cheeks!"

The sun touched down over the horizon as I reached the mountains. Sam had been right about Nick. All day long, he'd been caring for a child he didn't know was his. He had always been so good to her, and why hadn't I been honest? Was it really better for Willa not to have him around? Was it better for me to deny my embarrassment and shame?

Who was I actually helping with all these lies?

Coming home, the two already looked like a picture sitting in the kitchen. My heart clenched at the sight of Willa looking so happy. God, I'd tried so hard to be good to her, but I was a terrible mother. She could have been loved by two parents all this time, even if that man didn't want to love me too.

Nick must have kept her busy all day. Halfway through our first book, Willa went out like a light. She didn't even flinch when I ran my fingers through her tufts of wispy brown curls. They were so soft and precious. Watching her, I remembered that my heart wasn't mine anymore.

She was my pride. Willa carried all my deepest love and hopes. No matter what became of me, Dad, or even Nick, I needed to be honest for her.

I wasn't sure why Nick lingered in the kitchen. It had been hours since he'd been home. I figured he'd want to maybe stop by the bar or go change clothes, but he stayed there, packing up the leftovers in tinfoil and setting dirty plates in the sink. The light overhead brought out the sandy gold in his tousled hair as he turned around. Looking at him, my mouth became instantly dry.

As I pulled a glass from the cabinet, I heard him say, "Darcy, the other night, coming home from the bar . . ."

I pushed the glass against the water dispenser, already knowing what was about to happen. My pulse quickened, but I wasn't Nick. I couldn't keep my cool under such pressure. Taking a swig from the glass, I felt all my practiced lines leave me, flying out of my head and out the back door.

"What about it?" I wondered, forcing my voice not to crack.

"What did you mean when you wished Willa had my eyes?"

The question hung around us like static, unseen yet inescapable. Nick's piercing blue gaze took hold of me. He pushed up the sleeves of his black Henley and leaned against the kitchen cabinets. A checkered dish towel became a tight ball in his hand, and his expression pleaded with mine for an answer.

"I've been meaning to tell you," I began. "I've tried so many times."

"How many times?"

A pit formed in my stomach. "There was that night, after the party, and I tried to bring it up with you the night before. There was that spring afterward when I came home to tell Dad I was done traveling and to let you both know that I . . ."

"Just say it, Darcy," Nick urged me, his voice cracking. "I need to hear you say it."

"Her full name is Willa Grace Steward. I figured she should have something of yours since you're her father."

His silence cut into me. Standing there, I didn't move. I wouldn't even breathe too loudly. All the warmth I usually felt from Nick had vanished, and though his mouth drew into a hard line, I saw the pain in his eyes.

What had I done? Why did I think any of this was a good idea?

People called me smart. They saw me with my banned books, my grade school awards, and my college degree, thinking I had to be a genius. They were all wrong, though. Blinded by shame, I was a fool, and I'd ruined everything. How could I blame Nick for not loving me?

To be so selfish and reckless, I must have never loved him at all.

CHAPTER NINETEEN

NICK

Grace had been my mother's name.

All that time, she knew. She'd lied to her father and kept secrets from everyone. Part of me longed to be angry. I imagined screaming and ripping apart the towel in my hands, but more than anything, I *hurt*.

I ached in places I didn't know I had, watching as Darcy went over and shut the kitchen door that I'd never seen closed. She slumped into one of the kitchen chairs. Everything about her looked defeated. The radiant light in her eyes flickered out.

She began without prompting, "I was sick off and on for a few weeks. It wasn't until March when I reached the end of my three-month pill pack that I realized what could've happened. I came home that Easter because it was around Dad's birthday, but I figured I'd see you at his party. Of all people, I was shocked when you didn't show, and I . . . I decided you were avoiding me. You told me that morning that nobody needed to know what we'd done, so that's what I did. I made sure nobody here knew, not even you."

Running a hand over my face, it felt like my worst fears were coming true. I remembered that party. It wasn't special, just a dinner over at Mickey's, but I faked being sick. When I heard Darcy was coming home, I figured she wouldn't want me ruining her night. I convinced myself that I was better off keeping my distance.

"Why didn't you come to my place?" I asked anyway, feeling my pulse in my ears. "Why didn't you beat my door down and make me listen?"

Darcy's face hardened. "Why couldn't you face me? Were you really that ashamed of what we'd done?"

I shook my head. "No, it wasn't like that. I—"

"What?" she pressed me, rising from her chair. "What was it like?"

The truth was that I had been ashamed. I felt like I'd taken advantage of her. It embarrassed me to think that I could fold so easily, and for one moment, that I thought I was good enough. Trying to spit out the words, I groaned. The conflicting feelings were getting tangled up in each other. They all got stuck in my chest and throat until it all came bursting out.

"Well, just look at me!" I yelled, frustration filling every word. "I'm just a poor white bastard, the son of a woman who couldn't kick pills for her own damn kid! I've got no fancy job, no family, no nothing! And you..."

"What about me?"

Her voice sounded so much smaller than mine. Standing in the middle of the kitchen, I'd never seen Darcy look so fragile. She knew what I was. She knew my mother had gotten addicted to her prescription painkillers and died of an accidental overdose when I was sixteen, but she gave Willa her name anyway.

Darcy knew I'd been arrested trying to earn money for my mother's funeral expenses and my grandfather's mounting medical bills. Working my mother's old shifts at the local diner were nowhere near enough. Desperation and naivety got the better of me, and lured in by the money, I got wrapped up in a smuggling scheme far bigger than I knew. Hundreds of thousands of dollars in cigarettes were packaged in moving boxes for me to drive north and be sold for millions and to deny the government their share in taxes.

I told myself I wasn't selling drugs like the ones that killed my mother, and I couldn't leave her debts on my grandparents. When I was caught, the prosecutors in New York quickly realized I'd been a pawn. They let me be a witness to avoid criminal charges and do community service to expunge my record. It was during those hours when I met Bill.

He was the one who'd helped me get a better job and convinced me to take my first class at the community college, but people still whispered about me. Lies about what I'd done became commonplace. After a while, I had to teach myself that the fights and the shouting matches weren't worth it.

Growing up, Darcy heard every story. She knew the rumors and the unvarnished truth, but she still looked at me with those same dark eyes like I could be something more than what I was.

As if I could really be hers.

I shook my head and tried to make sense of it. "You're the girl who made good. You've been places, seen things. Dammit, Darcy, I still remember the day you got that scholarship to Duke. Bill always said you were the one who was gonna get off these damn mountains and make something of yourself. Not me, though."

I was born on this mountain. I was probably going to die there, just like all my family before me. That was my curse and my punishment.

Biting her lip, Darcy looked down at her hands, tracing the lines across her palm. Her breath grew heavy and intentional. Though she wouldn't look at me, I saw her eyes softening.

"It's funny," she mused. "Back when I was in college, I knew all these rich kids who couldn't fend for themselves. Hell, I knew one girl who didn't know how to make a doctor's appointment for herself, but Nick, you picked yourself up when you lost your mother. You were sixteen years old, helping your grandparents when you were just a kid yourself. You got your GED so you could get a job. You got yourself through community college, and you took care of your grandparents in their final years. I've always seen you as capable. In my eyes, you were never anything less."

Tears misted in the corners of Darcy's eyes. She chewed on the inside of her cheek while continuing to trace the creases in her hand.

My voice cracked. "Then, why didn't you tell me? Why did you keep Willa a secret?"

She met my gaze with a pain I wasn't prepared to see. All that armor she carried fell away, yet I was the one who felt defenseless. I was the one with a knife in my chest.

"Because you acted like you were ashamed of what we'd done," she answered. "I'm too proud. I know that. I thought I was making the right choices for Willa and myself, but I think I made them more for me. I . . . I'm just so sorry."

My mind turned back to that morning here in the cabin. Though I saw Darcy's face that day, I didn't recognize the wounded look in her eyes. I wasn't paying attention to how she retreated. I let myself believe she was showing me the disdain I deserved. Looking at Darcy that fateful Christmas morning, I never really saw her. We were both too wrapped up in our own emotions to see the truth right there before us.

The knife in my chest twisted. It carved out the wretched places inside me while tears rolled out of Darcy's eyes one by one. I couldn't bear it, not when I had the chance to reach out and wipe them away. Darcy tilted her chin up to me. Her lips gently parted as she sucked in a shuddering breath.

"I'm sorry I forced you into that situation, Darcy. I never meant to make you feel small."

She sucked in another long breath. "I wanted to be so angry. I tried to forget everything that's wonderful about you, but I can't. I don't want to."

"Then, don't. Give me a chance to make things right."

"Okay," she agreed, a small light of hope sparking in her eyes. "But you can't call me perfect anymore. I'm not perfect, Nick. I never was."

Wiping the last tear from her worn face, I smiled softly. Darcy and I had been far more alike than I ever knew. It was hard to stay mad at the one woman who'd given me a second chance at having a family. I didn't care if this was the ruin of me. Though I'd always feel some remorse for lying to her father, the feelings I held for Darcy overwhelmed it all.

"There will never be any woman as perfect as you, not to me."

No matter how we'd hurt one another, I still found myself lured into her kiss, falling all over again. Her fingers curled around fistfuls of my shirt. Her lips parted for me and coaxed me closer. The layers of clothing suddenly felt like too much. If there was anything in the world that could ease my pain, it would be having her again.

"Come to bed with me for a while," she murmured. "Let me make it up to you."

Following her became effortless. We moved one step at a time, and though I looked for it, the guilt that tormented me for all those months couldn't be found. Every shred of my body was overwhelmed by the sensation of Darcy, and every second of not having her felt like a worse pain. Reaching behind herself, she only let go of me to turn the knob of that closed door, letting it creak open as our resentment fell away.

Her hands slid down and up under my shirt. She pulled it back, and piece by piece, our clothes dropped like breadcrumbs onto the floor. It marked our path to the bedroom where we shut ourselves away. We didn't have to think about what had been left behind or what was to come. There was only the fragile moment and the light cutting through the blinds. It lit my way as I reached around and unhooked Darcy's bra.

"I know you're hurting," she whispered, her warm breathing tingling against my skin. "You can take it out on me. For what I've done, I—"

I cut her off with a kiss, stealing the words from the tip of her tongue.

"Don't worry," I muttered back. "You're going to get everything you deserve."

Through the torrent of emotions, my desire for her overwhelmed everything else. It drove my lips to the hollow of her throat as I pushed Darcy onto the bed. She moved with me at the slightest touch, letting me spread her limbs across the unmade bed and pin her body under mine. All the secrets and lies tore me apart, but I had a second chance to rewrite the mistakes we'd made. As my hands outlined her curves, inescapable thoughts haloed around me.

This is the body that made our child.

This is the woman who can break me apart and kiss it better.

Beyond Darcy, there was nobody else. No other woman's soft gasps could elicit such a reaction from me. With my mouth moving over the tops of her breasts, Darcy moaned for me, biting her lower lip as my teeth gently grazed over one nipple before soothing it with a kiss. Her fingers reached for my hair, but I pulled them away. I gripped her wrists and pressed them down into the bed.

I refused to let her take control. Darcy was going to know how she made me come undone. By the end of the night, she would echo my torment in every tremor of her body, exactly as she deserved.

"Tell me what you want," I urged her.

The rasp of want filled my voice. Letting my lips wander across her chest, I slowed to a glacial and frustrating pace, holding back until I had my answer. Darcy sucked in a small, sharp gasp.

"I want you deep inside me," she insisted breathlessly. "I want you to fuck me until we forget everything else. I–I don't want to know my name."

"What about mine?"

"Only yours," she said. "Leave me with nothing but your name."

My hand slid down her side and between her spreading legs. Her skin burned. Looking down at her, I caught how her eyes smoldered. Every piece of her was set aflame as my fingers traced her slick entrance.

"Then, say it," I pleaded.

"Nick," she whispered.

"Say it again."

Pushing two fingers into her, Darcy's breath caught before she whimpered, "*Nick.*"

The sound was enough to put a man in his grave. My gaze stayed fixed on hers as I coaxed another gasp from her lips. Instantly, my body reacted. My length grew with every one of her ragged breaths.

Darcy refused to shy away from me. She put her pleasure on display, grabbing fistfuls of the bedsheets and letting her hips roll into the sensation.

"Yes, Nick," she purred for me. "Just like that."

Even then, Darcy took hold of me. I had her pinned under me, her chest brushing against mine with every gasp of euphoria, but one word from her pulled every one of my invisible strings. She compelled me to keep going until the rest of me couldn't take it anymore.

I let my two fingers massage within while my thumb rolled over her clit. Darcy was on the precipice of satisfaction. With her toes curling and her spine twisting, she looked almost heartbroken when I pulled away.

"That's enough," I nearly growled, not having the strength to say more.

Once I licked my fingers clean, Darcy knew what I meant when my hands grabbed her by the wrists and guided them over her head. Slipping into her was slipping into silk. With our bodies connected, I pressed into her at full hilt, feeling how Darcy shifted to welcome me even closer.

My lips grazed over the crook of her neck and behind her ear. Breathing in the faint salt of her skin, I rocked into her again with purposeful intent. I longed to memorize every stroke, but desperation got the better of me. Slowly and then all at once, my pace quickened with the racing rhythm of my heartbeat. Darcy whispered my name again and again. Her voice rose higher with her building desire as her legs wrapped around me. It almost felt unbelievable . . .

What I could do to her.

How we could be.

After Darcy, there could be no one else. I'd never dared to find a replacement for her because she was one of a kind, rare and beautiful to behold. Falling for her was like falling for grace, but as I found myself on the edge of release, I silently said that this was my only chance for redemption. Darcy let her hot breath brush against my ear and took every inch of me until I heard the self-satisfied smile in her voice.

"Let go, Nick," she murmured. "Just . . ."

Her voice trailed off as her spine arched into me. I couldn't bear it anymore. Unable to hold back any longer, my grip tightened around Darcy's wrists. I felt the rush of my climax flow into her, echoing through her own euphoria. I gasped for cool air. Pulling back, I saw how her eyes were closed and that inescapable grin spread over her face. It was enough to make a poor bastard like me feel smug.

"Do you want me to stay the night?" I asked when I found the will.

Darcy nodded, opening her eyes. "If you can."

I didn't have the strength to be anywhere else. It took my final ounce of power to brush my teeth and splash cool water on my face. Before I knew it, my tired body was sinking into the mattress as Darcy pulled the covers over us both.

On paper, it didn't make sense for us to be together. Our lives seemed to move along lines that never should have crossed, yet we lay there bundled up together. Darcy pressed her body into me. Her fingers curled around my shoulders as I pressed my palm into the small of her back. Her dark eyes became all I could see.

"Nick, I hate to ask, but . . ."

"But what?"

Her expression became pleading. "With Dad's health the way it is, I don't know when I'm going to be able to tell him the truth. I don't know if he could deal with the stress of it all, and I don't want to make life any harder. There's so much going on and so much to do. Really, it's not fair of me, but can we keep this as *our* secret for a little while longer? Can we keep the truth, and well, whatever we are, between us?"

Nearly two years ago, I had made the same demand of her with far less reason. How could I deny her? Darcy wasn't going to keep Willa from me. I still could let my lips press against Darcy's forehead as her eyes half-closed.

"We can settle things between us first," I assured her. "This is enough for now."

We had so much to figure out. With her father in the hospital and my conflicting guilt sitting like a shadow in the corner, I had plenty to sort out on my own, but right then, I only had to shut my eyes and shut out the worries plaguing us both.

"You're right. This is enough," Darcy agreed softly. "*You* are enough."

Those three small words struck me at my core. Tightening my grip on her, I drew my lips to her cheek. Her fingers combed through the back of my hair, letting me bury my exhausted body beside hers. There were so many moments where I knew I didn't measure up, but that night, tangled up with Darcy, I didn't fight her. I allowed myself to be enough.

CHAPTER TWENTY

DARCY

When there were no guests around, hospitals felt like a different place. The nurses joked among themselves and with the patients, getting ready for the first round of appointments, trying to make it less awkward for the men they were about to give an all-body shave. I heard someone laughing on the other side of the beige curtain.

"I don't know if I've ever been this smooth," Dad tried to joke from the bed. "Is this what it feels like when you shave your thighs?"

I didn't have enough caffeine to laugh very hard. Between getting Willa to my aunt and uncle's and getting Dad to the hospital for his five o'clock check-in, the coffee hadn't had enough time to kick in. The sun itself wasn't even running at full capacity. Being in an oversized sweater with my hair braided was close to a miracle in itself.

Taking another swig from my travel mug, I replied, "I guess, but I've never let my leg hair grow for fifty years."

"I feel like a baby seal or like I'm a kid again."

"They've given you the first round of anesthetics, haven't they?"

Dad chuckled. "They've given me somethin'."

The curtain pulled back. The sharp sound of plastic rings scraped across metal, forcing me to wince. Rubbing my temple, I smiled up at the nurse who had years of practice to look so chipper so early. He flashed a crinkly-eyed smile and got to work.

"All right, Mr. Steward, let's get you feeling good, shall we?" the man said, already typing into the system.

It seemed not a pill or syringe was taken out without an insane digital trail. Swiping his badge, the nurse typed away before giving my dad another injection of something. Dad slowly blinked and tugged at the collar of his teal hospital robe. His brown eyes became more glazed than a hot yeast doughnut. His stoic expression relaxed into an intoxicated grin, and as the nurse went off to let the drugs settle in before taking him back, Dad turned to me. His words began to slow one syllable at a time.

"I love you so much, Darcy Rose," he said. "I've told you that, right?"

"Yeah, including twice already today. I love you too."

"And Willa, Lord, she's such a precious thing. She's gonna be a ball-buster, but she's precious. Where is she, by the way?"

Dad looked under his thin yellow blanket like a twenty-two-pound toddler could be hiding there. When she wasn't, he almost looked surprised.

"She's at your brother's. We dropped her off before coming here," I reminded him. "Since I wasn't sure when I'd be leaving, Aunt Erin was happy to spoil her for the day, and it would be easier for me to stay late here with you."

"Oh, *that's right.*"

Dad chuckled under this breath. Then, his smile began to fade. Something came to his muddled mind, and it weighed down his entire face. It put creases in his forehead and lines around his mouth.

"Mickey and Erin shouldn't have had to take her," he muttered. "Her *father* should be here. He should be at the house with her, lookin' out for her and bein' a damn man."

I sighed. "Let's not get into this right now."

Someone was about to crack his breastbone open and stop his heart. This wasn't the time, yet the more disgruntled he became, I realized the drugs were doing the talking. They loosened his lips and brought to the surface all the disappointment he'd held back for my sake. Dad's glazed eyes even flickered with a sadness I'd never even seen.

"I just wish you had someone in your life," he confessed. "I know how smart and strong you are, but it's hard raising a child on your own. The sleepless nights and worrying . . . you shouldn't have to deal with it alone. Nobody should. If I could've, I would've made it work with . . . with your momma, but she didn't want to stay here. It would've worn her down to dust, and I–I worry you're gonna end up like me. You're too special not to have someone in your life."

I reached over the hospital bed to take his hand, squeezing it until he stopped.

"We're okay, Daddy," I assured him softly. "Just focus on relaxing for me."

It had been so many years since I'd called him that.

Back when he still put me on his shoulders and declared me to be his favorite girl, my father was my whole world, but there were whole pieces of his world hidden from me. I shouldn't have been surprised that he downplayed his heart condition for so long. Over all those years, Dad had mastered the art of the hiding his pain.

"All right, Mr. Steward!" the male nurse declared upon his return. "Are you ready?"

"As I'll ever be."

Dad smiled again. Like all the masks I wore, my father hid away his dismay. He let me lean over the bed rail and kiss his cheek before the hoard of nurses arrived to cart him down the wide halls, back where I couldn't go. The hard red lines were painted on the linoleum floors, and I had to stand behind them and wave.

"I'll see you when it's all said and done," I promised him. "Love you."

"I love you too, Darcy girl."

The next eight hours would be like eight seconds for him. Somewhere back there, a team of medical professionals would stop his heart to save it, but I didn't get that convenience. Every slow, grating minute passed by in real-time. Ushered out into a small side lobby, I found myself sitting, waiting, wondering, and watching as a slushy, frozen mix fell outside the hospital windows. Work only kept me occupied for so long. The rickety wooden table and all my worries dragged my attention every which way.

If I had told my father that I was trying to find my someone or that Willa's dad was looking to be a part of her life, would he have been happy? I hated to envision the pitying look of frustration and resentment on my behalf, but in all honesty, I had no promises or guarantees to offer.

Nick said to do everything he could for Willa and me, but we lived two entirely different lives. I had no clear vision of what our life might look like in the future. My mind was too focused on my father's recovery and the tall, leather-clad frame walking toward me.

"Hey, Darcy," he greeted me. "Care for some company?"

"Sure, but I didn't expect to see you here."

Rising to my feet, I welcomed the hug from Nick. I smelled the cold air and the scent of pine on his knit sweater and chest. It couldn't be just the black soap bars he used. It must have permeated his very skin, but I didn't dare loiter there in his arms. I settled back into my seat before I started asking for too much. Nick sat across from me.

"I had to cover the keg deliveries and stop by the bank this morning, but I wasn't going to make you sit here alone all day," he insisted. "I figured we could use the time to talk."

"That's probably a good idea."

Our conversation and my confessions dissolved into spending the night together. Regardless of our impulses, plans had to be made. Willa and Nick couldn't be kept apart anymore, and with Dad's recovery, I needed Nick around more than ever. My stubborn independence had to be forgotten.

"How about we go grab a bite to eat, then?" Nick suggested. "You haven't eaten, have you?"

I shook my head. "Not since I left this morning."

"We're about to change that."

Helping me pack my work bag, Nick threw the backpack over his shoulder and matched my stride as we walked toward the hospital cafeteria. I didn't have much of an appetite for the soup of the day, but I needed to eat anyway. Swiping my credit card before Nick could pay, we found a table free of other visitors and tired-looking staff in colorful scrubs.

"I'm not gonna fight you for buying your own lunch," Nick said while opening his sandwich container. "You'll have to let me help you, though. Between your dad and Willa, you know I can help."

I dipped my bread into the cheddar broccoli soup. "I'll have my aunt and uncle. Dad's friends have been calling and asking when they can sit with him for an afternoon."

"So, you don't want my help?"

"No, I just . . ." I replied, my voice trailing off. "I don't expect you to drop everything to help me. If anything, I wouldn't blame you if you were mad at me. I figured you'd resent me now."

"You had your reasons. I'd rather spend the time trying to make things right, making a clean slate for us, and making the most of my time with Willa. Getting angry over the past isn't gonna do anyone any good."

"But—"

Nick held up a hand. "No more buts, Darcy. You're overthinking this. Sometimes, you just have to slow down and accept things as they are. Instead of hashin' out the past, we can start over with this lunch and take it one day at a time."

"One day at a time," I echoed. "I like the sound of that."

We turned a page in that cafeteria booth. As we ate, Nick and I planned times he could come over during my morning shifts. He could keep an eye on Willa and Dad while I worked over the next few weeks. There was no telling how long it would truly take for Dad to recover. We had to take it step by step, and Nick seemed determined to follow me every step of the way.

He stayed beside me as I worked that afternoon back in the heart unit's lobby. Thumbing through a book, he sat quietly while I tested code beside him. The world grew darker, and sunset arrived just as frozen mix started falling outside.

"Miss Darcy Steward?" a nurse asked as she came over.

I didn't know her, but I figured the ones working at dawn were long gone.

"That's me," I said, instinctively shutting my laptop.

"The surgeon would like to have a word. If you'll follow me, I can show you to the nearest consultation room."

In the closet-like space, mid-afternoon felt like midnight. My attention and awareness both began to fade. Twelve hours of tension were pent-up in every fiber of my being. I only needed to hear that Dad was okay, but the sight of his surgeon walking through the door with tiny flecks of blood on his white coat and scrubs didn't help.

"Miss Steward, I want you to know that everything went really well," the surgeon explained. "It was a textbook procedure. Your father will be recovering in the hospital as long as he's showing signs of drainage. I expect it will be about a week at most. The nursing staff are settling him into his room as we speak. You'll be free to see him as soon as you'd like."

"Thank you."

"Do you have any questions?"

I shook my head. My mind was too numb to think of anything but staying alive. Shaking his hand, I went through the motions of existing, following my feet as Nick led us both to Dad's new room. One nurse greeted us as the other nurses worked to rouse him under the bright ceiling lights. Pulling out tubes and hooking up monitors, they talked to Dad as if he were across a loud room, but Dad only mumbled back.

He had never looked so weak.

Part of me prepared for the worst, expecting to see him colorless and comatose, but Dad did have a faint flush on his face. The nurses stopped paying attention to us. After hours of life support, my father's body was automatically breathing on its own.

"Take in a breath for me, Bill," the male nurse with a buzz cut insisted loudly. "Do it as deep as you can."

Dad's chest hardly moved, but mine couldn't stop. Every breath he attempted to take brought out another ragged inhale from me. The nurses continued to get my father's body working on its own. With my back pressed against the soft yellow wall, I worried about being in the way. Every inch of me felt as if it was taking up too much space.

Was I stealing my father's air? Would it have been better for me to go? But if I left, would Dad know where I'd gone? Worries filled my head until I remembered that someone stood beside me. His head dipped down. Nick's breath tingled against my ear.

"It's gonna take time," he whispered, his hand squeezing mine. "It's normal for this to happen."

"Is this what your grandpa looked like?" I asked softly.

He replied honestly, "No, Bill looks much better. He's gonna get ahead of this."

"Feel free to come talk to him," a petite nurse told us, her tawny hands still moving over my father. "He probably won't answer, but it'll be good for him to know you're here."

"Go on, Darcy," Nick encouraged me.

Taking a few steps forward, I rested my hands on Dad's leg under the blanket. His breaths weren't strong or even, but the oxygen tubes in his nose made every faint inhale count. I wondered how long he was going to be like this. When would he open his eyes and smile at me again?

"Dad, it's me," I told him. "The doctor told me you did really well today. I texted your brother to let him know. He's gonna visit in the morning. Right now, Uncle Mickey and Aunt Erin are watching Willa. Aunt Erin sent me a picture of Willa's face covered in chocolate ice cream. It's really cute."

The corners of his mouth twitched. Dad really did hear me, even if his answer was merely a faint grumbling sound.

"Nick's here with me," I continued. "We wanted to be sure you were settled in for the night, but in the morning, we'll come back with Willa. I'm sure she'd love to see you."

"Mmm," Dad mumbled more loudly this time.

I turned to the male nurse still working around the room and asked, "When will he wake up?"

"He's got a lot of pain medication in his system right now," he explained. "Also, his throat is sore from the tubing. I wouldn't expect him to be fully awake until tomorrow, but stay as long as you like. Having you around is helpful. Just don't feel like you have to stay forever."

"Okay," I agreed with a nod.

For the next hour, I sat there at the edge of the bed as hospital staff drifted in and out. He was fine as long as I kept my eyes on him. Nothing could change or go wrong, but inevitably, my stomach started growling. Nick heard it from the armchair in the corner.

"I think it's time we head home," Nick declared. "Bill, I'm gonna make sure Darcy eats dinner and gets some rest. Try not to get into too much trouble while we're gone, okay?"

Dad's mouth twitched again, almost smiling that time. His cheeks felt too cold when I kissed him goodbye. It felt wrong to be leaving the hospital behind, but Dad wouldn't have wanted for me to sit there and starve. I had to take care of myself.

Taking my arm, Nick asked gently, "Where do you want to stop to eat?"

"We can eat at home," I muttered back.

"Oh, darlin', I don't think you're gonna make it that long."

He wasn't wrong. My head was already propping itself up on his shoulder. The weight of my body longed to lean against Nick's tall frame. Heading toward the parking lot, I felt my reserves of strength dwindling to nothing. I was running solely on fumes.

"How about a burger?" I suggested. "I'm fine with whatever."

"I'll see what's around here, and I'll take us through a drive-through."

"Who says you're driving?"

Taking the keys from my coat pocket, I wanted to stand my ground, but my fingers were weak. They betrayed me, letting Nick steal my keys and hide them away in his leather jacket.

"It's just something I like doing for you," he replied with a smile. "Just humor me, Darcy."

There would be no denying him. Silently, I wanted him to win. It had been too long since I had someone to lean against, and in my condition, I didn't have the strength to argue.

"Okay," I surrendered. "I'll humor you . . . *this time.*"

CHAPTER TWENTY-ONE

NICK

After a cheeseburger and a phone call with Willa, Darcy slept the whole way home. She snored with her cheek pressed against my shoulder, not that I minded. I let her fill the silence as I kept my eyes on the highway and the frozen weather.

"Darcy," I whispered as I pulled my keys from the ignition. "We're back, darlin'. It's time to wake up."

The night demanded for us to take shelter there in the house. As we rushed from my truck, whipping winds rattled the house windows. The storm kept every creature hidden and the night desolate. There weren't even stars to see as Darcy and I headed up the front porch. Inside, only the Christmas tree glowed. The technicolor lights cast a warm glow over us as we tugged off our coats, but there was no small child to greet us. There was nothing but the quiet of being entirely alone.

"I think I'm gonna shower," Darcy declared while taking off her coat. "Are you going to stay?"

I locked the door behind me, wondering, "Where else should I be?"

"The bar? Your cabin?"

"I promised Bill that I'd made sure you got some rest."

Darcy's dark eyes flitted my way. Her tired expression turned tempting.

"You'd have to watch me sleep," she remarked more softly. "You'll have to spend the whole night beside me if you want to keep your word."

"I'm well aware."

What Bill didn't know couldn't kill him, and though my feelings for Darcy were complicated by the truth, nothing altered my overwhelming desire. It lived in her hips and every breath she took. My reckless impulses were always there, simmering just under my skin, even as she got a glass of water from the kitchen and headed to the bedroom.

"I hate smelling like a hospital," she muttered under her breath before piping up. "Nick, do you want to use the bathroom?"

"No, I'm good."

Sitting down on the bed, I unlaced my boots, feeling that surreal simmer turn into a boil. Darcy didn't think twice about my being there. She took her clothes off piece by piece across the room, her body bathed in the yellow lamplight. With her back to me, Darcy didn't notice how I watched her carefully. She couldn't see how the faint light haloed her curves and the profile of her face. She slipped a thin black robe over her shoulders before turning my way.

"Are you sure I can't get you anything?" she asked while tying up the sash.

Darcy walked around the edge of the bed. With her eyes giving nothing away, she ran her fingers across my cheeks and into the sides of my hair.

"I'm okay," I mumbled back. "Don't worry about me."

"But your face is cold."

"A shower could make it warmer, if you don't mind the company."

Her dark lashes looked like a veil over her eyes as they held mine captive. Leaning into her touch, I realized Darcy wasn't the only one run ragged by the long day. We both needed to take shelter from the night. We both craved something more.

"Just give me two minutes," she whispered before kissing me and sealing my fate. *"Two minutes."*

"Two minutes," I repeated.

Every second felt like torture. I peeled off my clothes, leaving them in a pile on the floor. When the time finally passed, I walked out of the bedroom toward the cracked bathroom door in nothing but my underwear. I didn't have the balls to walk through another man's house naked, but the moment I saw Darcy, those anxieties vanished.

Steam clouded the mirror, and I began to feel the water's heat before stepping into the shower. It faintly flushed Darcy's skin, making every inch of her pink after coming in from the cold. She shrugged out of her robe and hung it on a hook beside two towels. Her nonchalance made it all so surreal. She pulled her hair up like we'd done this a hundred times before, and I found myself melting onto the penny tile floor.

"Time's up," I muttered under my breath.

"Just so you know, I don't have any pine soap," she teased. "You're going to have to suffer through citrus and ginger."

"I think I'll survive."

I wasn't worried about actually getting clean. I had showered before leaving the house that morning, but my mind filled with the notion of smelling like her. Darcy could leave scratches down my back and her perfumed scent on my skin. Under the running water, she filled the air with scents of orange and spice. Her back faced me again. I memorized how she ran her cloth over the nape of her neck and every other place I longed to be.

It took everything inside me to play along and not crumple into the old green tub. Infatuated with Darcy down to the stray baby curls stuck to her skin, I forced my hands to stay with me. I gave her the space to make herself clean before making a mess of us both.

"Here," I murmured. "Let me."

I gently took the washcloth from her hands. I only needed an excuse to touch her, letting my hand wander down her sides and back. Turning her head, the flash of her dark eyes ignited something wicked in me. It had my fingers itching for more and my body reacting.

"I didn't invite you in here to wash me," Darcy told me. "I thought you wanted to get warm."

"I'd get warmer if I were closer to you," I pointed out.

Inching closer, I pressed my lips against the nape of her neck. My arms curled around her soft frame, and her curves molded against me. Darcy had to feel what she was doing to me. My teeth grazing over her ear were nothing compared to the length brushing against her backside.

"It's too late to be doing this," she insisted between kisses. "We'll have to get up early."

"Are you saying you don't want this?"

Her head tilted to let my lips move more freely. "Well . . . not exactly."

"Then, why do you have to be so damn stubborn?"

My arms tightened around her. Dropping the damn washcloth, I let my hands rove over her, savoring the fullness of her breasts and the comfort of having her close.

"Old habits die hard, I guess," she mumbled.

With her blessing, my mouth moved over the side of her neck. Darcy's back pressed into my chest, relaxing into the feeling. She invited my hand to slide over her stomach and down between her legs. Unable to reach me, one of Darcy's hands braced my forearm fastened around her. The other pressed against the green tiled wall, already preparing for the rush of euphoria.

"Trust me, darlin', you don't need to fight," I vowed. "You're gonna like it when I win."

My two fingers slipped inside her slick folds, pushing deeper until my thumb found her little pink bud. I circled it with slow, damning intent, relishing the feeling and the patterns we were creating. As Darcy whimpered through her bitten lip, I got off on the sensation of her weakening under my touch.

It meant I wasn't the only one falling apart.

"Don't you like it?" I begged the question in a low rasp. "Isn't it better when you let me take care of you?"

Her hips chased the feeling, bucking back into me. Her head rolled back, and Darcy sucked in a quick breath.

"Yes . . ." she surrendered breathlessly. "Yes, it is."

Caught up in the moment, I coaxed the pleasure from her body and the gentle moans from her lips. I became lost in the current of our deed. Darcy beguiled me. With one word from her, I followed helplessly.

"*Faster*," she whispered between pleading gasps. "Yes, right there. *Don't stop.*"

I refused to relent. My fingers moved at a rapid-fire pace, and my heartbeat raced with them. Darcy's body begged to collapse. I only held her closer. I didn't quit until she stifled back a cry. Throwing her head back, her spine begged to twist as the climax tried to claim her, but it couldn't keep her forever. That night, Darcy was mine to have and to hold.

Between gasping breaths, she wondered, "What about you, baby?"

My lips pressed behind her ear. With one arm still braced around her, I reached for the shower handles. The water quickly ran dry.

"Don't worry," I assured her. "I'm not through with you yet."

I'd never dried myself off so quickly. Wrapped up in her towel, I carried Darcy to the bedroom. Her legs locked themselves around me, letting her skin brush against my dick and causing my will to weaken. As her lips moved over my neck, every step made the bedroom feel a million miles away, but we found it together. I lowered her onto the bed and let the large white towel spread under us. Already dripping in desire and on edge, it was nothing to guide myself into her. Darcy relished every inch I pushed into her, sucking in a sharp breath as she smiled.

"God, you feel so good," she purred for me.

I found myself chuckling before stealing another hasty kiss.

"Funny," I muttered. "I was gonna say the exact same thing."

Darcy anchored her grip against my shoulders as I thrust into her. It felt like elation and relief, and after the long day, the moment became an island for us both to take refuge. Darcy became a warm paradise on a cold night. With every push and pull, I found myself being lured closer. Her arms wrapped around my back. Our panting breaths moved together. In the heat of it all, I couldn't tell where I ended and Darcy began.

"Let me come for you, baby," she breathed in my ear.

It was enough to make me fall apart, but I held on until Darcy had her second wave of satisfaction. Her hips bucked. Her breath caught, and through her release, I found mine. A groan echoed deep within my bones as I collapsed beside her.

"*Damn, darlin',*" was the only thing I knew to say.

Every scrap of good sense I had got lost in the darkness. There, I forgot everything but the woman lying against me. Our worries were left outside the bedroom door. All I had to do was shut my eyes and listen to her soft, slow breaths as Darcy eventually fell asleep.

I couldn't fathom how I'd let her slip away or been stupid enough to hurt her, but as long as Darcy was home for the holidays, I knew it was my chance to set everything right.

In the morning, Darcy and I didn't linger under the covers. We had places to go and people to see. We each got to work, making our breakfast to-go, knowing it would be better to eat once we got to the hospital. Darcy itched to see Willa and Bill. Erin was already texting her about getting Willa into her coat and meeting us in Boone.

"Aunt Erin's made biscuits for everybody," Darcy told me as the coffee pot chimed beside her. "Should I mention that Dad can only eat broth for the next few days?"

I chuckled. "You think it's gonna be torture for him?"

"I don't know. Possibly?"

"Maybe he'd like to live vicariously through us. You can take a bite and tell him about it."

She seemed to like that idea better. With the wheels of her mind turning fast, Darcy moved quickly around the kitchen. She grabbed two steel travel mugs from an upper cabinet and some granola bars from the pantry. It would be about an hour before we were able to really eat. Darcy insisted that we would need something to tide us over, and I didn't argue. I simply grabbed our coats and let us press on.

Pouring the hot coffee into the thermos, she remarked, "You know, Boone's downtown holiday festival is next Friday. Dad should be out of the hospital by then. I was thinking I might go and do some Christmas shopping, maybe take Willa and show her the Christmas tree. I hate keeping her cooped up for too long."

"Sure, she needs some excitement."

She set down the coffee pot and paused. "Would you like to go with us, then?"

My eyes went wide.

"Um, sure, I mean, if you'd like," I mumbled like a fool. "You know I like spending time with you and Willa."

She nodded, smiling as she handed me a filled coffee mug.

"I figured it would be good for all three of us."

"I know what would be good for me right now."

Before Darcy could ask, I leaned over and kissed her fully on the lips, tasting the traces of mint toothpaste on the corner of her mouth. I wouldn't be able to do this once we reached Boone, but when next Friday came, things would be different. Darcy and I would be out and about together with Willa as a family for the first time. I'd finally know for certain what it felt like to be a family with them, and I could hardly wait.

CHAPTER TWENTY-TWO

DARCY

After going back and forth once a day to Boone, perhaps heading back should've been the last thing I wanted to do, but Dad was officially discharged from the hospital. He was settled in at home with my aunt and uncle keeping him company. I relaxed in the passenger's side of my Subaru. My eyes glanced to Willa playing on her doodle board while her father took the exit off the highway. The past week felt like one of the longest of my life. Being able to sit still was the best kind of reprieve.

"Is there anything you're looking for in particular?" I asked Nick.

Turning off the highway, he grinned. "You're the one who invited me here, remember? I'm just along for the ride."

"Says the man driving."

Nick chuckled under his breath. "Well, it might be nice to get some ideas about what to buy a certain someone in a car seat. I figured you'd know better than me about what she might like."

"She might not like them, but every time I turn around, she's not fitting into her pajamas anymore. She's already wearing clothes for eighteen-month-olds. I was thinking we need to go into the children's consignment shop and look around there, and there might be something in the antique mall that could make a good gift. Honestly, I thought I'd have a plan of action, but it feels like a miracle that I made it here."

Every day came with an endless to-do list. My fatigue seemed to laugh at every cup of coffee I drank. The strongest comfort I found was in Nick's hand covering mine over the console.

"You did make a plan of action," Nick reminded me. "You made an early dinner after work, you got Willa into her pajamas and coat, and now, we're going to go look at the Christmas decorations and see what the shops have on sale. Do you need more of a plan than that?"

"No," I had to admit. "I guess I don't."

That night, I was allowed to enjoy my evening, pushing Willa's stroller along the sloping sidewalks. Nick followed a half-step behind. His stride matched mine as we wandered through the closed-off streets where shoppers flowed in and out of the historic brick-clad buildings. Under the light of a massive Christmas tree, carolers sang over the noise of conversation and excitement. The smells of cocoa and coffee wafted out of the mobile coffee shop built into a vintage camper van.

It felt like we'd stepped into a real-life snow village, though there wasn't a flake to be found. My hand instinctively reached back, and Nick laced his fingers with mine. The horse-drawn carriage rolling around the block was icing on the holiday cake.

"You see the horse, Willa girl?" I asked, angling the stroller so she could watch the brown draft horse trot past.

"*Ooh,*" she said in awe.

Nick leaned in closer to me. "We could take a ride, if you want. It doesn't cost that much."

"Maybe later," I agreed. "For now, let's go see what we can buy."

"Whatever you want, darlin'. I'm just along for the ride."

It shouldn't have felt different from the day we went Christmas tree shopping. Back then, Nick didn't treat Willa any differently. The grin and joking remarks he offered hadn't changed, but for the first time, Nick and I were out and about like a hundred other families. The mundane had never felt so thrilling.

In the children's shop, we found a few things for Willa to wear over the winter, including a little knit cap that reminded me of her father's. Nick insisted upon buying it.

"I've gotta catch up, don't I?" he pointed out. "You've had plenty of chances to buy all the clothes and toys. I think it's my turn now."

He made it sound like a treat, and in a way, it was. Nick unwrapped the ivory mittens he found for Willa and slid them over her hands one at a time. He crouched in front of her stroller as she admired them.

"Do you like them, Willa girl?" he asked her.

Willa nodded, clapping her hands together though they hardly made a sound. Watching them together, I got lost in the sight of it all. Nick's blue eyes sparkled in the streetlights. He wasn't the kind of man to become visibly frazzled or upset, but I couldn't remember a time when Nick appeared so at ease. There was a calm in his expression that made me want to reach out and let his lips find mine. My heartbeat skipped at the thought, yet we weren't alone here. The secrets we'd promised to keep reared their heads.

A familiar face came crossing the street, stroller in tow. Her green eyes lit up at the sight of me.

"Darcy?" she exclaimed over the Carolers' rising chorus. "Darcy, oh my gosh, I can't believe it's you!"

I blinked in surprise. "*Lizzie?*"

It had been months since I'd seen her. With her own business, husband, and son, I didn't get to meet up with my old friend much these days. She had moved to the Charlotte area years ago. I was in Durham and then everywhere else, but hugging Lizzie always made the passed time pointless. Flinging her arms around me, Lizzie and I were back in our dorm room at Duke or in a cabin at summer camp as kids. Her upbeat energy and rosy-cheeked grin were just as infectious as ever.

"Funny running into you here!" I exclaimed as we pulled apart. "What are you doing in Boone?"

She gestured down to her half-asleep son. "Jacob and I are visiting my mom. Logan's off traveling for business, so I decided to get out of the house for a few days and come see her. Mom loves coming to this event. I don't know if she's ever missed it. She's around here somewhere, probably in the consignment shop."

"Oh, we just came from there. It's got tons of great stuff marked down tonight."

Lizzie's eyebrows went up. *"We?"*

Lizzie wasn't a fool. She knew my pregnancy was a surprise and that Willa's father had never been public knowledge, but as her son came only a few months before Willa, it felt easy to confide in Lizzie. We spent a lot of late nights coaching each other over the phone about the struggles of new motherhood. Lizzie's husband, Logan, had always been supportive, but that didn't make having a baby any less difficult.

Her bright, round eyes looked to Willa's stroller. She saw Nick's grip on the handle as he stood beside me. Thanks to her short frame, Lizzie had to glance up to meet Nick's gaze, but she saw who he was in a heartbeat.

"I don't know if we've ever met," she declared, extending her free hand to him. "I'm Lizzie. Darcy and I roomed together in college."

Nick accepted her handshake with one of his charming grins. "Oh, I know who you are. Darcy used to tell me about all the nonsense you two got up to in school, but it's nice to put a name to a face."

"This is Nick," I added. "He's my . . . my . . . well, we're old friends."

"I work at her dad's bar."

Lizzie nodded. "Well, it's sweet of you two to come out together as *friends*."

If she wanted to say more, Lizzie kept it to herself, only giving me a knowing sideways glance. We couldn't chat long on the sidewalk. Other shoppers were pushing past us, and Lizzie still had to find her mother. After a few more minutes, we waved goodbye and promised to meet up when we could. It had always been too long, and with our kids so close in age, Willa and Jacob were ripe for a play date. The entire time, Nick never faltered. We got our shopping done just as Willa began to poop out.

"I think it's time we head home," I realized. "I think we're all gonna start yawning pretty soon."

Following me out of the bookstore, Nick nodded in agreement. "And it's not like you don't have three bags full of everything here."

"It's good to shop local! I've got the bulk of my gifts now. I'll only have to get a few more things for her and you."

"Oh, you don't need to get me anything."

I shook my head. "Nope, no, I don't want to hear it."

"All right." Nick laughed. "Let's save that fight for another time."

We both conceded and turned around the corner. The crowds thinning out let us navigate the hubbub with a little more ease, yet I found Nick stopping at the corner. The parking lot was only one block away.

"What are you looking at?" I asked before I saw my answer.

That same old-fashioned carriage with the massive draft horse was unloading a round of passengers with nobody lined up for the next ride. I already suspected what Nick was thinking. He didn't have to turn around for me to know the idea lighting up his face.

"Let's go for a ride," he encouraged me. "Come on, it'll only take fifteen minutes, and Willa might even get to pet the horse. You know she'd like that."

"But..."

Nick shook his head. "You don't need to make up an excuse, you know. After this week, you've earned your fun."

He was right. I had decided to enjoy myself while we were out together. I wasn't about to spoil my own chances at a good time, and with the look in Nick's eye, I had no strength to deny him.

"You know what, sure," I happily surrendered. "If they've got space for a stroller, we'll go for a ride."

Of course, the coachman knew just how to pack our things on the free bench while Nick held Willa in his arms. Her tired eyes were wide with excitement as she stroked the horse, but by the time she settled into my lap along the old leather seat, Willa's last flicker of delight had her entirely wiped out. Nick pulled the complimentary blanket over us both and draped his arm around my shoulder.

"You know what I said before," he teased in a low tone. "You'll like it when I win."

I leaned into his side and smiled. "It's definitely nice."

If I shut my eyes, I could believe life had always been this way. Nick and I happily lived in this chilly but festive scene. The streets were quieter now, but the holiday lights still glowed. As we rounded the town's Christmas tree, I nearly nodded off like Willa, but Nick's sudden question stopped me short.

"Your friend, Lizzie," he began quietly. "She knew who I was, didn't she?"

"We lived together for three years," I reminded him. "Your name did come up once or twice, but . . . she did know about Willa."

Nick reached down and adjusted the blanket over our daughter. "Her son didn't look much older than her. What did she say his name was, Jacob?"

"Yeah, his name is Jacob, and Lizzie knows . . . enough. I'm pretty sure she put two and two together, not that I've told her about us now, or even Dad."

"There wasn't enough time."

"But . . . does that bother you?" I wondered, turning to look Nick in the eyes. "Do you not like people knowing about our history?"

"No, it's nothing like that. I'm not used to it, that's all. Eventually, people are going to have to know. I can't be a secret father forever."

"No," I agreed quietly. "You can't."

"But we're not gonna worry about that now."

Brushing back the few stray curls from my face, Nick made me forget it all with a kiss. I hadn't realized how the night breeze froze my cheeks. With his hand on my face, Nick felt impossibly warm. It coaxed me to nestle closer and breathe in the faint scent of pine that always lingered around him.

My eyes fell shut. My lips pulled away only to find his again. When we pulled up to my father's house, Nick and I couldn't kiss so freely. He had followed me back to my bedroom so many times, but that night, the television was playing faintly in the living room. Leftovers from dinner were still on the stove, and the hustle and bustle of life came back to me.

"I'll get goin'," Nick muttered where the others couldn't hear. "Thanks for inviting me out tonight."

"Thanks for driving."

If my arms weren't filled with Willa, I would have wrapped myself around him one last time, feeling the cold on his leather jacket and the strength of his chest. I didn't know how much time we had, though. Somebody could have walked into the kitchen at any minute, so Nick only gave me a brief kiss on the cheek and Willa a kiss on the top of her head.

"Take care, Darlin' Darcy Rose," he told me with one final smile.

The ghosts of Christmas past were all around us, following Nick as he headed out the back door. Like he said in the carriage, people would have to know one day. I only hoped we could hold onto our quiet happiness for a little while longer.

CHAPTER TWENTY-THREE

NICK

For the first time in days, I drove home to sleep in my cabin, leaving her back at her father's house with Willa and all their holiday shopping. I was happy for Darcy's sake that Bill was home from the hospital, but I couldn't wake up beside her anymore. Breakfasts with her and Willa were out of the question. In less than a week, I had grown used to the routine we'd made together. The meals at the table set for three became familiar, and Darcy's small bed became a comfort.

It showed me the kind of life I'd never dared to have.

The truck rumbled to a halt under my carport. Shopping bags in hand, I trudged up the back steps and into my place, but hardly anything about it felt right anymore. I set my things down on the kitchen table, but I couldn't settle myself.

The cabin had no spare bedroom or safety measures for a child. Back when I'd picked out the kit, I didn't plan on having much company, let alone a family, but things were changing for me. Looking around, all I saw were hazards for a curious toddler. It was somehow both too big and not enough. The stairs leading up to my bedroom even felt like a death trap.

"I need to buy a gate or something," I muttered to myself.

I had left my heart with Willa and her mother. While getting ready to shower, all I could do was think of them, wondering how they might fit into the cabin and the old order of my life. They didn't fit. It wasn't right, but heading downstairs toward the bathroom, I looked toward a gap where the kitchen cabinets ended and the fireplace began. My five-foot tall Christmas tree sat unlit. As I went over to flip its switch, a lightbulb went off in my head too.

They sell additions at the log cabin place, don't they?

Part of their whole marketing scheme was how customizable their home kits could be. I even vaguely remembered the saleswoman talking up the add-ons, but I'd declined. If I wanted to make things right with Darcy, perhaps the first step was showing they could have a place with me. I needed to make more room for Willa in my life, including, well, a literal room.

The rest of my night was filled with planning. With wet hair and a towel around my waist, I ran a tape measure over the empty wall. It was the perfect place for a door. I didn't need much, just a room big enough for a decent bed and a closet. I debated even closing off the loft to my room and making the overlook a full wall. Lying in bed, I tried to picture it all, and among the renovations, I tried to see Darcy there at the round kitchen table with her morning coffee and our daughter beside her. The fantasy followed me into my sleep.

Through the misty haze, I saw Darcy there in one of her many sweaters with mug in hand. Her smile warmed her tired eyes as Willa climbed up into her lap, not that she totally fit. A growing bump under Darcy's sweater got in the way.

Are you trying to eat my breakfast? Darcy asked teasingly. *Willa girl, what's the baby gonna have if you eat this?*

Willa reached for the half-eaten toast on her mother's plate and grinned. It showed off her baby teeth and the crinkles at the corners of her eyes.

Daddy's food! Willa declared in that small, silvery voice of hers.

I liked the sound of it too much. It didn't even matter that Darcy took the untouched bread from my plate while our little girl giggled. Everything looked too wonderful to be real. It was everything I never knew I needed. Simple and sweet, Darcy offered me a look better than any Christmas gift money could buy, and I finally noticed a familiar ring on her finger.

You two had better get going, she told me. *You've got places to be.*

Though my mind didn't know what Darcy meant, my body moved instinctively. I collected the dishes as Willa went and grabbed a backpack from a place I didn't see. Her small feet echoed as they hurried around the house. Some silent voice told me I was taking her to preschool before heading over to the bar. Darcy was going to work from our home that morning, but not until she kissed me goodbye at the back steps. She draped her arms over my shoulders and smiled again.

I'll see you when you come home, Nick.

Home wasn't the cabin. It was Darcy in all her glory. It was the little hand enclosed in mine. For years, I'd never dreamed up such a scene, but it filled my thoughts now. It pervaded every piece of me. If Christmas wishes were real, this was the life I would wish for every year.

Darcy, I . . .

I began to tell her something, but my words were lost. The scene began to fade away. Fighting, I tried to will it back, to hear what I wanted to tell her, but my eyes opened to the isolating silence of my dark cabin. The pale gray light of morning crept in through the windows. The sounds of giggles and Darcy's voice were long gone.

"What was I saying?" I grumbled, my voice dry and haggard.

Rubbing my eyes, I couldn't remember the words just about to leave my mouth. The scene was slipping away from me the more my body woke up, but I wanted it all back. My heart ached for a chance to make that fantasy something tangible and real. The only trouble was that it would take more than tacking on a spare room to my cabin. Between Bill, Darcy's life elsewhere, and all the complicated emotions in between, that same silent voice told me my troubles didn't stop at square footage. I needed something else too, something I'd never experienced in all my life.

I needed a damn miracle.

CHAPTER TWENTY-FOUR

DARCY

The day felt like some kind of comedy. Dad's hens making their usual morning kerfuffle paled in comparison to every hour after. From the moment I started making cheese grits for breakfast, time passed with a never-ending cycle of opening and closing doors, and I tripped over toys and my own two feet trying to juggle it all.

An occupational therapist came over between breakfast and my morning meeting, and the minute I turned away from waving goodbye to her, another kind of therapist showed up in the driveway. I began to lose track of them all. Doing my best, I half-listened to the monthly meeting being piped through my headphones while trying to keep track of everything happening right in front of me.

Nick was the only reason I survived.

As Dad showed one of his therapists around the house, Nick pulled up to stick around and mind Willa. He made sandwiches for lunch and chatted with Dad while Willa napped. I didn't have to jump up from my seat at the dining table every time somebody arrived. By the end of the day, I didn't know how I managed to get any work done before having Nick around.

"You've got some boxes here," he told me as was getting ready to head to the bar. "The mailman just dropped them off."

"I think those are for . . ." I replied before pausing to see if Willa was within earshot. "They're from *Santa*."

He cracked a smile and laughed. "Oh, that's how he gets around the world these days."

"He's very well-prepared. After Willa goes to bed, his elves will wrap those up in some special paper for the twenty-fifth."

"Are they gonna fit under the tree?"

Nick and I both looked toward the living room. A pile of colorful boxes with festive patterns was collecting under the tree. Strategic stacks kept it all from flowing out onto the floor.

"No, but they'll fit in my closet for now," I decided.

That too was a struggle, but I made room beside my shoes and securely shut the door. As Dad watched the football game, I realized I hadn't stepped outside the house all day long. I hadn't even stepped off the front porch all weekend, either. Dad's house suddenly felt confining.

"I'm gonna get some fresh air," I declared to Dad.

He looked up from the commentators on the television screen. "You goin' for a walk?"

That felt too far. I didn't want to go anywhere that wasn't in earshot of the house.

"No, I'll, um, be in the back yard."

Dad turned back to his program. "All right, I'll holler if I need you."

"Please do."

Noise from the television.

Noise from the house guests.

Noise from Willa who didn't know any better, God bless her.

Throwing my coat on, I hustled out as fast as I could. The screen door slapped behind me, and in the dark, everything felt bizarrely quiet. It was nothing like the chaos inside. The world had grown still for the night. The air smelled of ice. I needed to bide my time, but with the temperature only dropping, I didn't know how long that could last.

"Fire," I realized. "I'll make a fire."

I had done it a million times as a kid. Out at the old fire pit, Dad still had the same Adirondack bench he'd built when I was in middle school. I dumped a pile of logs into the brick circle and stole a blanket from the back of my car. I braided back my curls to keep them away from the sparks. One match failed, but the other worked like a charm.

In no time, my attention got lost to the fire. Time vanished like the embers floating up into the dark. I didn't even notice when the front door opened and the last guest of the night stepped out through the back.

"Bill said you were out here," Nick called. "All bundled up, and you still look cold, Black Sheep. Is your wool not keepin' you warm?"

Coming into the light, Nick's eyes looked tired from another night on the job, but his smile was as bright as when he left me. His familiar red knit cap pushed down his blond hair. Even if he was older than me, at the moment, he seemed to be the younger one. My body felt ancient, and my mind was numb.

I rolled my eyes and laughed. "It's doing its best."

"Then here, let me help it out."

Nick tugged off his hat and leaned toward me. He pulled it down over the tops of my ears.

"I've always wanted to look like Jacques Cousteau," I teased. "Now, what are you doing here?"

"Getting my fix of you."

I rolled my eyes. "Try again."

Nick flopped down onto the bench. I moved my fleece blanket to cover both of our laps, giving me the chance to inch closer. His arm draped over my shoulder.

"Your Dad had to sign some stuff for payroll, and I promised to let him see the inventory from the kitchen," he explained.

"He could see all that on his laptop if he used the cloud system I suggested. It would streamline lots of things for the bar."

"Oh, you're preaching to the choir."

I changed the subject. "How far along was the football game?"

"It was just starting the fourth quarter."

"Good," I muttered quietly. "That means we have plenty of time for this."

Under the blanket, my hand slowly trailed along the inside of his thigh. It hadn't been that long since we'd been together, but I had grown spoiled waking up to Nick every day. I missed the feeling of his body against mine as I slept. My aching muscles longed for the comfort of it all, and by the firelight, my needs flickered and flourished like the fire itself.

Nick reached under my old college sweatshirt, massaging my breasts as he cupped them. I wanted to moan from the delight of it all. There was nothing like his hands on me. No man could ever make me feel so good, but instead of whimpering into his feverish kiss, I *yawned*.

Horror ate my desire alive. My tired eyes shot open. If my cheeks hadn't already been pink, they would've turned bright red from the shame of it.

"I'm so sorry," I fretted. "I swear it's not you. I just had to wake up early to clean out that stupid chicken coop over there and get ready for a meeting with some company clients, and I just . . . I'm so tired."

It relieved me to hear him laugh it off. Tucking a curl behind my ear, Nick gave me a winsome grin.

"It's okay, darlin'. I know it's not your fault. What's that thing you're always telling me? That *this* is enough?"

"Yeah, something along those lines."

My brain couldn't exactly remember.

"Then, relax and let this be enough for now," he assured me, shifting himself to let me curl against him instead. "It is for me."

"Are you sure?"

Nick kissed my temple. "I wouldn't lie about that. Why don't you tell me what you want for your birthday instead? What do you like these days?"

"I'm pretty much the same person you've always known, even if I am getting a little older. I like my books and food and blankets and naps and pillows and sweaters and—"

Laughing, he nudged me. "Okay, okay, I get the message loud and clear."

I remembered when I'd tried to be someone else. Back before I traveled and just after college, I bought the stylish clothes and went out to the trendy downtown restaurants with my co-workers and friends. I wasn't unhappy, but somewhere along the way, I realized it wasn't exactly me. I didn't like trendy cocktails or small plates of food that left my stomach and bank account empty.

Being at home with him felt better than anything money could buy.

"As long as you come to my birthday dinner, I'll be happy," I promised him. "I don't need you to buy me anything."

"I wouldn't be anywhere else."

As we watched the fire together, I found my eyelids getting heavier and his chest becoming more and more comfortable. I didn't know what would happen if I fell asleep outside, but even if Nick had to carry me inside, I couldn't find the energy to care. It was only when something cold melted over my cheeks that I began to rouse again.

"It's snowing," Nick realized.

One tiny fleck hit my nose. More melted in the ends of my hair. By morning, it would all be washed away. The ground wasn't cold enough to let the frozen weather stay, but in that quiet night, it was beautiful to behold.

"I guess it's time for us to go," I whispered.

Nick's eyes met mine. They looked almost baby blue in the night-time, so soft and tender. Part of me wondered if we could sleep under the snow anyway, but Nick knew better. He pulled off our blanket and helped me to my feet. Taking my hand, he led me as far as the back steps.

"I wish I could take you inside right now," he confessed.

I sighed, leaning against him. "You and me both, baby."

Reluctantly, we said goodnight in the light of the back door. The quiet settled my tired bones as I smiled up at him. He leaned down, kissing me so gently that it broke my heart. His palms warmed my icy cheeks.

"Sleep well," he replied. "I'll see you soon."

"Drive safe."

Watching him go, I waited for the rumble of his truck to disappear before heading through the back door. The lights felt brighter. The sound of Dad's snoring drifted through the house, but it didn't leave me feeling as panicked as before. Perhaps I hadn't been able to get everything I wanted from Nick, but I got exactly what I needed.

CHAPTER TWENTY-FIVE

NICK

Delicate snowflakes floated on fishing line from the ceiling. Crêpe paper streamers spread to every corner of the dining room away from the brass chandelier. Darcy had never been one for big parties. Back when she turned eighteen, I remember Bill decided to throw a big surprise party for her. He closed the bar for the night and invited at least half of the town, yet Darcy had cottoned on. I found her parked in her old Mustang with a dead-eyed stare. I gave her a shandy and encouraged her to come inside.

That night, though, Darcy didn't need to be coaxed into having a good time. I cut through the kitchen and found her smiling from ear to ear. With her baby girl on her hip, Darcy appraised the decorations and the casserole dishes spread out over the table.

"Didn't Aunt Erin and Uncle Mickey do a good job, Willa?" Darcy asked with her eyes on the floral centerpiece.

I smiled at Willa's face lighting up at the sight of me. "I certainly think so."

"Da!" Willa chimed.

More of a sound than a word, the exclamation caught me off

guard, but a piece of me wanted to ask Willa to say it again. Darcy made a face in surprise before fussing with the bow pushing back Willa's curls.

"We're, um, working on that at bedtime," she explained. "I mean, she'll have to call you something, won't she?"

"Nicholas, maybe?" I tried to joke. "Mr. Wallace?"

"Who are you, Nick, her teacher?"

"Not unless you want her to fail at science and social studies."

Setting my gift bag with the handful of others, I laughed off the stirrings in my chest. This wasn't the place to get lost in Darcy's soft smile or want more than I should have. We didn't have the luxury of being alone.

"Where are the others?" I asked.

"Dad and Mickey are out in the garage talking about old cars, and Aunt Erin realized she forgot to pick up birthday candles with the cake. She'll be back any minute now."

"So, we have a minute?"

Darcy nodded and took a step closer. "One, at least."

Playing with fire, she gently pressed her palm against my chest before drawing my lips to hers. I told myself not to ask, but she offered it willingly. It was her day, after all. Who was I to deny her?

"You dressed up for me," she murmured, her fingers sliding up toward the collar of my green chambray shirt. "I don't know if I've ever seen you in this."

"I save it for the most special occasions," I teased back.

Smiling through her kiss, Darcy lured me back for a second time, but the squeak of the storm door threw us apart. An invisible wall formed between us as the sound of the brothers' raucous voices became clear.

"You can take the Mustang to the show," Bill declared. "If you win, though, I'd better get the prize money!"

"Oh, naw!" Mickey boomed excitedly. "I'd give it to our birthday girl!"

There was a sound of a large hand patting a back before Bill said, "Fair enough!"

The pair stepped into the dining room to greet me and see the spread for themselves. Not a minute later, Erin was back with her candles. Dinner was served, and through the meal, I refused to tempt fate by looking over at Darcy too much. The warmth of her touch still lingered, but Erin poured the wine more generously than she served her pot roast.

"What would everyone want from Oahu?" Erin asked eagerly, excited to talk more about their Hawaiian holiday. "Jordan says there's a great coffee roaster not too far away. We could bring everyone a bag to try!"

"Willa will take two," I joked.

As everyone laughed along, I found it harder and harder to settle in my seat, but I smiled anyway and played my part. I was the family friend, a guest at the table. I couldn't hold Darcy's hand over the table like Mickey held his wife's. Over the years, I got used to being happy with the small life I had, but looking at Darcy in her velvet dress and gold hoop earrings, she made it a struggle not to want more.

My hands braced themselves against my knees when they became too tempted to run through her cascading curls. When it came time to open her gifts, her expression had me crumpling faster than the colorful tissue paper. Erin and Mickey bought her a new scarf and some jewelry. Her father bought her a pair of pink suede flats that she'd apparently requested. It made me worry about my one small bag. Last but maybe not least, Darcy revealed the copy of *Lady Chatterley's Lover*, and a wide grin spread over her face.

"Did you know some booksellers were imprisoned for distributing this?" she declared to the table. "People called it filthy and obscene."

Erin cocked her head to the side. "What for?"

"For things that would make people a hundred years ago turn beet red," Darcy explained.

"Well, I know how much you enjoy banned books," I remarked. "When I saw that one in the bookshop, I couldn't remember whether you had a copy of it."

"I didn't until now. Thank you, Nick."

Meeting her eyes, I smiled softly. "You're welcome. Happy birthday, Black Sheep."

"Yes, happy birthday, sweetie!" Erin cheered along. "Let's go get that cake!"

The grocery store sheet cake was decorated in an array of holly piped in frosting, but I had no need of that sugary sweetness. Darcy's face glowed in those twenty-seven candles, her delight shining brighter than those flickering flames. I tried to follow the words of the song. My mouth moved, yet I became breathless. Darcy took it all, shut her eyes, and made a wish as her family clapped.

I only wanted to know what that frosting tasted like on Darcy's mouth. The small slice I ate with my teacup of coffee seemed so incomparable. As Darcy went to put Willa to bed, I helped clean up the remnants of the party, still wondering and waiting for the moment she returned.

"I promised to go help with closing tonight at the bar," I remarked when Darcy came back to the kitchen. "I guess I should head over there."

"Oh, sure, sweetie!" Erin remarked. "Thanks so much for helping me here!"

Darcy smiled. "Here, let me walk you out."

Erin was too buzzed on red wine to think anything of it. Darcy shrugged into her coat and followed me out into the night. With no moon overhead, all we had was the tall pole light out back beside the garage. I'd grown used to its yellow light sneaking through the gaps in Darcy's blinds.

"I don't have to run off immediately," I remarked, looking back over our shoulders.

Darcy laced her fingers with mine. "Well, it's a little too cold to stand out here, isn't it?"

The frozen grass crunched under our feet as we headed out past the chicken coop and a group of hibernating trees to reach the side door of the old shop. Darcy knew where her father hid the side door's key, and before I knew it, we were out of the chill and alone in the darkness. I reached over to click on the workbench light and cast our shadows across the smooth concrete.

As Darcy ran her hand along the hood of her car, I had to ask, "Do you ever think of selling your Shelby?"

"Never," she said. "This is Willa's college fund, and well, my Shelby's one of a kind, isn't she?"

"Just like her owner."

"I hope you don't think we came out here to talk about cars, though."

Slowly, I shook my head, feeling all those unmet desires brimming to the surface.

"No," I replied, already closing the distance. "I never thought that for a second."

She looked like a dream leaning against the hood of a car worth more than my life. Her dark eyes followed me as I came closer, flickering with a glimpse of all the feelings Darcy kept hidden. She had always been better at keeping her secrets than I was.

Part of me knew I was too old for these games, yet my hands reached out anyway. They slid up her hips and around her backside, pulling Darcy closer. I made a home for myself between her legs. Our lips found each other with ease, moving together in a dance we'd memorized. Darcy brushed her tongue against my lower lip, and with a low groan rumbling in my chest, I felt all those simmering desires close to boiling over.

"There's something else I wanted to give you, but it's not something I could put in a gift bag," I told her between kisses. "You could have it now or later."

Darcy's voice became low and sweet like the traces of sugar on her mouth. Admiring me through half-closed eyes, she shined with her knowing expression. Her fingertips were already trying to push past the buttons of my shirt.

"I think I have to have it now, don't you? It's not really a birthday gift if I don't get it today."

"You might get a little cold."

"But you'll keep me warm," she purred. "Won't you, Nick?"

Her free hand curled around the back of my neck. She beamed, and my pulse raced past the point of no return. My cravings consumed me. Not thinking twice, I kissed Darcy with all the reckless hunger I possessed. My hands slowly guided her back, lying her flat against the hood of the car. My answer was laced with the rasp of wanting.

"I'll keep you however you like, birthday girl."

Though she giggled, it got lost in a sigh. My mouth moved away from hers, traveling down the hollow of her throat. With her fingers reaching for my hair, I worked at undoing the bow keeping her dress together. It took one tug of a velvet sash to unveil everything underneath. It was like she already knew, and the thought compelled me to wander lower.

I kissed the tops of her lace-covered breasts before moving down her stomach. I felt every catch in her breath and the gentle shiver across her skin, yet she remained warm. Her soft curves radiated with that inescapable heat that ruined me a million times over. One hook of my thumb unveiled her most precious parts, and Darcy only spread her legs wider for me. She welcomed me between her thighs, her hands in my hair encouraging me to get closer.

"You always know how to treat a girl," Darcy whispered between panting breaths.

The only answer I needed was my tongue pressing into her folds before slowly circling her clit. Her body writhed against the pleasure, but my grip held her right in place. With Darcy's leg draped over my shoulder, I drank her in. I devoured every taste and claimed every sound of pleasure. There was only so much time before Darcy had to be back inside. The clock ran against me, yet I worked to make every one of her gasps and stifled moans count.

"Oh, God, *Nick*, I . . . I'm . . ."

She didn't need to finish the thought. Her nails scraped against my scalp as a climax consumed her, rippling through every inch of her body. I almost hated to see it end.

Though I pressed my lips tenderly against her inner thigh, I knew I couldn't linger. Darcy sat up and gathered herself. My aching fingers combed down my unkempt hair. The mess I'd made of her quickly vanished, yet my disappointment was reflected in her eyes.

"I can't go back in there and pretend," I thought aloud. "They think I'm leaving."

Darcy nodded. "I know."

With my forehead falling against hers, I dared to steal a few seconds more. I took one last kiss before heading out to the truck, letting Darcy follow me there. Releasing her hand pained me.

"I'll see you Christmas morning," she remarked. "You're still coming for breakfast, right?"

"There's nowhere else I'd rather be," I replied. "Happy birthday, Darcy."

She smiled and waved. "Thanks, Nick, for everything."

I watched Darcy bundle her long coat tighter across her body as I pulled away. The night felt so much colder without her there. In many ways, I didn't know how much longer I was going to last.

Pretending not to adore Darcy was quickly becoming the hardest thing ever asked of me, but for her, I would continue to keep up the charade. Whatever she asked, whatever she needed, I'd do it. For now, I just had to make those stolen moments enough.

CHAPTER TWENTY-SIX

DARCY

Was it possible to pack a man's six-foot frame into a suitcase or tuck him into a coat pocket? As the night waned on, I couldn't stop thinking about all the ways I wanted to keep Nick with me and beside me. I hugged my aunt and uncle goodbye. The house grew calm again, but the stirring feelings in my heart wouldn't settle.

I wanted Nick with me, but *how*?

My current life was nearly two hundred miles away. The bedroom Nick and I shared wasn't really mine anymore. I had a life and friends, not that Willa didn't keep me busy enough, but Nick's entire life was right there in the mountains. I couldn't throw him into my luggage and drag him back to suburbia. Nick would hate it, and deep down, I feared him hating me for it too.

I never expected that of Nick. Even if I wanted him to stay in Willa's life, I refused to have him blow up his life and follow me. It wouldn't be fair.

"You thinkin' about a second slice?" Dad asked as he stepped into the kitchen.

CHRISTMAS IN THE CABIN

I blinked in confusion. It took me a second to realize I was staring down at my half-eaten birthday cake. The clear plastic top reflected my pensive expression.

"Um, I debated it, but I'm definitely full," I lied. "After Aunt Erin's lasagna, I don't think I'm gonna be hungry for another week."

"She does know how to make 'em," Dad agreed with a smile. "You know, I noticed you and Nick were outside for a good while tonight. Call me curious, but it had me wonderin' what had you two out in the cold like that."

Picking up the cake, I watched as Dad slowly collected a stray piece of tissue paper. He remained careful of his chest and the discomfort in his healing body. I didn't really know what to tell him. It just had to be something believable.

"We got wrapped up in a conversation," I decided to say. "I guess it's been a while since Nick and I have really talked, but it's been good reconnecting. I . . . I think we've both been better for it."

I never knew what was good for me. My curiosity would definitely be the death of me. While Dad refreshed his water glass, I began to wade into treacherous territory, trying not to give away the secrets I'd worked too hard to keep.

"I mean, it was different when I was young," I continued, milling about the kitchen as if I was actually doing something. "Nick really only saw me when I followed you into work on the weekends. We didn't have much in common, but you know, we're both adults now. It's easier to talk, and he cares so much. He's good with Willa and you. He's . . . well, I don't know where I'd be without him right now."

"We'd both be in a pretty rough spot," Dad agreed. "Actually, I'm glad you two get along so well. You both deserve to get out more. Anytime I talk to him, I feel like he's always headin' to the bar, and you're always either mindin' Willa or worried about work. It's good for you both to spend some time away from your usual routines."

"It's definitely been nice to have the company."

"And it's been nice of him coming here to help you and watch Willa when he's not doin' a shift at the bar. It's just . . ."

"What?"

"I can't help but think that Willa's father should be the man doin' those things," he finished with a sobering look on his face. "It shouldn't have to be Nick."

My heart dropped into my stomach, forcing bile into my throat. Maybe it was a chance to come clean. Maybe, since it was my birthday, Dad wouldn't get too angry with me.

"Dad, I—"

He stopped me, holding up his hands in surrender.

"No, no, it's still your special day," he assured me. "I'm not gonna ruin it by makin' a fuss. I've got pills to take and a bed to see, so don't worry, Darcy. You just enjoy the rest of your night. Happy birthday, sweetheart."

I smiled, but my breaking heart wasn't in it. As he kissed my cheek, I thanked him and listened as his footsteps trod down the short hall. His door clicked shut, and I decided that a second slice of cake sounded like a good idea.

Alone on the couch, I ate every little crumb and bit of frosting. I pressed my fork onto the plate before drawing it between my lips. When Aunt Erin put that cake down in front of me, I had no clue what to wish for. The candles glowed like a Christmas tree in the dark. It beckoned me to dream of something impossible, to look beyond what I knew toward something sweeter.

That was the beauty of the holidays. Like love, it made the hollowest hearts wonder what was truly possible, and looking over the tree Nick and I bought together, I imagined that the life I wanted with him wasn't so far-fetched. I only had to shut my eyes and wish, so . . . I did.

When Christmas was over, when the lights came down and the darkness of winter settled over us all, I wished Nick could still be the man beside me. I didn't want him packed away with the stockings to collect dust in the attic. I longed to love him in the daylight, far from the shadows and secrets keeping too much space between us.

Maybe that was too much to ask of twenty-seven candles. They couldn't solve the complications of our lives, yet they had me hoping that Nick and I would figure it out. I didn't need to steel myself for that last night and final goodbye. Hope felt like a such a small thing, but sitting there in my father's living room, it was the best thing I possibly had to hold onto.

CHAPTER TWENTY-SEVEN

NICK

Christmas morning arrived with an excitement that I hadn't felt in years. I couldn't get my clothes on fast enough. My truck didn't move at the speed of light. For years, the twenty-fifth of December had been much like any other day. The magic of the holiday slowly dwindled away, but this morning was entirely different.

It was true what people said. Christmas was better with kids around.

Pulling gift boxes and bags from my passenger's seat, I was more than ready to have breakfast with Darcy, Willa, and Bill. I'd spent most holiday dinners with them. Except for that one morning two years ago, I never joined in as they ate their breakfast and opened presents, but times were changing. Darcy convinced her father that she wanted an extra hand around the kitchen and another to mind Willa. Regardless of the pretenses and pretending, I was just happy to see them.

"It's open!" I heard Darcy call out as the doorbell rang.

Feet scampered across the old floors. As I let myself in, Willa greeted me in her candy cane pajamas with the biggest smile on her face and the icing from cinnamon rolls on her cheeks. It looked brighter than any morning sunshine or fresh blanket of snow I'd ever seen.

"Hi!" she chimed.

I crouched down to meet her eyes. "Hey, kiddo, it looks like you need a napkin."

"She needs a whole shower with all the sugar that's on her," Darcy declared jokingly, coming into the living room. "Merry Christmas."

"Merry Christmas," I replied. "Have I missed breakfast?"

She shook her head. "Only Willa getting her first course while video chatting with my mom. There's coffee in the kitchen if you want it. Dad's in there fixing himself a plate."

I was so ready to lean into her. A half-step away, Darcy looked too lovely for words. Her curls were only a little unkempt. Sleep lingered in the corners of her eyes as she smiled. It wasn't much different from all the other mornings we'd spent together, even if she had already dressed for the day. If possible, I would've captured that moment and kept it in a golden frame, but one small reminder sent me reeling back to reality.

Every moment came with a cost. Across the long room, I caught sight of Bill waving at me from the open kitchen door. I refused to let my smile falter or fade.

"Darcy's lettin' us have bacon this mornin'!" he exclaimed. "You'd better come get some before I eat it all!"

"You can put the presents with the others," Darcy added, scooping up Willa. "We'll be back in just a jiff."

I nodded. "Sounds good."

This was a price I felt more than willing to pay. To sit at the dining table with Darcy and talk about dinner plans, to watch Willa pull out all the little goodies hidden in her stocking, I taught myself to smile and nod. We had a leisurely breakfast before opening gifts one at a time, and all the while, I watched Darcy as if she existed behind glass. The sight of Bill in his old armchair kept my anxious hands from ever reaching out.

I could see her there on the living room floor. I admired her as she held Willa in her lap, happily fussing over the new toys, books, and clothes. When Willa got to her bags from me, she tossed the green tissue paper into the air before pulling out the pajamas and slippers I'd found in her new size.

"I hope they'll fit," I told Darcy. "I got 'em from that store you suggested, and if you need it, I can send you the receipt."

Darcy slowly ran her fingers over the snowflakes like they were laced with diamonds or pearls. Looking up at me, her eyes said something she couldn't, something she was scared to let her father see.

"They're going to be perfect," she promised me. "Huh, Willa girl? Do you like your new pajamas?"

She nodded, already eager to discover the plush bear in the next bag. For a moment, Willa didn't know what to make of the teddy bear dressed as Beethoven. I had spent an obscene amount of time picking it out. Knowing her affinity for music, I figured it would be worth the cost, and when she pressed its paw, the music began to play. Willa's reaction was priceless to me. Her entire face lit up, and she gasped in surprise.

"It's a musical bear!" Darcy exclaimed for her. "Willa, isn't this fun?"

Crawling out of her mother's lap, Willa came to show me. She shuffled over to me with the bear half her size. It took her a second to climb onto the couch beside me. She showed me its musical paws and the biography of Beethoven written under his blue coat.

"Do you like it?" I asked her.

Willa grinned and nodded in response. Beside me, Bill chuckled in his armchair.

"I think you've got an admirer there, Nick," he teased lightly.

"Don't forget about your other presents," I tried to tell her, but she wasn't listening anymore.

Darcy laughed as she had to redirect Willa back to the task at hand. I considered it agony to not be able to kiss her as I liked. With Bill watching, I cemented myself onto the couch, but I realized this pain was nothing. I would've raked myself over hot coals to watch Darcy and Willa as I did. To be a part of that Christmas scene, I would've given every penny to my name away, but that wasn't necessary.

I got the chance to play with Willa before her nap and help Darcy make Christmas dinner. With Erin and Mickey off in Hawaii, it was just the four of us. Christmas became a quiet but cheerful affair, and I took my torment in stride. I allowed myself only the briefest of looks and faint, grazing touches. Even when we were alone in the kitchen, there was no telling whether Bill might decide to come in for a drink. It wasn't until he went to bed that I found myself breathing normally.

"Thanks for comin' over today, Nick," he told me before heading off to his room. "It's been good havin' ya here."

I kept my hands busy putting away leftovers as I nodded.

"I'm glad I could make it," I replied. "It's been fun seeing a kid enjoy Christmas this year."

"It certainly makes it more entertain'," Bill agreed.

Kissing Darcy's cheek, he bade us each goodnight before disappearing. I knew his pain medications would have him out like a light. With the strain of the day, he'd be out in no time, but that realization only made time with Darcy harder. Willa had long since gone to bed, clutching her new musical bear as she softly snored. There was nobody awake to catch me running my hand along Darcy's back or glancing her way.

"I'm glad you came today too, you know," she told me while packing away the holiday ham. "You made Willa so happy today, and you've made everything easier. I don't remember the last time Christmas felt so ... so ..."

"So what?"

"*Relaxing*," Darcy decided before turning toward the fridge. "It's usually a whirlwind, but with just us four, well ... I wish I'd gotten you something better than some socks and a new shirt."

"But I like that new shirt."

I was already imagining her fingers undoing the buttons before reaching the zipper of my jeans. The fantasy entered my mind the second she had me try it on, but more than anything Darcy could buy, she'd given me the gift of remembering what it was like to have a family at Christmas. I wasn't just a guest at somebody else's table anymore.

Everything good in my life all came back to her. Watching her from the stove, I studied how she bent over to make room in the fridge. Her curves were haloed by the bright white light, and the urgency to keep my distance dissolved. When she shut the door, my arms couldn't help but wrap around her waist from behind. Darcy twisted around in my embrace, and I didn't hesitate to kiss her, tasing the sweet red wine from dinner on her lips and tongue. She whimpered while her body relaxed against me.

"You've been holding onto this for a while, haven't you?" she teased before diving back into the kiss.

A day's worth of desires poured out. Her arms draped themselves over my shoulders. Every breath we took grew heated. As our feet moved together, Darcy and I slowly began to circle around. We were caught in this surreal sort of slow dance while the world began to spin faster and faster.

"You have no idea," I breathed.

Getting lost in the thrill, I felt my heart race, allowing my reckless desires to run free. My back hit the old white fridge as I held Darcy closer. My hands slid down her spine toward the full curves of her backside. With my pulse racing, I felt Darcy's lips part for me. She invited me to draw her in and take what I craved so badly, but I couldn't give into the impulse. We couldn't get carried away.

"*Darcy,*" I groaned the second I pulled away.

Her expression filled with a soft sort of bittersweetness that broke my heart. After all those nights together, I ached for more of the small moments with her. I harbored a desperate need to keep her close, to memorize every breath she took and feel her body move with mine. I didn't even have the right words to express how the damning desperation consumed me. I could only tell Darcy with a kiss, and by the way she kissed me back, it felt like she understood the pain too. It was a sweet, shared agony.

"You have to go, don't you?" she wondered quietly, regret lacing her words.

"It is getting late," I pointed out. "We can't stay like this forever."

Still, that didn't keep me from holding onto her. I slid my hands into the back pockets of Darcy's jeans and let her lean into my chest. Christmas wouldn't be over for another hour or so. The day didn't have to end, did it?

It was like the night by the fire all over again. I hated to leave. The thought of letting her go felt like torture, but I had to learn my limits. As long as we hid the truth, all my affection for her had to remain tucked away too. This had to be enough. I grumbled under my breath, letting out a long sigh. My forehead pressed against hers.

"I wish I didn't have to leave you," I muttered where only she could hear. "I've been good all day long. I can only take so much."

"You've been amazing," she whispered back. "Trust me, you weren't the only one, but . . ."

Her voice trailed off. Darcy didn't have to say it. We both already knew.

"I know. That's how things have to be."

"Well, maybe they could be different for a little while longer."

Looking up at me, Darcy smiled conspiratorially. Her dark eyes flashed with something mischievous and sinful. I sucked in a sharp breath, not knowing how to take it as she asked a question I wasn't prepared to answer.

"Do you think you can wake up before everyone else?"

CHAPTER TWENTY-EIGHT

DARCY

Nick flashed a wolfish grin, disarming and damning all at once.

"Who says I even have to go to sleep?"

"You will have to get some," I reminded him. "Enough to drive home."

He shook his head. "If I have you, Darlin' Darcy Rose, I'll get everything I need."

I didn't have the focus to argue. My hands were too eager to cast aside the clothes keeping us apart. My mind ran wild with all the things we could do and everything we could possibly be.

As our feet slowly shuffled to my room, we began to rewrite that Christmas from two years ago. Nick wasn't pushing me away anymore. He held me closer, kissing me with every ounce of desire a man could possibly possess. I couldn't lock the door fast enough. Turning to face him, I had my back pressed against the door in two seconds flat. An entire day of being good had Nick feeling anything but.

"Is this for me to unwrap?" I asked teasingly, stroking the length growing under the fabric. "I thought you'd given me my gifts already."

Nick let out a low groan. "Consider this the gift that keeps on giving."

The twin blue flames in his eyes flickered as he pulled off my clothes piece by piece. We were both eager to get past the fumbling and bated breath. I needed his mouth against mine and his hands gripping my breasts. After so many nights together, Nick knew all my secret spots and hiding places. His fingertips wandered and coaxed the whimpers from my lips. With his kiss wandering over the crook of my neck, I grew restless and impatient.

"We can't stand here all night, baby," I murmured.

Moving my leg between his, I let my thigh press against his hardening length. It was all the encouragement he needed. Nick backed off just enough to let me undo the zipper of his jeans. His clothes became piles of fabric on the floor, but I hardly saw where they went. My attention was too fixed on the bare chest laid before me. I let my hands feel the faint blond curls and the fading scar on his side. I felt stories to be told, but they had to wait for another time.

My fingertips were all too eager to tease his tip. As Nick sucked in a sharp breath, I felt how it was close to dripping with desire. The back of his knees hit the edge of the bed, and Nick fell backward. He invited me to crawl over him and let his mouth find my breasts.

"It's nice to know I'm not alone," I whispered.

I didn't want to be the only one going insane. Until Nick was in front of me, I considered myself levelheaded and under control, but one look from him and I found myself falling. I needed to anchor myself against him and be touched. I became a starved woman, and he was manna from heaven.

"You never are," he mumbled, his teeth grazing over my skin. "Not with me."

Nick and I were twisting, turning, and tumbling down this rabbit hole together. We were lost in the moment, lost to everything that had passed and the fears of the unknown future. All that existed was the shared need between us, and as long as I lived, I knew I would never crave a man so desperately as I did him.

Nick rose up to meet me as I slowly pulled away. He couldn't let my lips go.

"Don't think you're gettin' away from me tonight," he muttered in his low, seductive rasp.

"Not a chance in hell," I said to him. "I'm getting my gift tonight."

Nick's low rumble of laughter got lost in his groan. Our bodies connected. I lowered myself onto him inch by inch, but every piece of me was more than ready to meet the moment.

With my legs braced around his waist, I began to rock and grind against Nick, fastening my hands against his strong shoulders. His grip dug into my backside. He followed along with my rolling motion, and before I knew it, the slow, steady motion had my entire body burning in his captivating shade of blue.

"Nick, I . . . I . . ." I breathed, but I couldn't think of anything. "Oh, fuck it."

My lips flew to his, and my moan hummed into the feverish kiss. I couldn't pull away. There was no coming up for air. As the euphoria built inside me, I shuddered, ready to come out of my skin. My spine twisted and writhed as the climax sought to claim me, but I held on for dear life. I refused to let go of Nick or the pleasure we shared until it all became too unbearable.

Nick stole the air from my cry of sheer ecstasy. Satisfaction crashed over me like a wave, washing over me and cooling the burning heat of my desire. It flowed with Nick's release. It all coursed through me, but I welcomed the feeling. I buried my face against his shoulder. My chest heaved with every panting breath.

It was a long time before we came apart. Falling back onto the mattress, I let my head hit the pillow as the night air cooled my skin. My reeling mind finally began to slow.

"I'll be damned," Nick muttered. "That was probably the best Christmas gift anyone's ever given me."

One look at him, and I started laughing. I wasn't sure what possessed me. The childish giggling bubbled out of me like overpowered champagne. I had to bury my face into a pillow to muffle the sound, but Nick found me anyway. He fastened his tattooed arm around my waist and pulled me against his chest. Tangled together, we did our best not to wake the house. The world remained quiet and at peace, but all night long, I don't think that smile ever left my face.

I felt it when I woke up as my phone alarm went off. In the pale morning light, Nick's eyes were already open and brilliant with color. The chiseled features of his face were softened by gentle shadows. Studying him, my hand reached for his cheek to feel the faint blond stubble there along his jaw, but Nick turned his head. He shut his eyes and left a kiss in the center of my palm. It almost tempted me to linger.

"I'm gonna go make some coffee for us," I whispered. "Wait right here."

Nick showed me a sleepy-eyed smile. "As you wish."

I reached for my robe tossed on the desk chair. Nick feigned a pout as I tied up the sash and hid my body away, but he didn't make a sound. Tiptoeing out, I found myself enjoying one of my favorite parts of the holidays.

The house was quiet and still. Morning light left a cool shade over every room, but in the front window, the Christmas tree still glowed. The technicolor shades sparkled and shone. Every ornament looked like a happy memory captured in time, and it was all mine to admire.

Neither Dad nor Willa woke up as the coffee brewed in the pot. With two mugs in hand, I was free to tiptoe back to the bedroom where Nick was tugging on his socks.

"Here," I whispered, handing him the mug of black coffee. "Can I help you with anything?"

"Do you see my right boot anywhere?" he asked.

Sipping my drink, I searched around, finding it had slid under the dresser. I was a shame to watch him go, but Nick did me the kindness of not rushing off. He drank his coffee and pulled on his clothes little by little. All the while, I watched him, thinking about all the mornings we'd been like this and the many more I wanted.

Deep down, my heart whispered something, but I didn't understand it.

"Thanks for the coffee," Nick quietly told me as we reached the back door. "And for yesterday. I think that was the best Christmas I've had in a long time."

"Me too."

I kissed Nick there inside the back door, feeling his arm wind around my back. He held me there for only a minute. Outside, the day was breaking over the mountains. I needed to say goodbye, but there was something else on the tip of my tongue. I felt it but couldn't place it.

"Take care of yourself, Nick," I told him instead.

"You too," he replied before turning toward the door.

I let my hand fall away from his, and through the kitchen window, I watched him walk to his truck. I followed him through the dining room where the truck rumbled to life and into the living room as he backed away.

As I stood in the front window, watching Nick's truck disappear down the road, I realized what my heart longed to say. The simple words slipped off my tongue with such familiar ease. It was like I'd said it a thousand times before.

"I love you, Nick Wallace."

The declaration felt so good to say. I smiled to myself, wrapping my arms tighter around my chest. I was in love with the charming, kind, and ever-so-handsome Nicholas Wallace, and deep in my bones, I'd started to think that he loved me too.

CHAPTER TWENTY-NINE

NICK

Reaching through the kitchen window, I grabbed a basket of fried pickles and shoved them into the hands of one of the bar backs. Music blasted through the speakers over the crowd of drinkers and friends. After a million similar Saturday nights, my body moved through the motions of work before I could think about it. It jolted my system when an old regular chuckled at the sight of me.

"What's got you smilin' like that?" he wondered jokingly. "Or should I say *who*?"

I shook my head and smiled. "Oh, calm down, Earl. Just tell me what kind of beer you want."

"The usual lager," Earl replied, already handing me the exact change. "I gotta do something to calm down before I head home."

"Long day at the hotel?"

Earl had worked over at the Booths' resort for as long as I'd known him as one of their mechanics. After a shift or a night of being on-call, he always parked himself at the same stool and had a beer before heading home to his wife. We all had our patterns and ruts in the road.

As I handed him his drink, he shrugged. "We're preppin' for a long winter and checking over the ski lifts. They'll be opening next week."

"Are they already making the fake snow?" I wondered.

"Of course, they are, but if you wanna make me feel better, you'll tell me about the new girlfriend who put that smile on your face!"

Zoe sidled up beside me, laughing. Flipping her fine black braids over her shoulder, she reached for the soda nozzle. Her eyes went back and forth between us, watching me wipe down the bar top and clear away the cocktail glasses.

"Oh, Earl, *please*," she teased along with him. "We both know Nick doesn't do girlfriends. He'll go on dates, but lone wolves don't get serious."

Roger sipped his lager and smiled. "Well, that's the face of a wolf who's got a girl somewhere pickin' out a new den for spring. I got the same stupid look on my face when I married my June."

"I'll believe in her when I see her," Zoe insisted. "Besides, it's more likely that he's grinning over Bill giving him the bar."

My hand froze on the countertop. My fingers tightened around the old rag.

"What are you talking about, Zoe? That's not gonna happen."

She shrugged. "It's what the guys are saying in the kitchen."

"Well, they're yanking your chain," I said.

"Uh, I don't think so. They got it from the mechanics over at Mickey's garage. Bill's gonna be giving you the business."

"Hey, congratulations, Nick!" Earl chimed.

I smiled. "Thanks, but they've all got it wrong. Bill hasn't said anything to me, and I wouldn't be given the bar. I'd buy him out of it. That's the only honest thing to do."

I never wanted anyone to think Bill had taken pity on the poor boy he took under his wing.

Zoe threw up her hands in surrender. "That's the word on the grapevine. Don't shoot the messenger."

"I'm not shooting anyone," I replied. "I'm more interested in getting someone to bus the booths. Half of them needed to be cleared away five minutes ago."

"On it, Captain!" she agreed with a small salute before taking off.

Still, I saw the teasing look on her ebony face. Earl wasn't even the only one to make a comment about me. Other guys wanted to know who she is. Some of the local girls said I looked "sweet" and that my secret someone was "very lucky", but I was the lucky one. They didn't know how good it felt just to see Darcy's name flash on my phone screen. Long after I locked the bar doors, I bound bills at the register when the cell phone began vibrating in my back pocket.

"Hey, is this a bad time?" she asked.

"It's never a bad time for you," I joked with a small laugh. "Anything for my favorite Black Sheep."

"*Nick*," Darcy lamented, but it didn't sound like she minded the nickname.

"Seriously, the kitchen just clocked out for the night. I'm going to lock up here in a few minutes, so what can I do for you?"

"Nothing yet. It's more about what you could do for me on Monday. I got an email from my supervisor, Chris. He asked for an in-person meeting. He knows that I'm out of town and taking care of Dad, but he wanted to see if I could swing it. With my aunt and uncle in Hawaii still away, though . . . I can just tell him it won't work."

"What time do you need me to come over?"

A lilt of hope brightened her voice. "Are you sure? I mean, you don't have anything to do with the bar?"

"Zoe can handle Monday. It's usually a slow night anyway, except for the people watching the football game."

Our lone television on the wall didn't make Bill's the best sports bar, but Bill decided a few years back that not everyone could afford or get cable out here. The cost of a half-price draft on Monday night was much easier for some locals to afford than an overpriced satellite dish. Zoe knew how to take care of those regulars. On Monday, there was someone else I needed to worry about.

I wasn't used to feeling like this. Deep down, I felt my soul shifting and remembering how nice it felt to be needed. They called Darcy lucky for having my attention, but they were wrong.

I was the lucky one. I was the one indebted to her, and I took every chance I could to pay her back. If possible, I'd happily spend the rest of my life making myself worthy of her.

"It'll be a long drive there, so I guess I need to head out around eight or nine," Darcy mused. "I can get Willa and Dad up, if you'll just come over to watch them for the day. I should be home around dinnertime."

"Won't this interfere with your Monday work?"

"Yeah," she agreed. "It makes me wonder what Chris thinks is important enough for me to drive back and scrap a day of work."

"Yeah... I wonder."

A muffled sound echoed through the background. On the other end, Darcy said something I couldn't decipher.

"Oh, Dad's calling me. I think I've gotta go," she told me. "I'll, um, text you the details, okay?"

"Okay."

Saying goodbye, I felt a sneaking thought creep into the back of my mind. A day would come when Darcy had to go back for good. She didn't live in her father's house anymore. She had a life and a home back in that city, so much more than my small cabin not built for more than two people. I'd never enjoyed the traffic and noise of urban cities. The benefits never felt worth the headache for more than a long weekend, and that's all this visit was for Darcy.

She hadn't moved back to the mountains for good. For Darcy, this was her old winter breaks and Christmas vacations. Darcy never planned on staying like this forever. The patterns we created together weren't meant to last. Still, I had to be in Willa's life. We couldn't go back to what we were, so inevitably, we had to move forward.

I shrugged into my leather jacket and turned out the lights. The rosy glow of our Christmas day faded from my smile. Deep and unrelenting worry settled in its place. In the cold night, I felt that rare piece of happiness I'd found with Darcy already being torn in two.

I didn't want to be the one to trap Darcy here. I didn't want to be the one to destroy both of our relationships with Bill, but as the holiday season drew closer to its end, I knew things had to change. *I had to change.*

"I could learn to like the city," I muttered to nobody.

Climbing into my truck, I tried to picture it. I tried to fit myself into the life Darcy already had, but it was so hard to see past what I'd always known. Still, I had to move past it. I needed to be bold enough to risk it all for the chance at something better, for the chance to love my family as any man should.

There was one way to move forward that nobody could doubt. One question could keep Darcy and me from falling apart, but did she really want to hear it? It had only been a few weeks since we reconnected. The years with Darcy before didn't account for who she was right then. If I took this leap of faith, I didn't know whether my heart would survive it.

My entire existence hinged on her answer, leading to my greatest happiness or my ultimate destruction. With my life wrapped around Darcy's ring finger, I couldn't be certain what might become of me, but there was one way to find out.

I just needed to take care of Willa first.

CHAPTER THIRTY

DARCY

Nothing, not even Nick's secret kiss goodbye, taking the Mustang, or wearing my favorite office clothes, could make me feel good about heading back to Durham. My supervisor, Chris, rarely asked for in-person conferences. After years of having me on the road, we had learned our patterns and the best way to communicate virtually. It didn't even matter that I lived thirty minutes from the office, yet Chris knew I was out of town. Still, he emailed asking if I could come in anyway.

I agreed reluctantly. The closer I got to town, the more knots formed in my stomach. They twisted and tightened as I parked my car in the visitor's lot of the sleek glass building set back off the highway beyond a large grassy field.

Sleek and polished, the interior of my department's floor was largely composed of lacquered tables where people quietly typed away. Others sat with massive monitors and headsets blocking out the world. They didn't see the quirky chairs in primary colors or the snack bar by the long row of windows. It wasn't much different from when I worked in the office full-time or even as a hybrid worker. For a space designed to inspire collaboration and conversation, it appeared the bulk of my colleagues worked hard to tune the others out.

Few people spoke unless it was work-related. I knew their emails better than their faces, and so many of these people looked too young to be anyone I knew back in the day. Nobody but Chris stood out or even looked particularly friendly. They were all lasered in on their screens, frozen in place wearing their apathetic looks and stylish clothes.

"Hey, Darcy!" he greeted me with a wide smile and a large handshake. "It's so good to see you back here again."

As he led us into one of the few closed-off rooms, I replied, "Thanks, Chris. It's nice to see everything past your shoulders. I'd almost forgotten how tall you are."

His basketball memorabilia lined the floating shelves of the office alongside pictures of his family and dogs. Chris's bean-pole frame made it easy to see how he might've been encouraged into the sport as a teen. Scratching at his facial scruff, Chris settled into his chair with a laugh. I put my bag down and sat in one of the clear floating chairs across the desk.

"I know what you mean," he remarked. "My mental image of you is always a floating head, but I didn't call you into the office just to see if you still had feet."

"Well, that's a relief."

I tried to laugh, but the warmth of the sound felt tepid inside me. Chris grew antsy in his usual way. Looking around the room, he gestured to the water cooler.

"Would you like something to drink? Sorry, I meant to ask that first. I know I just made you drive, like, nearly three hours to get here."

"No, no, I'm okay." I held up my hand. "I've got a water bottle in the bag, but you know, I am really curious about what couldn't be said over a video chat. Don't tell me this is some kind of intervention, please."

Chris settled back into his rolling chair. "It's quite the opposite, actually. You've been working like a one-woman team for the last few years doing the work of three junior developers. You outperform most of this floor on a regular basis, if not all of them. When you emailed me about your father's condition and how you'd be working, I figured there would be some . . . *delay* in your project timelines, and that would've been totally okay. I know you have your daughter as well. My twins are definitely a handful even on their best days, so when you didn't miss a beat, well, to be honest, I nearly shat myself, I was so impressed."

Laughter bubbled out of me. Chris had always been different, a little off-beat maybe, but it was why he did well in middle management. He guided the people under him with respect and kindness while taking the heat from company leadership. It was a shame more men weren't like him in the office. Instead, the meetings were full of tech bros and self-important types who made me feel like so many others before them. They made me realize I'd become an old hat at feeling out of place.

"It did take me longer than usual," I pointed out. "I had to clock in some extra hours on the weekends, and I've been lucky to have my family around me in Boone. There are plenty of people happy to pitch in and give me a breather when I need it."

"That's great! I'm glad you have those people, so you know better than anyone the importance of having a support system and a team. That's why I want you to consider taking on a senior development coordinator position in the company."

"You mean like your job?"

Chris laughed once sheepishly, reaching for a pen.

"Actually, Darcy, I, um, I mean my job exactly. I've been offered a promotion, and they're asking me to recommend a replacement. I'd like for that to be you."

If anything had been in my hands, I would've dropped it. My jaw went slack, and my eyes widened. I had grown so used to the quiet pace of working from home. No promotions were ever on my radar.

"You're not joking," I realized dumbly. "Well, I'm flattered, of course, but . . . *why?*"

My face must've looked hilarious. It had Chris snorting with laughter.

"Come on, Darcy, don't tell me you didn't notice my options out in the office. Most of them are barely out of college. Most of your old co-workers have moved into different positions, and though you've negotiated several pay raises, I know you could be doing more. *You know you could be doing more.* I was five minutes from getting you to be a senior web developer last summer, but I know your daughter's care was a concern. She'll be eighteen months soon, right?"

I nodded, still trying to process it all.

"Yeah, she'll be eighteen months in February."

"Then, she can enter the tots class at the preschool down the road. Our company gets a discount there. They usually don't start kids until eighteen months. Although, I know from experience that they'll let in kids who might be a month or two younger if you go in to interview. You could start working here on a three-day in-office hybrid schedule, and then, you could move to full-time when she's old enough to do the five-day program. I know we've talked about your starting in like that next fall, but with this promotion, it would be the perfect time to start coming back."

"Sure . . ."

We had emailed back and forth about this after Willa's first birthday. Restlessly, Chris stopped twisting his pen and grew quiet for a moment. His eyebrows knitted together.

"Are you okay?"

Quickly fixing my face, I smiled.

"Yeah, I'm good," I lied. "It's just a lot to take in."

"Look, I get it. The applications won't start being reviewed until the first Monday of the new year. You've got time to think it over and polish up your resume. We'll open up the positions to all candidates, but like I said, it'll be yours if you want it. There's nobody better, Darcy."

That wasn't entirely true.

Leaving that small office, I shook Chris's hand and let my eyes sweep over the tables where I'd spent the first days of my time with the company. The memories of sitting among them remained fixed in my mind, but I never enjoyed them. A pane of invisible glass always kept me from being a part of this place.

I watched the world unfold from the outside looking in, and the comments and not-so-sly digs sent me running toward a fully remote position the second it was offered. It never helped that women were few and far between in the company. Leadership could only stop so much.

Even when I started shopping for other jobs, I realized this was a problem in almost every company. I heard similar stories from women I met on the road, women like my friend Sam. We all had moments where we felt slighted, overlooked, and undervalued. With this possible position, I could make the first step toward changing that. I couldn't save the world, but I had the chance to make life among those sleek and shiny offices more hospitable for the future females of the company.

Would it be worth it, though?

The question plagued me the whole ride over to my old place. It didn't feel right to call it home anymore. Somehow, after the last few weeks, the label wasn't apt anymore. I should've been over the moon. Dad would be beyond proud. Willa wouldn't know the difference either way, but what would Nick think?

Unlocking the garage door, I tried to talk through explaining the job opportunity in my head. Nothing sounded right. I stopped myself in the middle of the kitchen and looked around for a long, silent minute.

My duplex looked frozen in time. It didn't help that there were no holiday decorations set up. Everything had been cleaned by the monthly housekeeping. Willa hadn't spent the day scattering her life across the living room, and the lack of heat left a chill in the air. Rubbing my arms, I walked slowly over to the pile of mail on the dining table. Meaningless pieces of paper became a small mountain, and while filtering through it, I found myself reminded of everything I would be throwing away.

Taking Chris's job would be the ultimate chance for me. I would be the mentor and supervisor I'd always wanted. I could be an agent of change, but for that, I'd face the ultimate cost.

Nick would always stay in Willa's life. I knew that without a doubt, yet in my head, I saw the fragile life we were building together coming apart. He had a life in Banner Elk. He had the bar and friends, and I would be willfully leaving him there to enjoy it. The possible outcomes of resentment and distance began to play out in my head like a carousel moving faster until it blurred together. The junk mail in my hands dropped to the floor.

Everything I saw led to the same conclusion. It didn't matter which way I went or how I tried to spin it. If I took this job, Nick would stay in Willa's life, but he and I would never stand a chance.

CHAPTER THIRTY-ONE

NICK

"Well, well, Nick," Bill declared across from the kitchen table. "I didn't know you could cook like this."

I smiled to myself. "Don't start gettin' your underwear in a bunch. It's chili, Bill. It's not some fancy French food, and my grandma did need someone to help her in the kitchen."

"Peggy did know her way around the kitchen."

As took Bill another bite from his bowl, I wiped the ground turkey bits from Willa's face. I spent all afternoon reading and double-checking Bill's doctor-approved diet, but I didn't forget the person missing from the table. Darcy had sat right there that morning with her coffee and multigrain toast, looking too good in her forest green outfit. The soft knit material hugged her every curve. She left red lipstick on her mug and a kiss for me at the door.

I'd grown so used to our shared meals at the kitchen table. Bill filled the seat, but I felt a gaping hole without Darcy there. In some ways, I figured I should've felt guilty thinking of Darcy with her father right there. He couldn't know what was going on in my head. He hadn't seen the mornings she and I had spent together while he was recovering in the hospital or the nights I stole away to her bedroom like the shameless thief I'd become. Without realizing it, Darcy had given me so much that I craved to take more and more.

Part of me was crazy enough to want forever. Even if it destroyed my friendship with Bill, I needed Darcy to make a more honest man out of me. I'd do anything for her if she offered me that chance. Just thinking about it put a small smile on my face.

Stirring around his half-eaten dinner, Bill remarked, "Well, maybe you could add this as one of your specials once I sell you the place."

My spoon nearly slipped from my grasp. My wandering thoughts vanished without a trace. Of course, Bill and I had always talked about it jokingly. I made dumb remarks that started with "when I take this place off your hands" or "if you ever wise up and retire, Bill", but I hadn't expected anything like this any time soon.

It seemed the talk around the bar wasn't so far-fetched, after all.

"Yeah, sure," I tried to joke. "In a decade, maybe."

"Or in ten weeks," he countered. "Ten months, if you want a little more time."

Trying to ground myself, I looked for a task to act as my anchor. Willa was running out of milk. I gently took the sippy cup from her hands and moved to get her more.

"You know I'm serious, Nick," Bill furthered.

I shook my head. "I know, but . . . is there something you haven't told Darcy?"

"No, but havin' your heart stopped by a man in a white coat makes you think," he replied, reaching for his granddaughter. "I'm always spendin' Saturday nights in the bar when I could be down in Durham with this sweet little thing and her mother. I've had the place for, what, thirty years now? I think it's about time I pass it on to someone else, and well, let's not pretend that you're not practically runnin' the place yourself already. We might as well make it official."

I poured milk into Willa's cup. "But it's *Bill's*."

"And it still will be," Bill insisted before chuckling. "I didn't think you'd change the sign."

"I won't. I–I *wouldn't*."

Slowly, I brought Willa back her drink, letting her eagerly accept it with two outstretched hands. Bill reached up and patted my arm.

"You're always good at gettin' someone a drink," he teased. "Now, come on, sit down and finish your food. We'll talk about this some other time. I've got pills to take and a football game comin' on."

For him, the Monday night went on like any other. Bill took his medications and reclined into his armchair while I took Willa off to bathe and wind down for the night. Bill had read all kinds of books to his granddaughter while I cooked, but Willa was still eager for more.

After her bath, I struggled to keep her focused on getting into her pajamas. Darcy had laid out the ones I bought. I had to roll up the long pants legs, but I saw how Willa would be too big for them in no time at all. Bill wasn't the only one missing out on those fleeting moments with Willa. I could have stayed up all night watching Willa sleep, but inevitably, I had to go.

There will be other times, I told myself.

Seeing Bill quietly snoring through his game, I headed toward the kitchen to clean up. One day soon, Bill would realize the irony of his comments. He would have to know the truth, and if he still agreed to sell me his business, it might make my chances that much stronger. It gave me something real to offer Darcy beyond a tiny cabin in need of an extension.

I saw it all in my head. As some frozen mix tapped against the sink's window, I cleaned up the kitchen and began to make a list in my head. I needed to go to the jeweler's and then call up the people who sold me my cabin kit. They sold extension kits too. They could help me tack on two bedrooms onto the cabin, and the loft could be Darcy's office. First, I had to be sure she was willing, but we were so happy together on Christmas night and the morning after.

Who wouldn't want that all the time?

She said herself that she stayed in Durham to put distance between us, but that didn't have to be the case anymore. Even though there was so much to do and plan, if anyone could make the impossible work, it was Darcy. She'd know how to find our path forward, no matter how treacherous it seemed. The possibilities had me so pumped up that I nearly jumped when I saw car lights glowing outside. A pair of feet trudged up the back steps.

"It's me, not a burglar," Darcy called over the squeak of the back door.

"Hey," I greeted her. "How'd it go?"

She stepped into the light of the kitchen. The short walk from the car had nipped her cheeks rosy pink. A tired smile spread across her face. Without another word, she walked over and wrapped her arms around my chest. Her cold cheek brushed against my neck. As I hugged her back, it felt too good having Darcy come home to me.

"Three hours is a long way to drive," she muttered. "Are Dad and Willa asleep?"

"He's nodded off in front of some football game, but Willa's taking notes for him. She's gonna give him a full play-by-play in the morning."

I felt her laugh vibrate through my skin. "That's sweet of her. Was she that sweet all day?"

"She got a little hurt when I wouldn't let her wear her left shoe on her right foot this afternoon, but otherwise, we managed to survive without you."

"I knew you would."

I kissed the top of her head, feeling the faint flecks of ice melting in her curls. There was so much more I wanted. It reminded me of the growing weight in my back pocket and how I'd snuck into Darcy's room when Bill and Willa were both taking afternoon naps. Hopefully, Darcy wouldn't notice her old high school ring was missing for a couple of days. I'd put it back in her trinket box as soon as the jeweler was finished with it.

"Have you had any supper?" I asked. "There's some chili still here in the pot."

She shook her head. "I, um, had a lot on my mind. I didn't think to stop anywhere."

Over the last few days, I realized what I should have given Darcy for Christmas. I never thought the one diamond ring Grandma Peggy left to me would ever have a new owner, but as I felt Darcy's chest rise and fall against mine, every suspicion I quietly carried became a fact.

"Let me heat some up for you, then," I told her, already pulling away and reaching for a clean bowl. "So, other than the tiring drive, how did your day in Durham go? Did they offer a pay raise for working so damn hard?"

"Well, they kind of did, actually."

Darcy leaned back against the fridge as she watched me stick the old ceramic bowl into the microwave. I shut the door and pressed the one-minute button. Coming out of a lukewarm pot, I figured that was all it needed.

"They offered me the chance to double my salary," she continued. "I'd get to run my own team and work more with company leadership. It would even be a chance for me to help company culture. I don't know if you've heard, but um, the tech industry isn't known for being female friendly."

"Sounds like they could really use you, then," I replied with a smile. "I guess they know what they've got and they're tryin' to give you a hell of a promotion."

"They are. It's my current supervisor's position, and he's the one recommending me for the job. There's a catch, though."

"Oh, like what?"

I kept grinning like an idiot until my head turned. Darcy couldn't look up from her feet. She wrung her hands and rocked back on her heels.

"I won't be able to work remotely anymore. I could do the four-day week program and maybe work from home one day a week at most, but the majority of my time would need to be in the office."

Silence and the brutal realization crept under my skin. I wanted to be proud of her. God, I really was, but this . . . this changed everything. A sharp bell sound pierced my ears.

My time was up.

"Did you agree, then?" I had to know.

Darcy looked at me with pleading eyes. "I have to go through an application process first. They'll need to open up the job to the entire office, but Chris says if I put my name in, it's mine."

"Will you take it, then?"

She swallowed hard. "I . . . I'm not sure."

"Do you want to take it?"

"I'm not sure."

Her voice got so quiet, the words left unsaid were screaming in my head. I tried to act normal. Opening the microwave, I pulled out Darcy's dinner and turned to get a spoon. She may have wanted cheese and sour cream. It was still out on the counter, or no, I had already put the sour cream away. My thoughts began running faster and faster until they tripped over themselves and there was nothing but deafening silence in my brain. A cold chill blew through the room.

Why isn't she sure?

"What are you thinking right now?"

I snapped back to reality. Blinking twice, I struggled to meet Darcy's gaze again. The truth sat on the tip of my tongue, but I didn't let it out.

"Oh, nothing," I lied.

"Your face says otherwise."

I scratched the back of my head. "I was, uh, just tryin' to figure out where I left the stupid sour cream. I must've put it back in the fridge already."

Darcy stepped aside as I reached for the white door handle. The interior light nearly blinded me, but I kept moving. If I stood still for too long, I worried the electricity humming inside my body would shock me dead.

"Nick, I know it's getting late, and you're probably gonna have to head into the bar early tomorrow. I just—"

I stopped her short. "You're right. It's late. You've had a long day, and you need to eat."

With all her forbidden books and headstrong ways, she enjoyed being willful and seeing how far she could possibly go. She worked herself sick and lost herself in the service of others. Running so far ahead, she must have gotten used to running wild and alone, but now this pretty black sheep was looking back with her dark eyes trained on me.

I had already slowed her down once.

Darcy loved Willa with all her heart. There was no doubt about it, but standing there, I began to see all the ways my moment of weakness had dragged her down. She had settled herself away from the people who supported her just to avoid me. She became a single mother and made sacrifices.

I couldn't be the one who held her back again.

She had to see it. The cogs turned in her mind as she studied my expression. Darcy always liked the idea of things she couldn't have and places she hadn't been. It's what kept her restless and running all those years. She'd told me about it enough times for me to remember, and if that Christmas had never happened, if I'd never found her stuck in the snow, Darcy would have outrun me ages ago.

I swallowed back my feelings. No matter how badly I wanted Darcy to stay with me, I refused to let her be stuck by circumstance. The choice to be here had to be entirely her own. Nothing and nobody else could make it for her. If I swayed her at all, I feared she'd grow to resent me, and I would definitely resent myself.

"You could sit with me while I eat," she suggested softly. "You could, you know, help me figure it out."

"I don't think there's enough time for all that."

Reaching around, I took Darcy's coat, encouraging her to shrug out of the sleeves and let me hang it in the mud room. The small life I could offer her was nothing compared to the one she'd created for herself. I didn't know how long it would take for her to see it, but as I grabbed my jacket, I felt certain she'd see it for herself.

The smartest choice Darcy had possibly ever made was leaving me behind. After a few nights together, I'd somehow forgotten the exact reason I'd kept myself away for the last two years, even if it killed me. She was meant for more.

"Since you're home, I should go check on the bar," I offered as a cheap excuse. "I've made room in the fridge for the chili pot, and the toppings are all right there."

"You're leaving, then?"

I closed the distance between us for only a brief moment. Pressing my lips against her forehead, I reminded myself that Bill was snoring with only one thin wall between us.

"You deserve some quiet time," I replied. "Take care of yourself, Black Sheep."

Darcy didn't hide the disappointment in her eyes. Perhaps she couldn't.

"Yeah . . . you too, Nick."

Wanting more had always been dangerous. I knew it from the beginning, but I didn't let the burdensome truth crush me until I was in the safety of my truck's cab. My ragged sigh came out like a plume of smoke. Every muscle in my body ached.

I'd forgotten what it meant to love someone . . . or even two someones. Gritting my teeth against the pain, I couldn't believe I had forgotten the pain of watching someone slip away, but this was worse. Neither my grandparents nor my mother had the chance to come back from the cold clutches of death. Darcy was *right there*.

She had wrapped her arms around me so easily, yet I felt her slipping away. No matter how hard I ran, Darcy ran faster, and if I cared about her, I'd let her do what was best for her life. I'd let her give Willa the kind of life I never could. At some point, I had to accept that it was for the best.

My head slumped onto the steering wheel as I took in another ragged breath. Right there, I knew it had to be love. I must have loved them with every fiber of my being because only love could possibly hurt this much.

CHAPTER THIRTY-TWO

DARCY

The bag of discounted candy dropped into the grocery cart, joining its two friends. As a kid, I'd always loved pouring out my stocking to see what chocolates Santa had left for me, but as an adult, I learned the magic of chocolate, nougat, and nuts at seventy-five percent off. The store's bargain bins had already gifted me two rolls of wrapping paper, a bag of bows, a box of soft peppermints, and of course, *chocolate*.

"Oh, look, Willa!" I declared while holding up the bag. "It's peanut butter cups shaped like nutcrackers. That's fun, right?"

My daughter being, well, *my* daughter, agreed. Excited, Willa clapped as I dropped them in with the others. We had come to the grocery store to pick up stuff for New Year's dinner, but the sugar was an added bonus.

I needed collards, smoked turkey, and a long list of other ingredients for the foods Dad always made on January first. When I was small, I imagined we'd be stuck in a loop reliving the day over again like in *Groundhog Day* if we didn't eat this dinner. It was vital to ensure that January second arrived.

"Okay, now that we've got our sweets, let's get some real food," I declared.

Willa frowned, but she didn't complain. Wheeling the cart around the bustling store, I began to gather fresh vegetables before moving over to the butcher's section. Willa swung her legs from her seat, enjoying the music they piped through the speakers.

By all accounts, I should've been happy. This was my free day, and Willa had been extra-sweet from the moment she woke up. On top of that, Dad was doing amazingly well, according to his physical therapists.

He had taught himself how to get out of bed without his arms. It meant I didn't have to wake up in the early hours of the morning to help Dad to the bathroom. Still, purple shadows hung under my eyes like emotional baggage. Caffeine and concealer could only do so much, and chocolate could only be my self-medication for so long.

For the last two nights, I'd hardly slept. Tension made my muscles perpetually sore. I couldn't rest easily until Nick offered me any semblance of a sign. Even if it was a rejection, knowing somehow felt better than being left in the dark. My thoughts raced toward the worst. They were allowed to run wild even as I turned up and down the aisles of the grocery store looking for discounted items we could use.

"You like pasta, don't you, Willa girl?" I asked, already reaching for the boxes of half-priced ziti. "We could make some of Grandpa's spaghetti sauce and sneak in some veggies. Just don't tell Grandpa Bill, okay?"

The unexpected answer had me nearly jumping out of my skin.

"I won't tell him if you don't."

Whipping around, Kevin Booth stood there adjusting the frames of his glasses and holding a half-filled basket in his fist. He reached for the spaghetti as I took a step back. The memory of him by the campfire came crawling back. My adrenaline spiked in response.

"Hi, Kevin," I greeted him with clipped words. "You making pasta for *your fiancée* tonight?"

Guys like him were the reason I didn't go to parties anymore.

People made their assumptions, but being a mom had little to do with it. Sucking in a sharp breath, I gripped my cart tightly as he actually laughed.

"Tomorrow, actually," he answered. "We're going to look over florists for the wedding."

"How nice for you. Goodbye."

Quickly, I turned back and headed toward the next aisle, knowing we'd need more cooking oil. Hurried footsteps followed behind me. I couldn't be surprised that he'd followed me here. This was the nicest grocery store for at least twenty miles around, and the Booth family business sat just fifteen minutes down the road. He probably even lived nearby in one of those fancy condo communities.

Kevin grumbled under his breath before calling out, "Can you talk to me?"

I stopped only to pick up the first thing of vegetable oil I saw. I stepped lively down the aisle, and Kevin kept following with Willa looking at him.

"I just did," I answered wryly. "Did my hitting you impair your short-term memory?"

"No, that's not what I meant." He let out an exasperated sigh. "Look, I feel bad for how things went that night. I'd been drinking too much, and I guess . . ."

My footsteps slowed. Though part of me hated the idea, I slowly turned around.

"You guess what, Kevin?"

"I guess I was a jerk to you," he admitted.

My shoulders relaxed. We weren't alone on the shopping aisle. Some old woman was comparing flours at the far end, so I knew Kevin couldn't do anything too terrible. I had a minute to hear him out. The limits to my patience were far scarcer.

"Yeah, you were," I agreed. "You were not only rude to me, but you disrespected the woman you're planning to marry. I still have half a mind to tell her, you know. Jensen and I weren't exactly close, but she's not a bad person. She deserves a husband she can actually trust."

"I know. I know," Kevin said, scratching the back of his messy brown hair. "I guess just seeing you after all this time brought out something... I don't know. You were wearing that little skirt, and you had your hair all straight. It reminded me why I had thing for you back in the day. It made me want to be young again."

I rolled my eyes. "Why? You want to have acne and drive your momma's old minivan again? I'd rather eat dirt than be eighteen again."

"I can see why. You've aged well, Darcy. I almost find it hard to believe that kid came out of you."

The one sliver of redemption Kevin possibly had vanished the second his eyes swept up and down my figure. Revulsion mixed with my need to revolt in a toxic rage. Tired and already emotionally spent, I was beyond done with men messing with me, but Willa sat right behind me. I didn't need to make this overgrown boy cry in front of her.

"And I find it hard to believe that comment just came out of your mouth," I snapped back. "You'd better watch yourself, Booth."

He laughed again with a leering look in his eye. "Aw, come on, I'm just trying to pay you a compliment."

"Well, it wasn't wanted."

"You never make things easy, do you?" he scoffed. "Christ, Darcy, you don't need to get so bent out of shape. I thought women liked to be told they're hot."

"Not by scum like you. I—"

I was so ready to fire off my counterattack. Every feminist bone in my body looked to rage, but the sight of another cut me off. Nick came around the aisle with a look of happy surprise that instantly dissolved as soon as he saw Kevin's back to him. The man wasn't blind. He saw my expression and scowled. Kevin didn't even notice how Nick loomed up behind him like an ominous shadow.

"*Kevin Booth*," Nick began in a low, grave tone. "Are you botherin' Darcy? Did she not teach you enough of a lesson last time?"

Kevin's eyes widened. He tried to hide his fear behind a false bravado, but we already saw the panic. His feet rocked back as they turned to run.

He was such a coward.

"Why do you always show up to save her?" he fussed like a child. "We're just having a conversation, so go on and buy whatever crap you came here for."

Nick's laugh sounded like thunder. "Oh, you stupid little man. Darcy doesn't need me to deal with you. Right now, I'm saving *you* from *her* because based on the look on her face, you've got about sixty seconds before they call for a cleanup on aisle four. Have you already forgotten how hard she slapped you last time? Imagine how it might feel for her to kick you in the balls. Do you think that would feel good, Kevin?"

He swallowed. "You think you're gonna threaten me? You're just some white trash thug. You don't scare me."

"I'm not trying to scare you," Nick insisted, flashing a smile that could put ice in anyone's veins. "Although, I think I could make a problem for you if I talked with your future father-in-law. He's a good regular at the bar, you know. I guess being the sheriff can put a lot of stress on a man, so he and his wife like to come in once every week or so for the fish fry special and a few beers. They're nice people, but Kevin, would they be so nice if they knew how you were acting now?"

Kevin took a large step back. "You wouldn't."

"That's the beauty of working at a bar, Booth," Nick remarked, stepping around to reach for my shoulder. "You end up meeting a lot of interesting folks."

"Now, Kevin," I interjected. "If you know what's good for you, this is your chance to run away."

He didn't need to be told twice. Snatching up a bottle of olive oil, Kevin took off like a shot in the opposite direction. Nick's cold edge dissolved into a sweet smile for Willa. He tickled her underarms and let the peal of her tiny laugh overwhelm any bad feelings.

"It's funny running into you here," he actually joked. "I came lookin' for wool, and here you are, Black Sheep. I just don't see your three bags full."

I found myself actually smiling as I bantered back, "They're out in the Subaru. How many do you want?"

"None. I'd rather have you and Willa over for lunch. Do you have to go back to work?"

I shook my head. "It's a light week since we're closed for New Year's Eve and New Year's Day. I ended up taking the day off. Some of Dad's car club buddies are spending the day with him."

"Then, it should be no trouble to have you over."

"But I've got groceries," I pointed out.

"And they can't stay in my fridge for a few hours?"

Looking over, I couldn't help but notice how Willa gripped his thumb and grinned. Nick turned my heart into a torrent of emotions when he acted like this. He was aloof one minute and generous the next. I was too tired to know what to think.

"Please, Darcy," he encouraged me. "You could use the break, and I know I could use the company."

His blue eyes were too eager to deny. Even if he couldn't give me the answers I needed, Nick knew how to care for me in his own way. He offered me the chance to sit down and relax for a few hours. How could I possibly refuse that?

"All right," I surrendered.

Nick grinned. "Perfect. Just let me go grab some steel wool, and we can head over to my place."

My mind snapped like a rubber band, flinging itself two years back in time. Nick was really taking me back there. After checking out and loading up my trunk, I followed Nick back through the switchback roads and winding turns. There was no snow on the ground and the sun shone overhead. With Willa in my backseat, I had to remember that nothing happened the same way twice.

Nick wasn't going to love me and leave me high and dry for a second time. We were both different, and though my heart skipped at the sight of the log cabin with its metal roof, Nick and I were never going back. We were only moving forward, for better or worse.

CHAPTER THIRTY-THREE

NICK

The empty sandwich plates sat in a pile by the kitchen sink. Upstairs, Willa slept surrounded by a blockade of pillows with a blanket my grandmother had crocheted. I kept it in a box for all these years, never expecting to have any real use for it. I just didn't have the heart to give it away.

"I didn't know you owned a baby gate," Darcy remarked quietly. "When did you get it?"

"When I figured that if I was a parent, I needed to babyproof my house," I replied, stoking the flames slowly growing over the wood logs. "I didn't exactly pick out this cabin thinking that I'd have..."

Her eyebrows went up. "A child?"

"Yep."

"Oh, you're preaching to the choir," Darcy mused as her eyes glanced down into her mug before staring back through time. "I was in the process of building my place thinking I'd rent it out most of the year."

"To who?"

She shrugged and took a sip of her hot chocolate. "Vacation rentals are always booked up thanks to college football and basketball season, but anyway, it's nice to see you thought ahead."

"I wouldn't have invited you over if I wasn't prepared."

"That's good to know."

Across the living room, Darcy balled herself up on the end of the couch. Her sweater sleeves were pushed up to her elbows, and her hands wrapped themselves around the warm mug. Her hair piled up into a bun on the crown of her head to show off the soft features of her face. From where I stood, the sofa had never looked so welcoming.

That wasn't right, though.

It had been the most comfortable two years ago when Darcy's cheeks were flushed from sipping whiskey and her grin crinkled the corners of her eyes. I'd slept that night knowing what true happiness felt like, but when the morning came, paranoia told me to push it all away. I didn't want to think about it anymore.

"Will you be coming over for New Year's dinner?" Darcy asked, taking another sip of her hot chocolate. "Based on everything I just bought, we'll have enough for about twenty people."

"Should I come with a dozen friends?"

She almost laughed. "If you can fit them all in your truck, sure."

That was another thing I needed to replace. Though my grandparents bought that old blue Chevrolet back when I was a little boy, a car seat couldn't fit into its small three-seat cab. I couldn't borrow Darcy's car forever.

I sat next to her and took her into my arms.

"THE BAR WILL BE CLOSED on New Year's Day, but I'm guessin' most people have somewhere to be already," I mused. "Will your office be closed too?"

"For New Year's Eve and New Year's Day," Darcy replied. "Since I took today off, I'm going to have a five-day weekend, and then . . . I'll have to send an email to Chris about the job. He's expecting my answer that Monday."

Leaning forward, she set her mug down in a huff before flopping back into my arms. I hated how curious I was to know more about the thoughts racing behind her eyes. She grimaced a little and then sighed. I didn't even have to prompt her.

"It's only a few days," she muttered under her breath. "I don't know how they expect me to make up my mind so quickly. It might be different if I wasn't constantly thinking about Dad's recovery and Willa. I don't have the bandwidth to give this job offer any serious thought. Sometimes, I feel lucky to have a brain cell left at the end of the day."

"You know, you never told me how you got into coding," I realized.

Darcy shrugged. "It's not that exciting of a story. I always like learning new languages, and I guess I got that from Mom. She'd bring me little children's books from around the world when I was little. My favorites were these French books about these cartoon shoes. I was maybe able to read, like, five whole words in any book, but I liked thinking about a world beyond Banner Elk. An entirely different world and culture existed behind those words. When I was in high school, I took this community college class online, and the teacher explained coding like a language. It felt like I was learning another language again and diving into this whole world online, and after a while, I realized I was, you know, *good at it*."

"Aren't you good at everything?"

She laughed quietly. "I'm terrible at running and anything arts and crafts and so, so many things, but you know, I like how I work. I thought I found my niche in the company. The promotion would be a great move career-wise. I've just never been the type of person to think about that invisible ladder. Maybe people think that's bad, but if I have enough to be content . . . why do I need more?"

"Because nobody can sell you anything with that attitude."

"Oh, I waste my money on plenty of nonsense," she joked along.

Just tell her to stay here.

You can always be like this, together and content.

As Darcy rested her head on my chest, the thoughts transformed into a current under my skin. Her casual touch became a torture tactic. We were alone with time to talk it through, but the lavender shades under her eyes told me otherwise. Honestly, would it ever feel like the *right* time?

It felt like staring at a word for too long. Even if it was right, staring at something long made anything look wrong. The letters would seem out of order just as my feelings got all screwed up inside.

I didn't know how to do this anymore. As a grown man, it shouldn't have been this hard to let someone in, especially when her body was nestled against me. A small voice screamed in my head, demanding for me to be bold and honest, but Darcy had enough on her plate. The emotional labor of her everyday life left her with so little. She didn't deserve to be burdened with even more.

"What are you thinking about?" I heard Darcy ask quietly.

I glanced down to see her dark eyes looking curious. She had no clue what she was doing to me, how I started and ended my days falling apart. I struggled to bear the burden of watching her go, and even as her fingers slid under the fabric of my navy T-shirt, I hated the thought of this ending. My heart feared the storm looming on the horizon.

"That . . . you deserve a distraction," I finally replied.

Darcy's fingernails grazed over my waist, making my skin tingle from the touch. A knowing grin slowly spread over her face. Deep down, I knew I needed this more than her. I had to shut my eyes and shut out the worries of all the things yet to come.

"Did you have one in mind?" she murmured.

Her lips barely brushed against mine, and I was taken captive. My hand reached for the exposed nape of her neck. Breathing her in, I tasted the chocolate and sugar on her tongue. My quiet groan hummed into her mouth.

"I've got a few," I confessed between kisses. "But we can start here and see where it goes."

"Are you gonna let me win this time, Nick?"

With my hands sliding over her shoulders, I smiled softly. "Kiss me again and find out."

She readily took the bait. Darcy locked her lips with mine while her hand blindly wandered toward the zipper of my jeans. Her eyes couldn't see where she touched, but Darcy knew the way. She found the silver button with ease before pushing past the fabric. The grazing stroke of her fingertips already had me falling apart.

"Dammit, Darcy," I mumbled under my ragged breaths.

That didn't stop her. Her hand still reached for what it desired, wrapping around my reacting length like it was nothing. Her thumb circled my tip. Though she moved with an unhurried pace, Darcy knew just where to linger and press a bit harder. She set every nerve alive and gave a damn good reason for her smug little smile.

It didn't matter that I was the one pulling her rust-colored sweater over her head. She was the one pulling my strings all over again. Darcy twisted and made a home for herself in my lap.

"If you catch me screaming, we'll have to stop," she whispered.

"I'll stop you first," I said, even if she was teasing me. "You're gonna get your big finish, darlin'."

"And you will too, baby. I wouldn't have it any other way."

I hated to lose the feel of her hand, but as she yanked off my clothes, Darcy's body brushed against my dick. I felt the soft warmth of her skin as she straddled my waist. Gripping her backside, I let my head fall back to kiss her again, muffling the audible pleasure of Darcy lowering herself onto me inch by inch.

She was already so slick and so ready. Her body rocked against mine, moving to the tempo her own desires created. My fingertips dug deeper into her curves as I welcomed Darcy's taking whatever she craved. She could carve out my heart or leave me blind. My eyes were only for her, even if they had to watch her go. For one more moment, though, I had her.

Darcy whimpered into my mouth as her hips rolled against me. Her clit brushed against my skin, and the sensation sent a shockwave up her spine. I felt it all. I committed every second to memory before I had to let go.

"Don't give in," I urged her. "Not yet."

She agreed to my one request, slowing her rhythm ever so slightly. Her body pushed deeper as my hands slid up her back. Caught up in the moment, I forgot time and goodbyes existed. There was only her as her head fell back in the thrill of it all. Her parted lips gasped, and her nails dug into my shoulders. I kept my word, quickly reaching up to cover her mouth.

There was no holding on any longer.

Desperate need claimed us both. Darcy's pace quickened as her spine curled against the pleasure. Her thighs trembled around me, and before I knew it, Darcy let the climax course through her. Mine quickly followed.

Her head fell into my neck, and I found myself muttering, "Darcy, I..."

I didn't have the air to finish my thought, not that she heard me anyway. Between catching her breath and the fine pearls of sweat running along her spine, Darcy was drifting down from her great heights. The weight of her body slowly settled over mine, and I let the declaration get lost in the quiet of the afternoon.

I love you.

Even if I couldn't find the nerve to say it, I prayed she felt it. I longed for Darcy to feel it as I held her and as I kissed her goodbye. When Willa woke up from her nap, they had to go, so I helped gather their things. I settled our daughter into her seat before kissing her temple.

"Be good, Willa girl," I told her.

"Thanks for lunch," her mother offered with one last kiss. "I'll see you tomorrow night."

I nodded. "Tomorrow night."

It would the New Year's Eve party at the bar. Even though Darcy didn't like being Bill's girl at the bar, I knew she would come to send off the year with a fond farewell, but a countdown clock had already started in my head.

As Darcy headed toward her car, I could feel her walking away from everything we'd become. My feet were stuck on the front porch. My roots ran too deep in those ancient mountains. She hadn't said it yet, but a little voice told me this was the beginning of the end.

Darcy was kissing me goodbye.

CHAPTER THIRTY-FOUR

DARCY

Live video of the famous New York ball drop flashed across the screen. Drinks flowed over the bar faster than a rushing river, and everyone around me continued to talk over the loud music and each other. Standing in the smack middle of the party, I reminded myself that I put on my sequined dress and came here for Dad.

My father had hardly been out of the house except for a few doctor's appointments. The thrill of the night had him glowing like a new man. In his favorite shirt, he sat in the booth across the room, laughing with his friends as he sipped the token beer I'd allowed him. A sitter was watching Willa at home, and I wanted to be happy too. While trying my hardest, old acquaintances eagerly asked about my life and my work.

"You did a tour of Europe once, right?" a girl I knew from high school French class asked with a laugh. "Did you actually get to use anything we learned in school?"

"I heard Thailand is, like, super dangerous," another old classmate wondered later. "How'd a girl like you survive?"

A girl like me . . .

That had always been the age-old question around here.

Still, they hugged me like they meant it. They never tried to be malicious or rude, yet I struggled to get my smile to reach my eyes. There was more than one countdown clock in Bill's. One lived in my head, and with every passing moment, I felt it ticking down like a time bomb.

I had only two days left until I had to give my company an answer about the job. My two emails were already drafted—one for the hiring team with my resume and one to Chris as a polite refusal. Every night, I studied both. I had thousands of reasons my life could be arguably better in Durham. Beyond better opportunities for Willa, most of them now amounted to dollars and cents. The money would have made any intelligent person salivate, but one reason from Nick would overwhelm it all.

He just needed to give one measly reason.

Why was it so hard? Why had he kept me at arm's length over the last few days?

Behind the bar, Nick looked like the man I'd first been infatuated with all those years ago. His black sweater hugged the body I'd secretly memorized. His blond hair was swept back, giving me full view of his breathtaking blue eyes. Even from across the room, Nick radiated that casual charm everyone adored in him. My fingers itched to reached for him. In my head, I even imagined going over to the bar and grabbing him until my heart could have the closure it needed, but I kept my fingers curled around my glass of sparkling wine. My feet stayed frozen by my cocktail table.

I didn't want to start the new year with this weight on my back, but Nick was too busy being the man he was always meant to be. Dad had his reasons for wanting to sell Nick the bar, and though I craved some sense of direction, I had to ask myself whether I was really willing to make Nick leave his career for mine. Was it fair to ask Nick to leave behind everything he'd ever known?

The answer wasn't in the bottom of my wine, so I tried looking for it in a basket of French fries instead. The final hours of the year slipped away until there were only minutes left. Nobody had left the bar, but the rowdy room had settled into a simmering anticipation. People were hanging around those they hoped to kiss. Eyelids drooped from the good feelings that always came from a few beers. Making my excuses to the people chatting around me, I took my empty fry basket to the bar. Nick came through the swinging kitchen door with three more for the partygoers beside me.

"You lookin' for a second round?" Nick asked a little too nonchalantly for my liking.

"No, I'm bringing it back," I answered. "I figured you all could use it."

Taking the empty basket, Nick's eyes swept away, smiling to another man looking for a rum and Coke. He gestured to one of the bar backs while taking the guy's cash. I tapped the toes of my ankle boots impatiently. Too used to holding his attention, I didn't love having to be in third, fourth, or even fifth place. The sound of my second hand wasn't keeping time with the music blaring through the speakers, and with Nick's attention everywhere else, I found myself all out of sorts.

I blurted out, "I thought I might get a minute with you tonight."

"A minute?" Nick knitted his eyebrows together. "You seem to be plenty busy, and with Bill still out of commission, I've got my hands full."

"I can see that, but well, wouldn't *you* want to talk?"

Nick moved around behind the bar, looking more restless than relaxed. "Then, is there something you wanna tell me and get off your chest?"

"*Me*? What about you?"

"What about me?"

Nick had been too cryptic for one too many days. His masked expression made me want to rip the neon signs off the walls and throw them out into the night. The coming snow could bury them and me. If Nick and I kept talking in circles like this, my frazzled nerves would implode, and I'd never survive it. I ran a hand through my curls and tried not to scream.

Leaning over the bartop, I pressed him, saying, "Don't you want to spare a minute for me? We're friends or . . ."

My voice faded away. There was no good way to say it in a crowded room, not unless I wanted it to ripple over to where my dad sat with his buddies. Biting my lower lip, I heard the bass of a new song blare overhead.

"What?" Nick wondered, tossing the dish towel off his shoulder. "What did you say?"

"I need a little more than fries or wine right now," I replied like a fool.

No good words could be found. I watched Nick shake his head as another order came out, and he had to take it. I watched as he slipped around the bar and took out the grilled sandwiches to a table across the room. Fifteen minutes remained in the year.

Nick met me on my side of the bar. "Were you asking me for water? Are you feelin' okay?"

"No, I mean, having some water isn't a bad idea, but—"

People near the dart board began to cheer and clap. Others joined along for the fun of it, drowning me out and washing away my precious time.

"Dammit, I can't hear out here," he mumbled under his breath.

His hand slipped around my elbow, and before I knew it, Nick started pushing through warm bodies and toward the kitchen door. It swung behind us as we kept walking, heading to Dad's office down the hall. The world grew quieter, and I realized how hot and loud it was in the bar. Away from the commotion, I noticed my flushed skin and the ringing in my ears.

"I don't know how long I've got before someone comes for me," Nick said while shutting the door. "What were you tryin' to say back there?"

I sighed, folding my arms around my chest. The silly silver sequins I wore offered no warmth, but Nick's arms could. If I'd wanted a temporary fix, I could have wrapped my arms around him and said that I missed him.

It wouldn't have been a lie.

"We need to talk," I insisted instead. "The year's almost over, and I don't want to go into the new year without knowing what you think about my taking this job."

Nick's face grew grave. His mouth drew into a hard line, making my heartbeat pound like a drum. He refused to meet my eyes as he muttered his answer.

"So, you're going to take it, then?"

"Not necessarily," I replied. "It might be a good job, but work isn't everything. There are other things I have to consider that are more important."

"If you're talking about Willa, didn't you say she's got more opportunities around Durham? She'll have the chance to go to better schools and take those lessons you talked about. You can have a good life there."

"But will it really be good for everyone?" I begged the question, taking one step closer. "If I take this job, will it really be for the best?"

"You know that answer better than me."

I groaned. Ready to come out of my skin, I glanced over to the clock on the desk. There wasn't enough time to be coy.

"I can't answer for you, Nick," I asserted. "Taking this job would affect us all, including you."

"I'm not the one you need to worry about."

"But I am!" I huffed, throwing up my hands. "I've been lying awake for the last few nights wondering what you want me to do because you won't give me any kind of sign. Are you gonna come with us? Are you expecting me to plan out some kind of new joint custody? Do you even want any kind of life with me and Willa?"

Nick's blue eyes froze over. For the first time in ages, he wasn't my warm shelter from the cold. I felt myself taking two steps back, pulling away from his low, strange tone. The conversation was falling apart before my eyes, and I was crumbling with it.

"How could you even think that, Darcy?"

"Because I'm waiting for you to make a fool out of me again!" I fired back, doing everything in my power not to cry. "I need a reason from you because I'm not going to throw myself at you, only to have you push me away for a second time! I–I can't act like a few weeks together is enough to build a life on! I can't jump in blindly!"

"Nobody's asking you to do that."

"But you *are*," I said. "You're so desperate for me to make my decision, but you refuse to give me any signs about what you're willing to do."

Nick ran a hand through his hair. Pacing in front of me, he huffed and puffed. His nostrils flared, but it wasn't directed toward me. Nick looked angry with everything tearing us away from each other. He was mad at the situation and how quickly we'd come undone, but what did we expect? This had never been a stable relationship. We carried on in the shadows of the night. Nobody beyond that office door knew what Nick and I really were.

"How do you not know?" he wondered aloud. "After every night we've spent together—"

I cut him off. "Because wanting someone and loving them aren't the same thing. Just because you might like the idea of a life with us doesn't mean you're prepared to make certain sacrifices. I can't assume that everything's changed between us, but if you wanted me to stay, I would. I just won't cry and beg for a moment that's never going to come."

He finally stopped pacing. With his shoulders slumped, Nick had never looked so wounded.

"You think I don't want you two?" Nick's voice was hardly a whisper at first, but it grew like the pain stewing inside my chest. "You think it doesn't kill me every time I have to leave, after everything that's happened and after every damn night? How do you not see it, Darcy? How can you not feel it? For Christ's sake, Willa is *my daughter*! I..."

The room fell quiet, and the squeak of the door hinge pierced my ears like nails on a chalkboard. I didn't want to believe it. I longed to shut my eyes and not look at the one person I was always terrified to hurt.

"Dad, I . . ." I tried, but there were still no good words.

Nick might have looked wounded, but my father suddenly appeared ready to maim him and put him six feet underground. I didn't need to ask. Dad must have heard Nick's declarations through the door. After all the years of deceit and secrets, Dad finally knew.

CHAPTER THIRTY-FIVE

NICK

Darcy's eyes were filled with pain and the shame of sharing it. Under all the secrets, the last thing she wanted to do was put that exact look of betrayal on Bill's face. The mouth under his mustache thinned into a hard line, but his dark eyes said one thing.

How could you do this?

The room grew bone-chillingly silent. Though the party could be heard down the hall, it felt a million miles away. We were all cut off from the excitement, and instead, left in this strange standoff. I didn't know who was going to speak first. I hardly dared to breathe too heavily, let alone move.

Finally, I tried to say, "Bill, I—"

He quickly cut me off. Darcy had gotten her dark brown eyes from her father, but they never got flinty or flashed quite like hers. That night, though, Bill's gaze was hardened like iron while his mettle turned to immovable stone. He didn't need to raise his voice. Bill was terrifying all the same.

"Don't," he demanded, his words gruff and terse. "If I had the strength, boy, I'd be stranglin' you."

Not backing down, Darcy insisted, "Don't be mad at him, Dad. He didn't know about Willa until a few weeks ago."

"Darcy."

She continued, "I was the one who created this secret. I was the one who lied to you for all these years. You don't need to—"

"*Darcy*," Bill said, more firmly this time. "Go back to the bar."

"Why, so you can maim Nick and have an aneurysm yourself?"

He grumbled under his breath. "I will have that aneurysm if you keep testin' me."

Reluctantly, Darcy raised her white flag. She kept her head down as she walked to the door, her heels tapping on the concrete. One last swish of sequins, and she was gone. Bill slumped in the office chair with an exasperated sigh. He ran a hand over his pained face while taking in another uneven breath. His chest struggled against the sensation.

"Bill, are you okay?" I asked, forgetting myself and reaching out.

He swatted my hand away. "Don't you dare touch me right now. I'm mad as sin, but I ain't dyin'. After all these years, after sticking my neck out and giving you a chance, *this* is what you did?"

I swallowed hard. With his look of sheer disappointment and disgust boring into me, I shrank away. Darcy feared hurting her father. That exact look was what kept me lying awake at night. I'd never even seen it, but in a single second, I knew it was living the moment that terrified me. I didn't want it to come. I pushed Darcy away and tried to forget all the adoration and affection a man could possibly possess. That had all in been in vain. I still stood in that cramped office with my back pressed against the wall.

"How long?" Bill asked, though he looked almost scared of the answer. "How long have you two been . . . like *this*?"

"If you're asking what I think you're asking, I never once looked at her when she was young. I swear to you on my life, though I don't think that means much to you now. When Darcy was a kid, I never saw her as anything else. It was only two years ago that something happened, and then, well, I guess Willa came along."

CHRISTMAS IN THE CABIN

Bill looked like he was about to spit on the floor. Shaking his head, he muttered to himself.

"I can't believe this bullshit," he cursed. "After everything . . . after all this time."

I still remembered the day I met Bill Steward. As part of my community service, I worked at a fundraising event sponsored by the car club that Mickey ran. Bill had known my Grandpa Jim and my mother. That was the thing about owning the most popular dive bar around. You met people, you heard stories, and Bill had heard stories about me plenty of times.

I was the kid caught up in a black market scheme, the poor bastard looking for quick cash, but out of everyone, Bill was the first to sit me down and ask me about it. He bought me a soda and listened. At the time, I didn't realize that he knew about Grandpa Jim's health issues and funeral bills. He recognized the extent of my grandmother's debt.

"You made a mistake, but you were doin' it for the right reasons," he told me that day. *"That doesn't make you bad, Nick. It means you're human."*

Those words stayed with me through all the years. The next day, he offered me a job bussing and helping in the bar's kitchen. He trained me as a bar back once I was old enough, and little by little, Bill gave me all my worth. He'd offered me his trust so willingly.

I made the worst mistake betraying his trust, but I had done it for the love of Darcy. That had to be a right reason. Out of all the foolish things I'd ever done, loving her never seemed like one of them. It was the recklessness and deceit that placed me there at the mercy of an infuriated Bill.

Louder this time, Bill muttered again, "I can't believe it."

"I never meant for this to happen," I found myself saying as if it would make anything better. "I cared about Darcy because she was your daughter. She was part of the bar, part of the family, I–I never expected for my feelings for her to change. I'm not even sure when they did, and after I let myself get carried away the one time, I hated myself for betraying you, for not being a better man."

Bill scoffed. "I ain't talkin' about that!"

"Then . . . what?"

I blinked in surprise. Somehow, I was that jittery teenager again. I rubbed my arm and felt the urge to look over my shoulder. The whispering gossip loomed around me like a thousand tiny ghosts. I couldn't see past any of it. All I saw was Bill rising to his feet.

"I'm talkin' about how it was too damn easy for my daughter to keep this from you!" he fumed. "Two years, and you didn't do a damn thing. It took me nearly dying for you to find out, and when you did, you didn't have the balls to be honest with me! You lied right to my face!"

"I did what Darcy asked of me!" I exclaimed. "I only found out after your heart attack, but we were planning to tell you in time and in a better way than this!"

"That still doesn't account for your being so damn thick, boy."

I ran my hands through my hair, ready to pull every strand out of my scalp. I wanted to come out of my skin. I wanted to turn back time. Everything about the moment felt impossible and too much to comprehend.

"That's because I forced myself to forget her!" I pleaded, hearing the manic state of my voice. "I thought it would be better for Darcy to hate me and forget me. Until I came over back in November, I didn't even know Darcy was a mother! I thought she was still off traveling. I thought she hated my guts, and you know what, I wanted it that way because God, Bill, how could I ever measure up or be good enough for her? How could I be the one for your precious Darcy Rose? According to you, she was supposed to get away from this place, so I couldn't be the idiot who forced her to stay!"

Bill's hands balled up into fists until his knuckles grew white. The iron in his eyes sparked with an unmistakable fury, but his voice grew fearfully low again.

"*Get out*," he seethed, cutting his reply through clenched teeth. "Get the hell out of my bar, Nick. I don't know what to tell you anymore, but I sure as hell don't wanna look at you."

"But the bar—"

"Zoe and the others will manage the bar just fine. The party's gonna be over soon, anyway."

My voice faintly cracked. "And Darcy?"

"She's a smart girl," he huffed. "She'll figure it out."

I looked at the clock on the wall. Only seconds were left in the year, but I couldn't turn back. With Bill's sharpened gaze staring down at the floor, I could only get my old leather jacket from its hook and head for the back door. I had gone against him enough.

Outside, the night felt so cold and quiet. Snow was coming. I could feel in my ragged, heartbroken breath as the sound of counting echoed behind me.

"Twenty-nine, twenty-eight, twenty-seven!" the partygoers chanted behind me.

Standing there, I imagined Darcy in her sequined dress, alone and looking around. Was she missing me? Would she really know where I went, or would she think I'd abandoned her for a second time? Perhaps I should've fought harder to go see her before I left, but there was nothing to be done. Even if Bill knew, the rest of the crowd didn't. Darcy remained out of my reach.

My fingers flexed around the cold air they touched instead.

"Four, three!" they screamed louder. "Two, *ONE!*"

Applause poured through the heavy walls of the bar. In the distance, I heard the sound of fireworks going off like cannons in the night, but I didn't look to see their color or light. My eyes turned to my feet. My footsteps crunched against the gravel lot while my chest grew numb. It was a new year with the same old torment, and somewhere nearby, Darcy found herself alone again.

CHAPTER THIRTY-SIX

DARCY

The clock in Dad's old Bronco glowed red as the hour turned to one. Just as it changed, my father yanked his keys from the ignition and headed inside. He didn't look my way or even speak. I had only seen him like this one time in my life.

When I was small, my father took me out to see the ocean for the first time. The red flags flew, warning everyone on the beach not to go out in the water. Dad told me not to go. I promised him I was only looking for shells, but the water felt so warm. I had taken some swim lessons, so I thought it would be okay for a few minutes. It only took five for one large wave to crash over me and suck me into the undertow. Dad looked furious as the lifeguard pulled me onto the sand, and the look of pure pain burned into my retinas more distinctly than that seaside sunshine.

I had never just been stubborn to a fault. I'd been stubborn to the death of me, so sure I could escape if necessary. Too naive and too reckless, I wondered whether my father and I would survive this, but I didn't have the strength to ask.

My strength left me when Nick refused to give me a clear answer.

CHRISTMAS IN THE CABIN

My few bits were torn to shreds in the moment, and as the new year began, I stood there alone in the bar with the same worries and regrets. Dad came back out into the bar as people toasted the new year. Nick did not. The only answers I had were my father's stony looks and silence as he carried himself to bed.

"Thanks for taking care of Willa," I told the babysitter as Dad walked off. "How much do I owe you again?"

I was sure to be generous with my tip. The girl was a younger sister of a guy I'd known back in high school. Now a college girl herself, she was sweet, and she'd given up her night to let me have a bit of fun. I wished my evening had gone better for her sake.

I wanted to turn back time and stuff down my feelings like I had for years, but I'd shown Nick too much. Even as I got ready for bed, I felt the hollow hoarseness of the voice in my head. My insides screamed for an answer until I collapsed from within. Not even the sight of Willa sleeping peacefully made me feel better. Outside, snow began to fall.

I imagined it was covering me and all my offenses.

Leaving Willa to her dreams, I tiptoed back to my bedroom to watch the snow fall in the dark. Sleep was the last thing on my mind. I balled my body up under a blanket and let my toes twitch with worry. I had no clue what really became of Nick. A handful of his pine-scented T-shirts were still hidden in my drawer, but they couldn't replace him. An old tee advertising a local brewery didn't match up to the feel of his arms. With no note or call, I was only left to wonder.

Where had he gone?

Ice tapped at the window among the snowflakes. Something tiny hit the glass. Then, another was larger and more pronounced. I realized it wasn't ice at all. Beneath my window, a tall figure stood with snow collecting in his blond hair and his blue eyes pleading through the dark. I unlatched the window and threw it open. The snow nipped at my cheeks, but I hardly felt it.

"Nick?" I hissed, leaning out. "What are you doing?"

"I had to see you, Darcy. I couldn't finish my thought over the phone."

I shook my head. "What thought?"

"That Willa's my daughter. I have no other family but you two, and I'd die before letting you go willingly," he declared from down below. "I love you both too much and I don't think I can be fair about your job offer. No, that's not right. I *know* I can't be. I'm biased. I'm selfish, and I'm hopelessly in love with you. If you can't feel that, then that's my fault."

A blustering wind whipped up at my cheeks and my parted lips. I didn't know how long I held my breath, but I was terrified of exhaling. I feared one tiny huff of hot air would be enough to tip the scales and blow the fragile moment away. Still, Nick stood there. His boots sank deeper into the inch of snow already on the ground.

"I love you too," I answered so simply that it bewildered my already stunned heart. "Do you want to come inside?"

A smile toyed at the corners of his mouth. I watched the happiness swell from the tip of his toes to the corners of his eyes. His expression tried to fight the skepticism within.

"Is that even okay?" he had to ask.

"I don't care if it is. Meet me to the back door."

My hurried movements became a balancing act. I firmly shut the window before scampering toward the kitchen and into the mudroom. Nick was already there at the back steps. Snow melted in his hair, making it stick to his forehead and red-nipped cheeks, but his eyes burned the hottest shade of blue. There was no time for words. As soon as I threw back the dead bolt, Nick's cold hands flew toward my face. All the words I longed to hear had always lived there, electrifying Nick's lips as they found mine.

"You're so cold," I whispered.

With my eyes falling shut, I let my arms wrap around him anyway. My hands slid under his open jacket to feel the softness of his old black sweater. Nick would be warmer if he stripped off his wet things. My fingers curled around the well-worn cotton. They were so ready to peel off the confining fabric. I longed to share my body heat until I lost track of where Nick ended and I began.

"I think I forgot how I'm supposed to love someone," he muttered breathlessly between kisses. "It's been so long, but I promise I'll get better. I—"

I stopped him, taking the air from his lungs and his lower lip gently between my teeth before pulling away. A groan quietly rumbled deep within Nick's chest.

"It's okay," I assured him. "We'll figure it out together."

"*Together.*"

Nick echoed the word, letting it fill my ears. His grip slipped down to my shoulders and neck, and in the back of my mind, I knew there would be time to talk. Nick and I would figure it all out once we were safe, sound, and right where we belonged.

My feet already knew the way. Walking backward, my touch coaxed Nick into following. The silent house made every creak of the pine floors sound a million times louder, but we made it back to my bedroom. Nick's boots slid under my bed as the old brass lock clicked shut. Already tossing aside his leather jacket, Nick looked as determined as I felt.

"I'm too old to be sneaking around like this," he muttered under his breath.

Still, that didn't stop him from pressing my back against the shut door. His grip slid down my side and around the back of my thigh. With his grip pressing into my bare skin, Nick hoisted my leg against his waist. My hips rocked into the sensation of his growing bulge brushing against me, feeling delirious from the thought of it.

"Oh, baby." I laughed, kissing him again. "We're both too old not to get what we want."

I had never craved anyone like I did Nick. I slowly pushed him away, and Nick backed off without hesitation. He was mine to move and mine to bend. With my hands trailing down his chest, my fingers discovered the button of his jeans as my lips parted for him. It took no effort to tug down Nick's clothes, yanking them all out of my way. Wearing nothing but his wolfish grin, Nick leaned back against the bed as I crawled over him.

"Can I show you how much I love you?" I whispered teasingly.

My hands were already running where they longed to go, wrapping themselves around the semi-hard length going rigid at the slightest touch. I wasn't even waiting for an answer. My lips slowly wandered over the crook of his neck and down the center of his chest. His tattooed arm reached for my hair.

"You can do whatever you like, darlin'," he replied. "I'm yours to use."

"Then, you tell me when you can't take it anymore."

Pushing my curls back from my face, Nick took in a sharp breath. His head fell back against the bed while his eyes shut tightly, giving in to the sensation. Something inside me felt set free. Eager to revel in the moment, I licked his length from base to tip and relished the soft sound of Nick's low groan. He was mine to have and to hold, and it didn't matter if he wasn't perfect. Nick was absolutely perfect for me.

My fingers became an extension of my work, stroking as my head bobbed with measured intent. Nick tightened his grip on me in reaction. With an indiscernible curse, he shuddered against the growing pleasure, allowing me my satisfaction until it was all too unbearable.

"*Enough*," he declared in a raspy tone.

Hardly a heartbeat passed before I found myself being twisted around, shifting and gaining the weight of him. Nick let go of my hair to take fistfuls of my T-shirt.

"You don't know what it does to a man to see you like this," he muttered, yanking the shirt over my head. "To have you in my clothes, *between my legs . . .*"

His voice trailed away as he hungrily kissed the tops of my exposed breasts. Cupping them, he worked over each nipple with his thumbs until they were like pebbles to the touch. He couldn't get enough of me. There was no such thing as close enough.

"There's not a second of the damn day that I don't want you," he said. "It's always there . . . just underneath . . . I've been living with it for years now."

"Don't act like you're the only one."

I'd pined for this night for two years. All that time felt like one like eternal winter. My heart went to sleep, but there beside him, I came alive again. My entire body burned in the newness of it all. It compelled me closer. Even as our bodies connected and Nick slipped into me, I pulled him closer. We twisted around, turning like the world on its axis.

Three simple words.

They shouldn't have meant so much, yet everything had changed.

Side by side, we locked ourselves together. Nick thrust into me, pushing deeper than he ever had before. With my leg draped over his waist, my hips bucked against him and rolled into the feeling. Each breathless gasp leaving my body gave Nick the chance to steal another kiss and consume another part of me. Even when I didn't have the strength to kiss him back, he didn't relent until I found myself overcome in every sense of the word.

"I love you," he said against my skin like an unbreakable vow. "I love you so much."

"Nick."

My head fell back as my spine began to arch. His name was the only thing I knew, the only word left as every scrap of sense left my body. With his teeth grazing over my shoulder and neck, Nick left with me with nothing but a feeling of deep satisfaction and the truth that I was loved.

Like a prayer, I pleaded his name, saying, "Nick, *Nick*, I . . ."

Every muscle in my body was claimed by the climax overtaking me. It rocked me to my core and had my fingers digging into the nape of Nick's neck. If it hurt him, he didn't show it. He was too lost in his own release and too focused on keeping me as close as a man possibly could.

I wasn't sure how long we lay together like that. Time crystallized and grew still. Catching our breath, Nick and I refused to let go of each other. We didn't want to leave the moment behind.

"I love you," I vowed the second I had enough air. "I don't just want to come home for the holidays, Nick. I want to come home to you. I want to come home to you every day of my life for however long that lasts."

"But where will our home be?" he wondered.

With his head still buried against my neck, Nick pressed his lips gently against my shoulder. The fine mist of sweat around my neck didn't stop him. His palms pressed flat against my back, and with our bodies still connected, I knew my home didn't need four walls and a roof.

"Wherever we want," I whispered back. "As long as you and Willa are with me, I don't care where we go."

I felt the smile stretching over his handsome face. His words came out low and rich.

"That was supposed to be my line."

We talked it over in the faint glow from the light pole outside. Half-dressed and teeth brushed, we locked ourselves away and talked through it all. I loved the work I did, but I didn't care much for the company culture or the endless onslaught of the suburban commute. If my father could learn to forgive Nick, there was a chance the bar would still be his. Nick would have his own business. His life would still be here, but if not . . .

"I'll go back to Durham with you," he promised. "Even if you don't want to keep working for these people, you could find another company you liked better or start one of your own, and I'll bet there are plenty of restaurants who would like a good-lookin' bartender like me."

"But you never liked big cities. I've heard you say that."

"I didn't like wanderin' through big cities by myself, or fancy, pretentious places," he amended. "If you're there, if my days are spent with you and our girl, I wouldn't consider that a bad life."

"And my place is close to Eno River. We could take walks through the state park or go over to some of the small towns nearby. It doesn't feel much different from Boone, really."

It sounded like I was trying to convince myself that it was a good idea, but geography wasn't our biggest problem. There was a chance that Dad would never get over the secrets and the lies. When the time came, we would have to face the world outside my bedroom door. The problem had never been about where we were going.

"We won't be able to keep secrets like this," I thought aloud. "People have to know."

There was a good chance they wouldn't like it, either. Nick retreated into the hills where the whispers of small minds couldn't reach him. If they decided to condemn us as well, it felt like the city would be a place to seek refuge and escape. That's what it had been for me those past two years, and with Nick around, maybe it wouldn't feel so lonely.

His hands pressed more firmly into my back. "I know, but I don't wanna spend another year pretending I'm not in love with you. Dammit, Darcy, I'm not sure if I could take another day of it."

"You won't have to. We'll figure it out."

As the snow made the world pristine and new, Nick and I hid ourselves under the bedsheets, letting our bare legs tangle together. His arm draped over my waist. We faced each other in the darkness. Not bothering to draw the curtains closed, I let the faint glow of the night cast its silvery shadows over us. My palm pressed into Nick's chest as I whispered.

"I'm glad you came over."

"Thanks for lettin' me in. I don't think I would've been able to stay outside for much longer."

Something about the way he said it made me laugh. It spread a childish grin over my face and made me bury my face against his chest. When the dawn rose, Nick would have to go, but I didn't have to worry. My time with him wasn't over. With the new year ours for the taking, our lives together were only beginning.

CHAPTER THIRTY-SEVEN

NICK

Twelve hours after digging out my tires and heading home to shower, I was back at Bill's place for dinner. I'd been invited for New Year's dinner every year. The offer had been opened to me like every other year, but that was before the party. Casserole dish in hand, I trudged up through the snow not yet scraped away from the gravel path. Bill still smiled at me back then. Now, he was greeting me with a hollow look in his dark eyes and a sobering grimace beneath his push broom mustache.

He grumbled under his breath. "Well, it looks like you actually showed up."

I figured we weren't doing niceties. Darcy said she'd talk with her father. Over the phone that afternoon, she insisted that they had spoken over breakfast and I was still supposed to come over for dinner, but with Erin and Mickey in Hawaii for a couple more days, I had to brace myself for the tensest meal of my life.

It's for Darcy and Willa, I kept telling myself the entire drive over. *You're going to grovel for them, not for your sake. Everything's for them.*

"I brought cornbread," I replied. "It's, um, Grandma Peggy's old recipe."

Not much more than doctored-up box mix, the cornbread was a paltry peace offering, but no side dish would put a smile on Bill's face. The only grin I got came from the sweet little girl who shuffled her way to the door. She clutched her grandpa's knee and smiled up at me.

"Hi!" she chirped in excitement.

"Hey, Willa," I greeted her, reaching down to accept her outstretched hand. "Do you want up or . . .?"

If Bill didn't want me in his house, it was too late. Willa was already pulling me inside, showing me where she played in front of the television. Bill didn't say a word. He only settled back into his old armchair. His hawk-like gaze followed me as I made it to the kitchen. There, Darcy was on her own again, fussing with a pot of black-eyed peas and checking the oven-fried chicken.

I set down my dish on the kitchen table, asking, "Can I help with anything?"

Her head shot up from the old cast-iron pot. Wiping a few beads of sweat from her forehead, Darcy smiled. She smudged her pink lipstick on my cheek with a kiss.

"It looks like you survived the gauntlet," she joked quietly. "I was trying to see if I needed to intervene, but I couldn't hear anything you guys were saying."

I shrugged. "There wasn't much to hear. I think Bill's resting on the old 'if looks could kill' bit."

"Just try to make it through dinner. I promise we'll talk once Willa's gone to bed."

"And if it doesn't work?"

I hated to be the cynic. We all wanted to make things right with Bill, to help him understand, but I feared the moment where the hope in Darcy's eyes might flicker out. For her, hope was not a delicate or pretty emotion. Hope was a bloodied soldier coming home half her weight. She'd seen it all, done things she didn't care to talk about, yet she'd survived all the same.

Right then, I needed a bit of Darcy's hope. It felt stronger than anything I'd ever known.

"It will work out," Darcy said in a whisper. "My dad can't be mad forever. He can't just cover his ears and shut his eyes."

"Kids do it all the time."

"Good thing he's not Willa's age then," Darcy tried to tease, but I saw how she worried.

Worry and anxiety were hope's dinner dates that night. Around the table, few words passed between us. Bill sat at the head of the table, glaring at his plate. In an act of sheer diplomacy, Darcy sat between us, leaving me to tend to Willa for the meal. It was all intentional. Even through dessert, I felt Darcy's attention shift back and forth. She studied Willa before flitting back to Bill and seeing if he was noticing how I looked after my own child. By the time I put Willa to bed, it felt like I was the one who needed to crawl into the crib.

"Get a little sleep for us both, okay?" I encouraged her, stroking her soft curls. "Good night, Willa girl."

She smiled up at me. Tucking her blanket under her chin, she tried to answer back.

"'Nigh, Dada," Willa answered in her small, high voice.

I didn't know where I was for a moment. Taking in a deep breath, I felt the weight on my back grow a little lighter. I found myself smiling, tempted to ask Willa to say it again.

There will be other times.

As I straightened my shoulders, I held onto that promise for all I was worth. I carried it into the kitchen where Bill and Darcy were having a Western-style standoff. Shoving up the arms of her knit sweater, Darcy pursed her lips.

"I'm not going to rehash what happened anymore. I told you everything you need to know this morning," she insisted. "At the time, I thought I was doing what was best for Willa, but my reasons were built on shaky circumstances and several misunderstandings. You know I have my pride, but that didn't make me right."

"No, it doesn't," Bill mumbled in agreement, folding his arms over his chest.

CHRISTMAS IN THE CABIN

They didn't seem to notice me in the doorway. Their dark eyes were trained on each other. Too stubborn for their own good, both Darcy and Bill tried to strong-arm the other. Neither Steward wanted to surrender their dogged opinions of the situation.

"But I'm allowed to make mistakes," she countered. "Every adult is, which you agreed that I am. You agreed that Nick and I are both adults after my birthday dinner. You said yourself that things had changed, and I wasn't just your kid anymore. Those were *your* words."

Bill huffed. "I didn't say 'em for you to use against me."

"I'm not trying to use them against you. I want you to make peace with this. This doesn't need to be the thing that comes between us."

"But it's okay if it takes time," I added in. "It might be a new year, but it's not even been a day."

Darcy and Bill quickly shifted their attention to me. I was right. They hadn't noticed me coming back, but as Darcy looked at me, she tried to seem hopeful. She wanted to believe the worst of the storm was over. Bill's expression said nothing.

"Darcy, why don't you go wait in the living room?" Bill declared from where he stood by the sink. "I think Nick and I should talk alone."

She picked up her glass off the kitchen counter. Her eyes darted back and forth between us. It was clear that she didn't want to leave us alone, but Darcy forced her feet to move. She let her free hand graze over my arm as she walked past me.

"*Good luck*," she mouthed silently.

On the surface, Bill Steward seemed just as I'd seen a million times. His uniform flannel hid his surgical scar. His expression remained stoic and silent. As he leaned back against the counter's ledge, Bill let a long, exasperated sigh. He didn't speak for an agonizing minute. I wouldn't dare open the conversation.

"She's been running circles around me all day," he muttered. "It's been hard to get a minute of quiet."

"Do you not actually want to talk, then, or . . .?"

Bill shook his head. "No, I got somethin' to say to you. It's been on my mind since I threw you out of the bar last night."

Hesitantly, I shut the kitchen door and walked over to one of the old wooden chairs. I lightly scraped it against the floor as I pulled it out to sit down. With my hands folded in my lap, I waited and listened.

"You know, part of me feels like I should be happy," he began. "I don't know how many times I'd wished Willa had her dad. It feels like a lesson in bein' careful what you wish for. If I'd known, I would've... well, I don't know what I would've done. Darcy told me *something* happened between you two that Christmas Eve she spent over at your house, and then things got messed up Christmas mornin'."

I swallowed hard. "It was something like that."

"She said you were worried about what I'd think."

"I was worried what everyone would think," I admitted. "People around here already like to call me a criminal. It would've been easy for them to call me a cradle robber too, and God, I didn't want them sayin' anything about Darcy. People have given her enough grief for not being like everyone else here."

"You could always leave, you know," Bill suggested, playing the devil's advocate. "I know people've been hard on you, Nick. I've nearly hit plenty of 'em, but you always stayed."

"Well, where was I supposed to go? I didn't have any family that I knew of. I didn't have some girlfriend to follow. Since my grandma died, you... you were all I had. Living around Banner Elk was all I knew. I wasn't like Darcy or even you. I didn't feel free to come and go as I pleased, so I stayed. I taught myself to get over it all, but if I'd known about Willa, if I'd realized how badly I had screwed everything up, I would've been gone in a heartbeat."

"I know."

My eyebrows knitted together. *"You know?"*

"I always knew the kind of man you were. That's probably why I never suspected you of such bullshit nonsense like skippin' out on your girl. Back when I met you, Nick, I saw myself in you. I saw the kind of kid I might've been if I didn't have anyone to lean on. You tried so hard, regardless of that, and it wasn't like I was plannin' on having kids. Lord knows, Darcy had never been a part of my plan, but

I decided if I could figure out fatherhood, I don't know, I could figure out how to help you too. Now, you're even more like me, with a girl you're tryin' to figure out what to do with, but you're doin' what you can."

"You did help me," I said to him. "Bill, you saved me."

He almost smiled. "I don't know about that."

But he had. Back when I had nowhere else to go, he gave me a job at the bar. He gave me someone to talk to about my problems and the chance to take classes at the community college. It wasn't much, but it was something more than I'd ever expected for myself. He made me feel like I deserved more than what others put upon me.

It was perhaps how I grew reckless and selfish with Darcy. At the end of the day, it all came back to Bill. He gave me a chance and a choice.

"Everything I have, I owe to you," I continued. "Nobody was willing to give an idiot teenager with a criminal record a job. They didn't care how it happened or who I was, even after my record got washed clean."

Bill shook his head. "But they don't matter. With all these heart troubles, I've had a lot of time to think about things that really matter. It doesn't matter what doctors do to me. One day, I'm gonna be dust in the ground. These mountains will be hills, and what's gonna matter is what you did with the little time you had. Lord knows, I'm angry that you've been lyin' to me. I'm annoyed that Darcy actually kept your damn secrets, but I'm not promised any amount of time with you all. I'm not guaranteed any amount of years with my girls, so I'm not going to be damn foolish enough to waste what I've got. Now, my question for you is what are you gonna do with your time?"

"I'm going to make things right with Darcy," I vowed. "Whatever she needs of me, I'll be there. If she wants to keep living in Durham, I'll go with her. I'm not going to waste my second chance, Bill, I promise."

"You'd damn-well better," he muttered back. "People are gonna talk, but you'd better be ready to deal with it."

"I am."

Bill nodded, crossing the kitchen floor. He closed the distance between us, and pausing for a beat, he outstretched his hand.

"Now, don't read too much into this," he told me. "I'm gonna be pissed with you for a while."

Looking at his hand, I waited for it to punch me in the face, but it didn't come. I took it, shook it, and smiled. Bill and I weren't back to what we were. Our friendship wasn't ever going to be the same, not that I wanted it to be.

We weren't friends anymore. We were family, and I intended to make that true in every sense of the word. Knowing how to keep my promises, I stood up from the chair and took in a deep breath.

"I hope you'll be mad at me," I told him, a new kind of excitement swelling inside my chest. "I wouldn't have it any other way."

CHAPTER THIRTY-EIGHT

DARCY

My knees bounced to near vibration. Trying to sit still on the couch was impossible. Even my fingers tapped against my thighs as I tried to make out what Dad and Nick were talking about in the kitchen. A few mumbled sounds came through the door, but nothing I could decipher as actual words. It would've been easier if I had gone for a run, not that I ever did that in the whole of my life. With all the anxiety building inside me, I sprang from my seat the second I heard the faint squeak of the kitchen door's hinges. Nick's footsteps slowly padded across the floor. My dad didn't come out with him.

He wasn't bruised or buried in the back yard, so that was a good sign.

"How'd it go?" I asked quietly.

Nick went over to grab his coat, saying, "I think you should talk to him about that. I've got to head into the bar early tomorrow morning for deliveries, and I have some, uh, other things to take care of."

"*Other things?*"

"Let's just say it's for me to know and for you to find out."

As I crossed the living room to meet him, Nick offered me a small smile and a kiss on my cheek. I didn't fully know what to make of the look in his eyes, but I felt the smallest stirring of hope inside me. I'd believed the worst for so long. Now that those hypotheticals were reality, maybe I didn't have to be so worried. All the possibilities were officially in the past.

I wasn't ready to see him go. After the most uncomfortable evening of my life, I still wanted Nick to stay. My bed didn't feel the same without him there, but I consoled myself that this separation wasn't permanent. Eventually, Nick would be able to do more than kiss me goodbye and drive off into the night. Even my father and I might discover something better than what we once were, but that could only happen if I dropped my guard and faced him honestly.

In the kitchen, Dad worked on loading the dishwasher. His eyes wandered through a place I couldn't see. With two coffee mugs in his hands, Dad didn't move, clearly forgetting where he was. His thoughts must have been laid out before him on the kitchen counter.

"Hey," I greeted him hesitantly. "Can we talk?"

Dad let out a small, bitter laugh. "I've done a lot of talkin' today. I can't believe you haven't talked my ears off already."

"Dad."

Folding my arms across my chest, my face silently pleaded with his. This cold war needed to end. My father was just as important to my life as Nick, both vital in different ways.

"All right, all right," he surrendered with a sigh. "What do you want me to tell you, Darcy? You want me to say I ain't mad? Do you need me to forgive you for lyin'?"

"No, I don't expect that any time soon. I just . . . I want you to understand *why* I did what I did, and I want to be clear that this was my choice."

"How?"

My hip propped against the kitchen cabinets. Staring down at my cold toes, I couldn't look my father in the eye while making my confession. The words were already caught in my throat while my pulse quickened. We had scratched at the surface more than once that day. It was time to plunge deeper.

CHRISTMAS IN THE CABIN

"After telling myself that Nick didn't want anything to do with me, I didn't want you to be mad at him or use you to lash out," I admitted. "I knew how much you meant to each other, and well, I didn't want to have you think less of him . . . or *me*. You had such high hopes for my life, Dad. When I decided to have Willa, I couldn't help but think I was disappointing you."

Dad's body deflated.

Seeing the misting tears in my eyes, my father shook his head and closed the distance between us. His immovable arms wrapped themselves around me while I buried my face in his well-worn flannel softened by decades of wear. It didn't matter how old I was. Standing there with my dad, I felt like a child again. I went back to the days of student clubs and school projects, each one steeped in the pleading hope that they deserved my father's overwhelming delight.

"I've been so scared of not being the daughter you wanted," I muttered into his chest. "You were always so proud of me, and somewhere along the way, I don't know, I began to feel like maybe I was a fraud. I was terrified of letting you down."

"That'll *never* happen," Dad said. "You'll always be my girl no matter where you go or what kind of life you make for yourself."

"But you were so upset when you heard I might be giving up that job offer."

Pulling back, Dad let out another long exhale. "It wasn't like that, Darcy."

"Then, what was it like?"

He shook his head slowly. Resting his hands on my shoulders, Dad held the weight of the world in his expression.

"I've seen too many women get stuck in tiny towns," he began. "People like to say you got the travel bug from your mother, but before you, I was determined to see every corner of this country."

"I know. That's how you and Mom met."

"But no matter where I went, I always saw 'em. I'd meet women like Nick's mother workin' in diners or gettin' by cleaning my hotel rooms. They were overlooked, underestimated, and too often mistreated. You know, there are even times when I wonder what my own momma could've done if she hadn't married my father and given up teaching school. When you were born, I was so happy to have you in my life, but I–I worried what would become of you. I never liked what the world did to women. As God is my witness, I promised I'd do everything in my power not to let any foolish boy or small-minded place stop you from bein' all that you could be, and look at you, Darcy. You saw more than some old country highways. You bought yourself a passport and saw the whole world, but even if you hadn't done that, you would still be my girl. I'd still do whatever it takes to make you happy."

"So . . . you're okay with this?"

"Oh, hell, no," he muttered with a quick laugh. "I'm still madder than a hornet's nest for you lyin' to me, but I ain't gonna pretend I have a say in who you like . . . or, you know, *love*. I'll just be happy that you're here and that I can still be a part of your life. I'm not dumb enough to push you away over this. You're too damn special."

"Is that what you told Nick too?"

"Not exactly, but we've got a different kind of relationship, you know. When it comes to that boy, I'm not such a sucker."

"I love you, Dad."

Dad pulled me into him again. My head tucked under his chin, and relaxing into the feeling, I felt his wide hand pat my back.

"I love you too," he mumbled into my hair. "Now, you remember it's my job to be annoyed with him. Nobody gonna be good enough for my Darcy Rose. I don't even think I'm good enough for you."

"Oh, please. You're the best dad anyone could ask for."

I felt the smile on his face as my father kissed the top of my curls. All these years, I'd been mimicking him as I played parent. I used the same tricks Dad used on me with Willa, and secretly, I harbored the same feelings of inadequacy. We had always been two peas in a pod, Dad and me. I couldn't expect him to get over everything overnight, yet for the first time, I wasn't agonizing over his reactions. I didn't worry that these revelations would make him drop dead from a wounded heart. The quick-turning wheels of my mind began to slow.

The new year finally looked bright.

CHAPTER THIRTY-NINE

NICK

The bright sun made the blanketed fields of white snow look blinding to the naked eye and the asphalt even more black. Our bizarre errand had become the perfect excuse for me to take Darcy into town, but the pack of little plastic favors didn't make much sense. She knew exactly what to look for at the party store. The cashier kid at the register didn't bat an eye either. Even in the afternoon light, I was still in the dark.

I had to know, "What are these babies for, anyway?"

"They're for the king cake," Darcy explained, adjusting my truck's radio. "You're supposed to hide these little babies in the cakes, and whoever finds one will have luck in the new year."

"And . . . they're supposed to be baby Jesus, right?"

"Exactly, and these baby Jesuses are going to give the gift of drink vouchers for the bar tonight."

I chuckled. "It's like the new version of turnin' water into wine."

Bill and Mickey's mother had grown up in Louisiana, so they had grown up with these kinds of traditions like Darcy. I heard Bill talk about it from time to time. I'd seen the ring-like cakes decorated with purple, green, and gold sprinkles in the grocery store, but this was the first time the bar would be having any kind of Mardi Gras party. The kitchen was cooking gumbo and these cakes while different kinds of cocktails were going to be on special for the weekend. On the ride to Boone and back, Darcy gave me the whole history of the seasons and the colors, distracting her from my detour away from the highway.

White snow piled up on either side of the road where tractors had already come along. It made the cloudless sky brighter and the sun that much more piercing. There wasn't a shadow in sight. While heading onto a small road not yet cleaned off, Darcy sat taller in her seat. She finally took notice of where we were going.

"We're not going to the bar," she stated plainly.

"You're right," I agreed. "We're not."

"Then, where are we going?"

Turning my head, I gave her a smile instead of a real answer. Darcy's dark eyes narrowed, but she played along. Her head fell back in the seat while the radio filled the cab. She didn't need to fill the silence. Her eyes were elsewhere, watching as she waited to see where I'd stop. By the confused look on her face, I knew Darcy couldn't make heads or tails of where I parked.

"It's . . . *a field?*"

I hopped out of the cab and shut my door. Coming around to her side, I tried not to laugh at Darcy staring at the snow-covered clearing. She tugged down my red knit cap over her head in frustration. Her sunglasses hid her eyes, but I saw the frown she fought at the corners of her mouth as she surveyed the landscape. Only animal prints marred the gently sloping surface. They made their path around the treeline where the pines were frosted over with ice of their own, and in the chilling breeze, the branches crackled as they swayed.

"I think it was a field once," I remarked, sliding my hand around her waist. "Or maybe it was a pine forest. Either way, they're gonna put houses here now. The land's been divided into like, ten or so lots, I hear."

"From who?"

"From the man I bought this lot from," I answered.

Darcy jolted. She threw off her sunglasses in shock.

"Excuse me?" she asked incredulously. "You're buying this piece of land? What for?"

"It's kind of a long story . . . I think you should sit down for this."

It really wasn't, but I had an image in my head of how this was supposed to go. Taking Darcy by the hand, I led her around to the back of the truck and pulled down the tailgate. The metal latch groaned, but she slid on it easily. It put her eyes just above mine as I stood there before her. For all my practice in the mirror, there was nothing like meeting her perpetually determined gaze. My mouth couldn't ruin this moment, regardless of how it wanted to run away with itself.

"It seems that wearin' the same pairs of jeans for nearly twenty years has let me put more money aside than I realized." I began to lead Darcy on a little. "You've given me so much—a family, your love, and probably more chances than I deserved. I figured that I should give you somethin' in return."

"A piece of land?"

I nodded. "It's twenty-some minutes from the bar, fifteen minutes from a good charter school, and as you saw, it's not too far from the highway. It would be no trouble for us to go to Boone or for you to head to Durham every once in a while. It's just the right spot for you and Willa."

Of course, Darcy got clever with her employers. She never wanted to give up her flexibility and her freedom. She didn't want to leave me for a place that wouldn't bring her any joy, so with all her clever charms, Darcy convinced them to create a new position just for her. The job would be just like the other, coordinating work as part of middle management, but Darcy was now going to manage all the remote workers like herself. She was even working with her new colleagues to help make the transition from hybrid to remote a more seamless experience, and she never had to give anything up.

Darcy had done everything to set the scene for us. Now, I only had to ask the right question.

"Oh, would it be?" Darcy played along, reaching for the sides of my hair. Her fingertips tickled the tops of my ears. "And you're going to sign this piece of land over to me so I can, what, pitch a tent?"

"I was thinkin' more along the lines of a house than a tent."

She grinned, coaxing me an inch closer. "That does sound better."

"But there's a condition."

"That you'll have to move in with us?"

"Not exactly," I replied, reaching into my coat pocket. "I was thinking more along the lines of us getting married and moving in together."

There was no more teasing in Darcy. Her expression softened as she pulled me closer.

"Really, Nick?"

"I'll get on my knees if you want," I said to her. "I don't care about the snow or any mud underneath. Just say you'll marry me, Darcy, but don't do it for Willa's sake or anyone else's. Marry me because I don't want to spend another day without you in my life and you feel the same way. Marry me because even if Willa had never come, you know I'd still be hopelessly in love with you and want a dozen kids just like her."

"That's a lot of kids," she joked lightly, but I saw the tears misting at the corners of her eyes.

As Darcy grinned, my only regret was not doing this sooner. Perhaps we hadn't been together long, but this moment had been over two years in the making. We both knew it.

She continued, "Besides all the babies, that honestly sounds like a dream."

"Then, my Darlin' Darcy Rose," I began, pulling out the ring for Darcy to see, "will you take this ring and give me the chance to be a good husband to you for as long as we both shall live?"

"Yes, Nick," she readily answered. "A thousand times, *yes*."

Sliding the white gold band over her finger, Darcy admired how the lone modest diamond caught in the light. The old-fashioned band had been engraved with fine scrolling details. To some, it may never look like much, but it was all I had to give. Everything I had, all that I was, was wrapped around Darcy's finger.

I confessed, "If I was gonna walk into that party on your arm tonight, I wanted people to be certain I was serious."

"There's no doubt about that," Darcy mused. "You've got a ring, a home for now, and one to build. You really planned everything out, didn't you?"

"Well, I know how much you like thinking ahead."

"Almost as much as I like you."

"Only like?"

Darcy reached for my face, brushing back the hair from my forehead. In the bright light, she had never looked so breathtaking. I had every intention of getting Darcy in nothing but that engagement ring. She would finally spend a night in my bed, and plenty more besides, but right then, feeling her fingertips comb through the sides of my blond hair, I had more than enough.

"Love," she amended for me.

When Darcy kissed me, it felt like the final piece of the puzzle falling into place. All the hope and happiness I ever needed lived right there in her embrace, and I had it. Though it didn't amount to dollars and cents, I considered myself the richest man alive.

"You always smell like pine, even now," Darcy muttered between kisses.

"It's *Pine Sol*," I explained. "It's an old trick my grandma taught me. It disinfects the clothes and helps keep the washer clean. Do you not like it?"

Darcy threw back her head and laughed like a kid. The sight of her was more blinding than any sunshine.

"No, no, I love it, Nick!" she exclaimed through her fit of giggles. "I love everything about you, and I wouldn't dare change a single thing."

"And I wouldn't change anything about you, Black Sheep. I love you and all your wool just as it is."

The last of her laughter began to float away in the winter wind. Over the field of sparkling white, there was nothing but possibility and hope for something better, and it was all ours for the taking. Daylight shone over us both that day in the snow, and our future together looked nothing but bright.

It was all a man could ever wish for.

EPILOGUE

DARCY - ONE YEAR LATER

I had never experienced so much life in a single year. By the time winter thawed, Dad's cold shoulder toward Nick had warmed up too. He couldn't deny how pleased he was to see Willa have two parents who loved her, and the decades of loving Nick like a son couldn't be forgotten. Sure, there was gossip among those who didn't understand. I learned to deflect the pointed questions because at the end of the day, they never mattered.

When Nick and I said our vows on a late June afternoon, I only saw the smile on his face and the unmistakable blue of his eyes. The fourteen years between us couldn't be found. We were as ageless as the evergreen mountains and as alive as the flowers growing in the gardens of that historic bed and breakfast. Nothing dimmed my delirious grin that day or during the week-long honeymoon in Italy that came after, but the day we came back, everything became a whirlwind of life moving forward.

Dad's surprise reception at the bar certainly put everything in the fast lane, taking us off guard after picking us up from the local airport. By the next day, we were already looking at finishes for the new cabin, preschool orientations for Willa, and managing to live in a one-bedroom cabin as a family of three. Nothing about it ever felt expected. Any serious plan we attempted to make fell by the wayside, but life was the thing that happened while we stayed busy making plans.

It felt like heaven when we finally unlocked our front door for the first time. With my we-still-appreciate-you pay raise from my company, Nick and I were able to get the house furnished in record time. I figured it would be a quiet holiday getting settled into the new place, but when it was suggested that we have a housewarming party the weekend between my birthday and Christmas, well, the plans snowballed from there.

I couldn't be angry at all the family and friends eager to fill our new house to the brim. Between spiked holiday punch on the kitchen counter and Christmas music playing on the living room television, the cold December night felt festive and filled with possibility. Even Willa was ecstatic to stay up past her bedtime being passed around from friend to friend. Crawling into Lizzie's lap, my daughter happily listened to me talk about her as we all sat on the new sofa.

"She's doing really well in preschool," I explained to my friend. "She's made some new friends, and we're looking into enrolling her into a dance program next spring. One of her classmates goes twice a week to an after school class that's a combination of ballet and tap. Her parents say it's great and that the teachers are all supportive."

Sipping her punch, Lizzie grinned. "That sounds perfect for her! Logan and I have been talking about getting Jacob into something. It feels like all the babies at his fancy-schmancy preschool are bilingual and in three different extracurriculars."

"And Jacob?"

Lizzie adjusted Willa in her lap. "He's more into snacks and sleeping. I can't exactly see him playing the violin or taking Spanish lessons just yet. I mean, he's only going to be three next spring!"

"It's the perfect time to start applying to the Ivy League schools," I joked lightly. "That's what they mean by early admissions, right?"

"Oh, you know my in-laws are going to revolt if our kids don't all go to UNC. It's their family tradition."

"And what if Jacob wants to go to Duke like his mom?"

"Then I'll be very proud," Lizzie vowed. "He and Willa can attend their summer orientation together. Maybe they can even rent an apartment together like we did."

"How about a play date first? Next time you visit your mom, we can make a plan to come out and do a little day trip together. I'm sure Jacob and Willa would like it. Wouldn't you like going on an adventure, Willa girl?"

In Lizzie's arms, Willa yawned and smiled. "Yeah, Mama."

She settled herself deeper into Lizzie's scarlet striped sweater, treating it like a blanket to snuggle up against. Glancing over at the clock, I knew it was high time Willa took an adventure upstairs and into her bed. Her eyes were in a losing battle with the need for sleep.

"Unless you want to be stuck here all night, I think I should get Willa into her pajamas," I told Lizzie. "Here, let me take her off your hands."

Lizzie gently lifted Willa from her lap. "I should probably go figure out where my husband went, anyway."

"Last time I saw him, he was chatting with Nick about beer in the kitchen."

Hoisting Willa up onto my hip, I noticed Nick still stood by the edge of the kitchen island, playing bartender. He chatted easily and showed off his handsome smile, but even through the crowd and the noise, he caught me studying him. The corners of his mouth twitched. Pushing up the sleeves of his old fisherman's sweater, Nick carried on with talking, but I saw the renewed gleam in his eyes. Like every other day of our marriage, I found another piece of him to adore.

It warmed me from within, making my heart swell as I headed toward the stairs. That man was *my husband*. Friends told me I'd lose this sensation in a year or two, but I honestly didn't believe them. Nick Wallace gave me a home to make ours and the beautiful daughter I was tucking into bed, but more than that, he offered me the freedom to be exactly who I was. We loved each other without exception or pretense every day of our shared lives. It lived in every casual glance and touch, and that night was no different.

I got Willa into her nightgown and under her covers before she passed out, and with her door shut tight, I found her father standing near the mistletoe hung between the kitchen and the dining room. Food covered the long table, and with all eyes on my arrival, I got at least ten knowing looks.

"As if I'd need a stupid weed to kiss you," Nick muttered before kissing the corner of my mouth. "I saw you put Willa to bed. Did she make much of a fuss?"

Leaning into his embrace, I savored the feeling of his arm draped over my shoulders. The spice of the winter beer faintly lingered on him. Breathing it in was as close as I could get to any of the drinks, but the taste in his kiss was enough to get me buzzed. I grabbed a cookie off the table to help me sober up.

"She's passed out up there," I told him. "We could shoot off fireworks, and Willa wouldn't know."

"Damn shame we don't have any, then," he teased. "Maybe your dad's got some back at his place."

"Oh, don't tempt him. I'm sure he does."

I looked back across the open room to see Dad laughing over a beer with an old family friend. Back in September, he'd finally sold the bar to Nick, and it turned him into a new man. A weight left his shoulders. He went on more trips and even got a dog, a yellow lab mix that Willa named Sunny. The only burden Dad had these days was the secret we refused to let him share.

Nick and I told him over my birthday dinner, and he'd been close to busting at the seams ever since. We agreed that tonight would be the night we'd announce it. It would be like ripping off a bandage, and my father would have the freedom to talk.

Turning toward his ear, I whispered, "Do you think we should make our little speech before everyone gets too toasted? I don't want to wait too late."

"It's only eight thirty."

"And most of these people will probably be leaving in the next

CHRISTMAS IN THE CABIN

hour," I pointed out. "People have to pace themselves for Christmas parties. Even we've got to go to Uncle Mickey's to welcome Jordan back from Hawaii tomorrow."

"We could wait until the New Year's Eve party at Bill's."

"Come on, Nick," I urged him. "It's not like I can hide under oversized sweaters until June."

He laughed under his breath. "I'll buy you a rain poncho, then."

"As if that wouldn't be suspicious."

"Point taken," Nick conceded with a smile and a sip of his beer. "All right, darlin', should you get their attention or should I?"

"I've got this."

Kissing him one more time, I pulled Nick's arm off me and led him by the wrist. The glint of his golden wedding band caught my eye in the lamplight. Sometimes, it felt like I put it there yesterday, but walking through the crowd, it felt like a lifetime.

This was where we were always meant to be—together and happily content. We let the fools talk and the jealous ones roll their eyes. Hopping up onto our tree root coffee table, I knew nothing could touch me but Nick's warm hand. He handed me the remote to pause the music for a minute before lacing his fingers with mine.

"Hey, everyone!" I called over the conversations. "Before you all get lost in the beer and barbecue meatballs, Nick and I just wanted to say thank you so much for coming out tonight. It's been wonderful seeing how many people we can fit in the house. Maybe in the summer, we'll see how many more we can fit on the porch!"

I got a few claps and cheers of encouragement, but everyone saw I intended to say more. The words were humming on my lips. For over a month, Nick and I had kept it between us. It had been ours to talk about under the covers, but love and joy weren't meant to be hidden away. Some things had to be shared. Taking in a deep breath, I glanced down at Nick and found my nerve again.

"I'd also like to particularly thank the few of you who offered to get me a drink tonight and your graciousness when I said I wasn't having any of the punch I'd made. I'm sure it made you suspicious, and I don't think this dress helped either," I continued, using my free hand to gesture to my teal turtleneck dress while pausing for some light laughter. "Well, in case there are any bets going now, we wanna let you know that Nick and I are another having another baby!"

The whole first floor erupted in excitement and questions. The baby was expected to arrive in June. No, we didn't know if it was a boy or a girl, not that we actually cared either way. Yes, this was very much planned, but secretly, Nick and I hadn't expected for it to happen so soon. We figured it would take months or even a year. We had Willa and the house and work, so of course, we should've known the pregnancy would happen right when life was at its most hectic.

As I talked it over with friend after friend, I realized how far my future was from what I had expected only a few years ago or even the Christmas before. My entire world had turned upside down, and I only felt grateful for it. Only in my wildest dreams did I find comfort in Nick's arm wrapped around my waist. Back then, my love for him was mere infatuation. I never once imagined having one child with him, let alone two, but there we were. Hand in hand, we stood by our brick fireplace and tall Christmas tree, answering every eager question without any reservation or doubt.

It might not have been expected, but that didn't make it any less perfect.

"I hope you're not getting too tired of this," he whispered at one point. "I'd hate to have to carry you to bed like Willa."

With his blond hair falling across his forehead, I flashed a teasing grin at the man I loved that Christmas and a thousand nights before. No shadows were cast over his handsome face. No bitter cold nipped at his cheeks. Every piece of him looked golden and devastating.

"Don't lie," I murmured back. "You'd *love* that."

His lips brushed against my ear as he replied, "You're right. I absolutely would."

I shook my head and went back to the onslaught of questions and inquiring minds, but the warm glow Nick offered didn't fade. It kept me warmer than the fire itself, giving me comfort in the beauty of being at home. Although Nick and I could have been in the mountains that raised us, the streets of Rome, or in the rocky wilderness of Tibet, home wasn't a log house on a hill. It lived in the people who loved me and who I loved in return, and the party proved how extensive my home could be.

Everything else was simply geography.

Of course, none of them quite compared to the man who held me a tad bit tighter when he mentioned the baby and our plans. *He* was where I planned to build my life with our children. He was the one who offered me more support than the walls around us or the green metal roof overhead. For the first time in too long, I was home for the holidays, right where I happily belonged.

EPILOGUE II

SAM

I didn't know how Darcy still had the stamina to stand there in the living room after two hours of questions and celebration. Everyone buzzed with the news, and her dad was grinning from ear to ear. After hearing the news, it made sense as to why Darcy invited me to come stay for the weekend and why Nick kept fretting over his wife while setting up for the party. All those comments about Darcy "taking it easy" finally came into focus.

"Nick and I aren't worrying if it's a boy or a girl. I do have plenty of hand-me-downs from Willa in the attic," I heard Darcy explain. "Between everything I couldn't bear to donate, I think we'll have a few things that'll work for the baby, even if it's a boy."

Nick's low voice carried over the Christmas music. "Even if we put a boy in a pink onesie, it's not like he'd actually remember."

The group around them laughed lightly, and inconspicuously, Nick gently tightened his arm around Darcy's waist. They fit together so well, almost a matched set. The blue of her dress made the spark of excitement in Nick's eyes brighter. Darcy leaned into the crook of his shoulder and laughed. I could say that Darcy looked like completely different from the friend I met on the road, but that wasn't entirely true.

In her new home, Darcy looked at peace with herself. She was the woman she was always meant to be, glowing with that self-assured contentment everyone aspired to find. Admiring the scene, I heard a buzz come from the back pocket of my jeans.

It turned out Darcy Steward-Wallace wasn't my only friend with good news. In a group chat with the only two girls I kept up with from grade school, one of them was texting in all caps. I nearly dropped my punch glass at the sight of it.

LOOK AT WHAT PARKER GAVE ME TONIGHT!!!

THE INTENSE MESSAGE came with a photo of her manicured left hand adorned with a boulder of a diamond. After five years of officially dating her boyfriend, it looked like Cassidy Mills got exactly what she'd been hoping for since the first night they met. Her picture-perfect childhood was slowly turning into her even more perfect adult life, but Cassidy deserved it. Our other friend, Delilah, agreed.

That's so amazing! Delilah gushed via text. *I can't wait to celebrate with you, Cass!*

A holiday party wasn't the place to be standing in a corner and texting, but I couldn't miss the chance to chime in. Stepping over to the corner of Darcy's dining room, I began to message back.

I'll be heading home tomorrow morning. Should we do a holiday get-together while we're all in town???

No question! You know you two have to be my maids of honor, and NO, I'm not picking between the two of you, Cassidy replied. *Parker doesn't have any sisters, and you know you're the only two I want beside me. We can talk plans and possible bachelorette party ideas. It'll be so great!*

I quickly messaged back. *I'll let you know when I get into Charleston.*

I could see it now. Cassidy was bound to have a massive society wedding, if her mother had anything to say about it. There would be a few hundred guests at the least, and several days of pomp and circumstance. My travel plans would likely have to be put on pause, but I'd do it for her. I'd stay in South Carolina and face everything I'd left behind.

Sliding my phone into my back pocket, I threw back the last of my drink and began weaving through the crowd. I had plenty of packing to do, and after leaving this home behind, my entire day tomorrow would be spent driving from high mountain peaks to the sprawling Low Country. I didn't need to spend my entire night getting tipsy on Darcy's cranberry punch.

"Hey, I think I'm gonna head downstairs," I told Darcy as I reached her. "There's some stuff I need to get done if I want to head out tomorrow morning, but if you need help putting away the food tonight..."

Nick showed off his charming grin. "Oh, I'll take care of it. Just don't plan on skipping out before breakfast. All my girls would be heartbroken."

"Willa, especially," Darcy agreed.

"I wouldn't dream of it!" I assured them both. "I want to hear all about this new baby and have one more coloring session with Willa over coffee."

Pulling away from her husband, Darcy threw her arms around my neck. "That sounds perfect."

"Congratulations on everything," I replied while hugging her back. "If you need anything, Darcy—"

"I know," she promised me quietly. "You always said everything would work out in the end."

"And it really did."

The day we sat together on the cold tiled floor would always stick in my mind. Our backs pressed against the paper-white wall. Rain tapped at the window overhead while Darcy turned the positive pregnancy test over and over in her hands. Torn to pieces over how to tell Nick, she never imagined the truth would lead her here. She didn't let herself believe or even hope.

I had never been so happy to see a friend be wrong.

At that party, Darcy and Nick made love look like something everyone should want, and maybe, if the planets and stars aligned, I might find someone who could make me settle in place.

Marriage and babies always seemed to be something for friends.

Always a bridesmaid and never the bride, I was delighted to toast another couple's happy ending, even if I didn't need one for myself. Not every life required a minivan and a white-picket fence. Still, I couldn't rule it out.

There was always a chance for miracles. Looking at Darcy one last time, I saw all the proof right there before my eyes. The hope for it all lived in the least expected places. I only had to open my eyes and see it.

Thank you for reading Nick and Darcy's story.
In mood for another holiday romance from this series?
Checkout Accidental Daddy here.

My vacation itinerary:

Meet a stranger.
Sleep with him.
Lose his contact info.
Get pregnant.

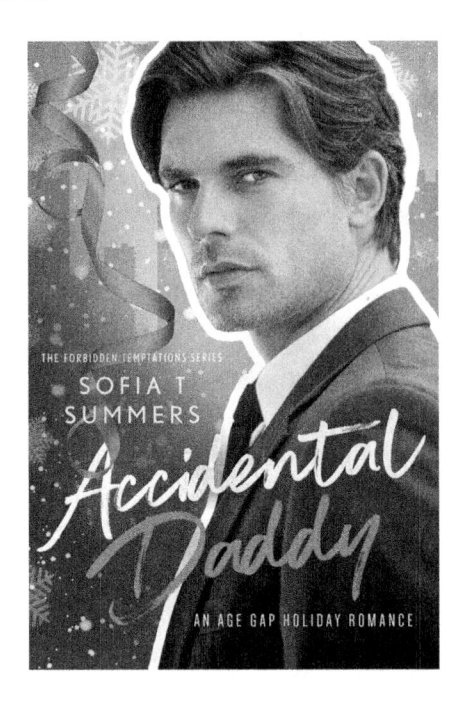

Let me be clear.
My daughter was the best thing that ever happened to me.
And I *never* expected to run into her dad again.
What were the odds?
But life surprises you, and it my case, life shocked me.

Her dad was none other than the son of my family's biggest rival.
I supposed that it made us enemies.
But the electricity between us was undeniable.
So were the secrets.
Oh, the news was going to piss him off.

Would the holiday cheer be enough to make a family our of sworn enemies?
And could we even find a place for love where there had only been hate?
Download Accidental Daddy - An Age Gap, Holiday Romance, NOW!

ACCIDENTAL DADDY (PREVIEW)

My heart
If you enjoyed Romeo and Juliet when you you're young and impressionable, then this will bring you back to that feeling and have you wishing for your very own HEA.

1 in a thousand Great read!!
Loved this book! 10 stars easily L O V E

and definitely a favorite I will read and fall in love with all over again. Now I want to read all of the author's books.

<u>Swoony</u>
This book will make you swoon on every page. Ambrose is #bookboyfriendgoals and little Mia is adorable. I loved every minute of this book.

Intrigued? Continue reading the preview on the next page, or get the book here.

PROLOGUE: AMBROSE

I was struggling to keep my eyes on the art. As a cacophony of techno music played overhead, the massive modern paintings were becoming just as mundane as the white walls on which they were hung. She had stepped into the gallery an hour earlier, and it became harder to look away with each passing minute.

Her black satin cocktail dress was scattered with an array of flowers. The full skirt's hem swished around her knees, while the corseted top contoured itself to the feminine curves of her chest. She didn't drink from the champagne glass she carried. She tucked a piece of caramel brown hair behind her ear as I wondered if it was due to worry over smearing her lipstick or that she just wanted to be polite to the wandering wait staff.

Two more minutes passed, and I gave up. I could no longer ignore this living, breathing work of art. She was just too alluring.

"Ciao," I greeted her casually.

Her attentions left an abstract painting of swirling splotchy colors on a field of orange, and the young woman's eyes flicked to mine. The green and gold inside them looked more vibrant than any shade on that canvas. I was sure my brown eyes paled in comparison.

"Don't worry." She laughed lightly in her warm American accent. "You won't need to stumble through Italian with me."

"That's good to hear," I remarked with a small smile.

"I've been misusing words all day myself," she told me. "I think I might've insulted my waiter over breakfast this morning, or maybe he was just having a bad day."

As she laughed at the thought, I replied, "Let's say it was the latter."

"I'm Stella, by the way."

"Ambrose."

For the first time, Stella allowed her pink lipstick to stain her champagne flute. Her heels clicked along the brick floor as we moved on to the next painting. The smell of ripe peaches, honey, and springtime flowers lingered in the air around us.

"So, Ambrose," she began, pausing by a colorful self-portrait of the Italian artist. "What brings you here to this little gallery in Rome? Business or pleasure?"

"I haven't decided," I answered her. "You?"

"Business," Stella replied, smiling. "But I could be persuaded otherwise. It's my birthday. Maybe I should have a little fun."

I thought she was joking for a moment, but Stella's eyes were serious. This lovely creature had been wandering around Rome all by herself, and on her birthday, no less. It seemed like such a waste.

"You know," I remarked, finishing the sparkling wine in my hand, "I have reservations for the last seating at my hotel's restaurant, but I don't have any company."

"Would you like some?" she asked.

I shrugged. "Only if you're interested."

"Dinner with a stranger," she mused, laughing under her breath. "I'm pretty sure I was told *not* to do things like this in college."

"I could give you my social security number if that makes you feel better."

Stella's laughter grew, drawing the eyes of other stiff-lipped gallery patrons. Men in tailored suits and women in elegant clothes whispered, but Stella didn't pay them any mind. She abandoned her half-empty flute and smiled at me. Her hazel eyes were sparkling.

"All right, Ambrose," she agreed. "I can be your company for the evening."

We stepped out onto the cobblestone side street together, leaving the haughty art connoisseurs behind. In the night air, Rome felt warm and quiet. Many of the city dwellers were on vacation. Bakeries and coffee shops were closed, blaming the holiday season. Still, there were plenty of travelers flocking to the Eternal City. Stella and I wandered into the busy Piazza Navona, heading toward my hotel until an empty taxi wandered our way.

Soon, we were in the backseat of a tiny white hatchback, buzzing past retired palaces and ancient landmarks. Our driver sped around the Trevi Fountain before delivering us to our hotel. I handed the portly man his euros before he took on new passengers.

Stella looked up at the tall white façade of the old five-star hotel. The brown hair brushing against her shoulders billowed in a summer breeze wandering off the river. She swept the waves of hair from her eyes as the doorman ushered us inside.

"This is quite the view," Stella remarked as we were seated in the top-floor restaurant. "Is that the Basilica dome over there?"

"I think so," I replied.

Rome was laid out before us from our little table for two, glowing in the golden August night. It was a captivating landscape, but I couldn't admire it for long. My new companion was far too enticing. She studied the scene just as she'd studied that art. After taking our order, our waitress quickly arrived with a bottle of chilled white wine before vanishing tactfully.

"You said you were at the gallery on business," I recalled while fixing the cuffs of my light blue dress shirt. "What business are you in?"

"I've opened a gallery in Manhattan," Stella answered. "I want Politi to make her stateside debut there."

"Will she?" I wondered.

Truth be told, I'd wanted the same thing, but the Italian painter agreed to put some of her works up for auction with my company. It appeared that Politi was a hot commodity.

Stella nodded as she sipped her wine. "Yes. Tonight was just a formality. What about you?"

"What about me?"

"You implied that you weren't there for sheer enjoyment," Stella noted as our fried squash blossoms arrived. "Should I consider you my competition?"

"I run an art auction house in London," I admitted. "I think we're both safe."

"You don't sound British."

"I grew up in Connecticut," I explained. "I moved to London for work."

Her bright eyes captured mine as she sighed. "Shame, though. I always enjoy a little friendly fire."

It was hard to ignore how her full breasts pressed against the boning in her top. As Stella toyed with the gold pendant around her neck, her body became only more tempting. The worst part was that she wasn't even trying. Her shoulders curled over the table as she rested her elbow on the ivory tablecloth. Everything about her felt relaxed and unhurried. It compelled me to slow down as well.

We dined on roasted eggplant and peppery pasta as Stella told me of her tour of Europe. She'd visited Paris, where her father restored art and her cousins in Brittany owned a pastry shop. The way Stella described it made me feel like I'd seen the vivid blue seas of northern France for myself. I'd tasted the sugary sweetness of her cousins' macarons and smelled the coffee her father made each morning. As we shared an Amalfi lemon cake, I began to wonder how such tart sweetness would taste on Stella's lips.

Looking at my watch, I remarked, "It's a few minutes before midnight. This place is closing then."

"Then I should get going," Stella sighed softly. "I have a two-fifty flight out tomorrow afternoon. I'll need to check out of my hotel and pack."

"I don't know," I considered aloud. "How long do you need to pack? An hour, hour and a half?"

"I guess so," Stella answered with a knowing smile.

"So, you could stay here until nine and have plenty of time to pack up your things."

"Just nine hours?" she mused, her head tilting to the side. "Are you really sure that's enough time?"

"For you," I confessed, "I'll take all the time you're offering."

I didn't know if it was my words or the expression on my face that convinced her, but I found myself undressing in the cream-colored bedroom of my penthouse suite. Shades of violet and deep blue painted the night skies, but I couldn't see them. My eyes closed as I tasted the lemon on Stella's tongue and the white wine on her lips. After pulling off my shirt, her polished fingers teased my waistband.

"It's not my birthday anymore," Stella murmured, her hand pushing past layers of fabric to wrap around my aching length. "I don't know if I deserve a gift like this."

Stella's zipper quickly unzipped down the length of her back. My hands tugged at the thick black straps of her dress, and I knew she was being a tease. It was clear in her smile and eyes glittering with sin. She was enamored with the moment, and it was carrying us both away.

"It's still your birthday somewhere, Stella," I reminded her, my voice darkening. "Besides, you're the one wrapped up like a present."

"I guess you should finish unwrapping me then," she said.

Stella invited me to kiss the skin I exposed. Casting aside her bra and lace underwear, my hands sought to memorize every inch of her glorious body. I adored how my fingers pressed into the softness of her inner thighs before reaching her burning heat. A gasp escaped Stella's lips, and I captured it with another kiss.

I could feel her body melting into me. Her hands were getting caught up in my dark hair as she whimpered again. Eager to explore, my finger traced up the folds of her entrance. It circled her little nub before slipping inside her. Her legs spread wider in reaction, and it wasn't long before neither of us could take it any longer.

Her coy expression long gone, Stella breathed, "I want you inside me, Ambrose."

"I wouldn't want to be anywhere else," I swore raggedly.

I easily connected my body with hers, and it felt like I'd entered paradise. Having Stella's body twist around me was a heady feeling. As I pushed deeper, her hips rose to meet me. Her legs tangled around mine as her breathing became more desperate. She was too far gone to kiss me back, but I didn't care.

I would take the very breath from her body. Whatever she offered, I'd gladly accept.

Stella let out a soft moan as a wave of satisfaction rippled through her body. It sent me over the edge and left me breathless, but it wasn't enough. I don't know how much sleep we got that night. My eyes would shut for five minutes, maybe, but then I'd feel Stella's body against my six-foot frame. Her fingers would brush against my jaw or chest, and I'd come alive again.

I cursed the sun when it rose over the eastern horizon. The violet skies were becoming a soft blue, and my time with Stella was over.

"Why don't we go out for coffee?" Stella suggested as she pulled her crimson heels back on. "Is there a good place nearby?"

Perched on the edge of the bed we'd ruined, I considered the notion. My mind was still hung over from my night with Stella, so it took longer than usual for me to think of a place.

"There's a little café on the corner, Amelia's," I recalled. "They've got excellent cappuccinos and cornettos."

"Sounds lovely."

She linked her arm with mine as we headed out into the early morning. Nobody seemed to care that we were in rumpled dress clothes. If they did, I didn't notice, but my senses were still overwhelmed with Stella. With my shirt sleeves rolled up, her fingers pressed into my bare forearm. She was fresh-faced and smiling beside me.

Even without a stitch of makeup, Stella was undoubtedly pretty.

She crossed her legs at the metal bistro table and sipped her coffee with both hands. Stella was lovely to admire, but I hated to be letting her go so soon. Pulling her hair back with some pins from her little red purse, Stella sighed in disappointment.

"I guess I really should be leaving now," she admitted. "It's after nine."

"I know," I agreed. "But I was wondering, do you ever find yourself in London?"

"Sometimes," she replied with a smile. "I've seen a lot of Heathrow."

I laughed lightly. "If you ever find yourself with an extended layover, I'd be happy to keep you company. It would only be fair since you've been such wonderful company for me."

"Yeah," she mused. "I think I'd like that."

After paying the bill, I hailed Stella a cab on the street corner. I handed her my gray and gold contact card embossed with my private number, and she slipped it into her bag. Moving to leave, her hand lingered on the handle before she turned back one last time.

"Take care of yourself, Ambrose," she told me softly.

"You too, Stella."

Her free hand brushed against my jaw as Stella kissed me one final time. I tasted the coffee and sweet pastry on her mouth, and it gave me hope that it wouldn't be the last time I'd see Stella again. I believed I would get a chance to rediscover her lips and her laugh. However, it wasn't meant to be.

Stella never called, and I was left with nothing but a beautiful memory.

STELLA - THREE YEARS LATER

The summer sunshine warmed my bare arms as I walked down the sidewalks of Sixth Avenue. A soft breeze blew through the streets of Manhattan as I stopped at the street corner to wait for the crosswalk. It made my top's little ruffled sleeves flutter around, while my hair blew against my cheeks.

"Dog, Mommy," Mia said, pointing across Sixth Avenue. "It's big!"

I looked to see someone walking their Great Dane out of a building. The big black and white canine was heading toward a little green space at the center of the triangular intersection. Excited, Mia grinned a gap-toothed smile as her golden-brown eyes met mine. Her sneaker-clad feet bounced, making the whole stroller shake with enthusiasm.

"Yes, sweetie," I agreed. "It's very big."

"Pet him?" Mia asked curiously.

"No, sweetie, Mimi is waiting for us. We're all having pancakes together, remember?"

My daughter clapped in agreement. She'd been buzzing with excitement ever since I reminded her that we were meeting my mother for brunch. As expected, Mia was my happy little sweetheart, even if she had been quite the surprise.

I thought I'd been careful enough. It wasn't like me to have sex without a condom, but it wasn't like me to drink half a bottle of white wine, either. Intoxicated and infatuated, I got swept up in the magic of Rome and a very debonair man. I contented myself with the fact that I took birth control pills, but there was no such thing as perfect contraception

Eight months, two weeks, and one day later, Mia came into the world as seven pounds of preciousness. She had rosy cheeks and her father's shade of chestnut hair. I figured she had some of his personality too, but I couldn't be sure.

There was so much about Ambrose that I didn't know because I never got the chance.

His contact card vanished amid the chaos. I could've just left it in the back of that Roman taxi. There was a chance it fell out going through security gates time and again. I hunted high and low for that stupid thing once I realized our baby was coming, but the lovely gray card with a satin finish and gold letters was nowhere to be found.

I tried looking for him. The trouble was I couldn't remember his last name. I knew it was Christian, Andersen, or something along those lines. Still, it proved difficult to find a man in another country with just one name. I had to give up eventually and focus on raising our little girl, but part of me always wondered what could have been.

Mia was the gift Ambrose never intended to give me. Wherever he was, I just hoped he was happy. I hoped that more than anything.

Pushing Mia's stroller through the crosswalk, I hustled toward the familiar Italian farm-to-table restaurant with green awnings and lush plants hanging in the long row of windows. The place was bustling with the weekend brunch crowd. Patrons were sipping mimosas and eating homemade focaccia bread with their eggs. In the rustic romance of the open dining room, my mother was already sipping her frizzante wine.

"Darling!" Mom gushed as I arrived. "Oh, this lilac eyelet blouse is divine on you! How is my birthday girl?"

Hopping up from her seat at the square, Mom kissed both my

cheeks before kissing the top of Mia's head. My daughter's grin widened with delight.

"Hi, Mimi!" Mia exclaimed, already reaching to be picked up.

Offering her warmest smile, Mom replied, "Good morning, Mia."

My mother didn't falter. Although a high chair had already replaced one of the four wooden chairs, Mom had to hold Mia for just a moment. She had to fuss over Mia's curls and blue floral romper. The outfit almost matched the blue silk of my mother's blouse. Mia, in turn, had to admire the jewels and gold adorning my mother's fingers. Mia ran her thumb along the smooth ruby ring and toyed with the bangles around my mother's wrists. When they finished fawning over each other, we were all able to settle down.

"So," my mother began. "How was France?"

"Very French," I replied, my lips curling into a grin.

Mom rolled her eyes. "Twenty-six and still a spitfire. Let's have a real answer, shall we?"

Picking up her wine glass, her slender fingers wrapped around its stem. My mother had always been lithe, a gracefully aging beauty. She never colored the silver strands lightening her auburn hair, but she had always taken care of herself. Years of sun protection and facials kept her face vibrant. Her timeless style kept her from falling out of fashion. The only thing giving away her age was maybe the beginning of crinkles around her dark eyes. Otherwise, you could never tell that she was over forty-eight years old.

It didn't help that she was never larger than a size eight. She was the kind of person who never had a voracious appetite. She could even *forget* to eat. Against all laws of survival, I could never imagine forgetting a meal, but Mom did. She would get wrapped up at work and forget all about lunch or dinner. Our weekly meals together were the only ones that she wasn't prone to forgetting.

"Paris was empty for the summer holidays," I recalled. "My favorite bakery was shut up for the week. It's not the end of the world, though. My cousins were all doing well, and Dad too."

Mom huffed under her breath. "Oh, I'm sure he's quite happy with that little girlfriend of his. How old is she, anyway? Twenty-five, thirty?"

"Thirty-two," I amended. "And Chantal is his wife now. They got married last month."

"Of course they did," Mom muttered under her breath. "This is Hercule's, what, fifth wife now?"

"Fourth," I amended for a second time. "But you'll always be his first."

I smiled as Mom sipped her wine with a resentful expression. She could fuss all she liked. She could complain and pout, but I knew the truth. Their wedding photo from the Las Vegas chapel was tucked away in some bedroom drawer. Married by an Elvis impersonator, my mother was twenty-two and exuberant. She wore a white sequined mini-dress and laughed over how campy the whole affair was.

After all this time, some secret part of her was still smiling over that night. Eloise Phillips and Hercule Lavigne had been young and absolutely intoxicated by one another, but they sobered up after a few months. The recklessness of young melodramatic love lost its appeal.

I wasn't even born before they called it quits, but I knew all too well that brief marriage offered just enough time to conceive me. One fateful night, they were reveling in their success in acquiring a prized Frank Stella painting. My mother and father shared a few bottles of fine wine, started listening to some David Bowie albums, and, well, I showed up nine months later.

It was awful how many times Mom told that story.

The last time I asked about the painting, I learned it was tucked away somewhere in some overpriced storage facility. Dad took it in the divorce, but it didn't go with the "aesthetics" of his new Parisian apartment. Mom liked to joke that I was much more versatile and far more priceless.

"You suit any room, Stella," she would tell me with a laugh. "Perfect for any mood or season."

That was her version of high praise. Polished but slightly eccentric, my mother was already beyond her begrudging as she cast her eyes upon Mia.

"Tell me, Princess," Mom asked her. "What did you get up to in France?"

"I swam," Mia answered as she started to color the pages I provided. "I ate Papa cookies, um, macky-roms?"

"Macarons," I amended softly. "Mia adored the rosewater and strawberry ones."

"They sound heavenly!" Mom gushed. "Now, have you made any special plans for Mommy's birthday tonight, Mia?"

"We've got cake!" Mia exclaimed.

"I ordered a cake from the neighborhood place," I added quickly. "We're getting pizza delivered and watching a movie."

"Oh, Stella," my mother bemoaned, shaking her head. "It's your birthday. You should be out and about, enjoying your youth."

"I did that, remember?" I reminded her with a laugh. "We both know how that ended."

As I shifted my gaze toward Mia, Mom shook her head. "Having your romance was probably the smartest thing you ever did. What woman needs the heartache of marriage?"

"Actually, Mom, a lot of women."

I could've said more, but the waiter arrived to take our order. Getting the lemon mascarpone pancakes for Mia, I ordered the eggs Benedict for myself. She quickly chose the carbonara before sending the ginger-haired man off to fetch her a new glass of frizzante. I seized the opportunity to change the subject.

"I'm more focused on getting Mia ready for the new school year than my birthday," I remarked before sipping my sparkling water. "She's starting preschool in just a couple of weeks."

"That reminds me. I need to send them money," my mother proclaimed, fishing her phone from her black Chanel purse. "Tell me, Stella, how much is tuition again, thirty-something?"

"Mom," I sighed. "I'm perfectly capable of paying for Mia's preschool."

"I'm well aware," she assured me. "You're successful, capable, and altogether wonderful, but I have more money than sense! It's much better that I waste it on something constructive than on another one of those shopping trips I take with those skinny harpies."

"You mean your friends, Mom?"

She laughed lightly. "It's a term of endearment, darling. Trust me. They call me much worse to my face."

I didn't doubt her. Her wine and book club friends were just as eccentric as my mother, but we were getting off subject. Mom was still fumbling through her phone to find her accountant's number.

"Mom, don't call anyone," I asserted. "I'm paying for Mia's education. You can waste the Phillips fortune on her some other day. She needs new school clothes. Maybe you could buy her a couple of outfits?"

"I can do both," Mom proclaimed. "Spoiling my granddaughter is my favorite indulgence. Don't deny me my little pleasures, Stella."

Shaking my head again, I opened my mouth to answer, but the phone in her right palm began to vibrate suddenly. The silvery chime of a robotic bell sounded as my mother looked genuinely annoyed. It wasn't the feigned pouting from before.

"Why is Franklin calling?" she grumbled. "He knows I'm with you two today. God, somebody had better be dead."

Complimenting Mia's skills at coloring a tropical fish, I pretended not to hear the frazzled, anxious voice of my mother's assistant. He always reminded me of the rabbit from *Alice in Wonderland*—frantic and panicked over too little time. Franklin never failed my mother. He just lived in a state of worry that one day, he might.

I was going to suggest to Mom that Franklin deserved an extended trip to a spa or some kind of meditative retreat, but her expression made me forget it all. Her eyes were going wide. Her bejeweled hand was clutching her chest in shock.

"Okay," she told Franklin. "Yes, yes, all right. Thank you. No, Franklin, I'm glad you called. I wouldn't want to hear this anywhere else. Goodbye."

"Mom," I hissed across the table, "what's wrong?"

She set her phone back into her bag while her face kept its sober look. Looking around, she leaned toward me before swallowing hard.

"It's Tobias Sutherby," she shared with me.

Sutherby's was my mother's top competition in the family business, and Tobias had less appeal than Satan himself. Why was Franklin calling about him on a Sunday?

"What about Tobias?" I had to know.

"Stella," my mother murmured with fearful hesitation, "he's dead."

AMBROSE

Checking one last time, I hadn't left anything in the jet's seat. The flight attendant was quietly clearing away our meal plates as the handful of others from my old office were already sauntering down the gangway. They'd come for my uncle's funeral, not to take over his job.

"Thank you as always, John," I told the pilot, extending my hand for one firm shake.

"Of course, sir," he answered with a nod.

"We're so sorry for your loss, Mr. Christensen," the attendant offered with a sympathetic smile. "I'm glad we could be of service to you in this unfortunate time."

"Thank you, Gina."

It could've been called an unfortunate time, but not in the way she presumed. I'd just spent the eight-hour flight going over all the to-do lists and points of concern I had for the New York headquarters for Sutherby's. When I took over the London office ten years earlier, I had done the same thing. I requested that every scrap of information be compiled, analyzed, and summarized for my consumption. I needed to see what I was working with to move forward in an orderly fashion.

Whether the world knew it or not, Sutherby's in New York had been running like a slap-dash circus. The amusements were rusting and falling apart, and the workers were denying everything.

Of course, I couldn't blame anyone but my uncle. Years of cigar smoking and brandy finally caught up with him. Although he forced it into secrecy, Tobias Sutherby spent the last six months of his life battling an aggressive form of lung cancer. It spread to his weakened kidneys and his bones. There was nothing to be done but to quietly pass the Sutherby's torch onto me, just like he'd always planned.

This was the moment I'd been groomed for since getting into Yale's business school at only twenty years old. It's why I was sent to run the art auction houses in London, and later, the office in its entirety. My whole life revolved around this fated moment.

"Ambrose," my cousin called from across the private airport. "How delightful to see you. How long has it been?"

"Since last Christmas," I answered without any warmth. "Hello, Candace."

Standing by the sleek black sedan, my bags were being loaded up by my cousin's chauffeur. She might have been dressed in black, but she didn't look forlorn at all. If anything, she looked spiteful. Her muddy-brown eyes were filled with resentment toward me, but her burgundy lips had an artificial smile forced upon them.

She had the infamous ice in her veins, just like Uncle Tobias and everyone else in our family, including me.

My mother had been that way to some extent, too, but my parents were just more aloof. Regardless, I was used to Candace's storm clouds. She had always projected her displeasure onto other people, but this passive-aggression was a little more warranted. If she'd been a boy, Candace would've been taking her father's crown, not that she even wanted it.

She was happy sipping vodka tonics while her husband practiced his professional golf swing. She'd once been an Olympic tennis player herself, but Candace quit all that when her twins were born. She was content with living the lap of our family's luxury, but the snub over her gender remained a sore spot. Honestly, I didn't blame her. I just wished she would stop glaring at me when she thought I wasn't looking.

"I've come to take you to your new rental," Candace proclaimed in her silvery false voice. "I thought we could chat about the funeral on the way."

"Fine," I relented, adjusting the cuffs of my white dress shirt.

There was no arguing, not when she was already there. Her chauffeur quickly took off toward the Tribeca address I provided, weaving through the evening traffic as the sun set over New York City. It felt strange to be back, knowing that I was staying for good.

Flipping her dyed-blonde hair over her bony shoulder, Candace crossed her legs as she settled in the back seat. Her stilettos looked like weapons angled in my direction. Her bemusement was her protective shield. Classical music lightly resonated around the car's dark interior, but it didn't relax the tension building in the air.

"I've settled everything with St. Mary's," Candace declared while staring out the tinted window. "They have their own little team of people for funerals and such. Dad had plenty of requests already laid out for his service. It didn't leave too much work for me, thank God."

"Like what?" I pressed.

Candace's smile looked frigid. "He wanted you to speak at the funeral, being his heir apparent and all."

"That's funny," I remarked, my voice flat. "I thought you were the one inheriting Uncle Tobias's money. What was his estimated net worth again? Twelve billion?"

"Eleven point eight," Candace quickly corrected me. "But you're getting his controlling interest in the company as CEO. Those stocks are the more profitable portion of his estate."

"I'm sure you can dry your tears with the rest of your father's millions, Candace," I told her, glancing out at the traffic around us. "His home in Aspen would be a beautiful backdrop for your wallowing."

My cousin let out one lone laugh.

"Always so clever, Ambrose," she replied as a quasi-compliment. "I'm sure you'll do just fine with your little eulogy."

I knew before Candace said anything that Uncle Tobias wanted this from me. He'd declared it on one of his cough-laden phone calls this summer. He wanted it to be a signal of strength, a sign that he had never been weak and that I was no less soft. However, commemorating a sexist, xenophobic workaholic was more tedious than some might've imagined. It would be difficult to find a generous word for my uncle, but I would manage something, even if it wasn't entirely true.

I had ways of twisting stories to put them in their best light. I figured everyone else did too.

"I appreciate your faith in me," I sighed. "How are your twins?"

"Poppy and Patrick are doing quite well in California," she remarked, her voice brightening. "Poppy enjoys the equestrian program at their boarding school. They'll be leaving for the fall semester right after the funeral."

"I'm glad they enjoy it out there," I offered, not knowing what else to say.

"Yes," Candace agreed.

We hardly spoke for the rest of the ride to my new temporary penthouse. Candace didn't bother to get out of the car as the chauffeur and building's doorman quickly gathered my things. She was already staring at her phone, moving on to some other task.

"Do you need anything else from me?" I asked. "For the funeral, I mean."

"No," Candace answered. "It's covered. A car will be picking you up at one o'clock on Saturday."

"Okay then."

There was no need for any kind of goodbye. Candace was already making a phone call as I shut the door behind me. I thanked her driver before he shuttled her off, and I was left to go inside my temporary home.

With tall white walls and massive black steel windows, this furnished rental was just the kind of place I'd grown accustomed to owning. It was clean, modern, and suited all my needs. There was a gym downstairs and a housekeeping service. I'd already arranged for a private chef as well, and the first meals were already waiting in the spotless steel fridge.

It was quiet here. The rooms were so wide and tall that the silence echoed around the penthouse. It carried through the two spare bedrooms and the neat home office. I could see Tribeca unfolding through every window, but I was too far away to hear the bustling city. I was high up on a pedestal built upon years of generational wealth. Now, that mantle was mine to carry.

After fixing myself a drink, I unpacked my wardrobe in the walk-in closet, categorizing and organizing based on the storage provided. It didn't take long before I was finished. My last few personal items weren't going to arrive until I purchased a place, so technically, I was all settled into my new abode. I just had to pull back the bedroom's golden curtains and stare out at the early evening sky.

Somewhere out there, Stella existed. The rosy shades of light brought back memories of her laugh and sweet perfume. It had been her birthday the day before. The anniversary was impossible to forget.

I just hoped she hadn't spent it alone again.

I'd begun to think that she wasn't real after some months of silence. She'd never called or sent me an email. She simply . . . vanished.

Still, I remembered talking about her gallery plans over dinner. She had purchased a place somewhere downtown back then. I was never in New York long enough to look her up before, but things were different now. The variables had changed, and I didn't have anyone else.

How many women named Stella worked in Manhattan's art industry, anyway?

It didn't matter, though. First, I needed to get a firm grip on the company's reins. The clocks hadn't stopped when Uncle Tobias passed. There were still luxury auctions to monitor, real estate rentals and sales happening, and our newer diamond venture was primed for expansion. The rich were getting richer, and Sutherby's hinged its success on such excess being wasted with us. Otherwise, they would flock to Phillips-Bonham or some of our foreign competitors.

Personal matters would have to wait. If Eloise Phillips gained an advantage in this pivotal moment, my uncle would be rolling in his grave. The woman was far from stupid. She had to know by now of my uncle's death, so she had to be making battle plans of her own.

Finishing my drink, I wandered toward the home office. The beige room was dressed in dark woods and golden brass accents. Little pieces of figurine art adorned the half-empty bookcases, while the long wooden desk sat in the center of the room without a speck of dust. I brought in my briefcase and got to work.

"Tobias Sutherby was . . ." I muttered to myself, my voice already trailing off. "A jackass, a very rich jackass."

Going to fix myself another glass of bourbon, I knew it was going to be a long night.

Continue reading Accidental Daddy here in Kindle Unlimited.

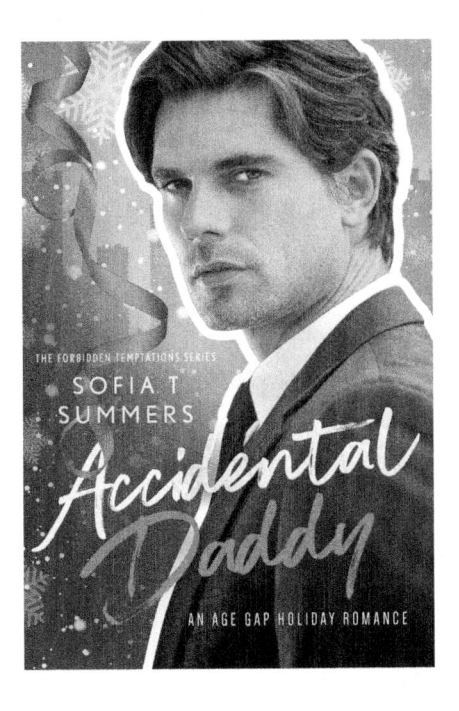

Accidental Daddy - An Age Gap, Holiday Romance

A Marriage of Convenience, Age Gap, Surprise Pregnancy Romance

READ THE ENTIRE FORBIDDEN TEMPTATIONS SERIES HERE

Sofie's books are full length, standalone romances with HEA and absolutely no cliffhanger.

Read ALL books in the Forbidden Temptation series in Kindle Unlimited NOW!

Daddy's Best Friend

My Best Friend's Daddy

Daddy's Business Partner

Doctor Daddy

Secret Baby with Daddy's Best Friend

Knocked Up by Daddy's Best Friend

Pretend Wife to Daddy's Best Friend

SEAL Daddy

Fake Married to My Best Friend's Daddy

Accidental Daddy

The Grump's Girl Friday

The Vegas Accident

My Beastly Boss

My Millionaire Marine

The Wedding Dare

The Summer Getaway

The Love Edit

The Husband Lottery

CONNECT WITH SOFIE

Want to receive extended epilogues, sexy deleted scenes, freebies, and new release alerts?

For all things Sofia, join her VIP Hangout here.

Printed in Great Britain
by Amazon